Stephen McCranie's

SPACE BOY

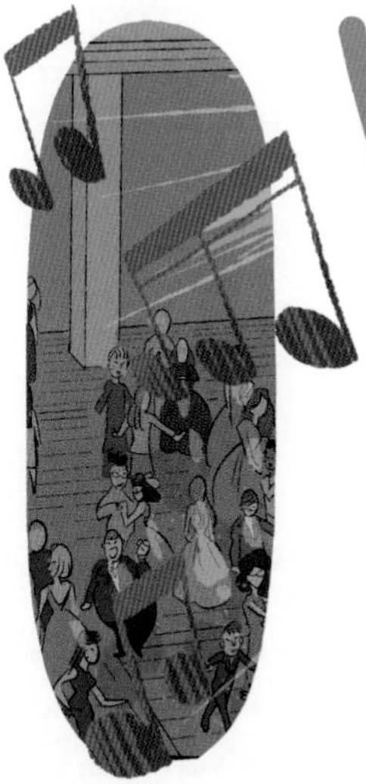

VOLUME 8

Written and illustrated by
STEPHEN McCRANIE

DARK HORSE BOOKS

President and Publisher **Mike Richardson**
Editor **Shantel LaRocque**
Associate Editor **Brett Israel**
Designer **Anita Magaña**
Digital Art Technician **Allyson Haller**

STEPHEN McCRANIE'S SPACE BOY VOLUME 8
Space Boy™ © 2020 Stephen McCranie. All rights reserved. Dark Horse Books® and the
Dark Horse logo are registered trademarks of Dark Horse Comics LLC. All rights reserved.
No portion of this publication may be reproduced or transmitted, in any form or by
any means, without the express written permission of Dark Horse Comics LLC. Names,
characters, places, and incidents featured in this publication either are the product of the
author's imagination or are used fictitiously. Any resemblance to actual persons (living or
dead), events, institutions, or locales, without satiric intent, is coincidental.

This book collects *Space Boy* episodes 111–126, previously published online at
WebToons.com.

Published by Dark Horse Books
A division of Dark Horse Comics LLC
10956 SE Main Street | Milwaukie, OR 97222
StephenMcCranie.com | DarkHorse.com

To find a comics shop in your area, visit comicshoplocator.com

First edition: October 2020
ISBN 978-1-50671-402-8
10 9 8 7 6 5 4 3 2 1
Printed in China

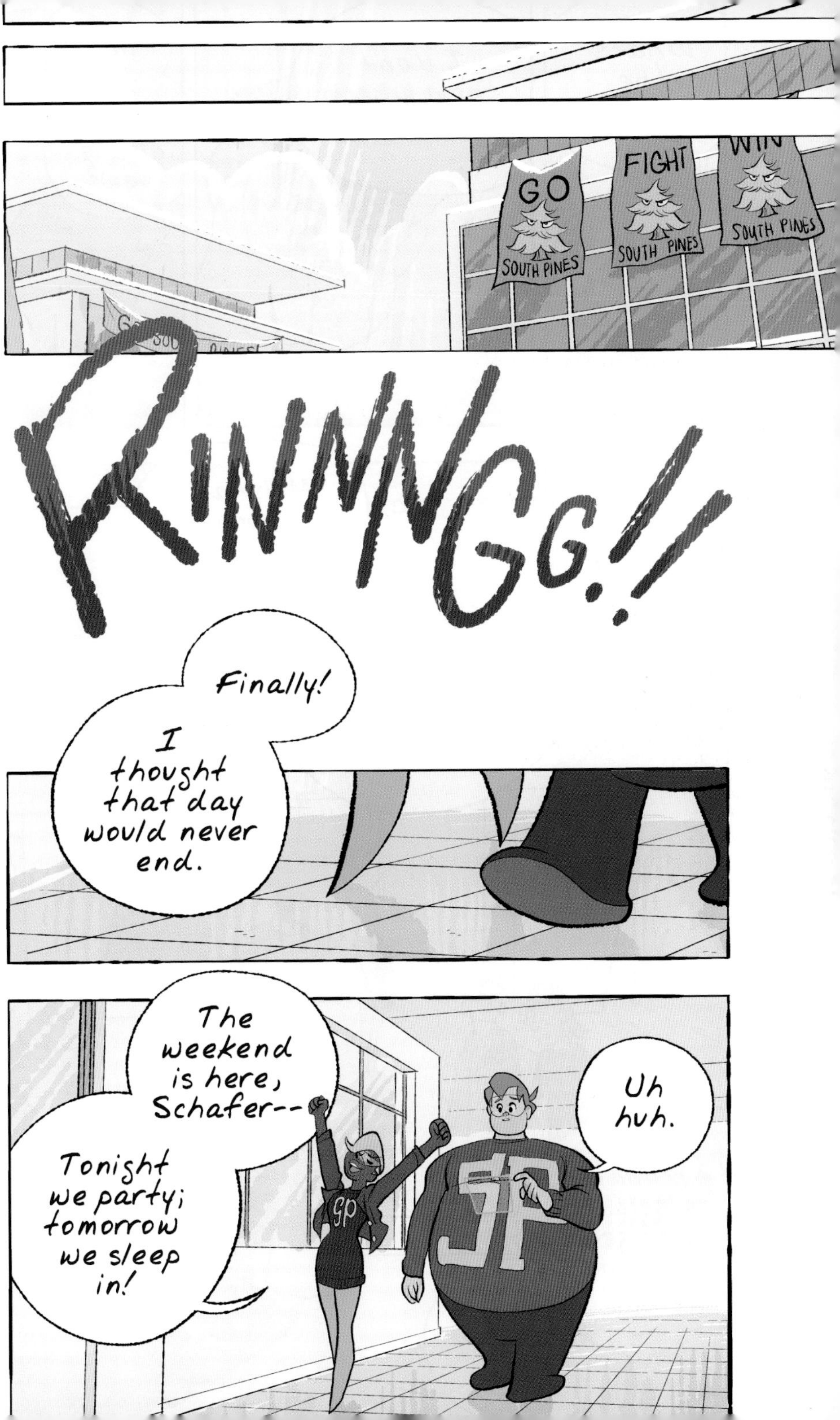
GO SOUTH PINES
FIGHT SOUTH PINES
WIN SOUTH PINES
RINNNGG!!
Finally!
I thought that day would never end.
The weekend is here, Schafer--
Tonight we party; tomorrow we sleep in!
Uh huh.

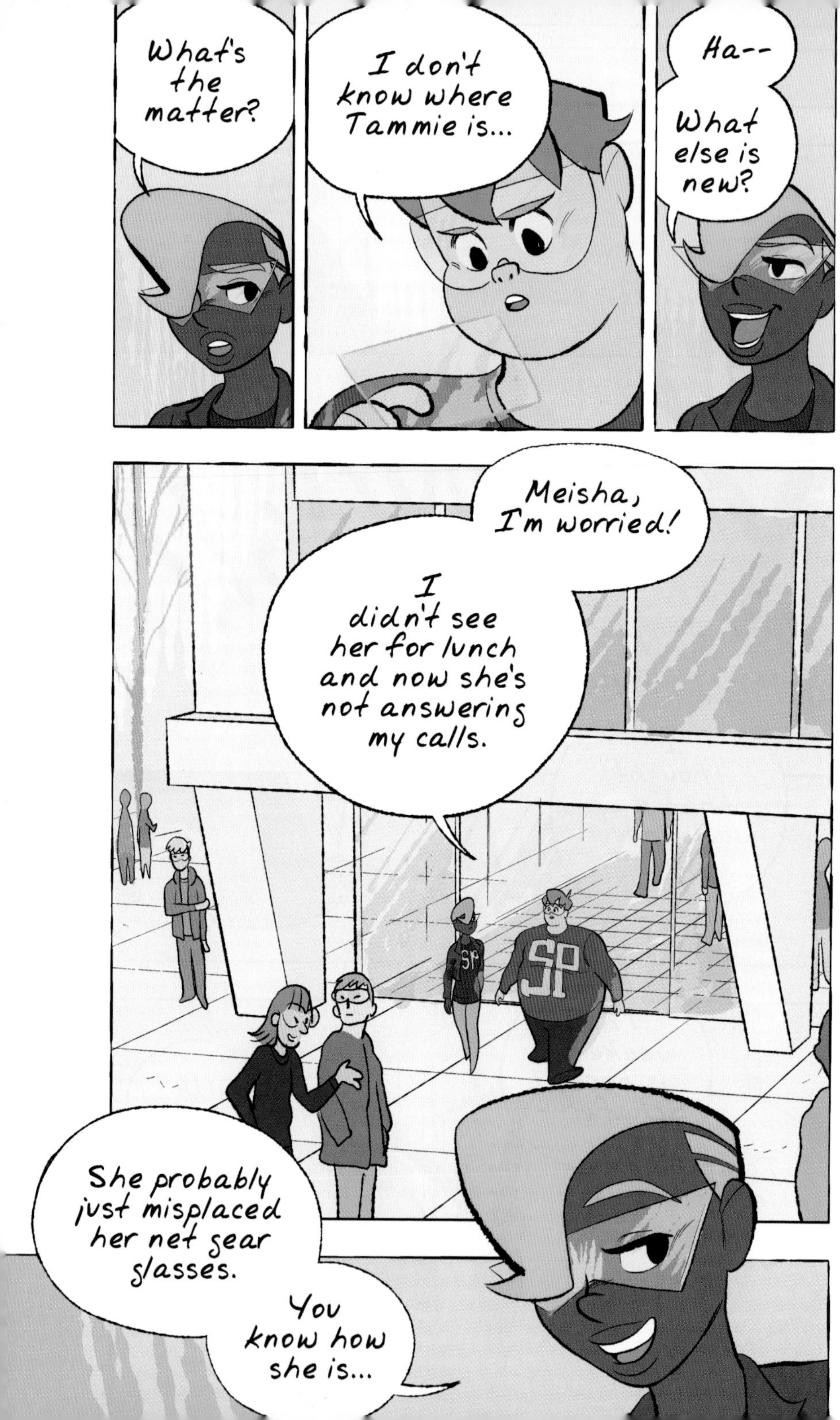
What's the matter?
I don't know where Tammie is...
Ha--
What else is new?
Meisha, I'm worried!
I didn't see her for lunch and now she's not answering my calls.
SP
SP
She probably just misplaced her net gear glasses.
You know how she is...

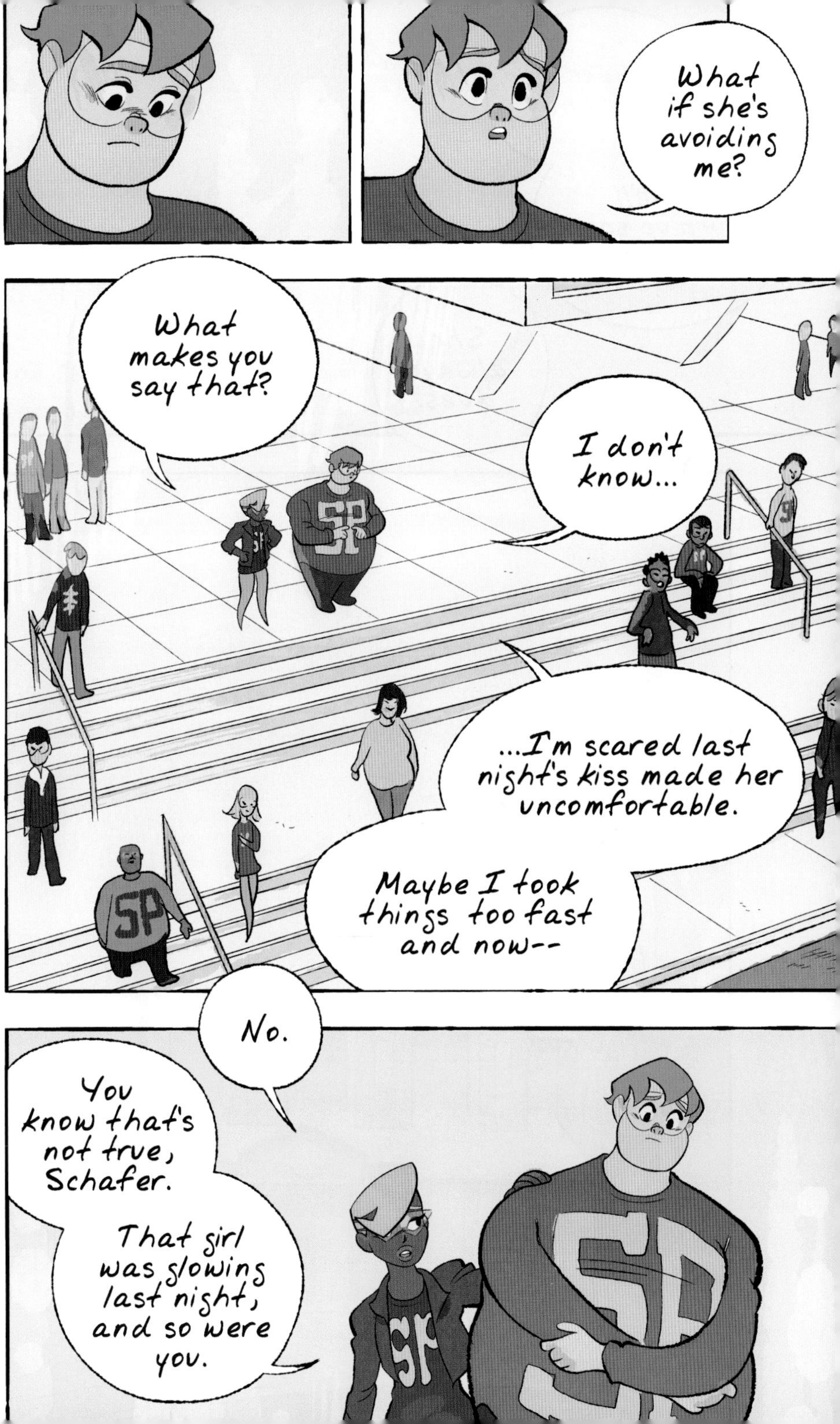
What if she's avoiding me?
What makes you say that?
I don't know...
...I'm scared last night's kiss made her uncomfortable.
Maybe I took things too fast and now--
No.
You know that's not true, Schafer.
That girl was glowing last night, and so were you.

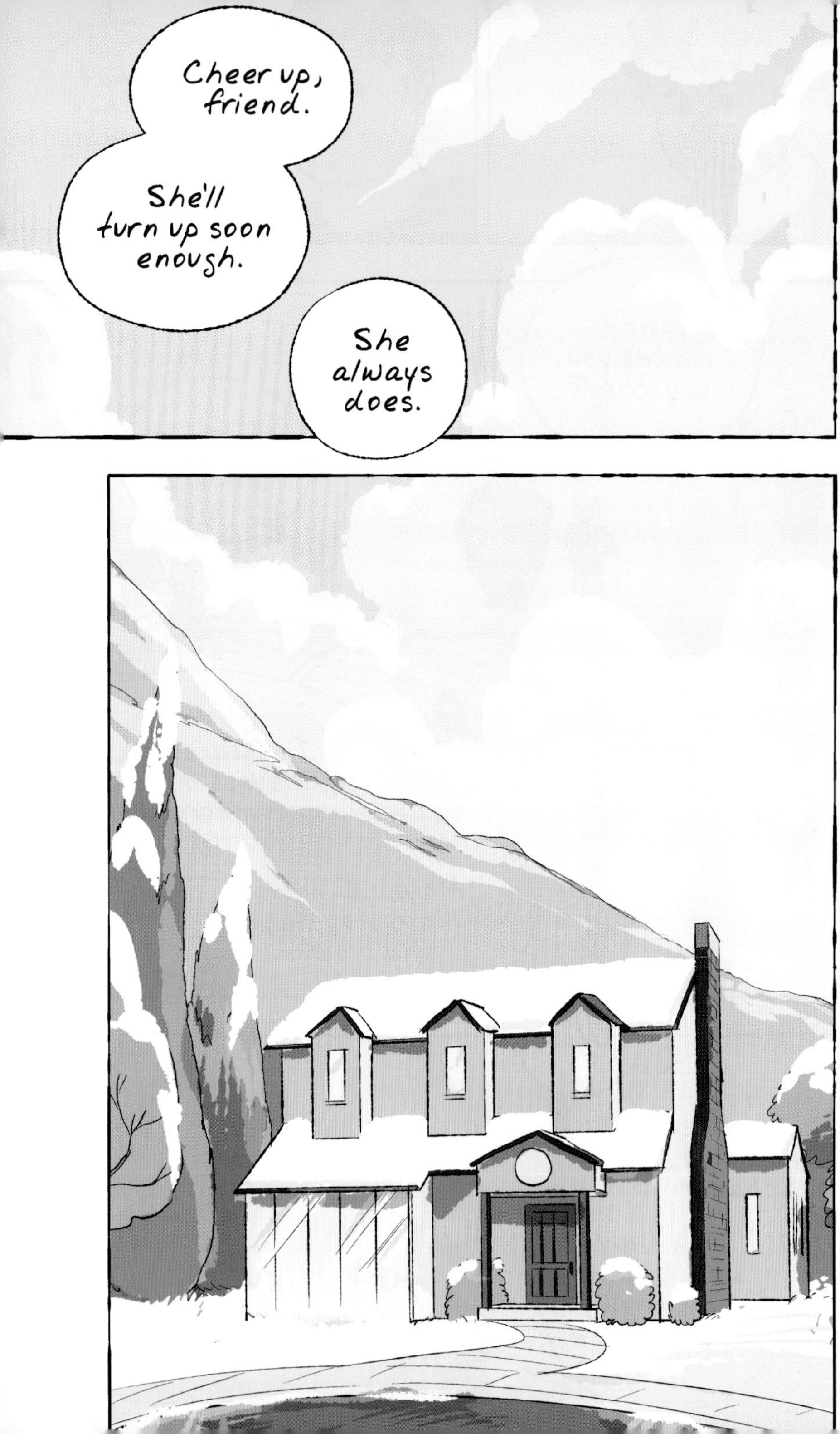
Cheer up, friend.
She'll turn up soon enough.
She always does.

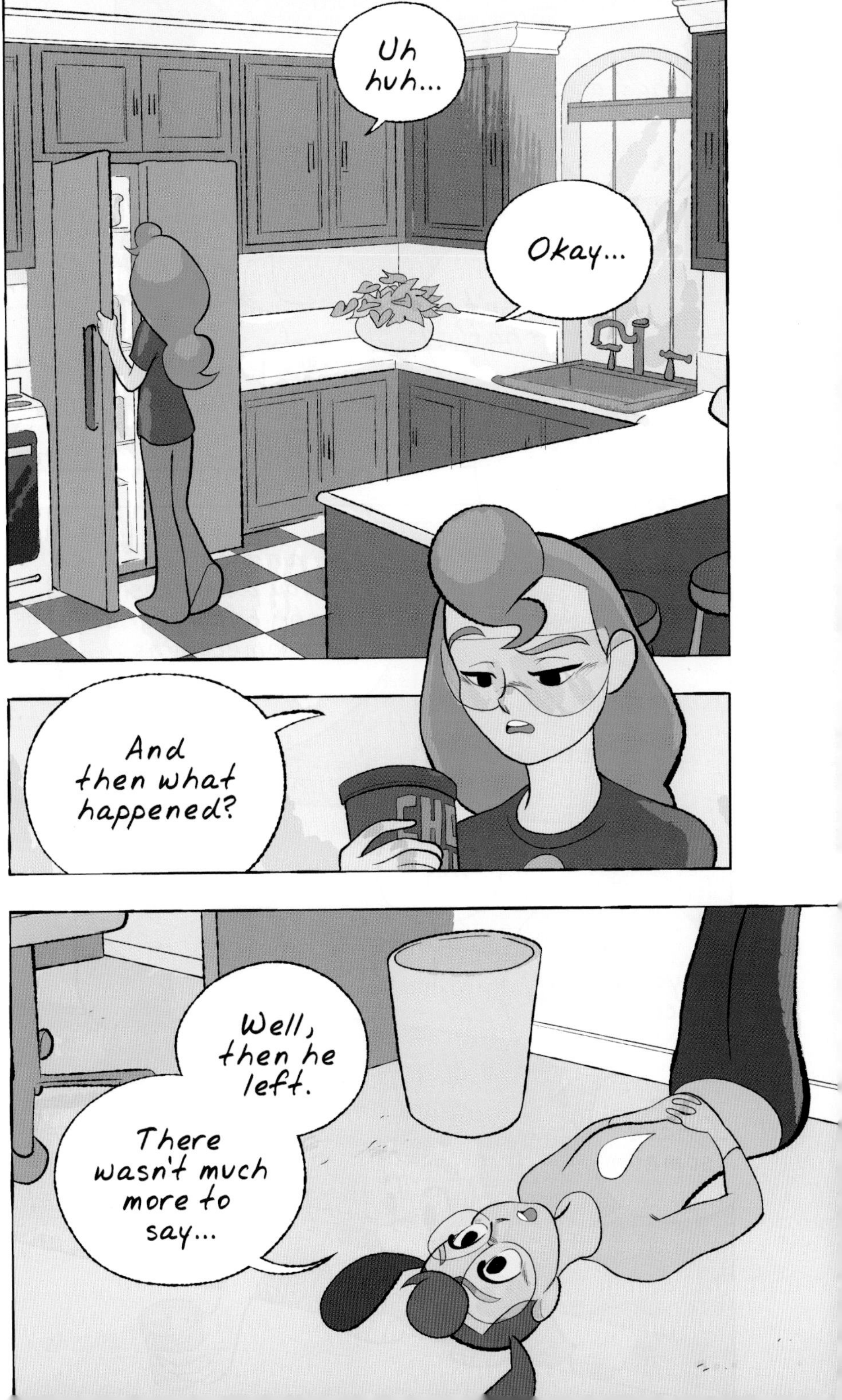
Uh huh...
Okay...
And then what happened?
Well, then he left.
There wasn't much more to say...

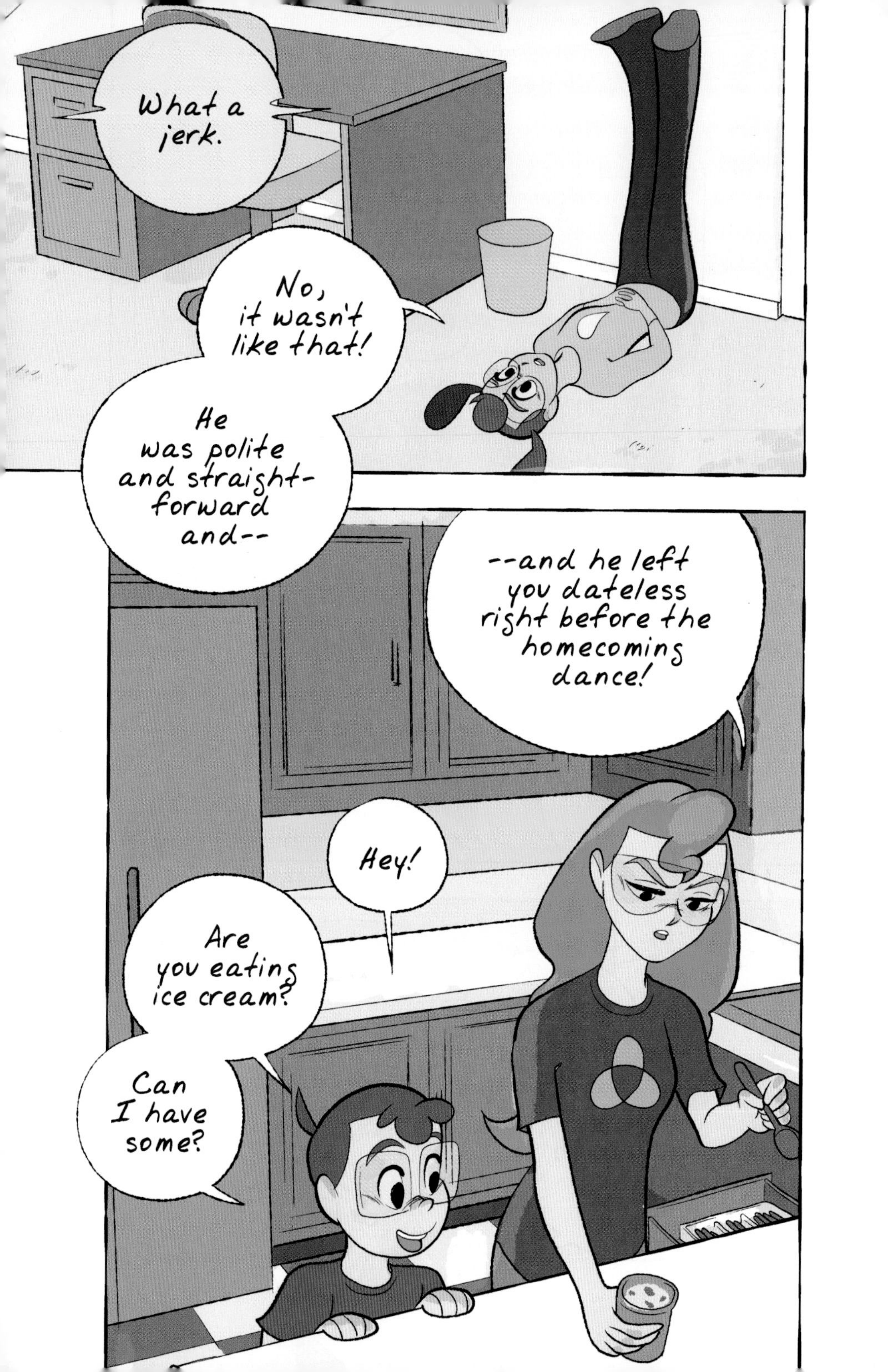
What a jerk.
No, it wasn't like that!
He was polite and straight-forward and--
--and he left you dateless right before the homecoming dance!
Hey!
Are you eating ice cream?
Can I have some?

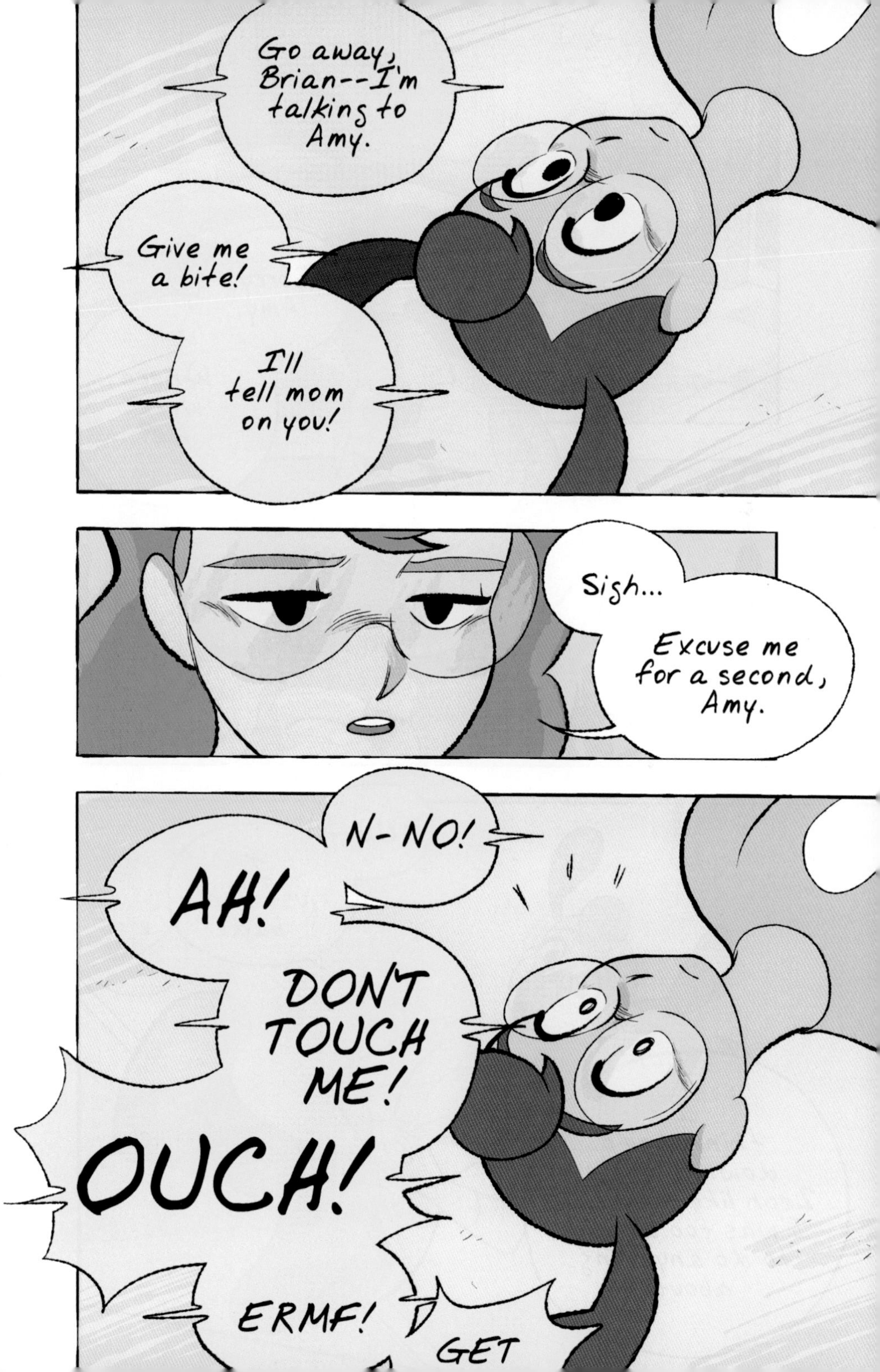
Go away, Brian--I'm talking to Amy.
Give me a bite!
I'll tell mom on you!
Sigh...
Excuse me for a second, Amy.
N-NO!
AH!
DON'T TOUCH ME!
OUCH!
ERMF!
GET

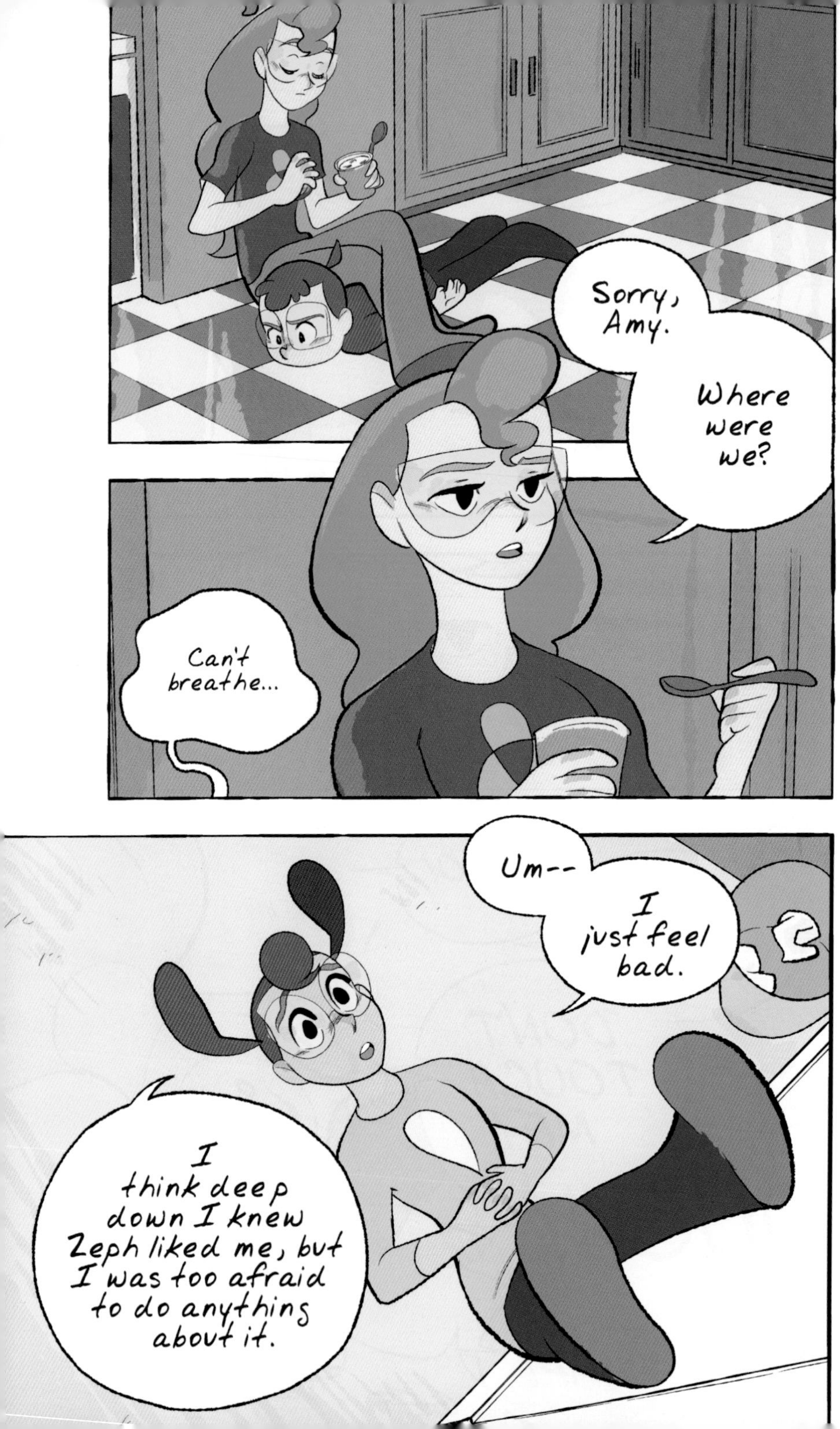
Sorry, Amy.
Where were we?
Can't breathe...
Um--
I just feel bad.
I think deep down I knew Zeph liked me, but I was too afraid to do anythins about it.

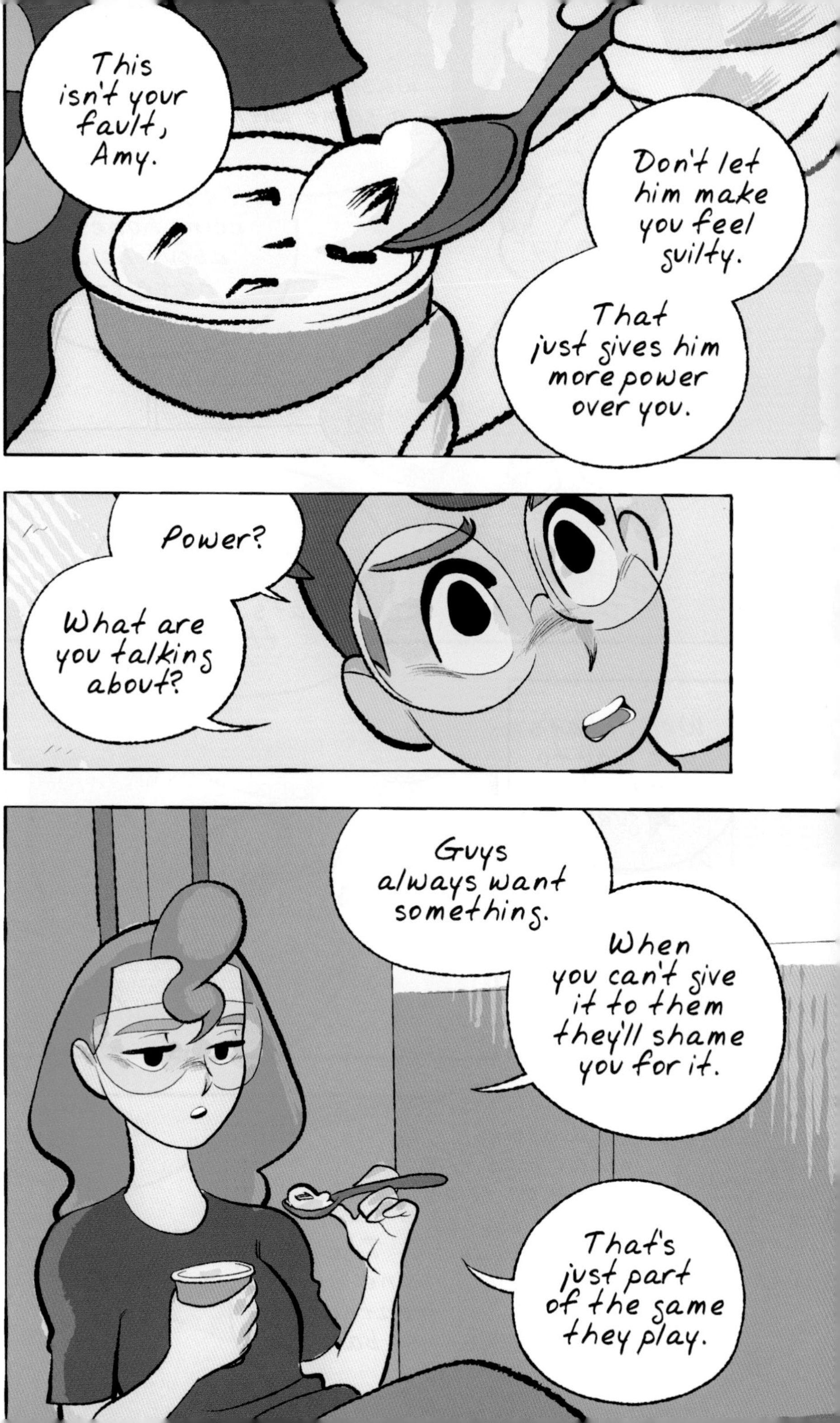
This isn't your fault, Amy.
Don't let him make you feel guilty.
That just gives him more power over you.
Power?
What are you talking about?
Guys always want something.
When you can't give it to them they'll shame you for it.
That's just part of the game they play.

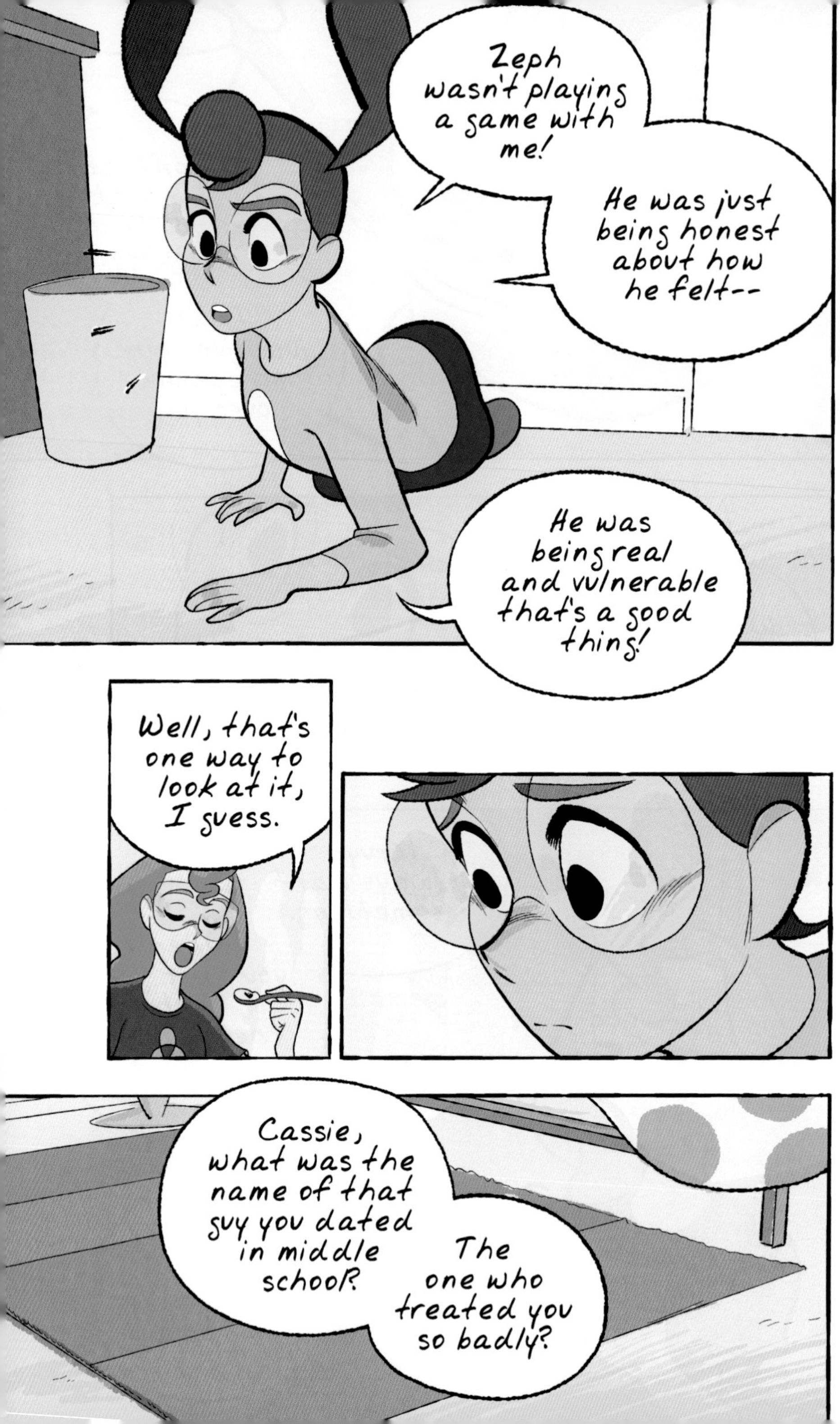
Zeph wasn't playing a game with me!
He was just being honest about how he felt--
He was being real and vulnerable that's a good thing!
Well, that's one way to look at it, I guess.
Cassie, what was the name of that guy you dated in middle school?
The one who treated you so badly?

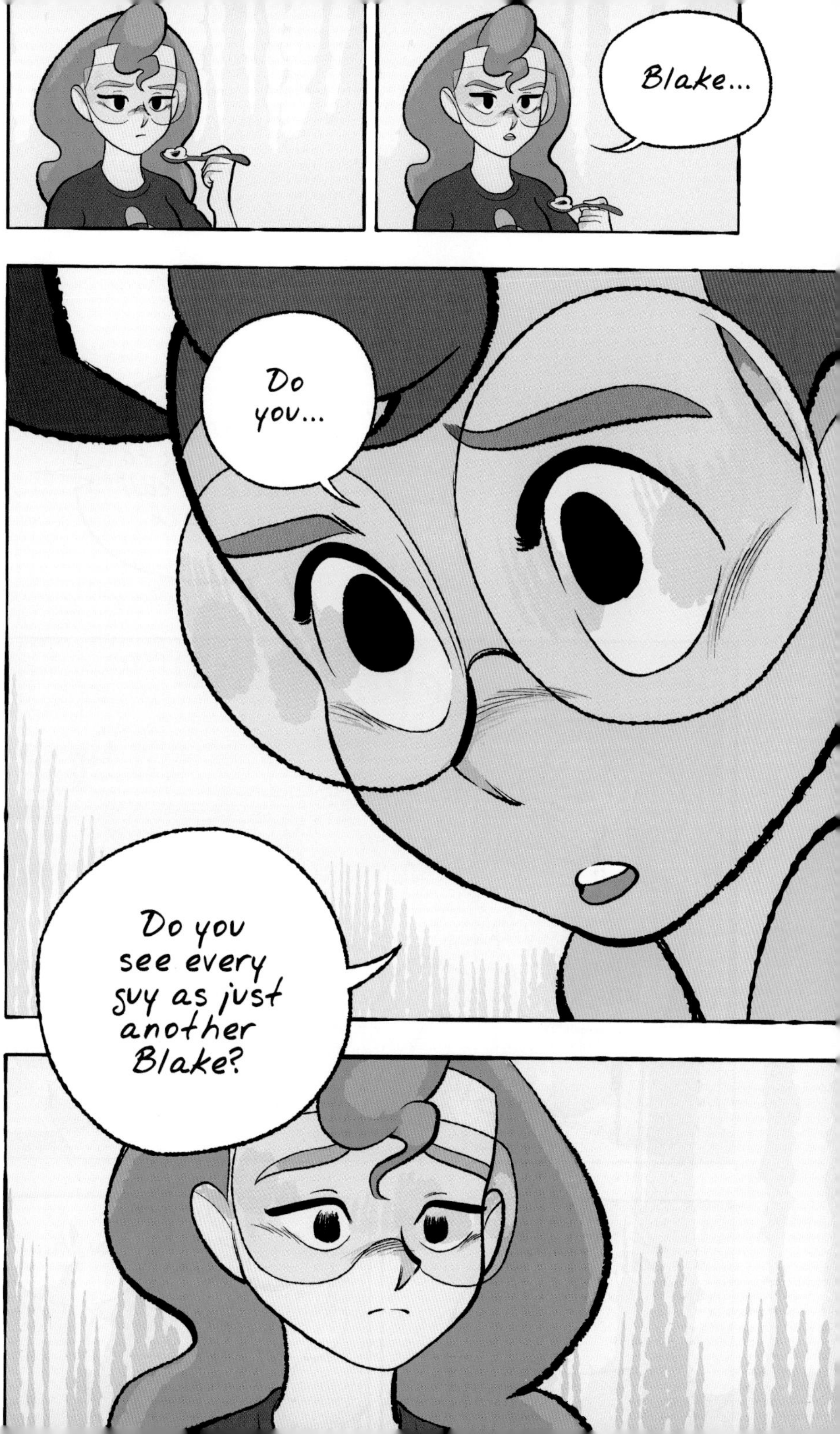
Blake...
Do you...
Do you see every guy as just another Blake?

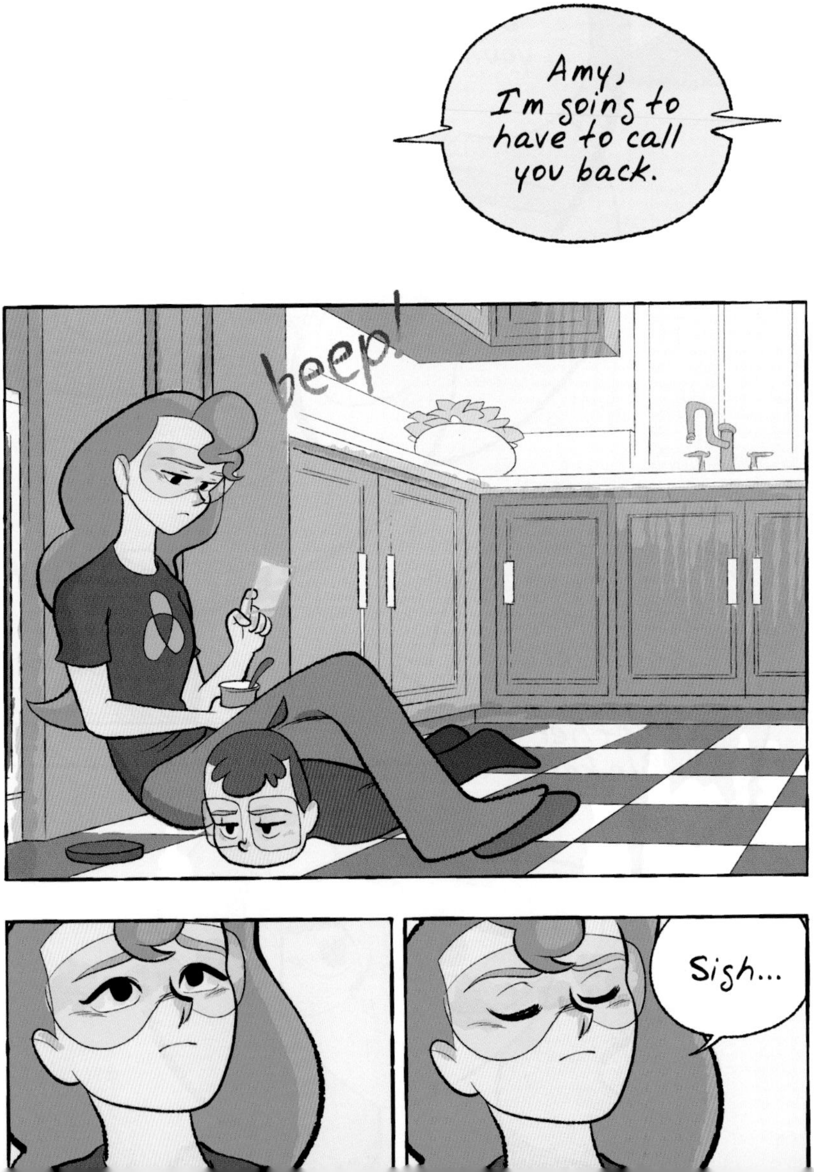
Amy,
I'm going to have to call you back.
beep!
Sigh...

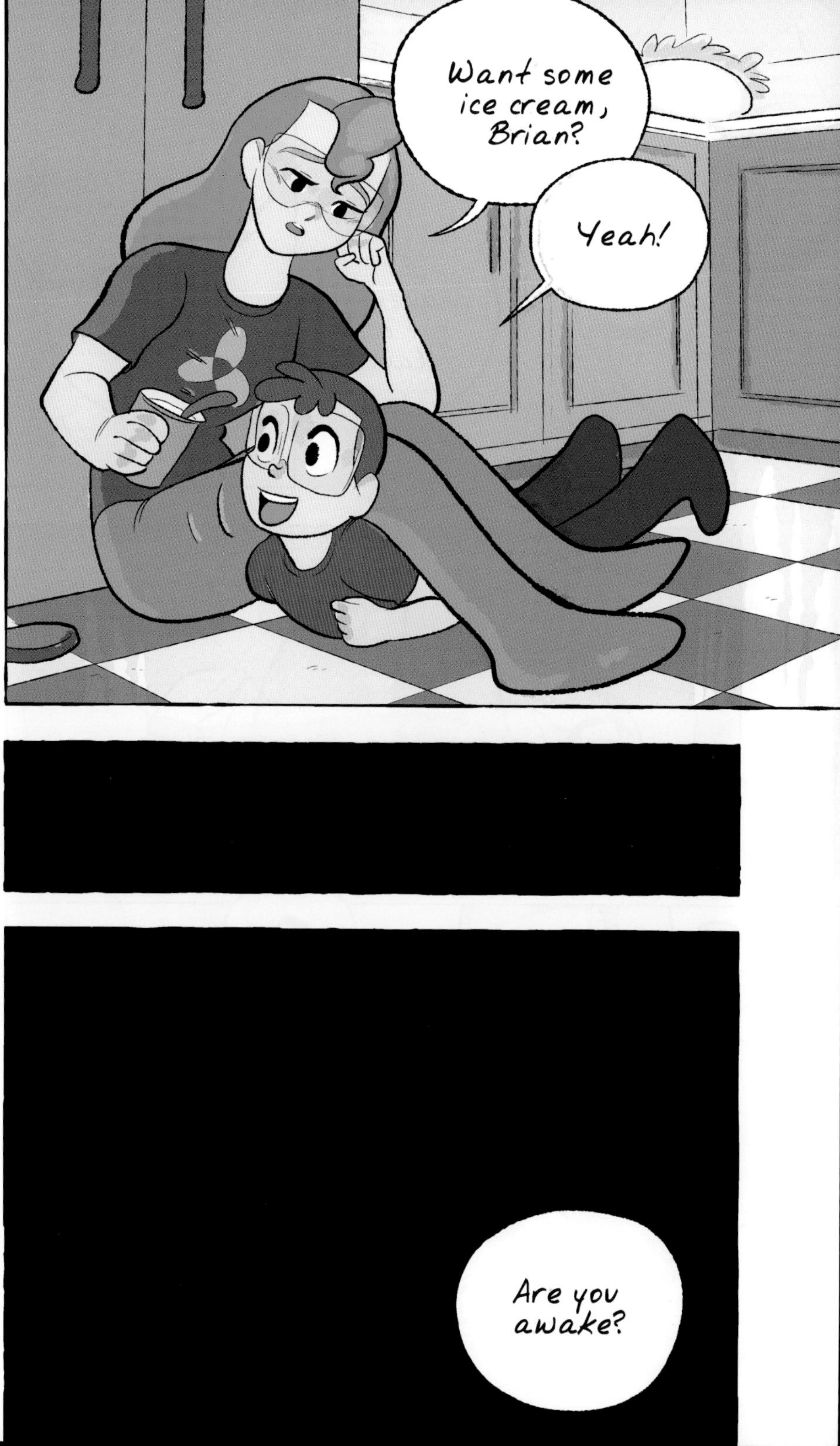
Want some ice cream, Brian?
Yeah!
Are you awake?

Come on.

I haven't got all day.

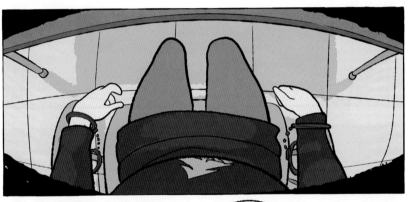

?

Tamara...

Look at me, please...

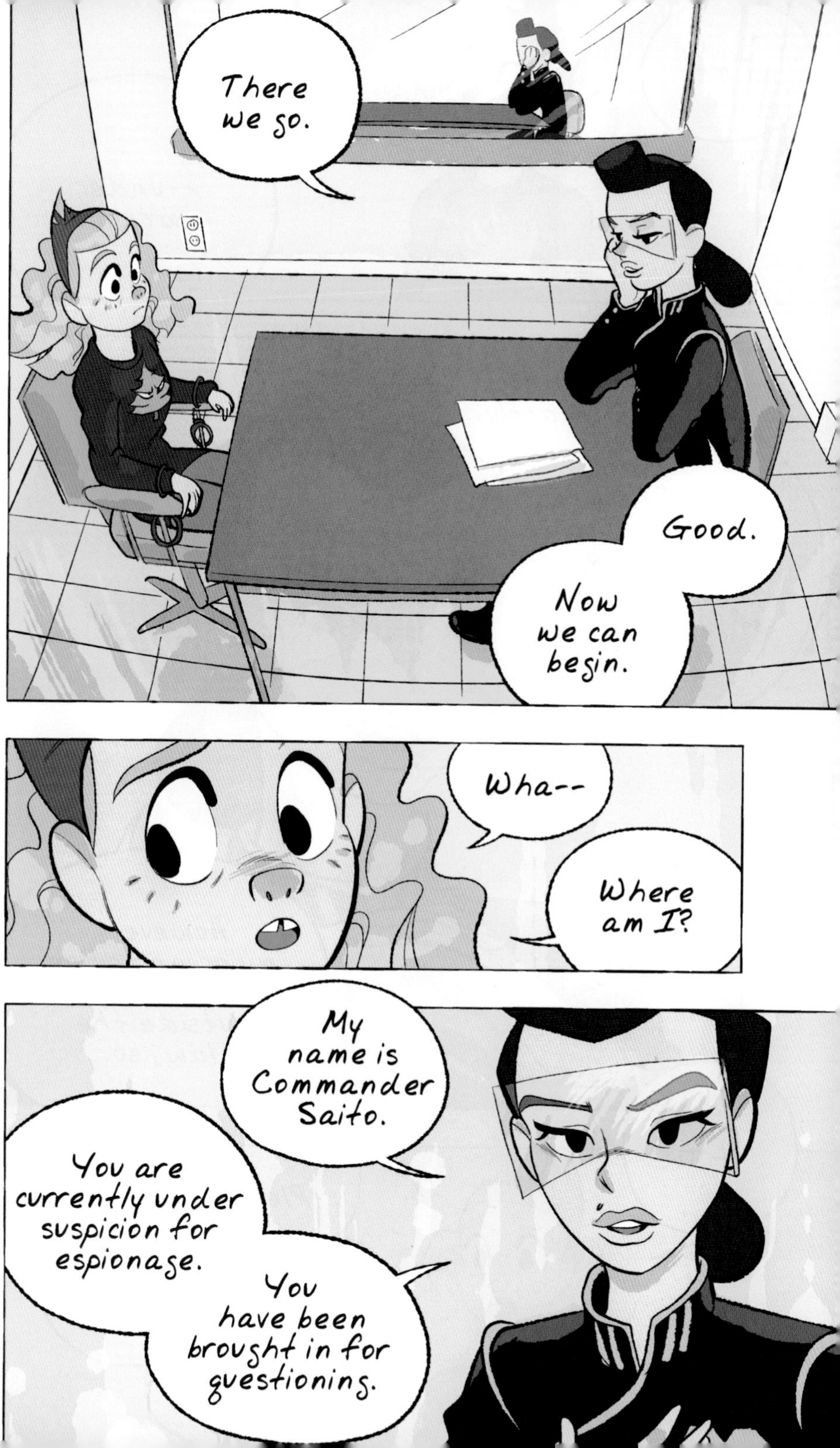
There we go.
Good.
Now we can begin.
Wha--
Where am I?
My name is Commander Saito.
You are currently under suspicion for espionage.
You have been brought in for questioning.

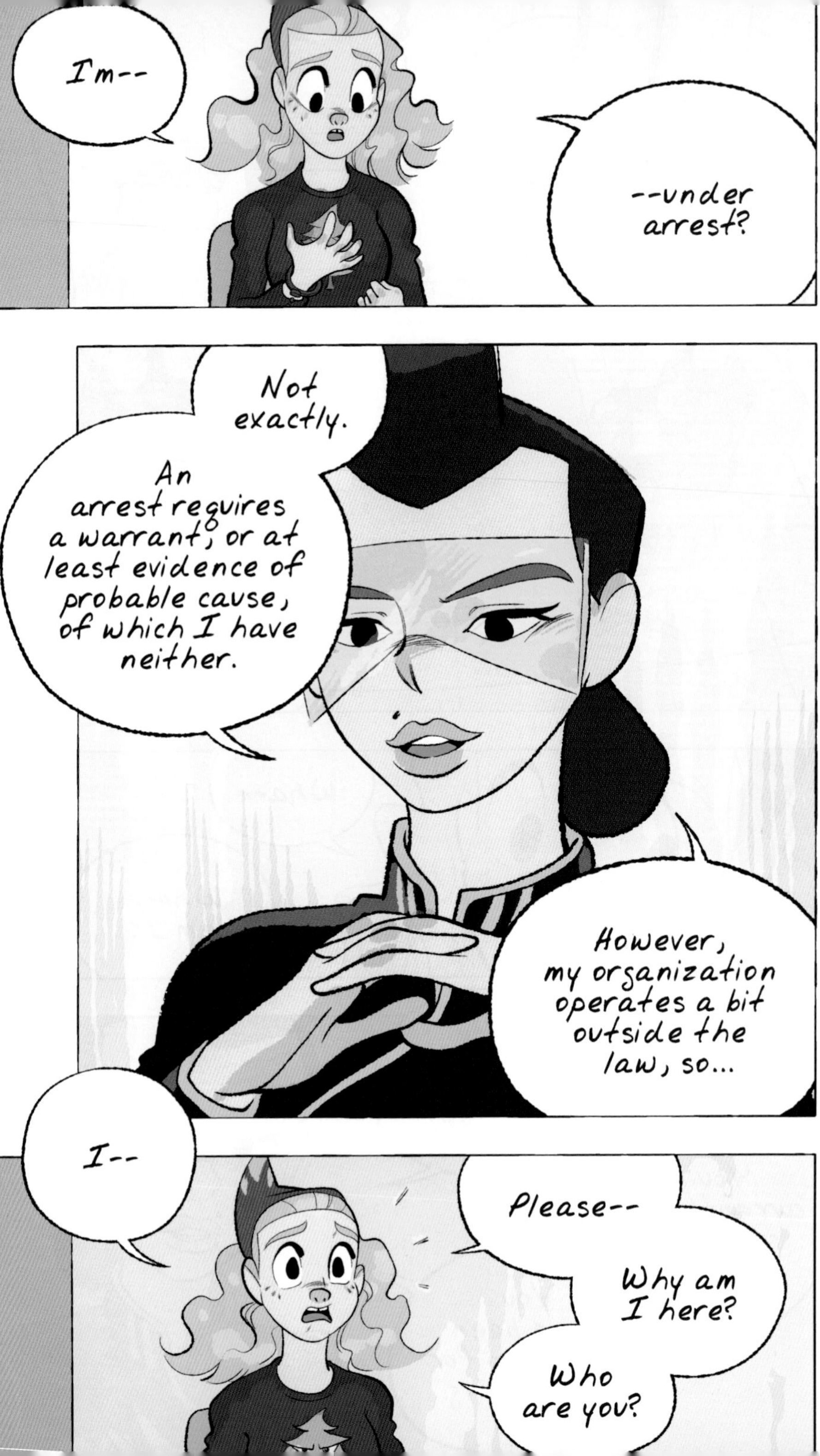
I'm--
--under arrest?
Not exactly.
An arrest requires a warrant, or at least evidence of probable cause, of which I have neither.
However, my organization operates a bit outside the law, so...
I--
Please--
Why am I here?
Who are you?

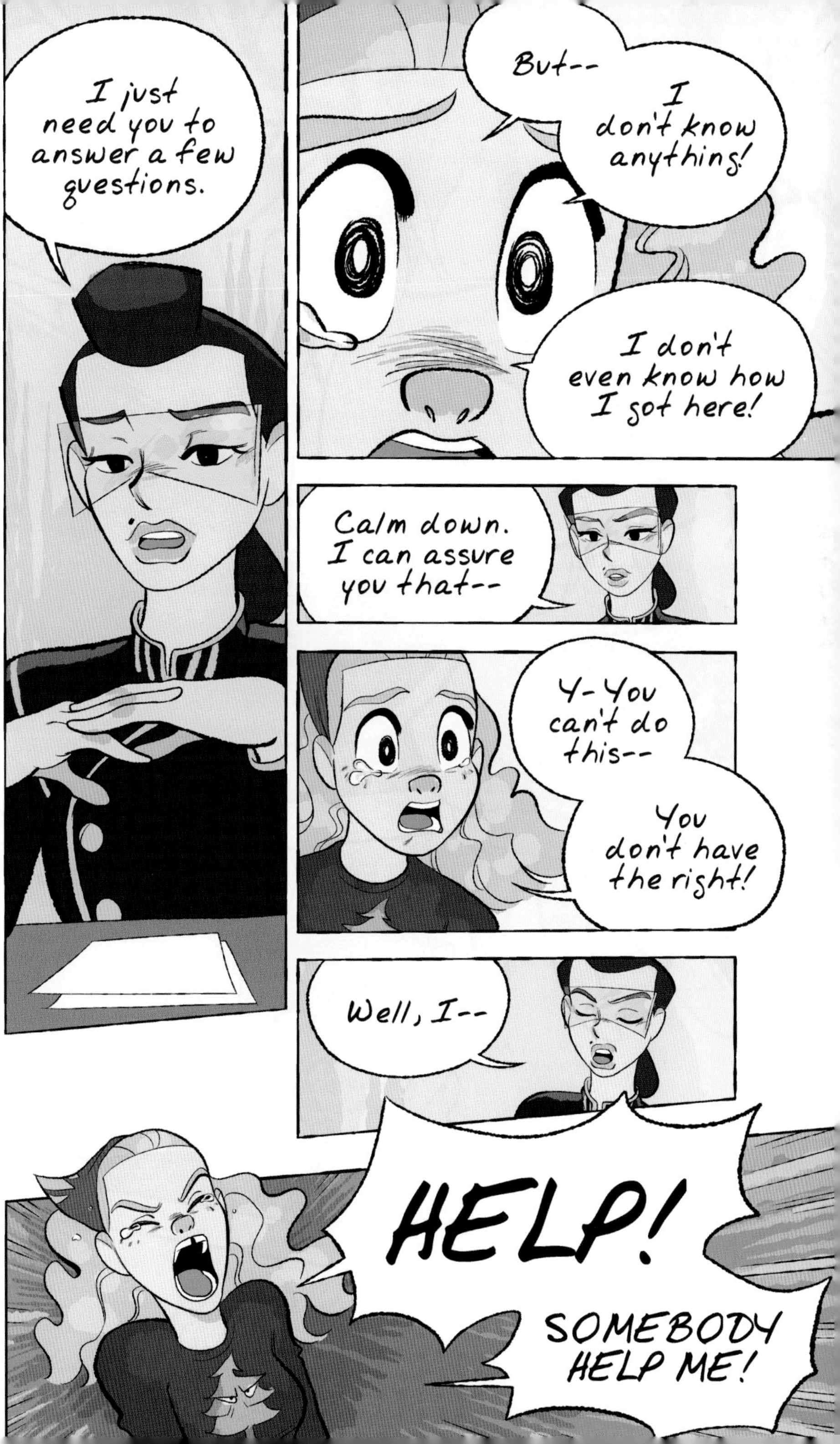
I just need you to answer a few questions.
But--
I don't know anything!
I don't even know how I got here!
Calm down. I can assure you that--
Y-You can't do this--
You don't have the right!
Well, I--
HELP!
SOMEBODY HELP ME!

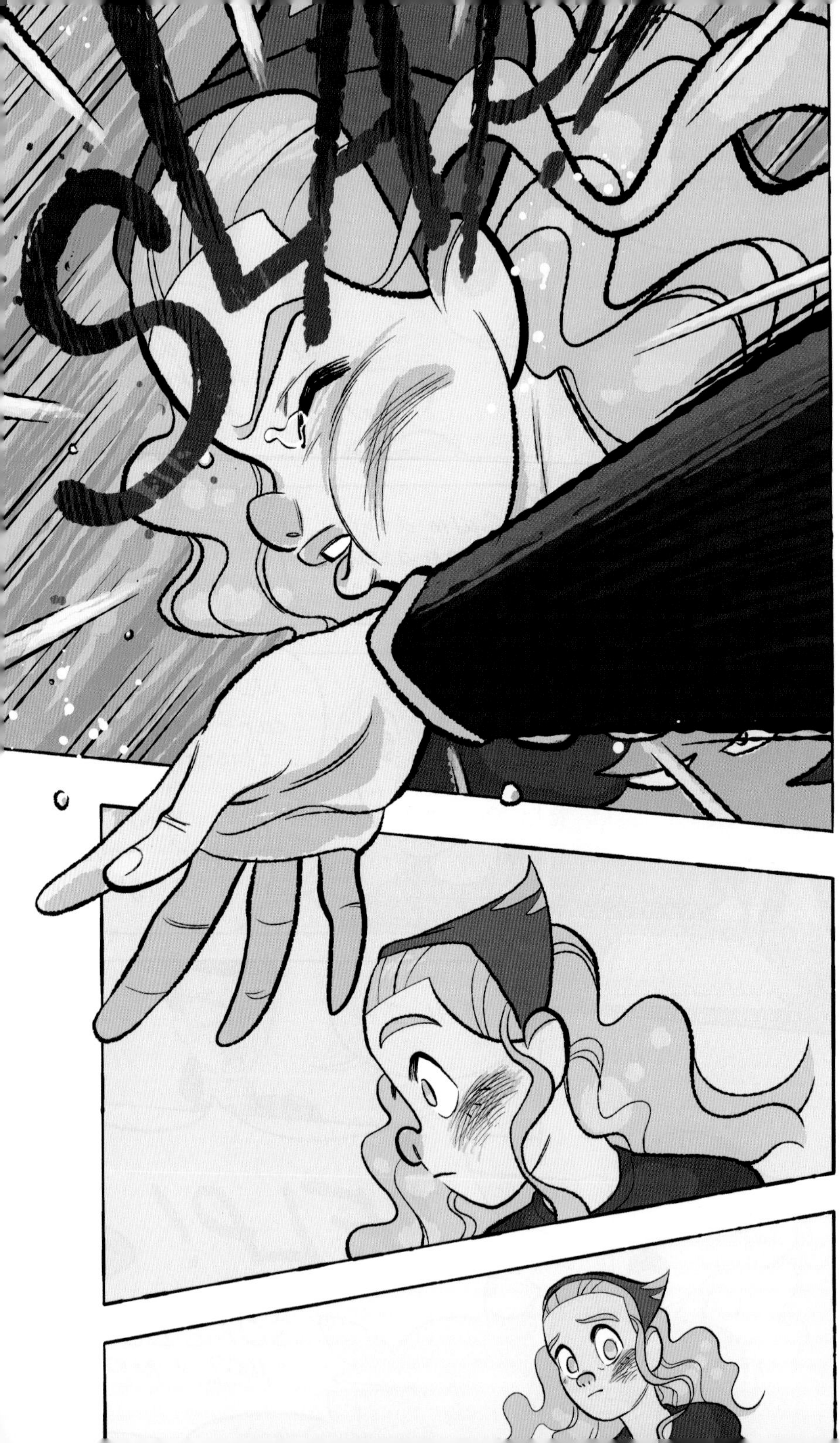
SLAM

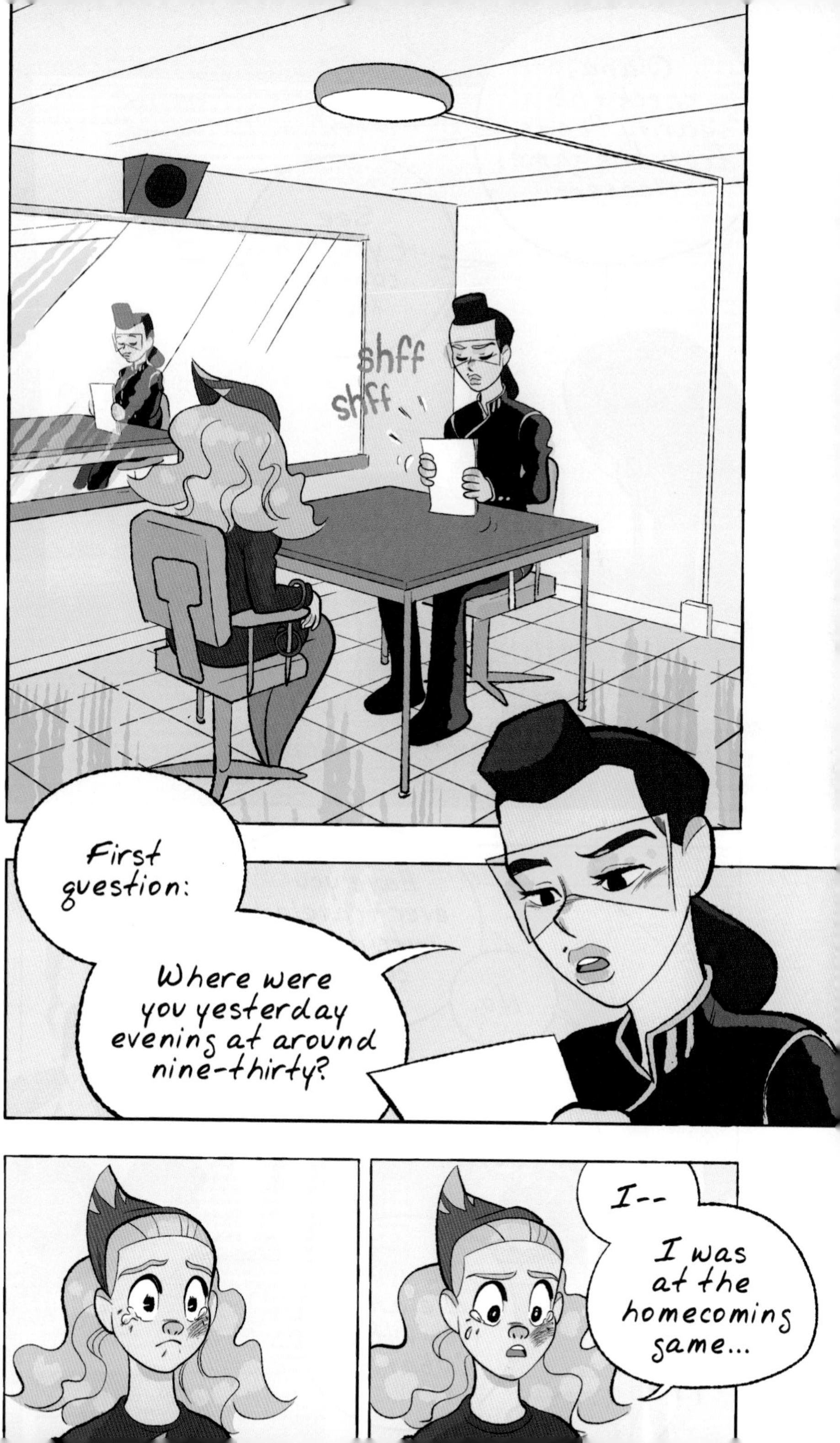
shff shff
First question:
Where were you yesterday evening at around nine-thirty?
I--
I was at the homecoming game...

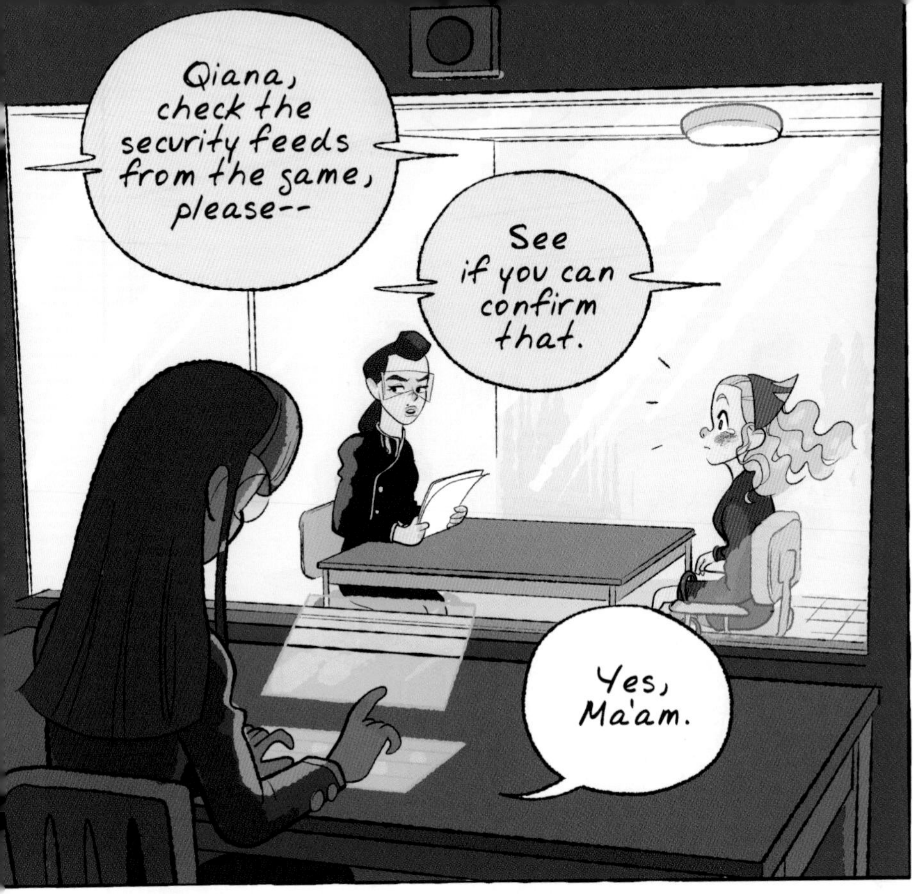
Qiana, check the security feeds from the game, please--
See if you can confirm that.
Yes, Ma'am.

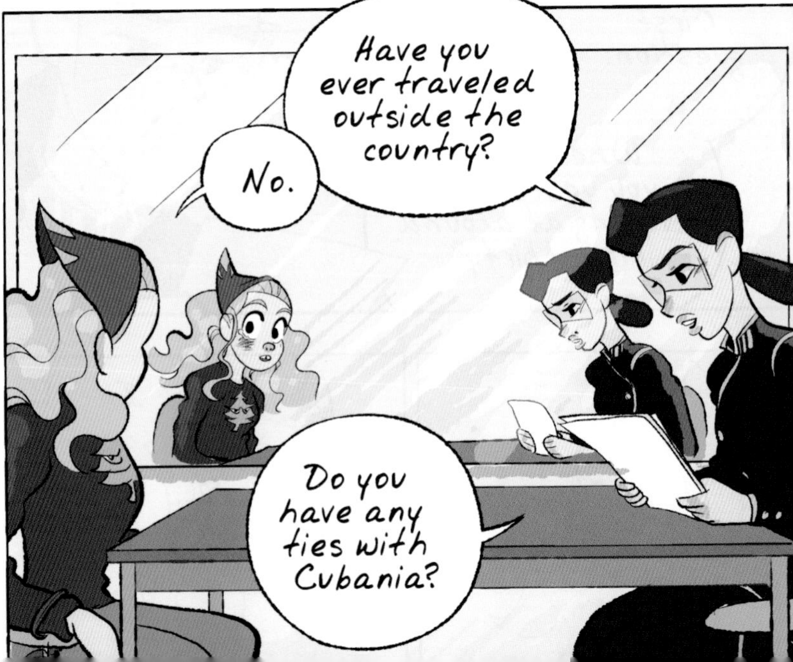
Have you ever traveled outside the country?
No.
Do you have any ties with Cubania?

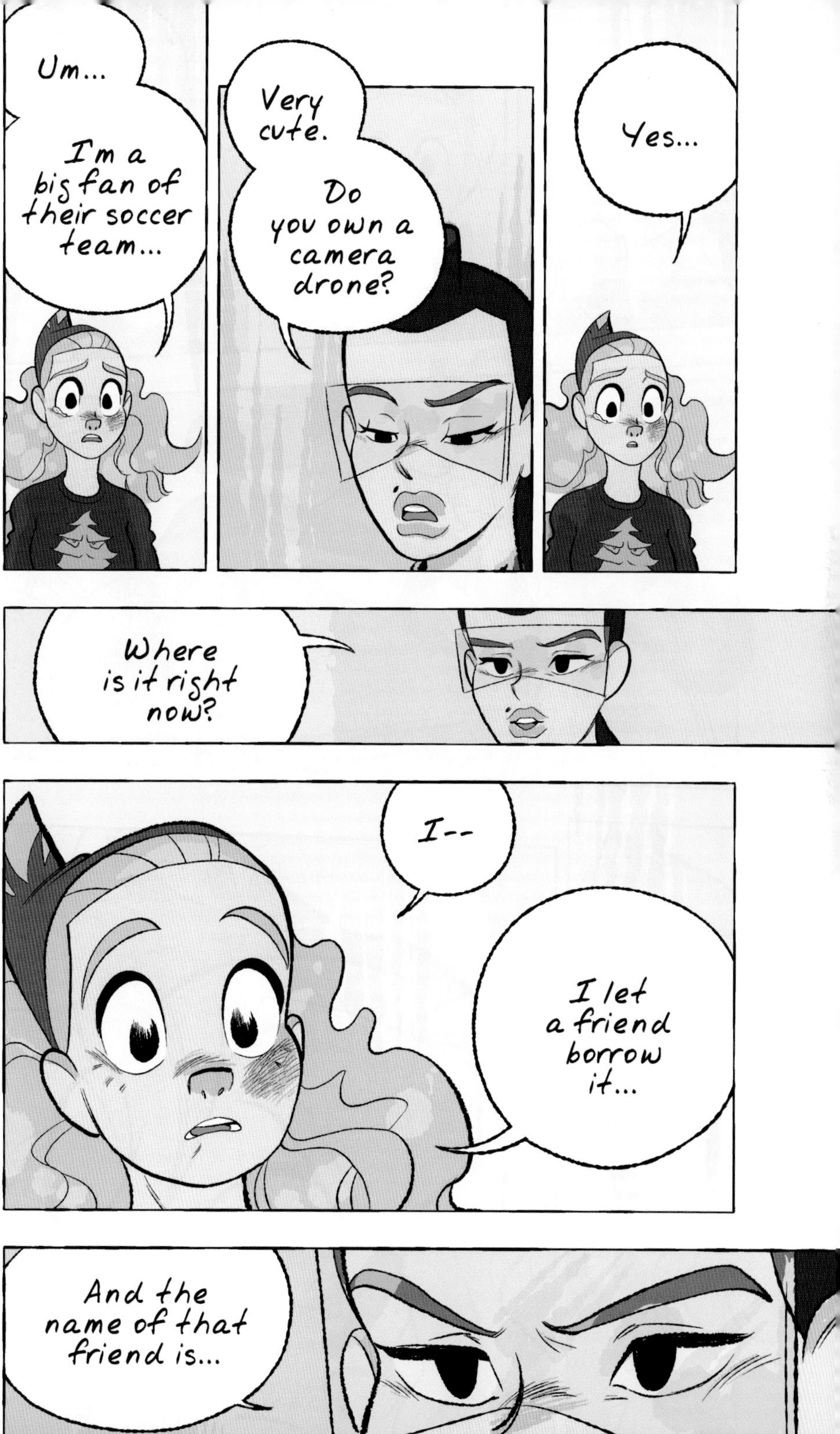
Um...
I'm a big fan of their soccer team...
Very cute.
Do you own a camera drone?
Yes...
Where is it right now?
I--
I let a friend borrow it...
And the name of that friend is...

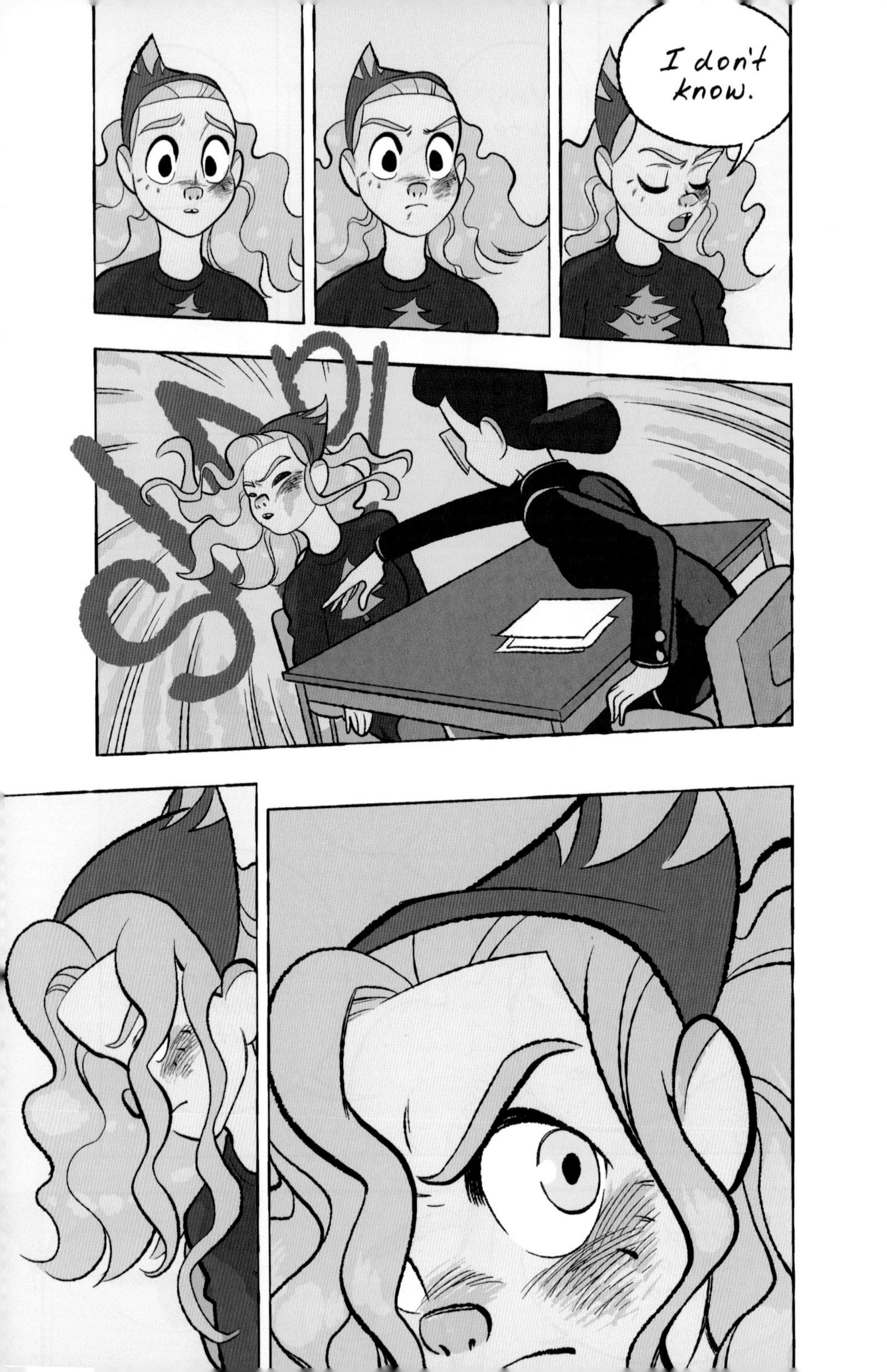
I don't know.

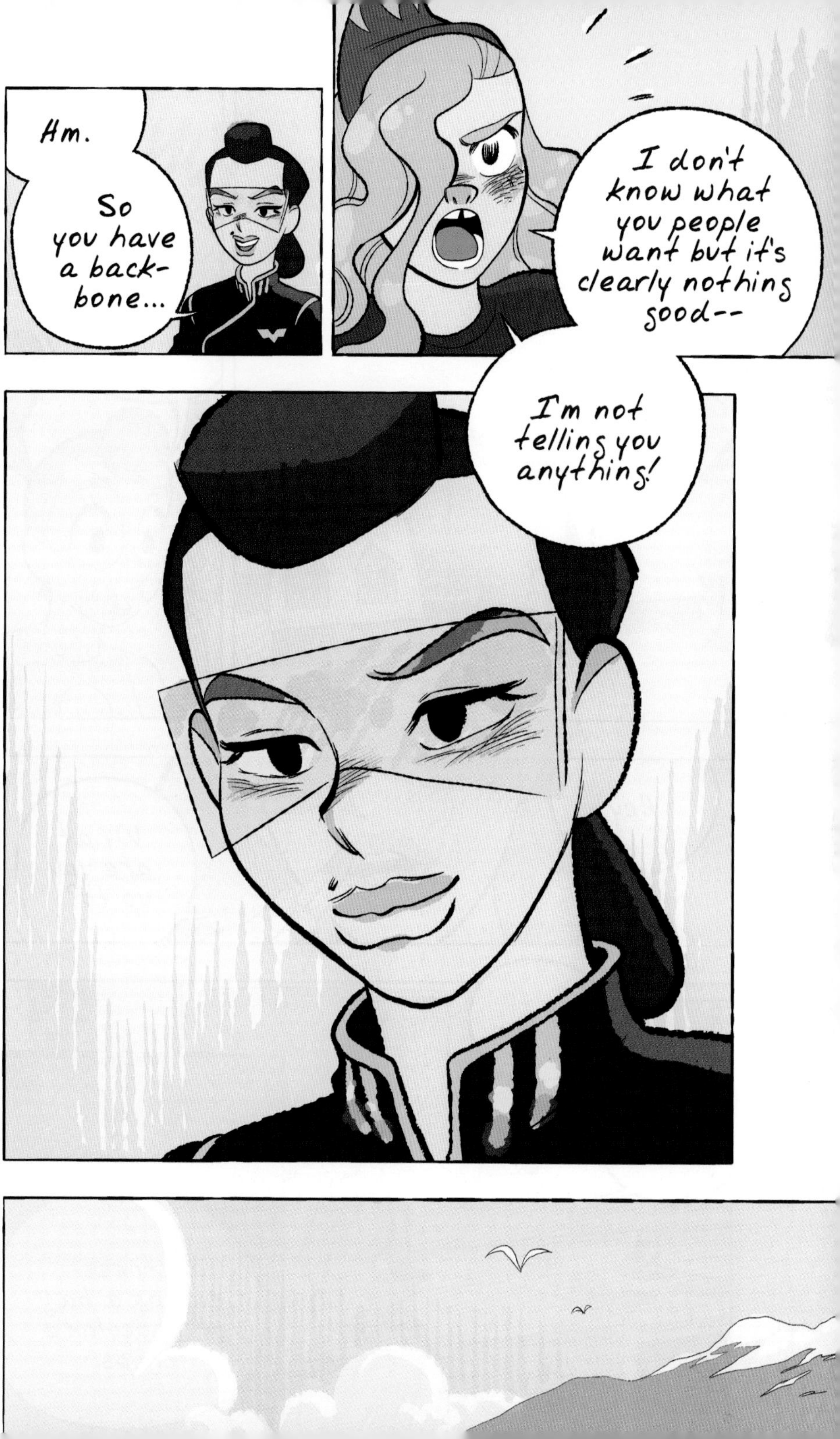
Hm.
So you have a back-bone...
I don't know what you people want but it's clearly nothing good--
I'm not telling you anything!

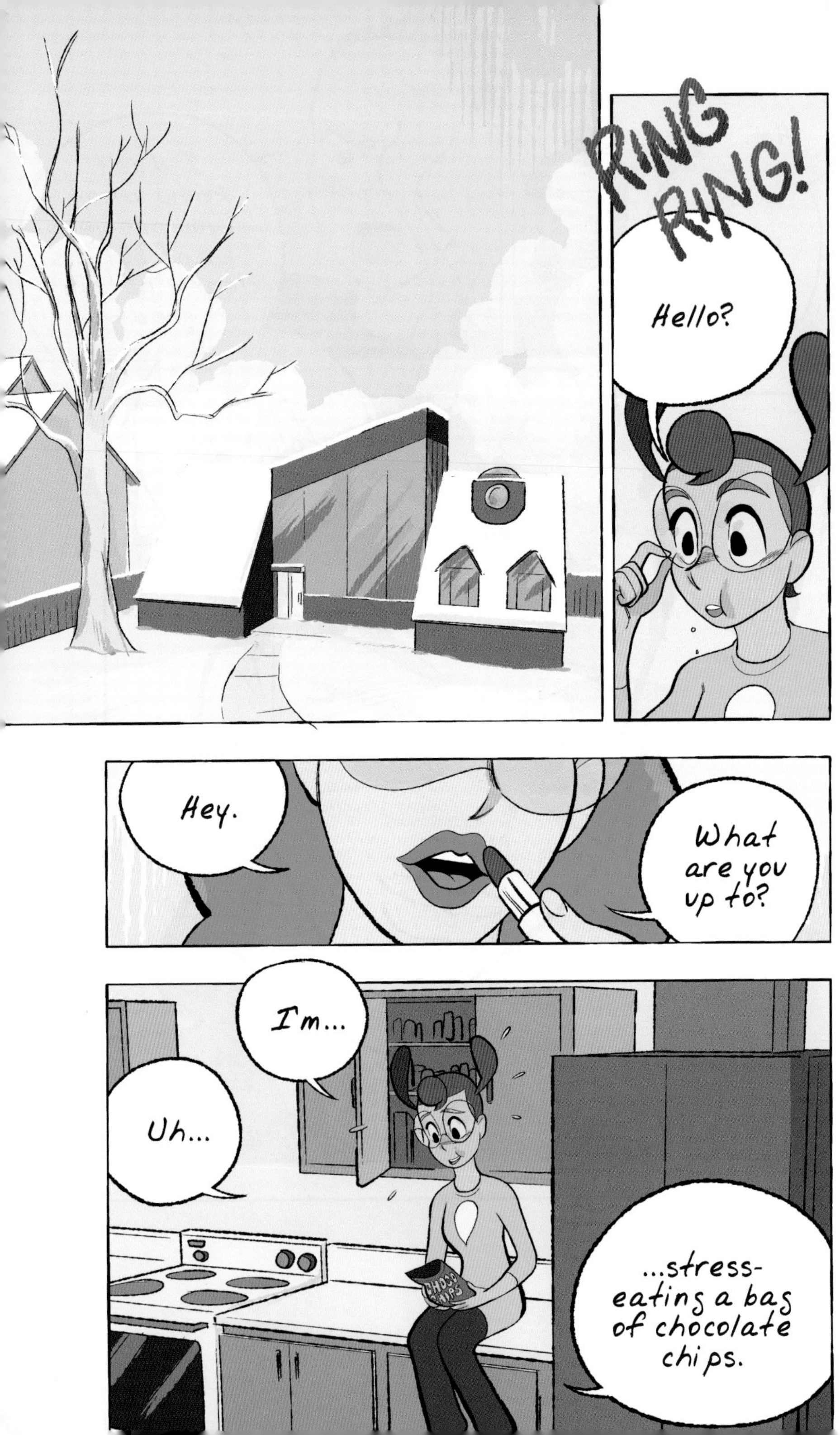
RING RING!
Hello?
Hey.
What are you up to?
I'm...
Uh...
...stress-eating a bag of chocolate chips.
CHOCO CHIPS

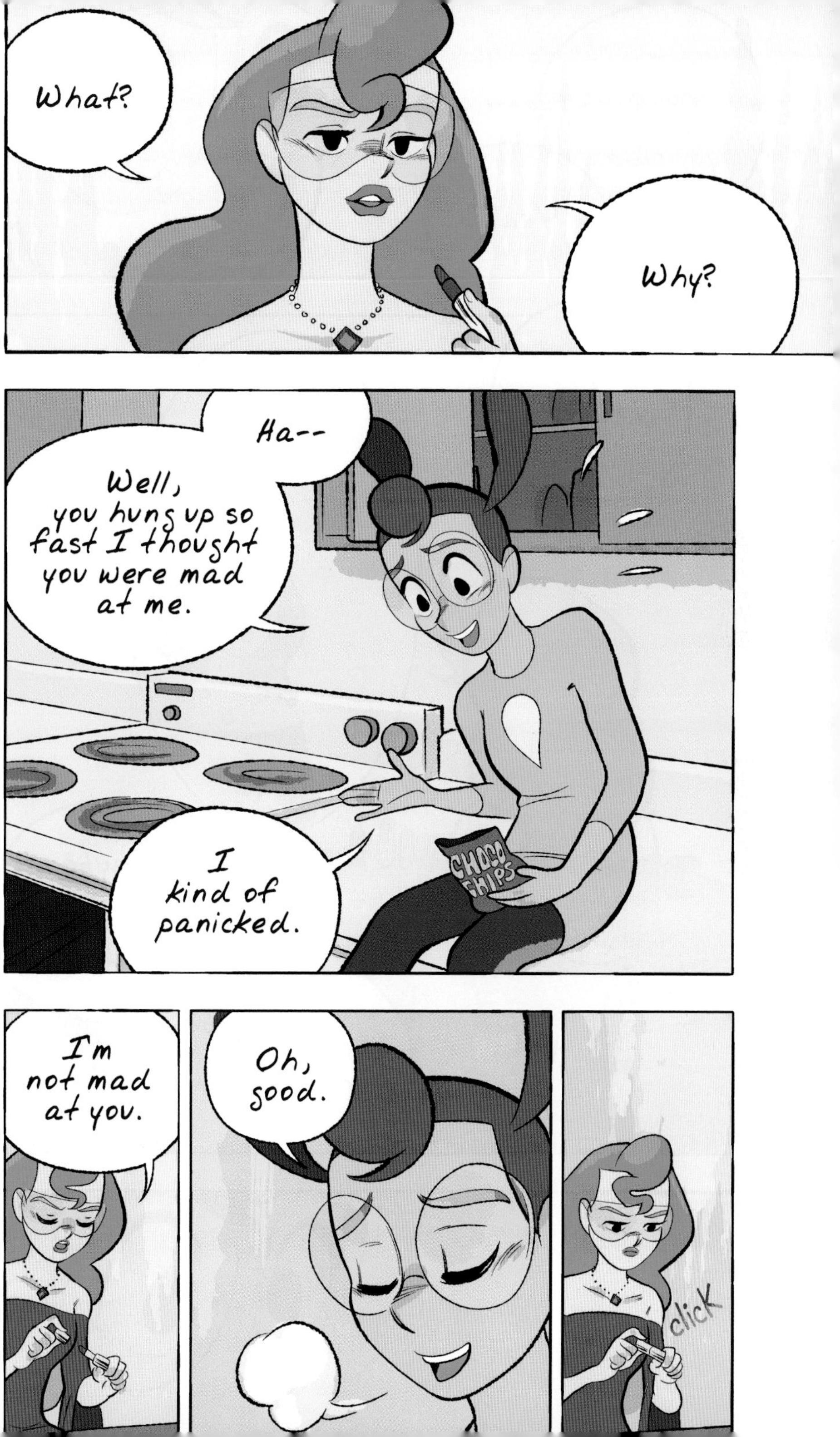

What?
Why?
Ha--
Well, you hung up so fast I thought you were mad at me.
I kind of panicked.
CHOCO CHIPS
I'm not mad at you.
Oh, good.
click

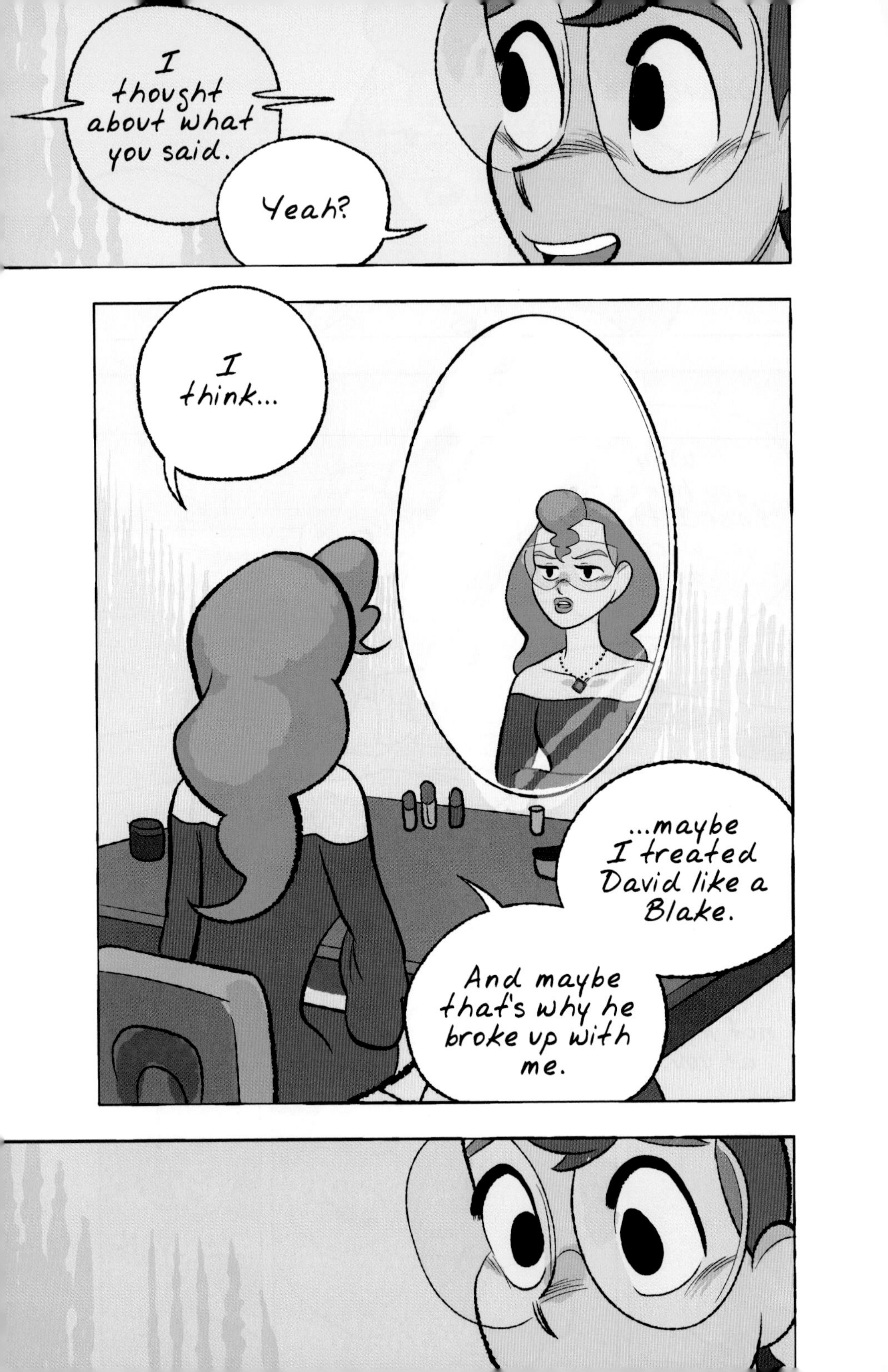
I thought about what you said.
Yeah?
I think...
...maybe I treated David like a Blake.
And maybe that's why he broke up with me.

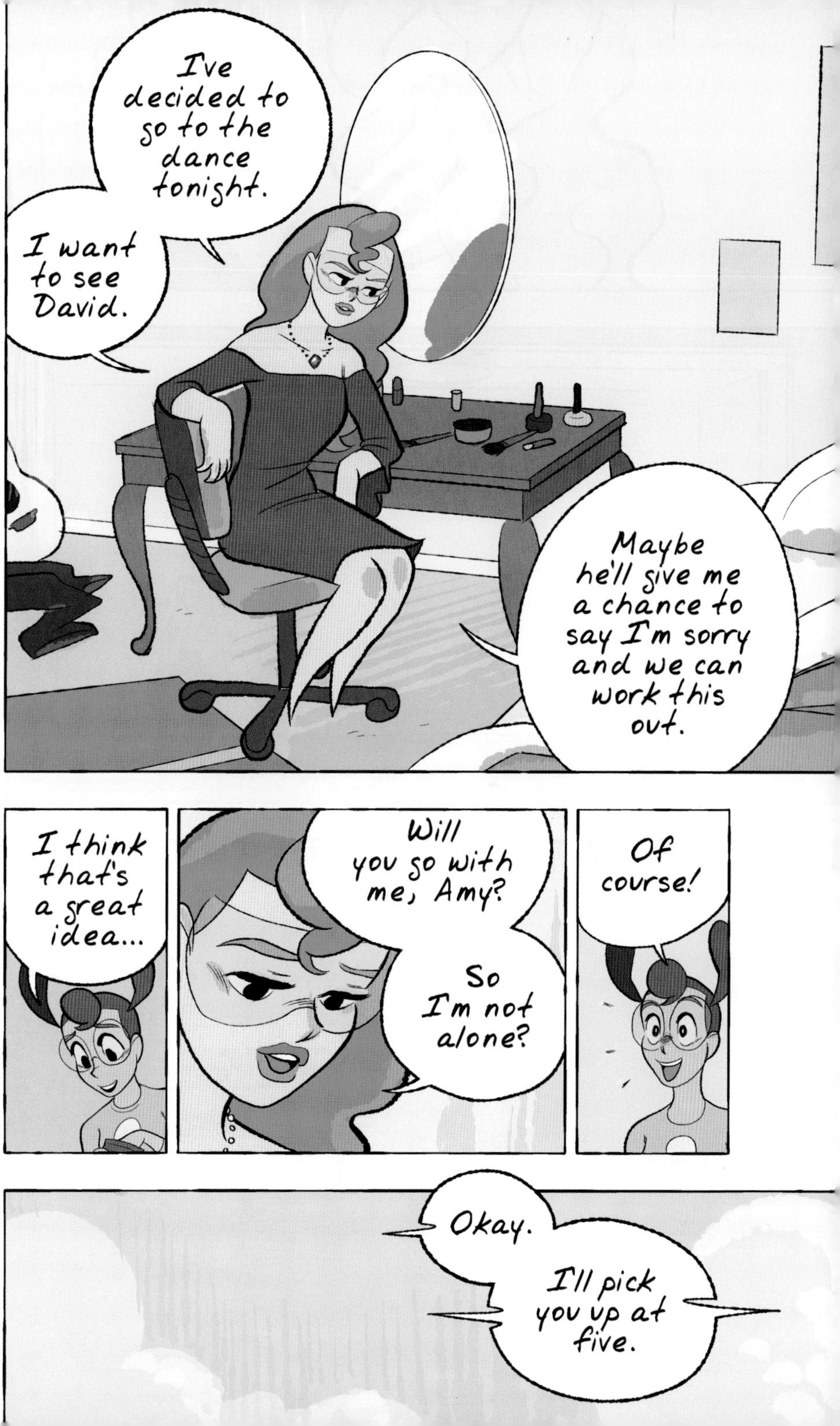
I've decided to go to the dance tonight.
I want to see David.
Maybe he'll give me a chance to say I'm sorry and we can work this out.
I think that's a great idea...
Will you go with me, Amy?
So I'm not alone?
Of course!
Okay.
I'll pick you up at five.

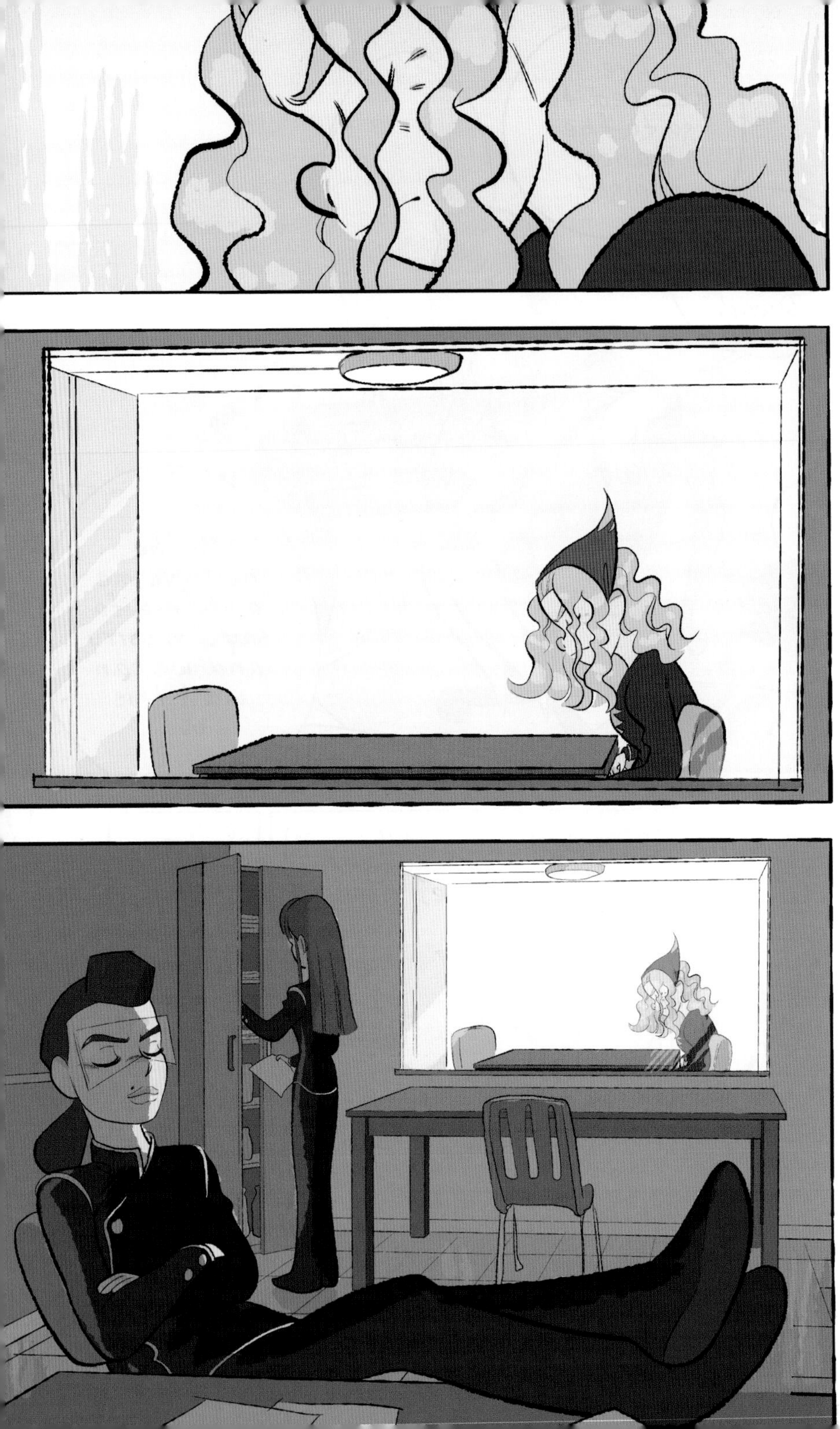

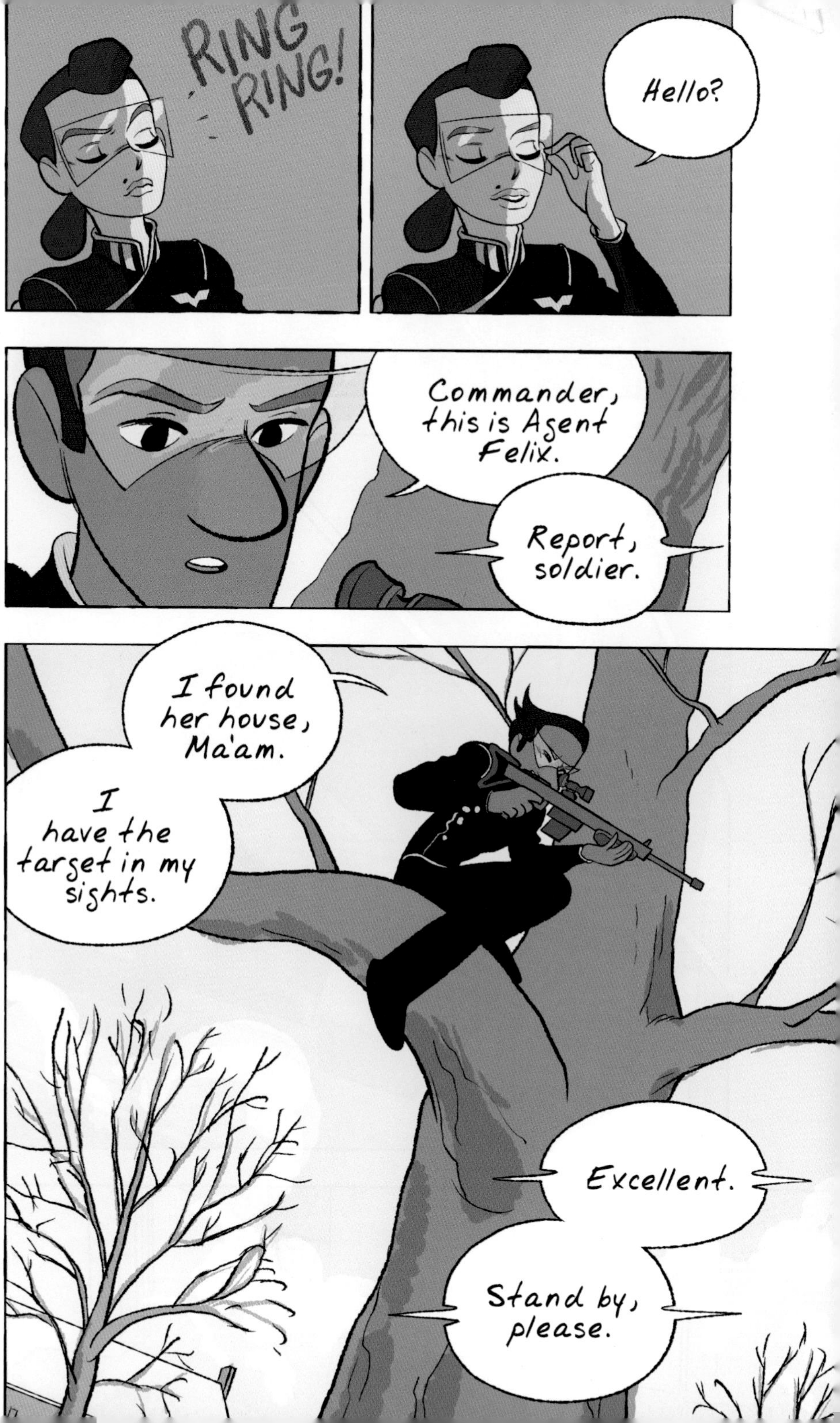
RING RING!
Hello?
Commander, this is Agent Felix.
Report, soldier.
I found her house, Ma'am.
I have the target in my sights.
Excellent.
Stand by, please.

Qiana--

It's showtime.

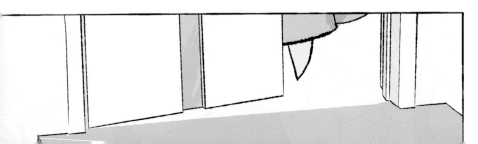

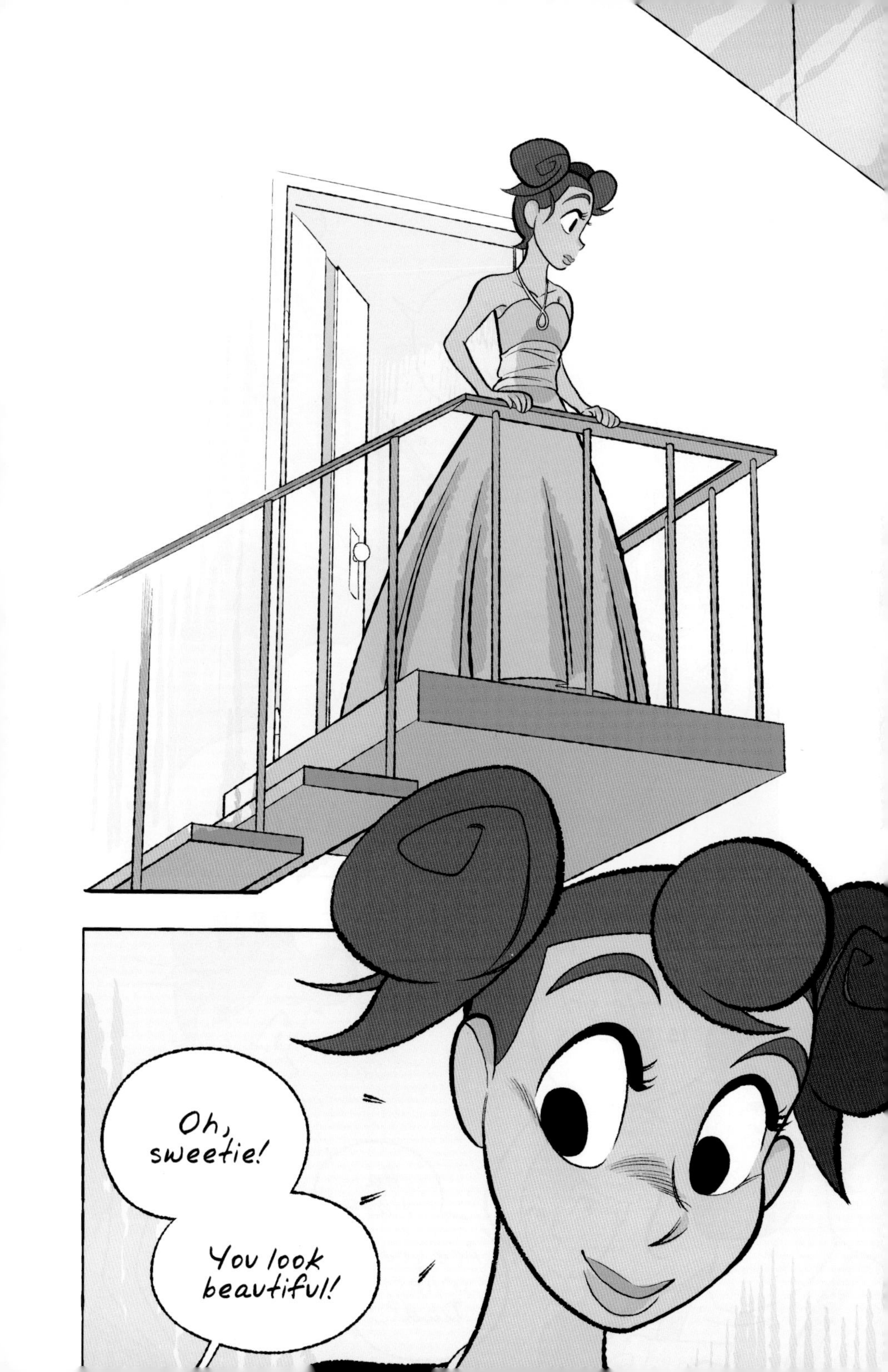
Oh, sweetie!
You look beautiful!

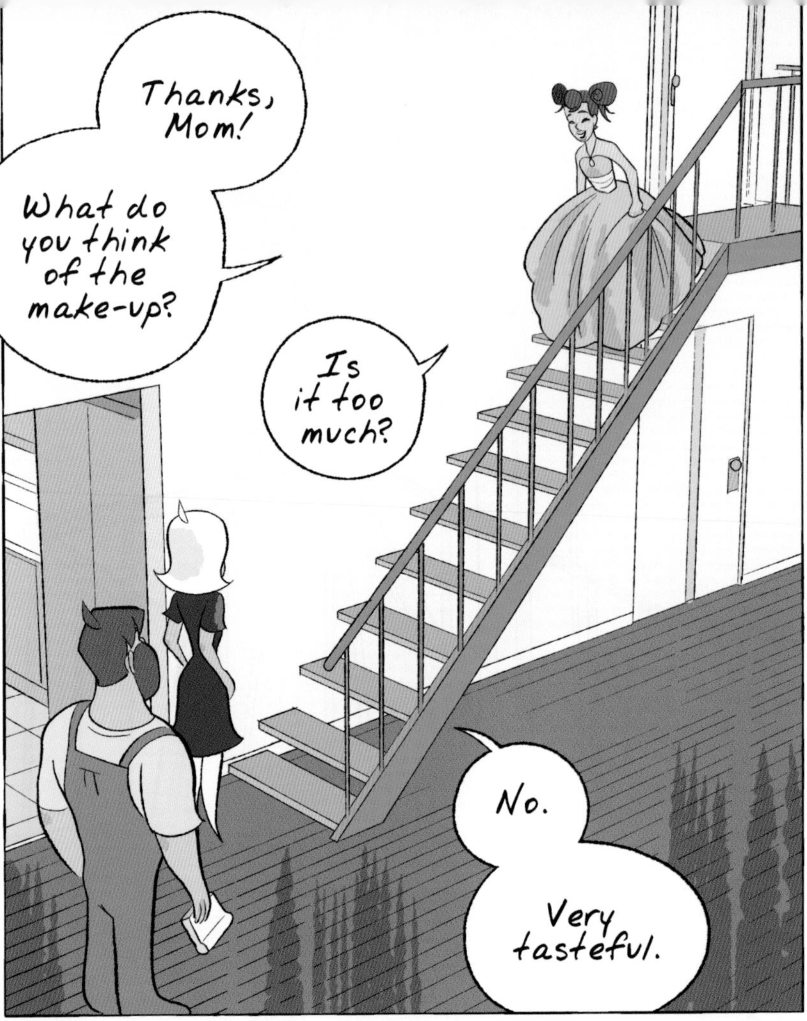
Thanks, Mom!
What do you think of the make-up?
Is it too much?
No.
Very tasteful.

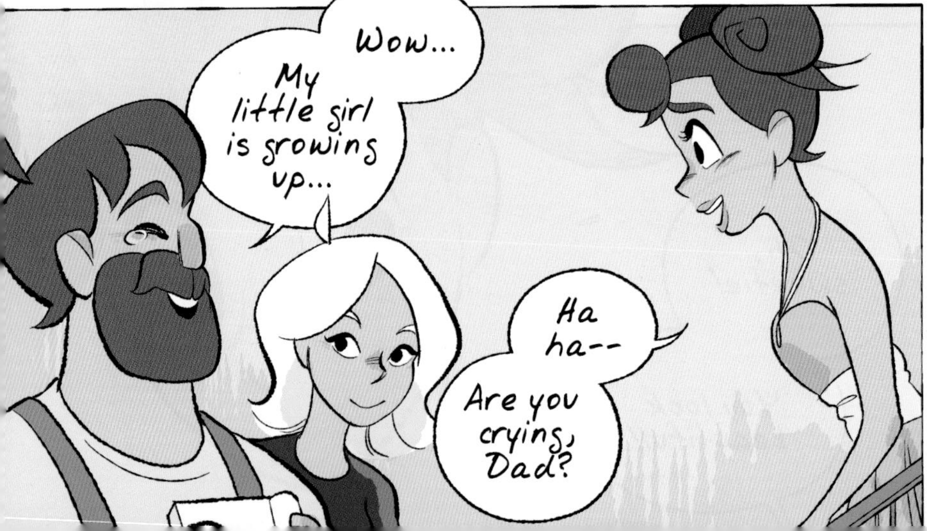
Wow...
My little girl is growing up...
Ha ha--
Are you crying, Dad?

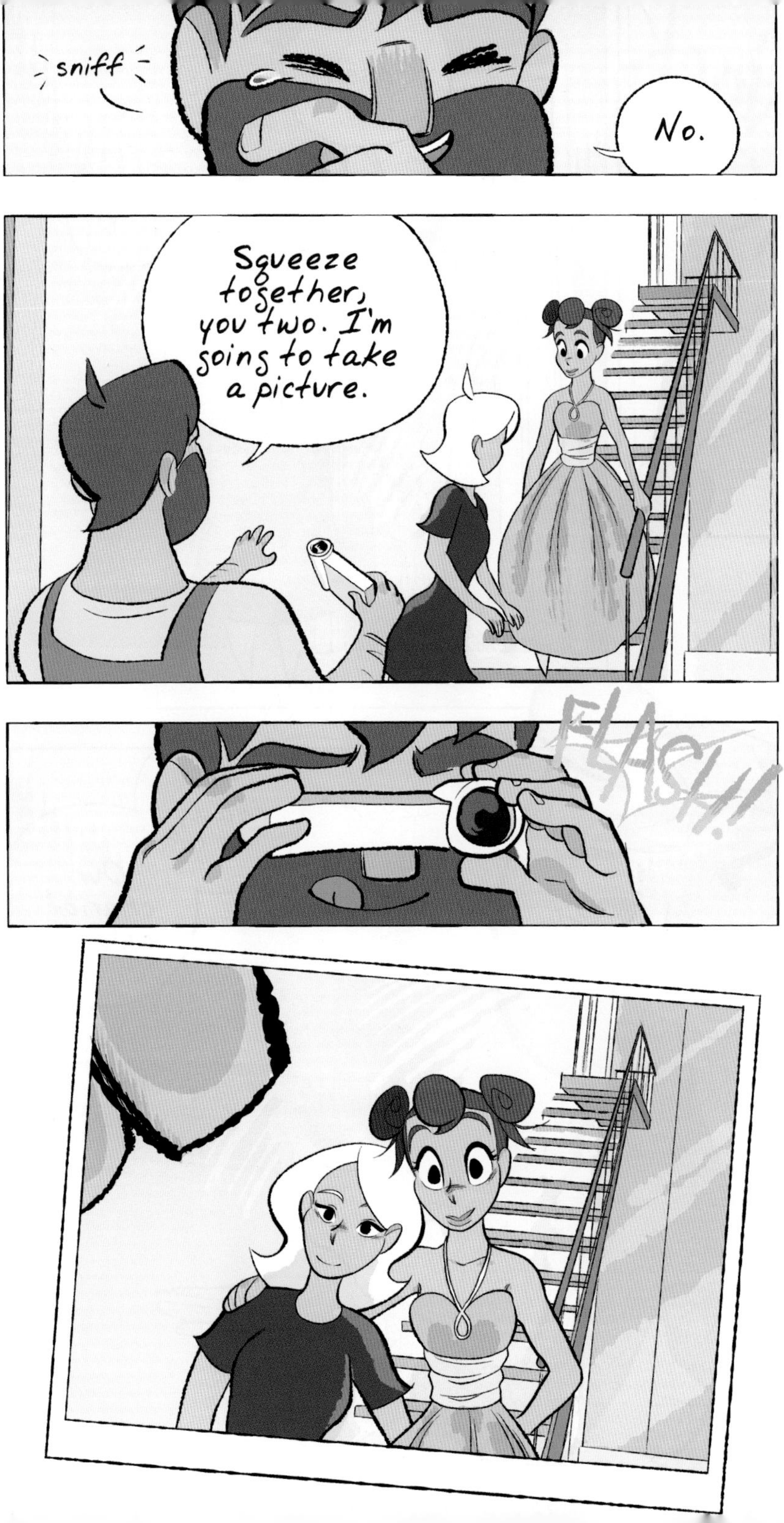
sniff
No.
Sqveeze together, you two. I'm soins to take a picture.
FLASH!!

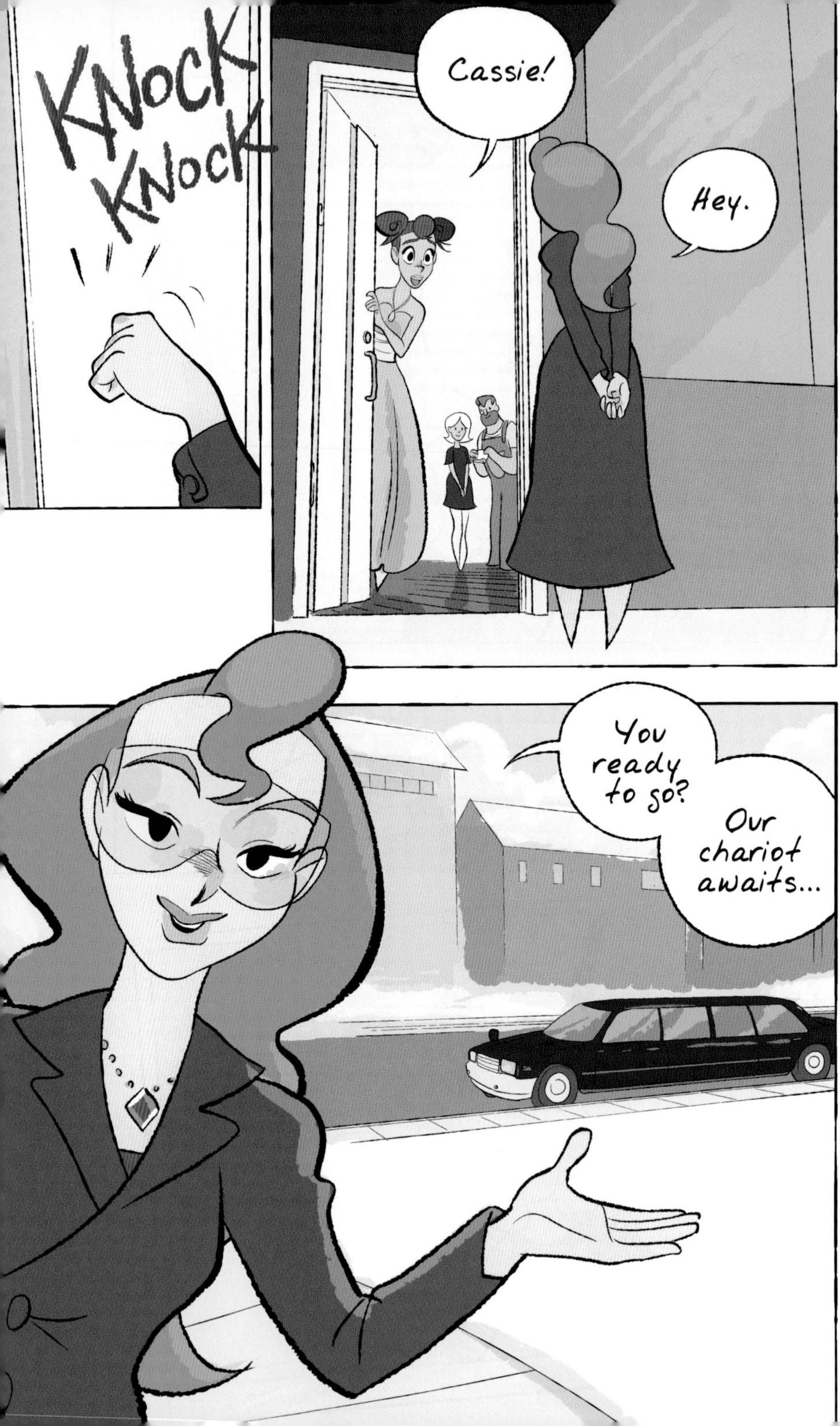
KNOCK KNOCK
Cassie!
Hey.
You ready to go?
Our chariot awaits...

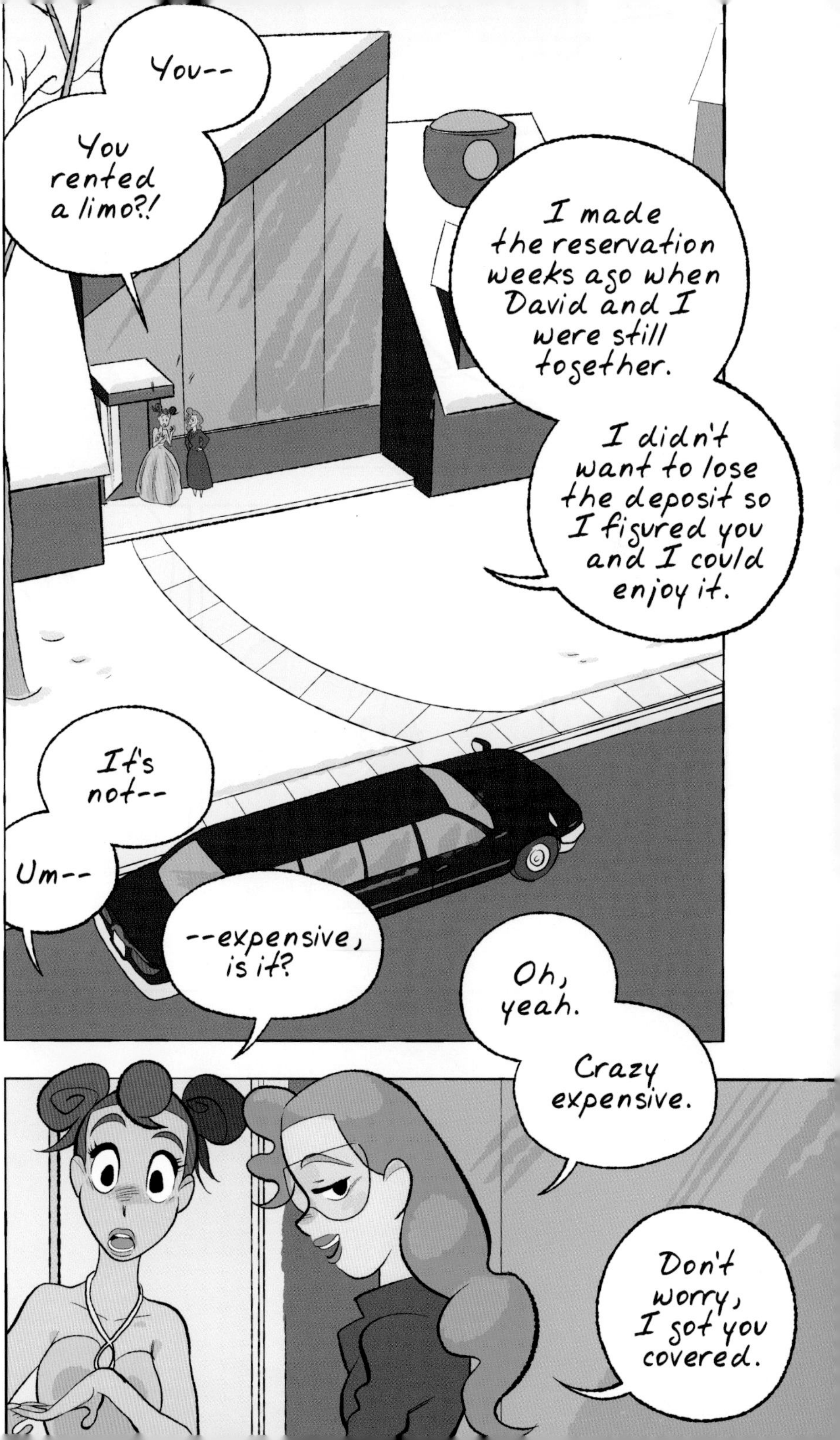
You--
You rented a limo?!
I made the reservation weeks ago when David and I were still together.
I didn't want to lose the deposit so I figured you and I could enjoy it.
It's not--
Um--
--expensive, is it?
Oh, yeah.
Crazy expensive.
Don't worry, I got you covered.

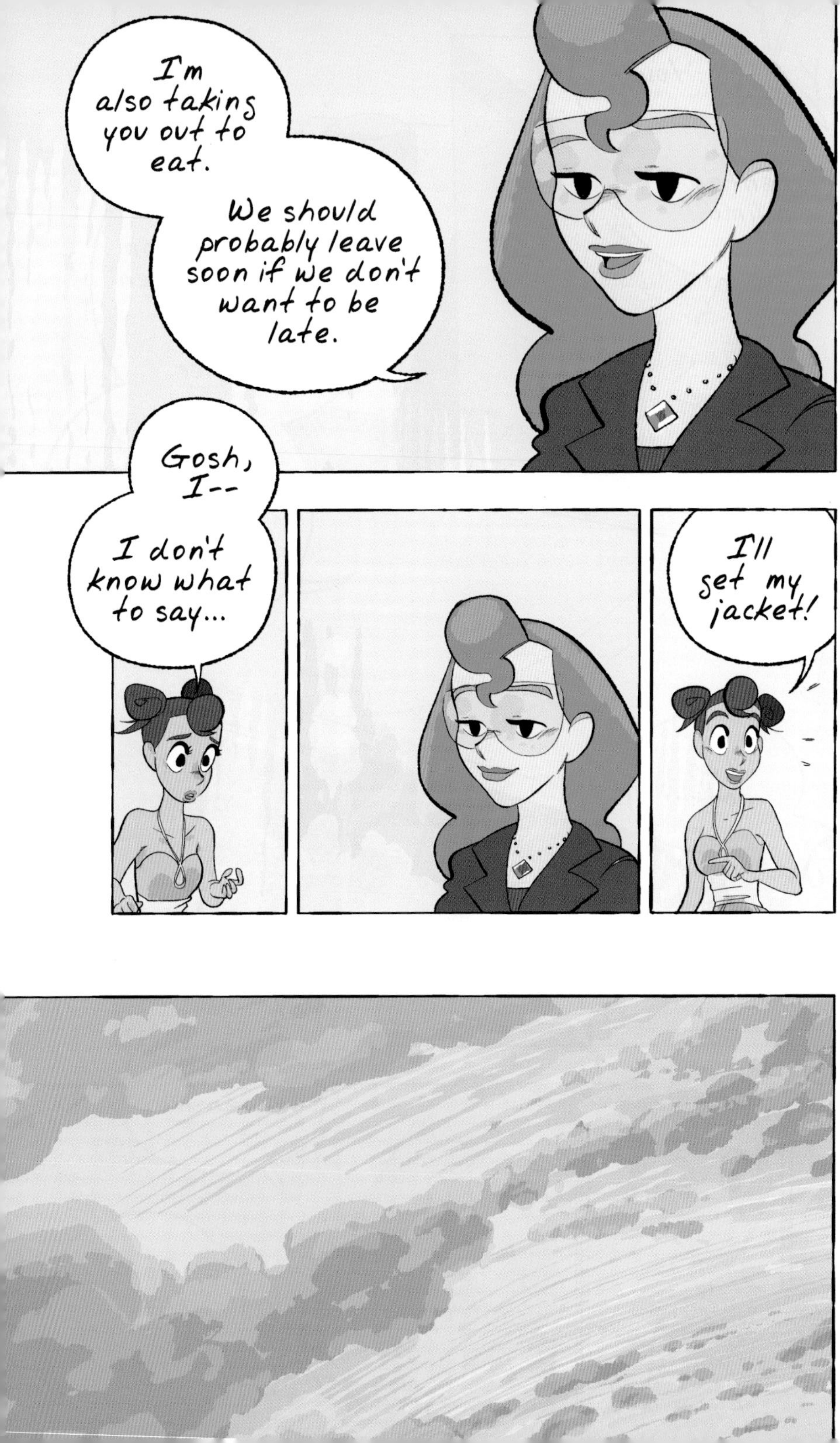
I'm also taking you out to eat.
We should probably leave soon if we don't want to be late.
Gosh, I--
I don't know what to say...
I'll get my jacket!

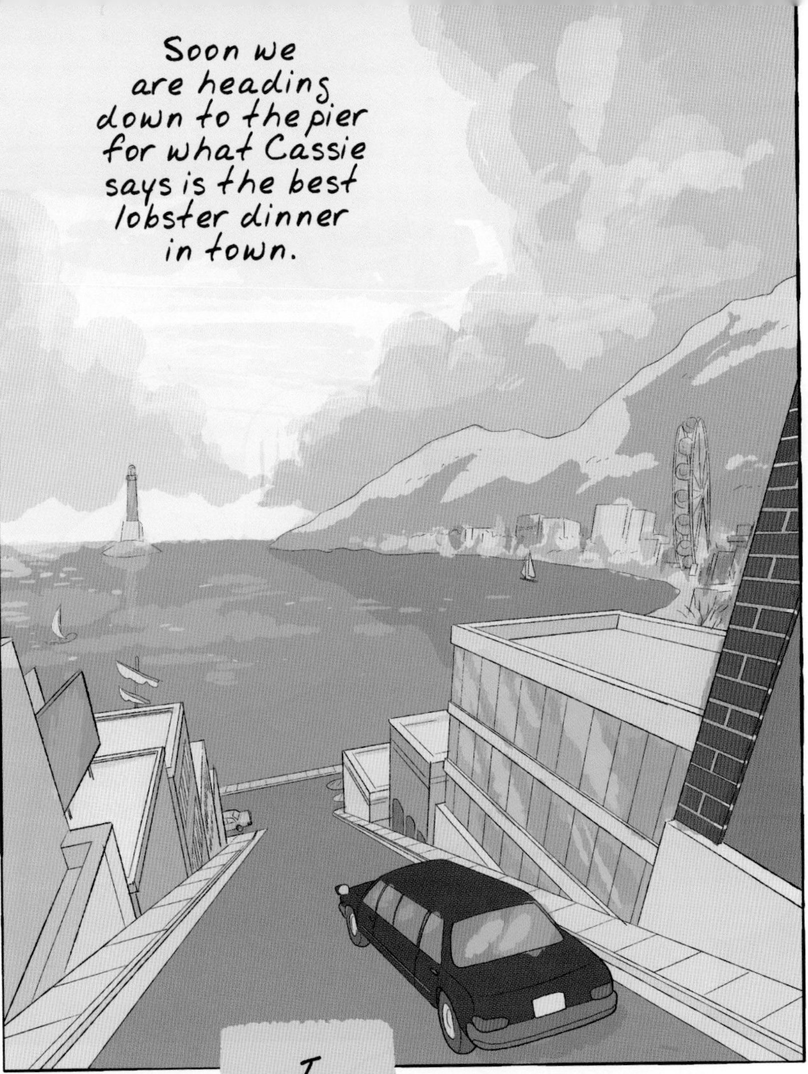
Soon we are heading down to the pier for what Cassie says is the best lobster dinner in town.

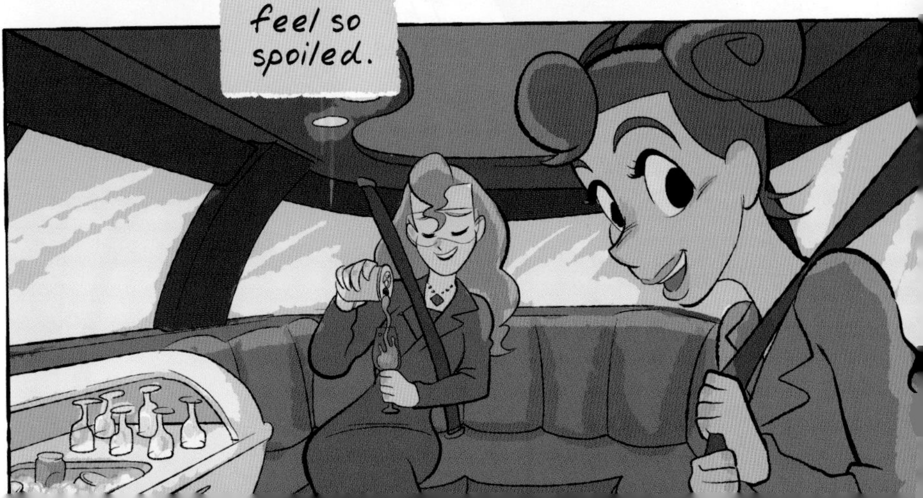
I feel so spoiled.

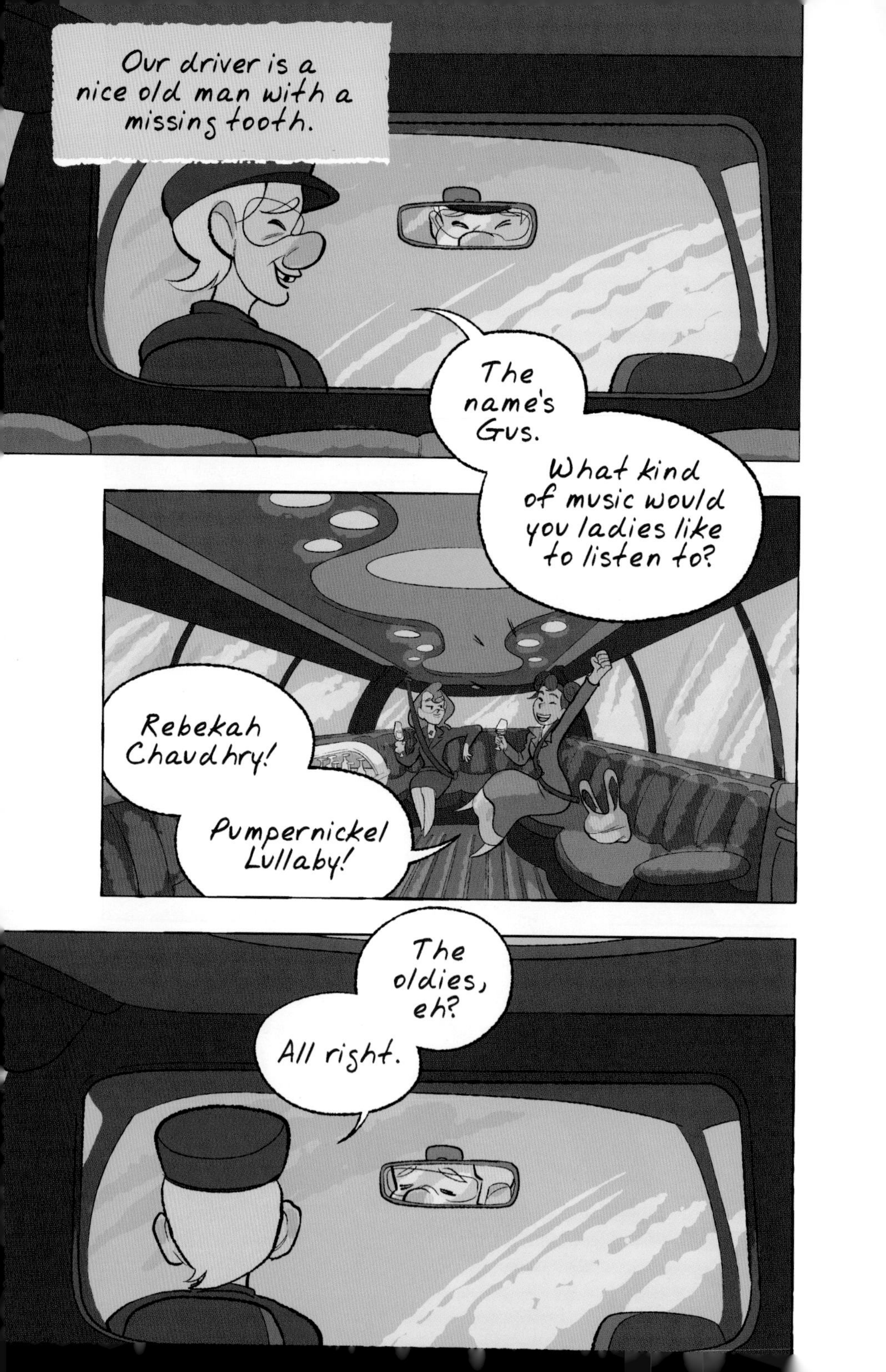
Our driver is a nice old man with a missing tooth.
The name's Gus.
What kind of music would you ladies like to listen to?
Rebekah Chaudhry!
Pumpernickel Lullaby!
The oldies, eh?
All right.

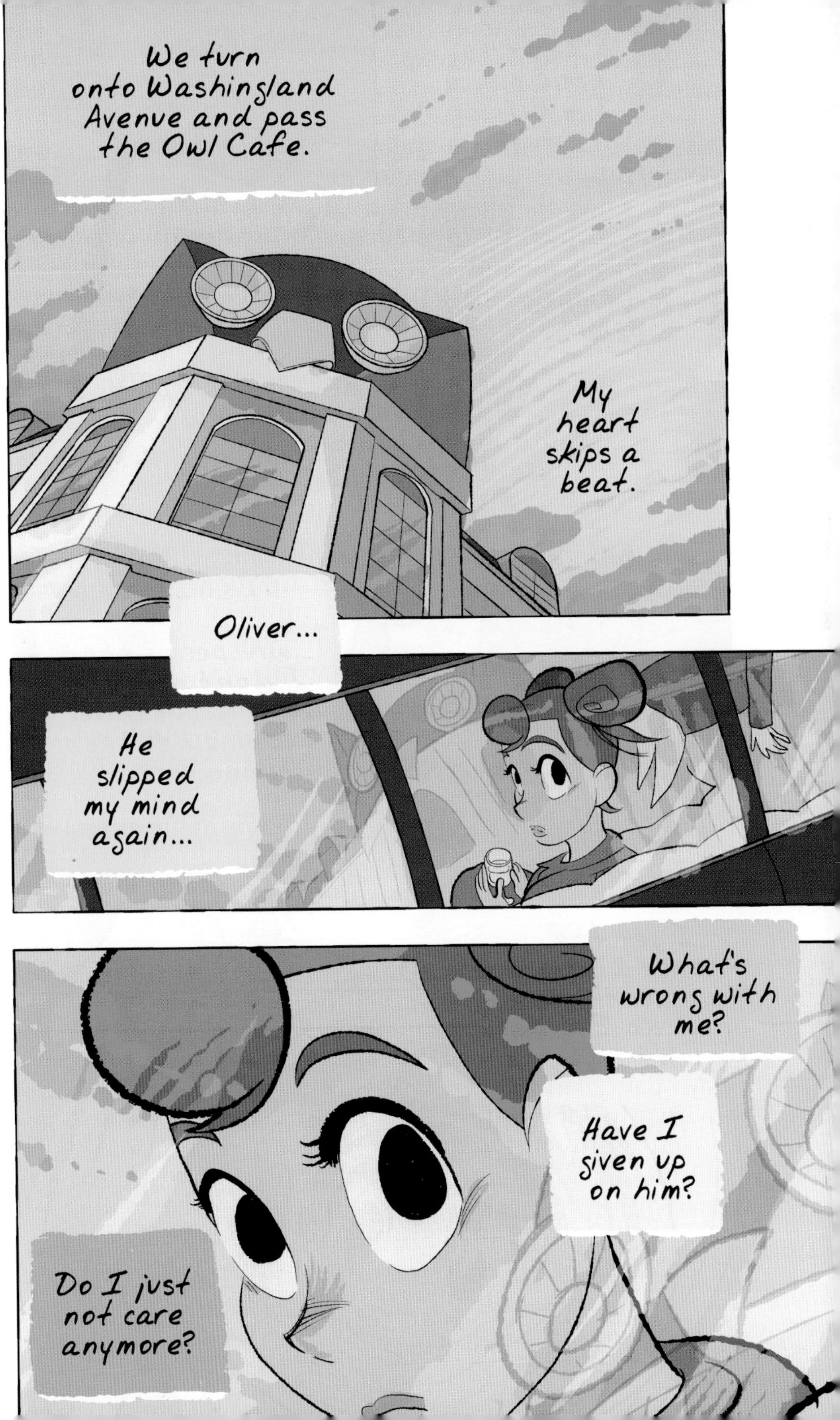
We turn onto Washingland Avenue and pass the Owl Cafe.
My heart skips a beat.
Oliver...
He slipped my mind again...
What's wrong with me?
Have I given up on him?
Do I just not care anymore?

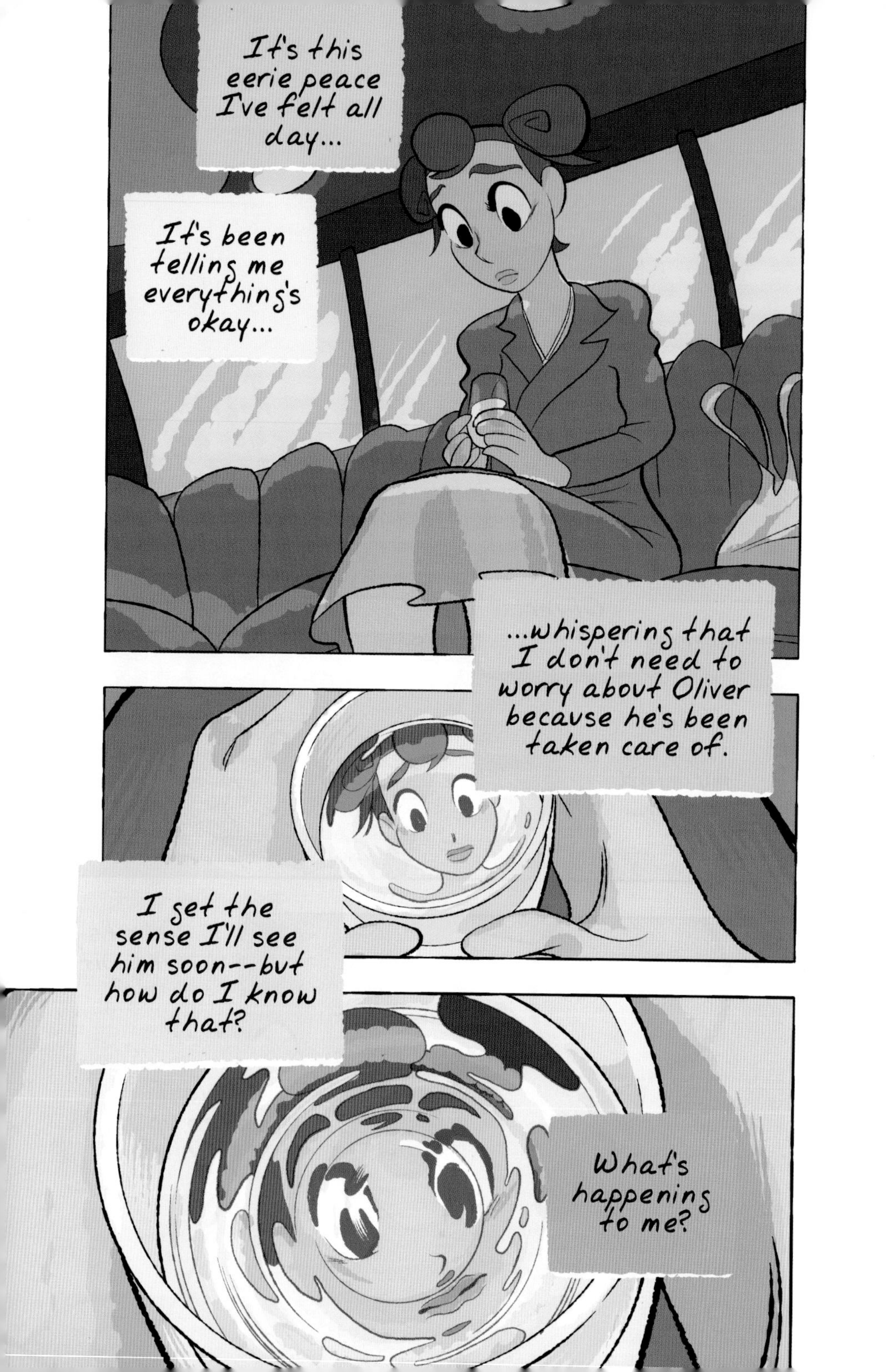
It's this eerie peace I've felt all day...
It's been telling me everything's okay...
...whispering that I don't need to worry about Oliver because he's been taken care of.
I get the sense I'll see him soon--but how do I know that?
What's happening to me?

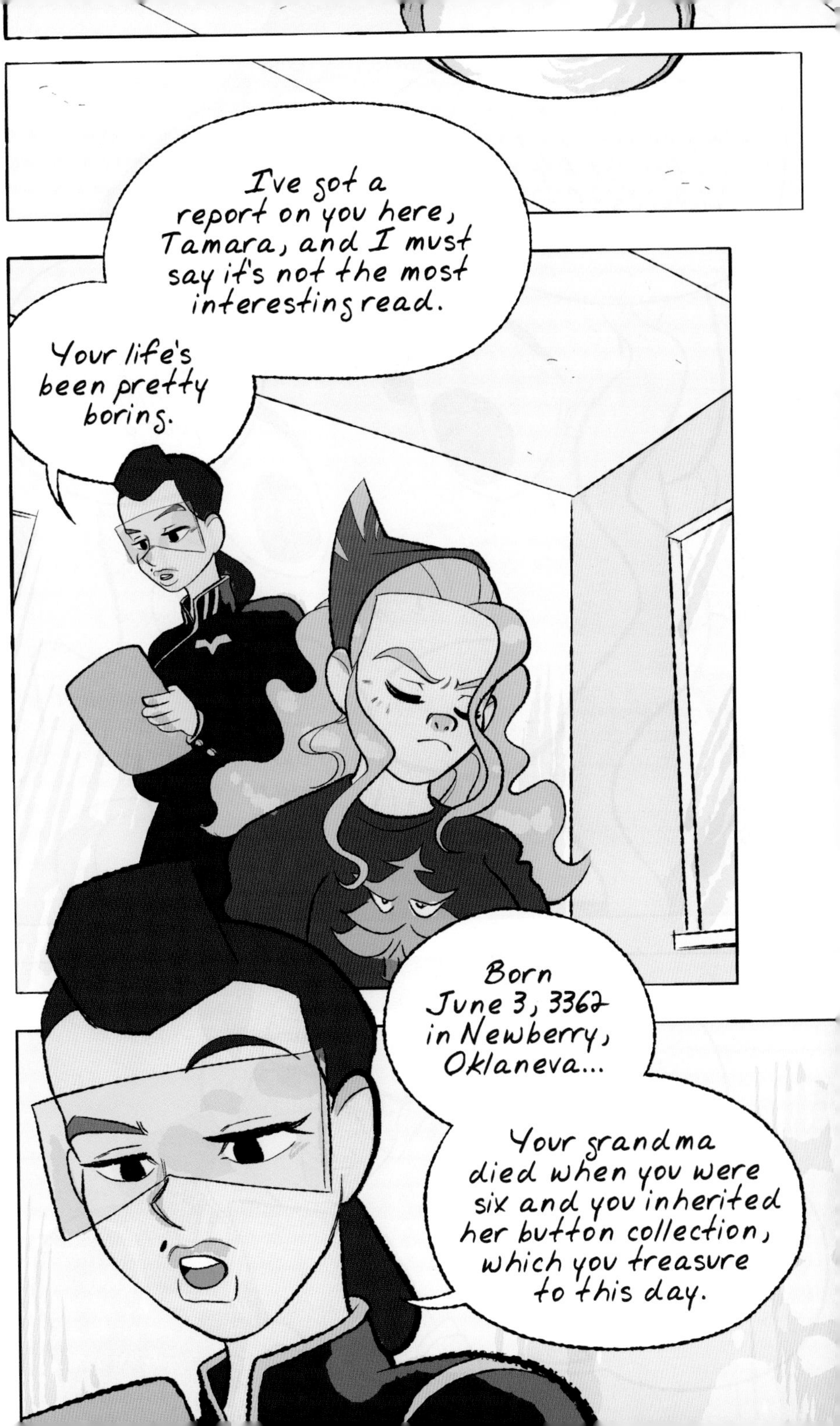
I've got a report on you here, Tamara, and I must say it's not the most interesting read.
Your life's been pretty boring.
Born June 3, 3362 in Newberry, Oklaneva...
Your grandma died when you were six and you inherited her button collection, which you treasure to this day.

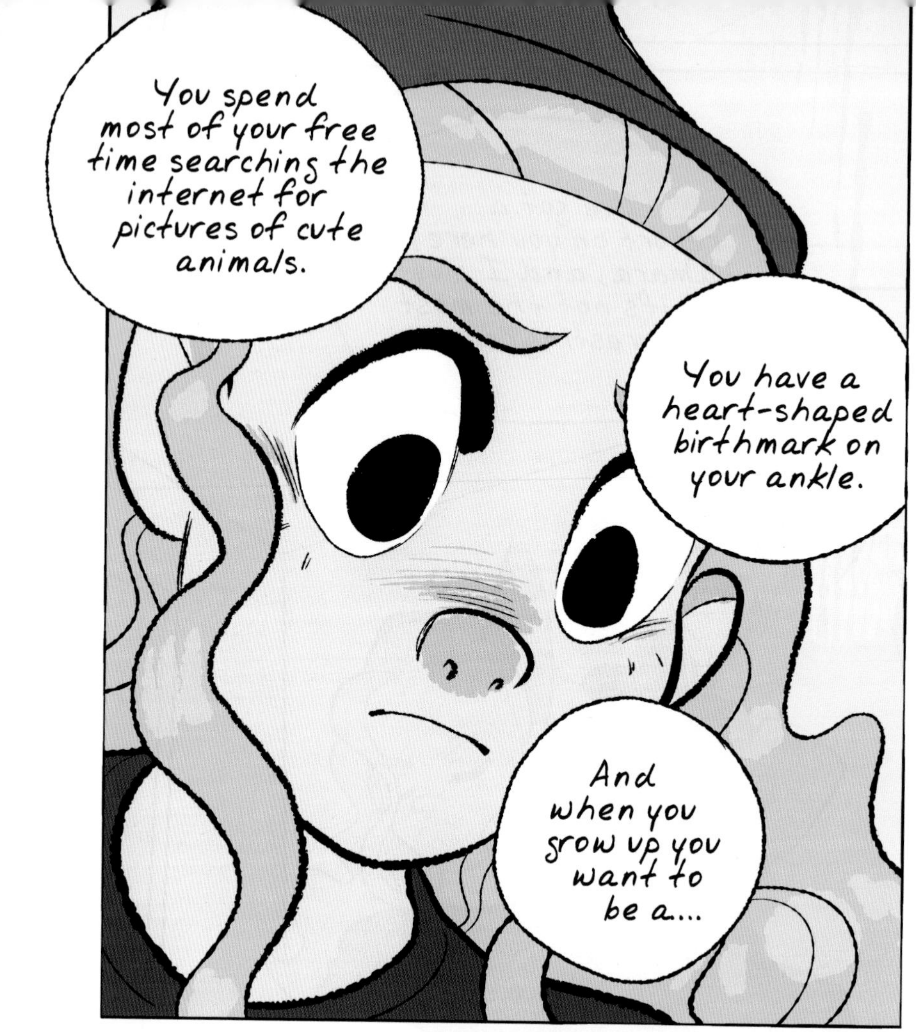
You spend most of your free time searching the internet for pictures of cute animals.
You have a heart-shaped birthmark on your ankle.
And when you grow up you want to be a....
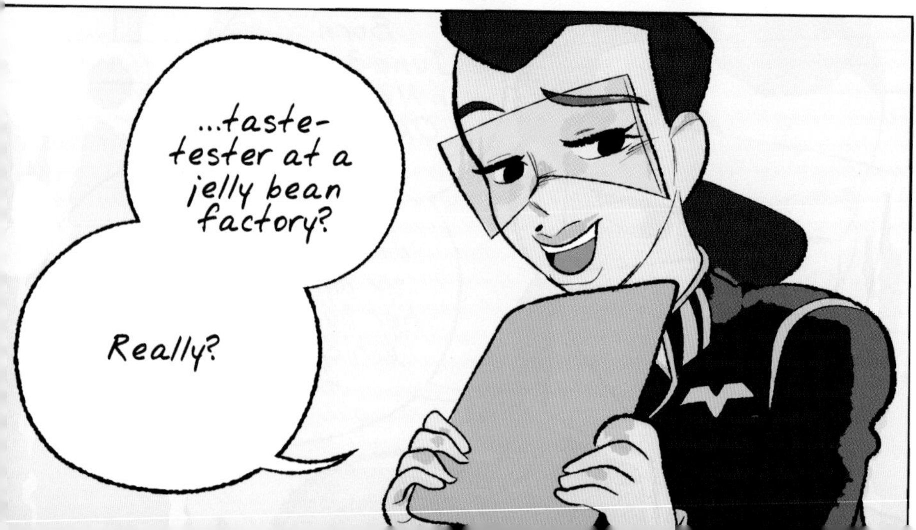
...taste-tester at a jelly bean factory?
Really?

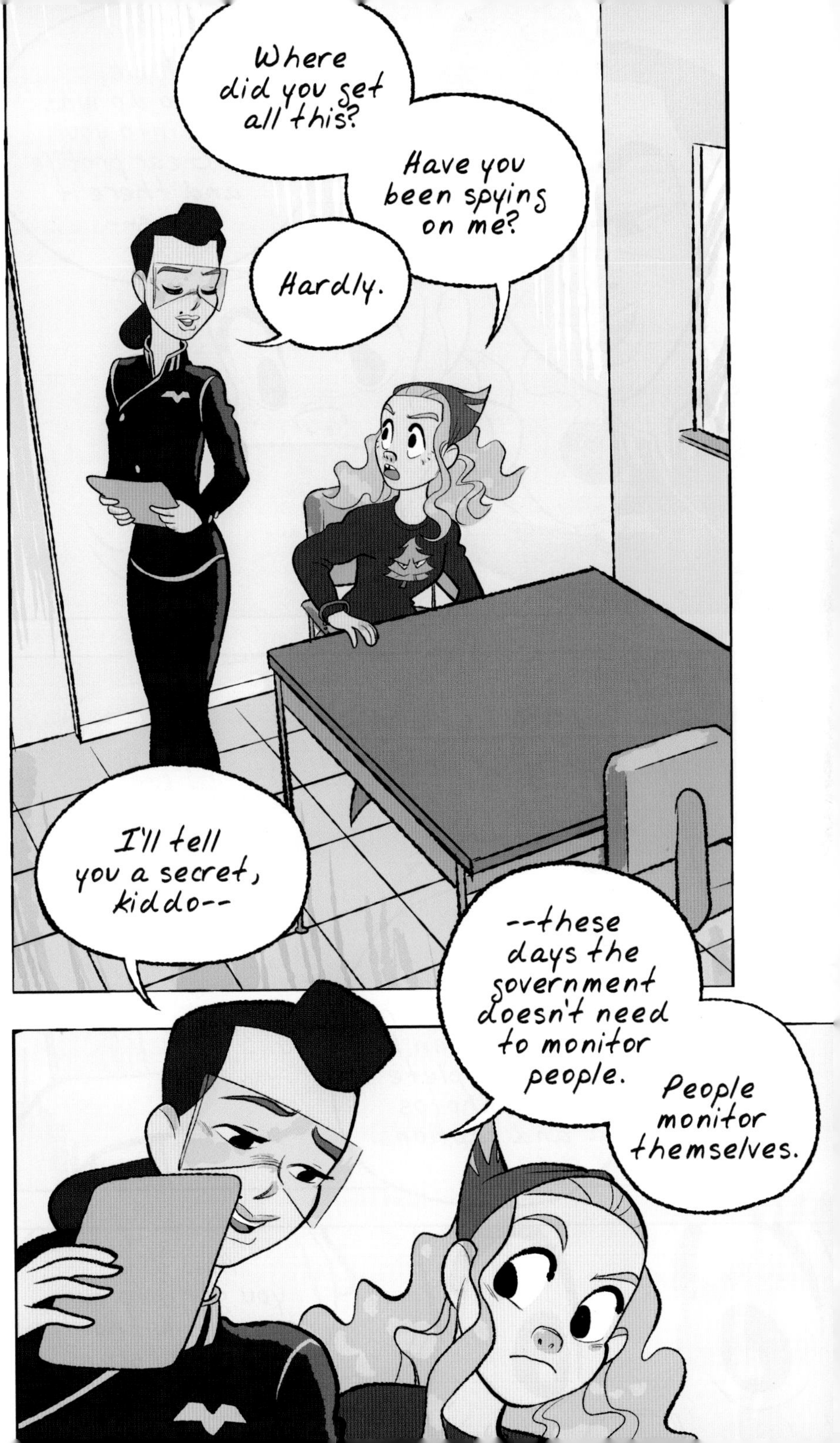
Where did you get all this?
Have you been spying on me?
Hardly.
I'll tell you a secret, kiddo--
--these days the government doesn't need to monitor people.
People monitor themselves.

All we had to do was hack into your Net Gear profile and there it was--

--a detailed record of your life, written by you, complete with photos and captions.

Tamara

Tamara

...l like waking up early today ...til noon. Whoops!

...w what those things ...e end of the ...not sure.

...st house keys ...think I misplaced ...hen I went for

How did you get into my account without a retinal scan?

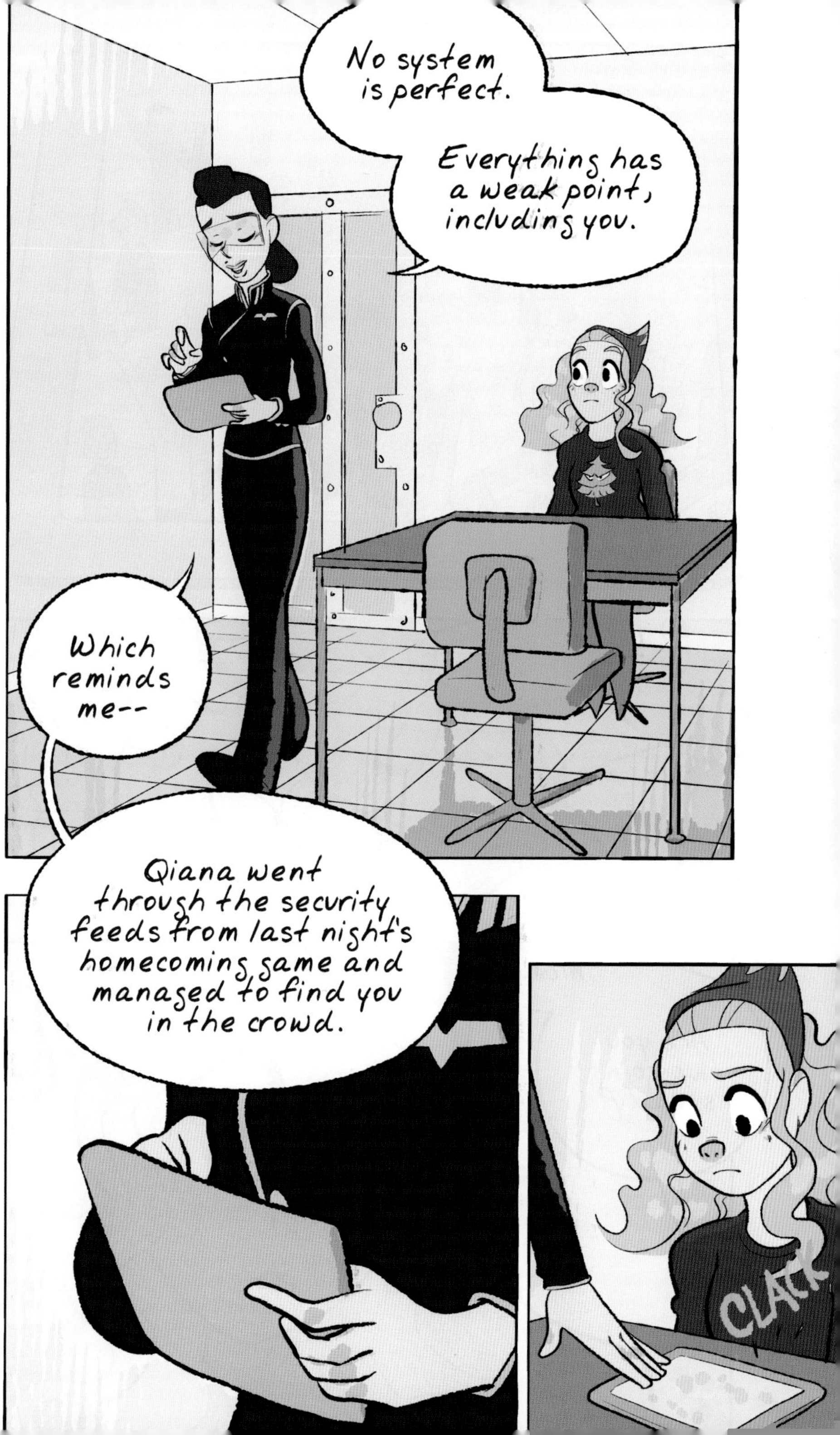
No system is perfect.
Everything has a weak point, including you.
Which reminds me--
Qiana went through the security feeds from last night's homecoming game and managed to find you in the crowd.
CLACK

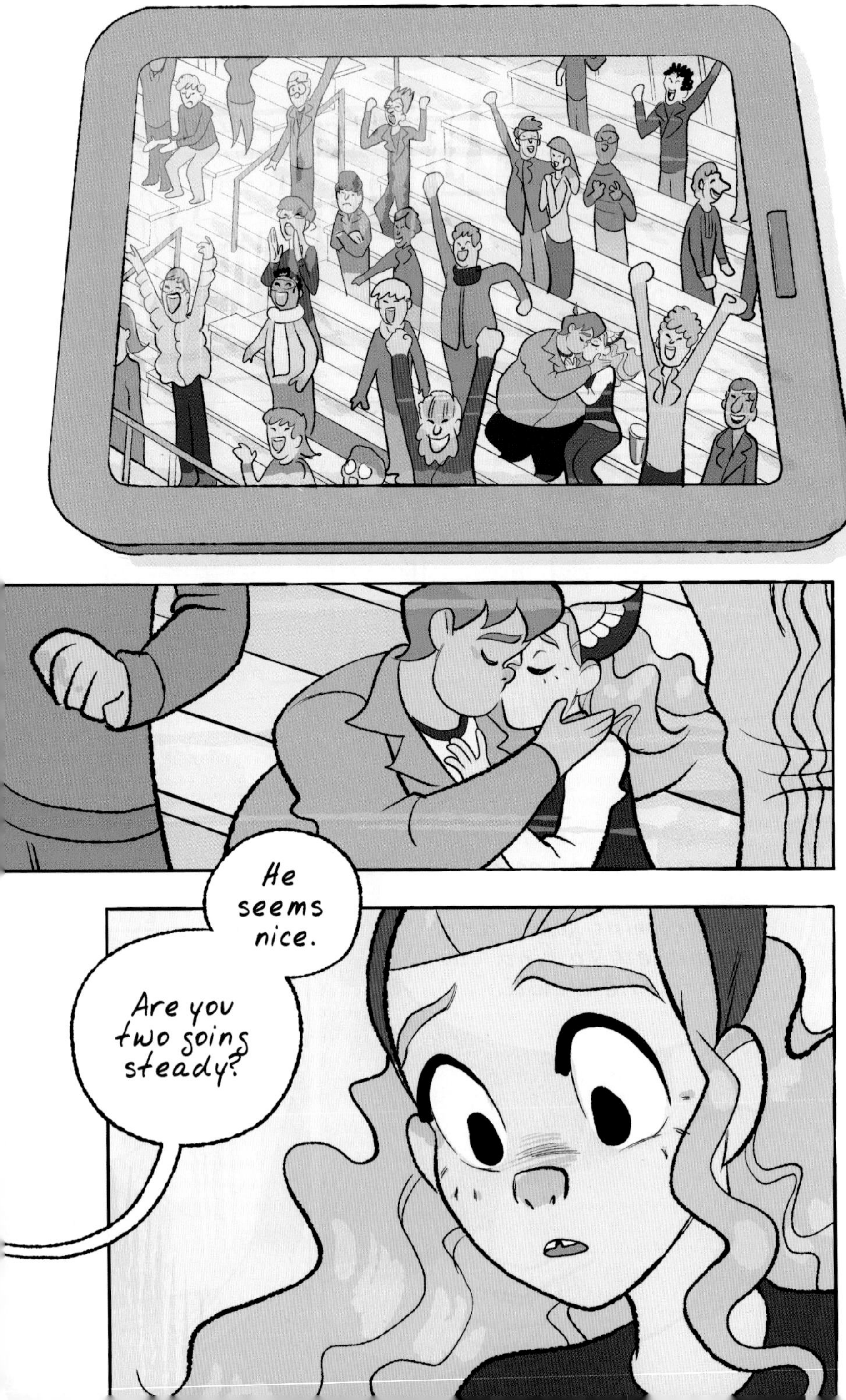
He seems nice.
Are you two going steady?

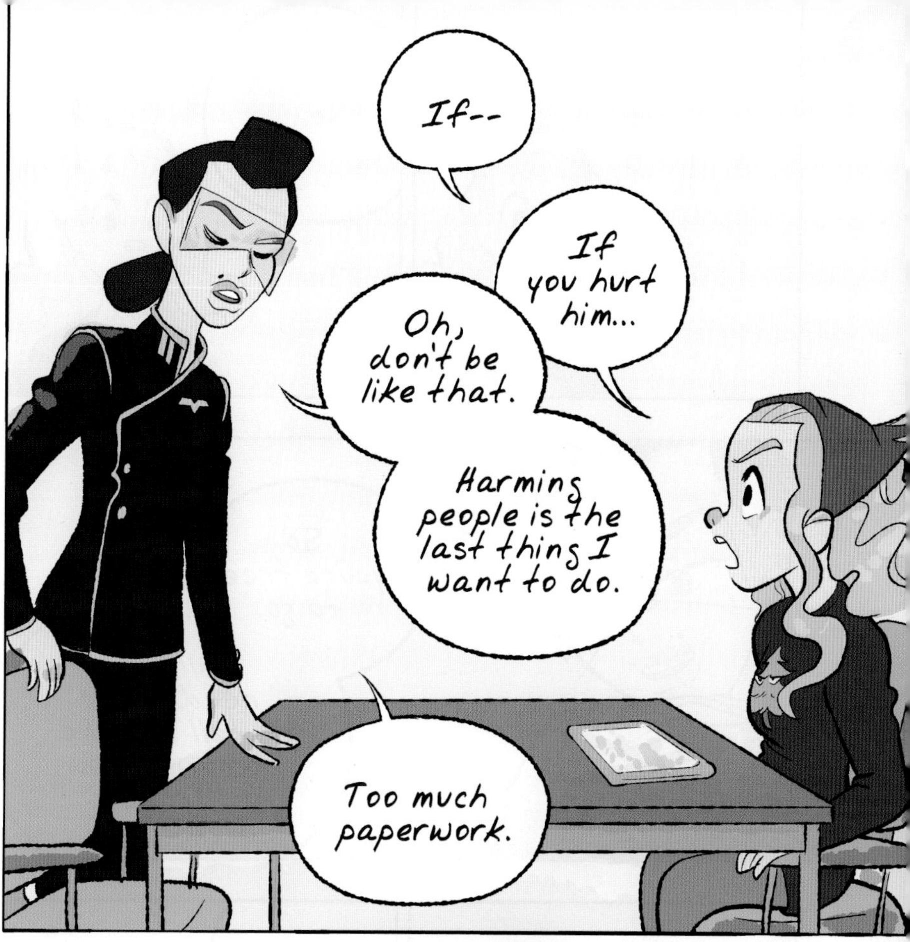
If--
If you hurt him...
Oh, don't be like that.
Harming people is the last things I want to do.
Too much paperwork.
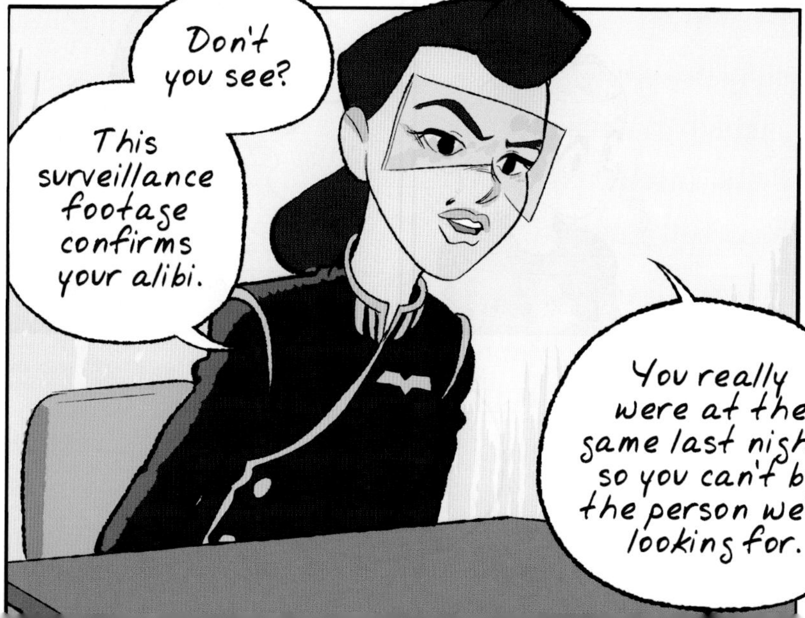
Don't you see?
This surveillance footage confirms your alibi.
You really were at the game last night, so you can't be the person we're looking for.

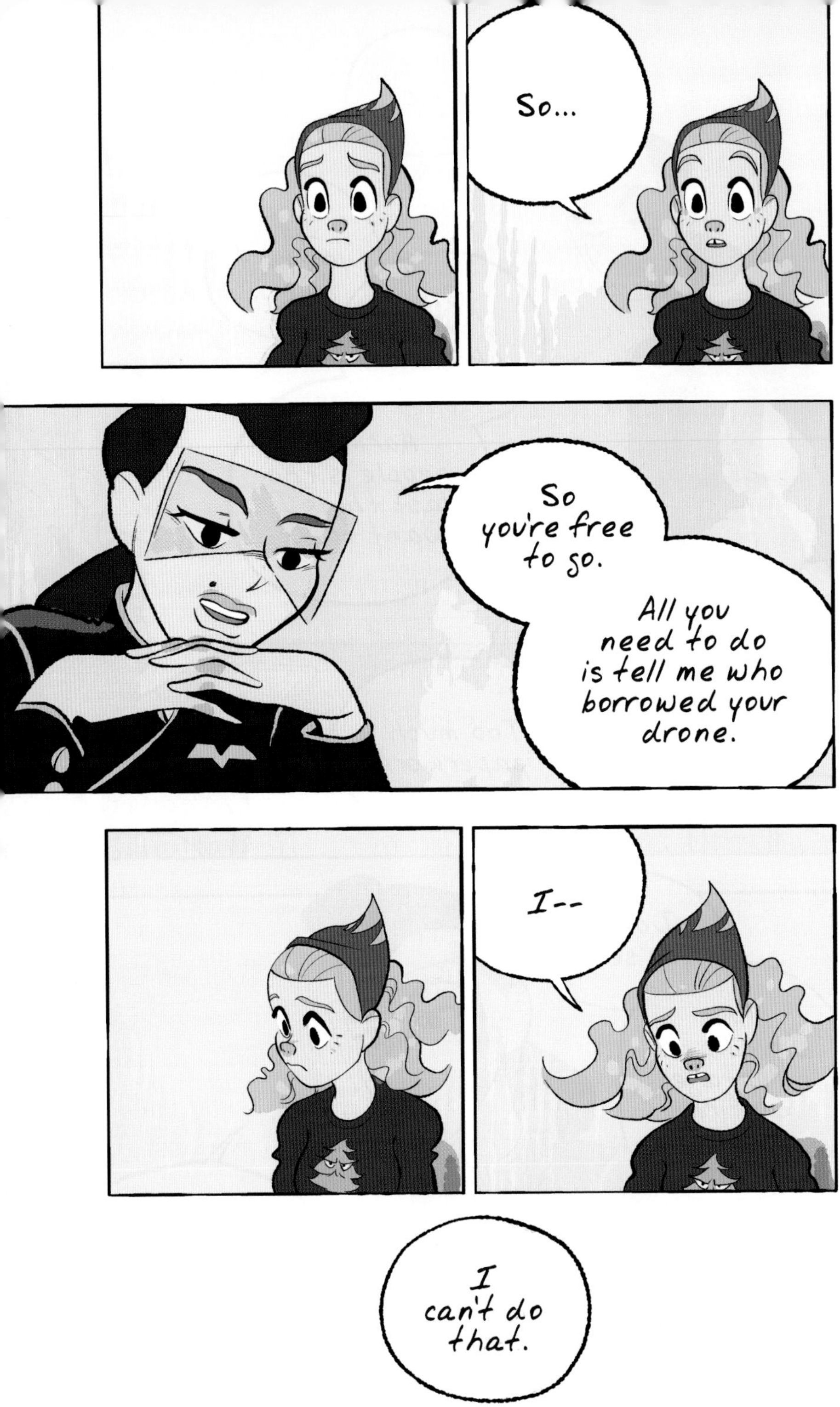
So...
So you're free to go.
All you need to do is tell me who borrowed your drone.
I--
I can't do that.

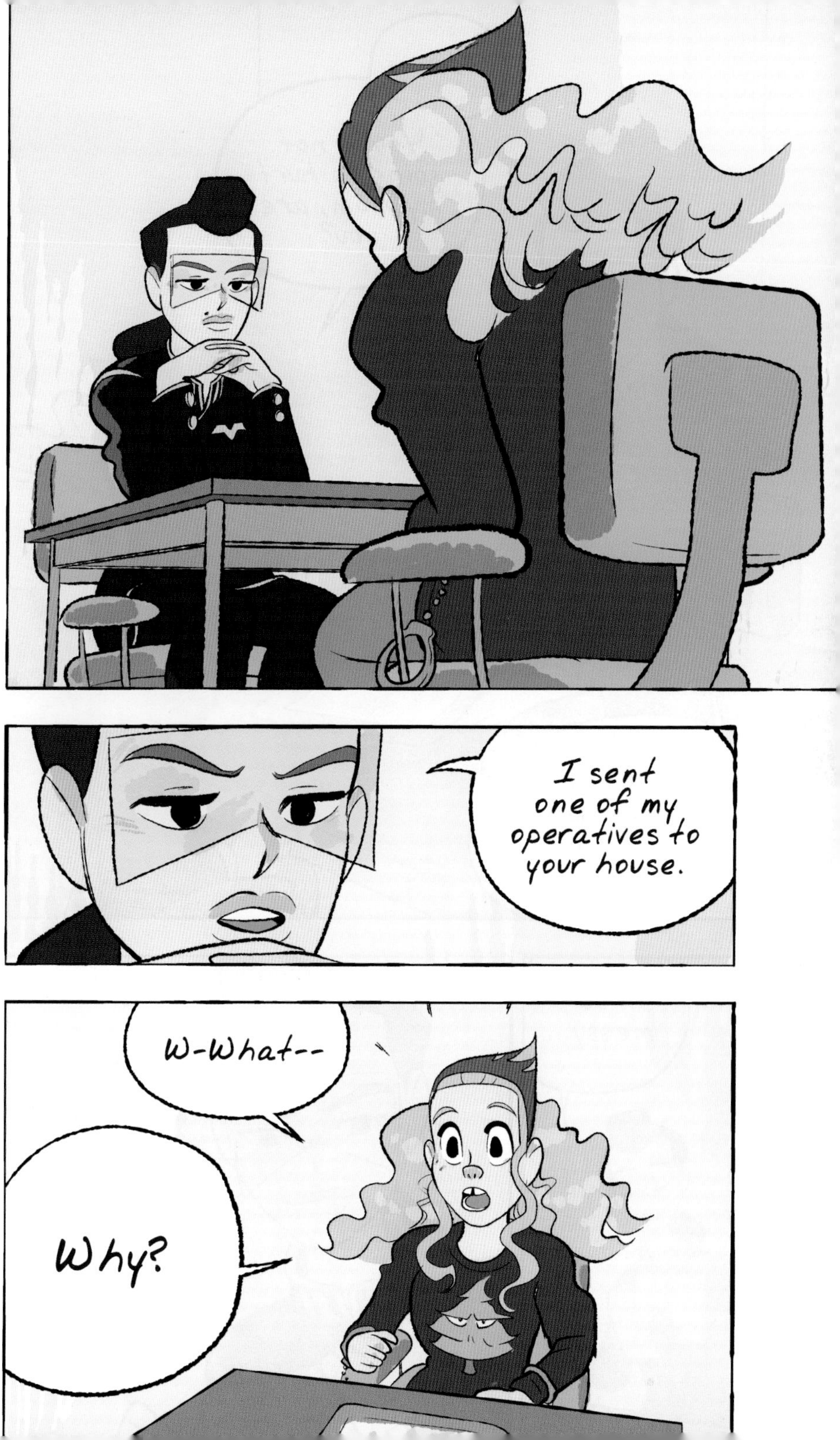
I sent one of my operatives to your house.
W-What--
Why?

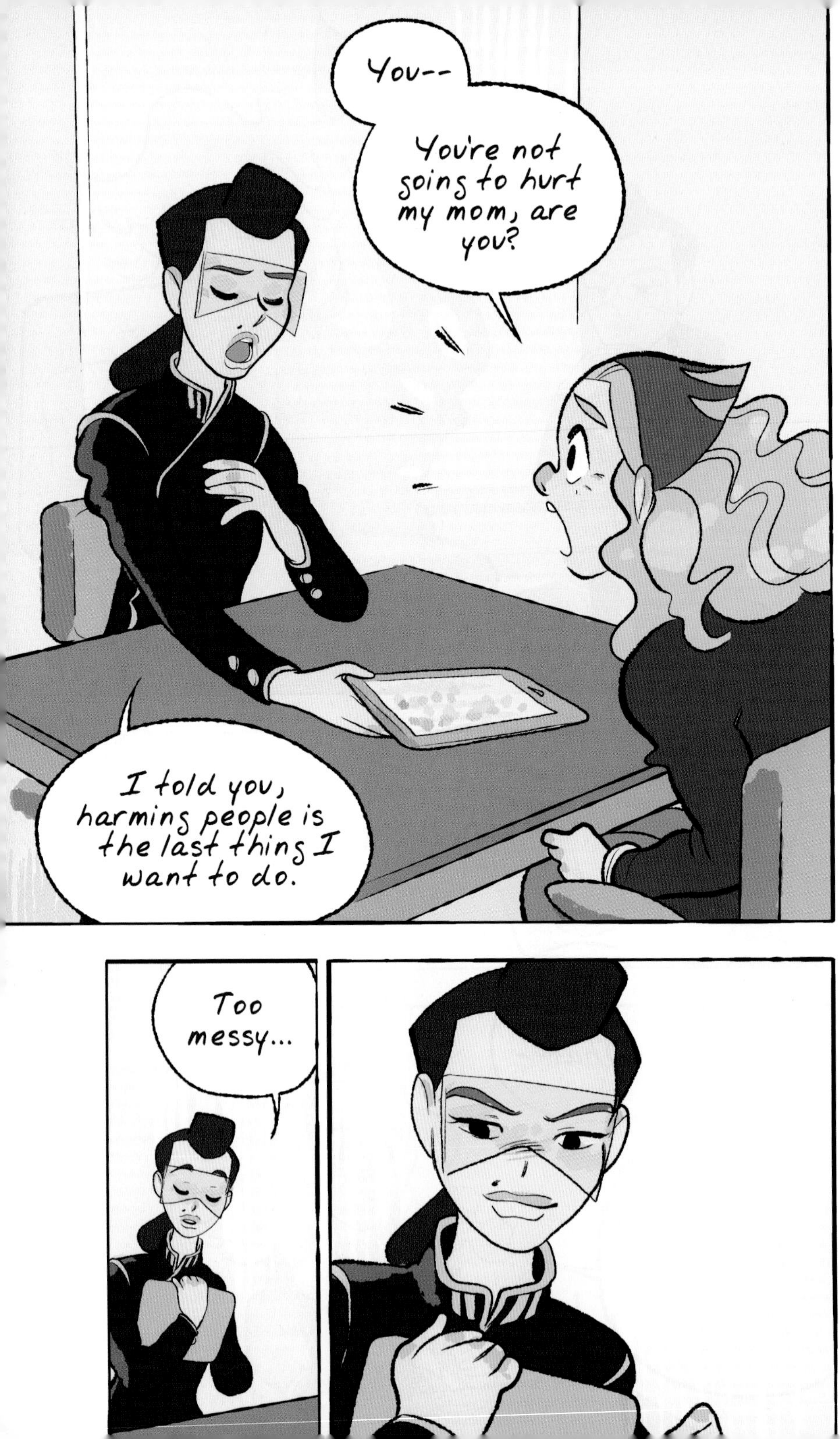
You--
You're not going to hurt my mom, are you?
I told you, harming people is the last thing I want to do.
Too messy...

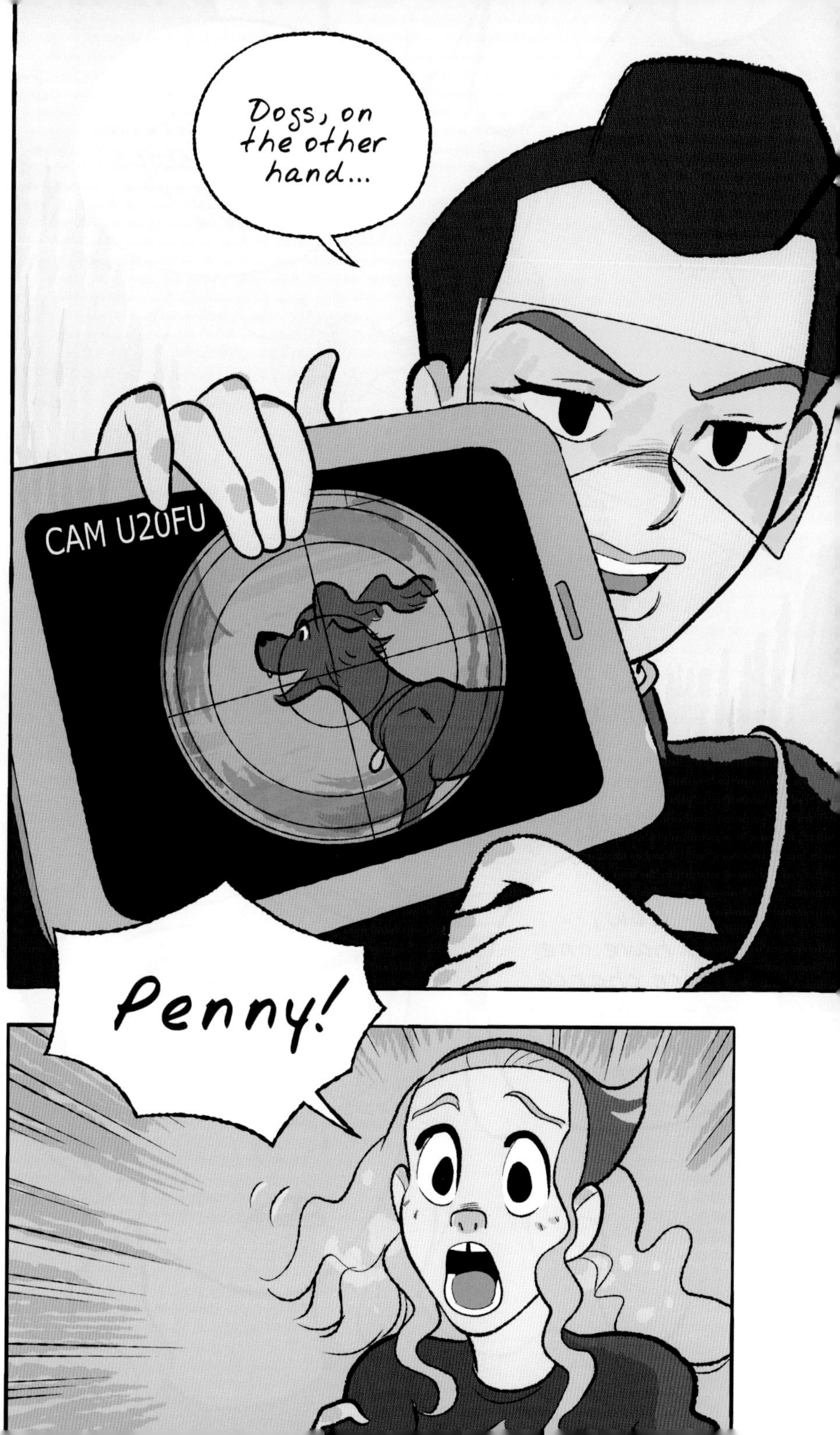
Dogs, on the other hand...
CAM U20FU
Penny!

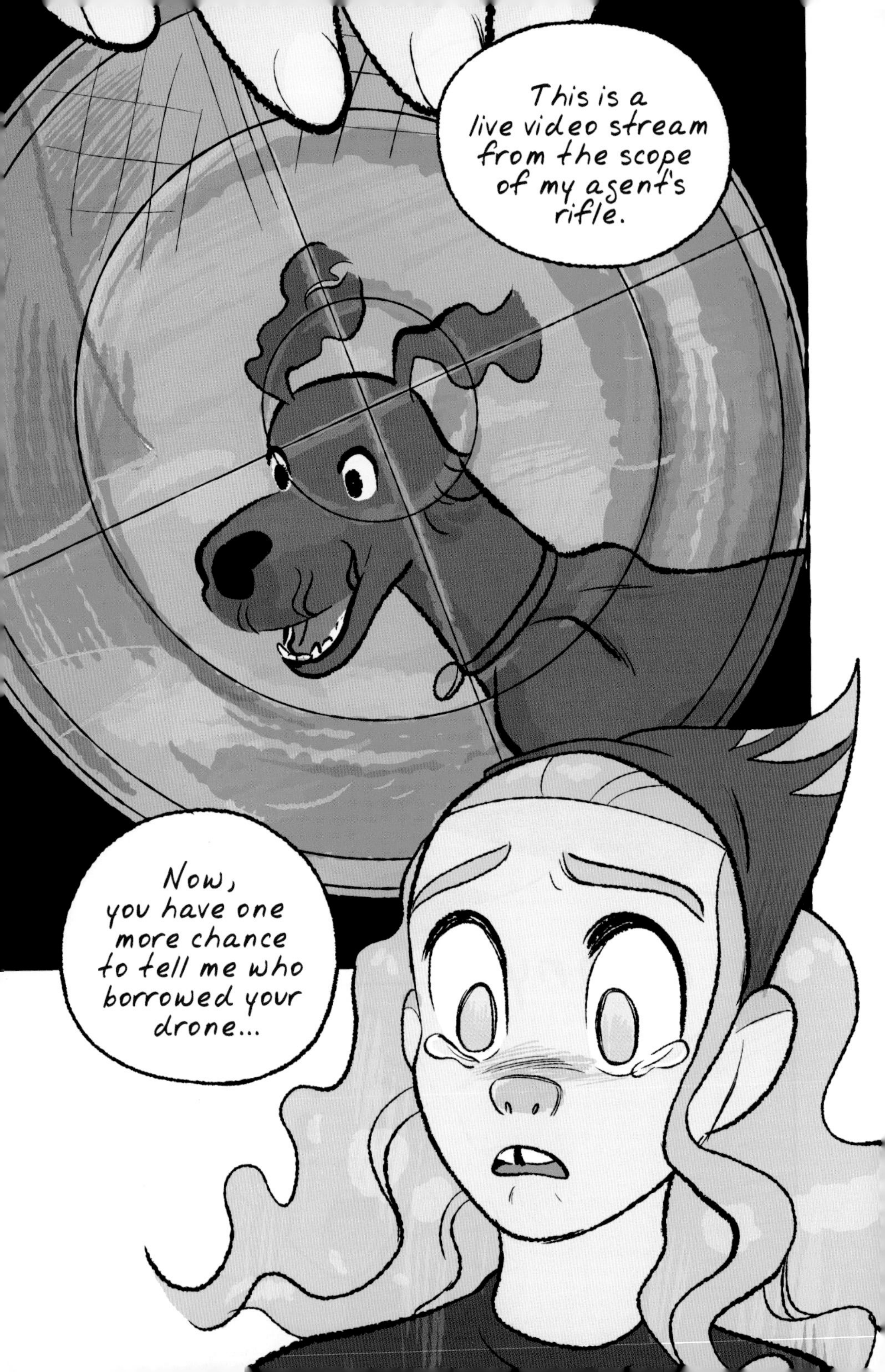
This is a live video stream from the scope of my agent's rifle.
Now, you have one more chance to tell me who borrowed your drone...

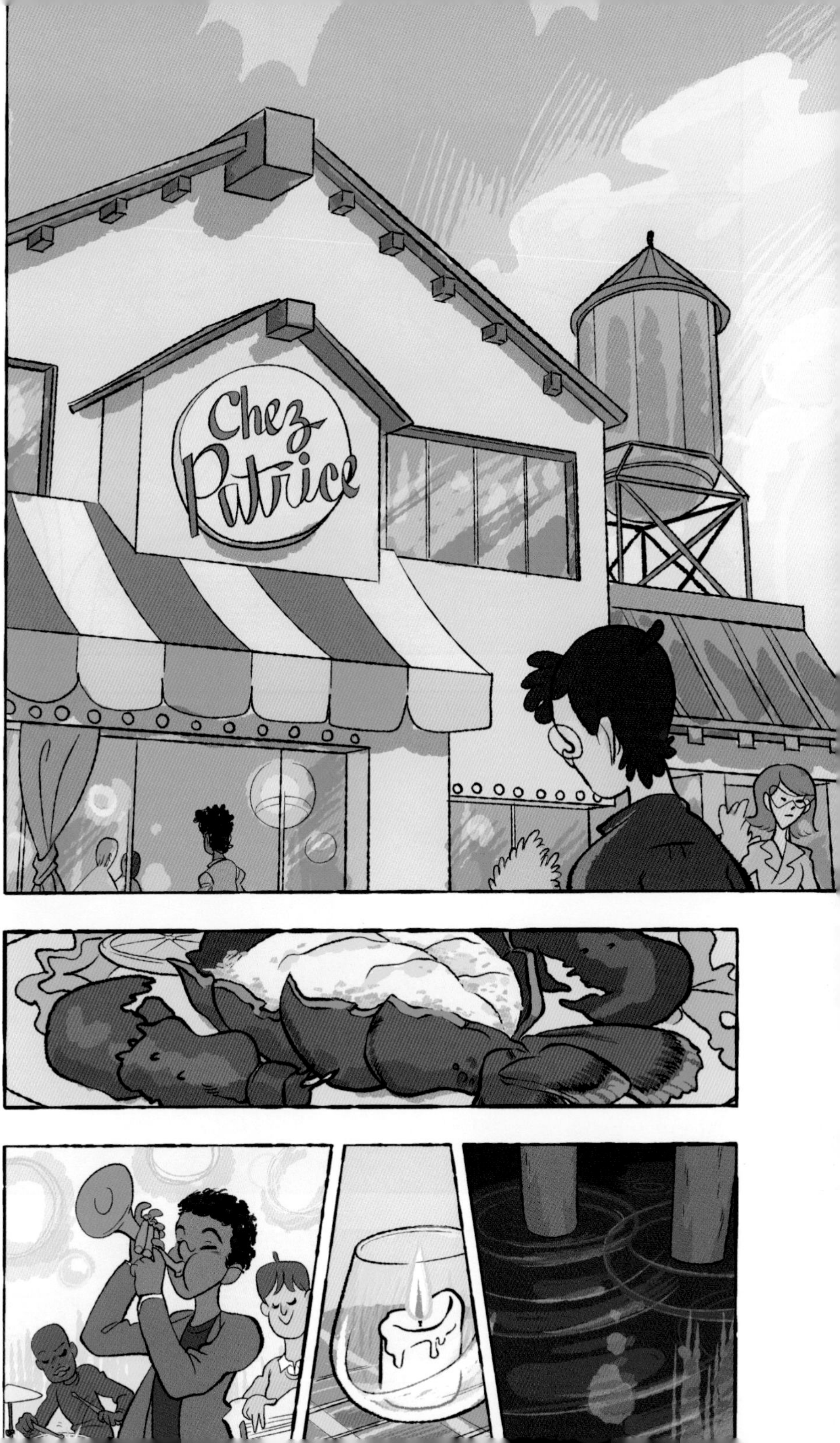
Chez Patrice

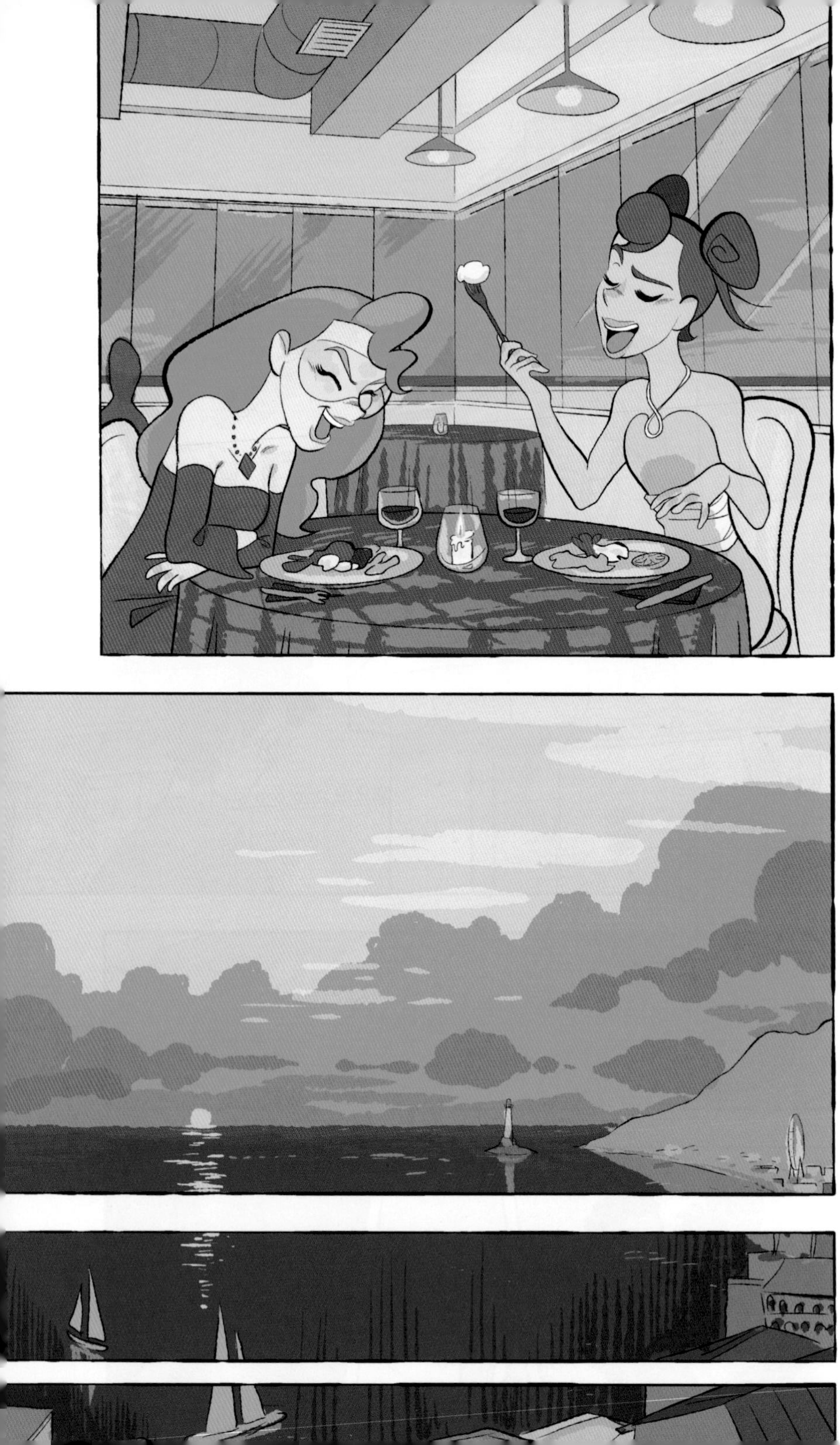

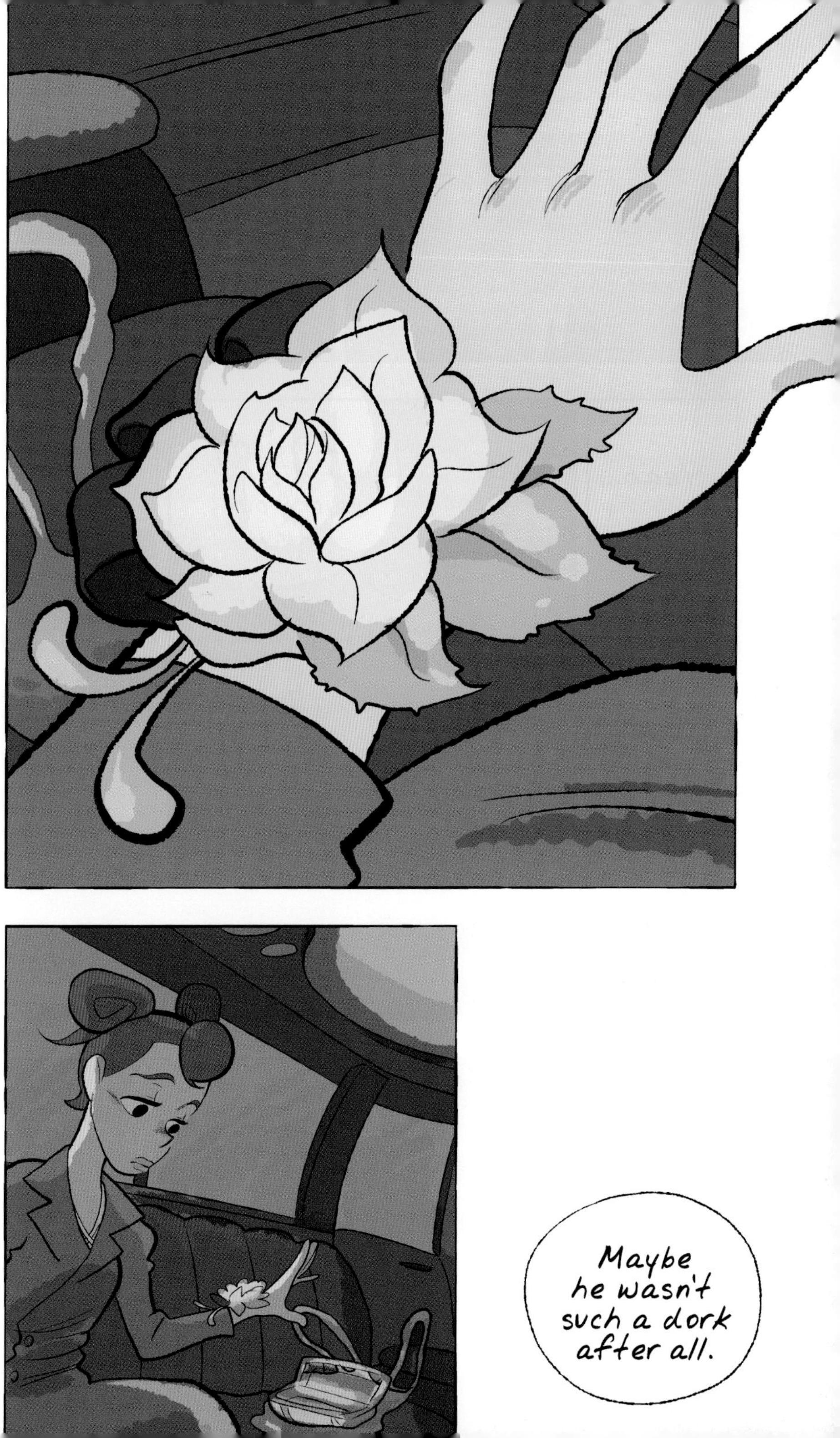
Maybe he wasn't such a dork after all.

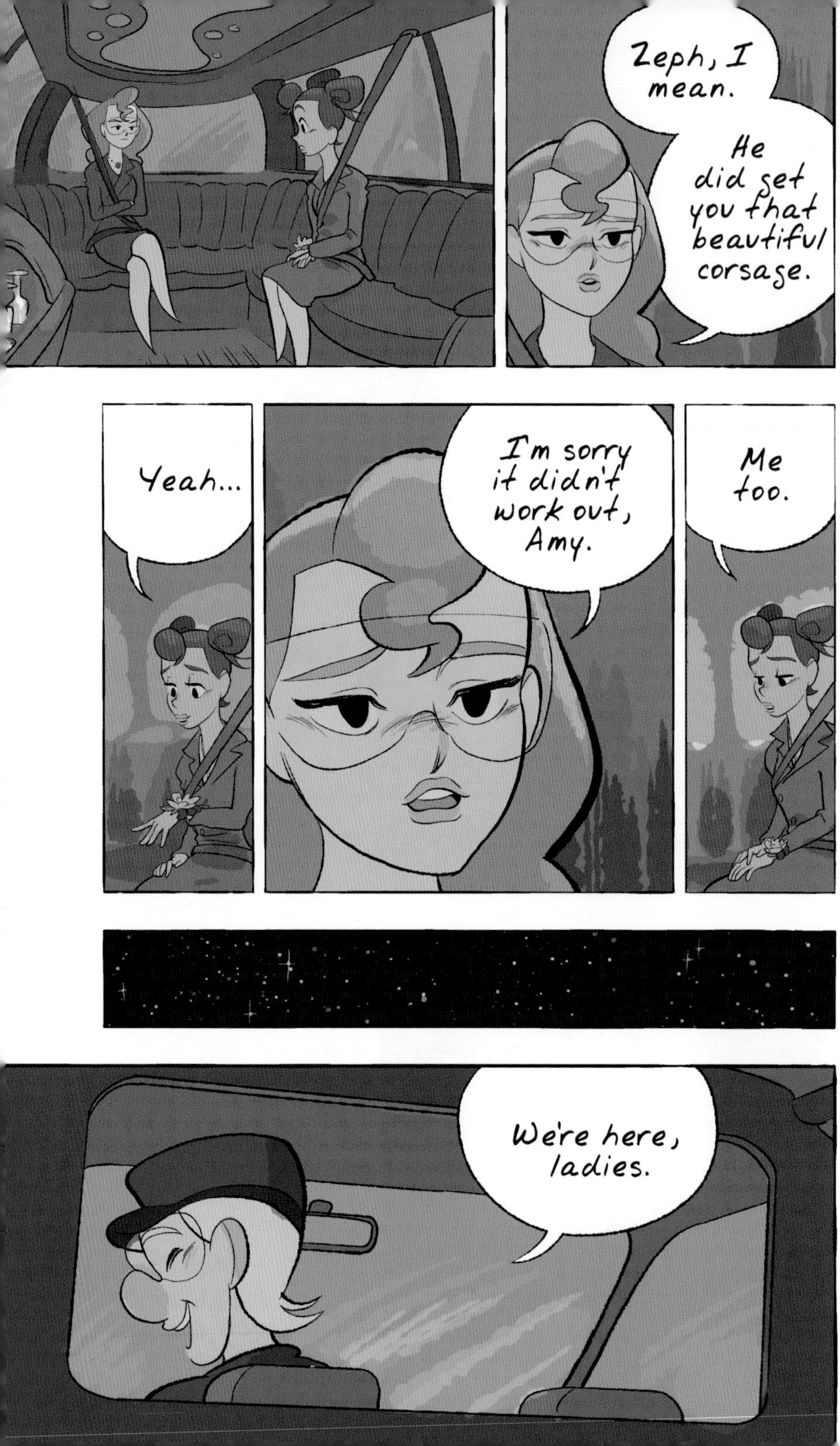
Zeph, I mean.
He did get you that beautiful corsage.
Yeah...
I'm sorry it didn't work out, Amy.
Me too.
We're here, ladies.

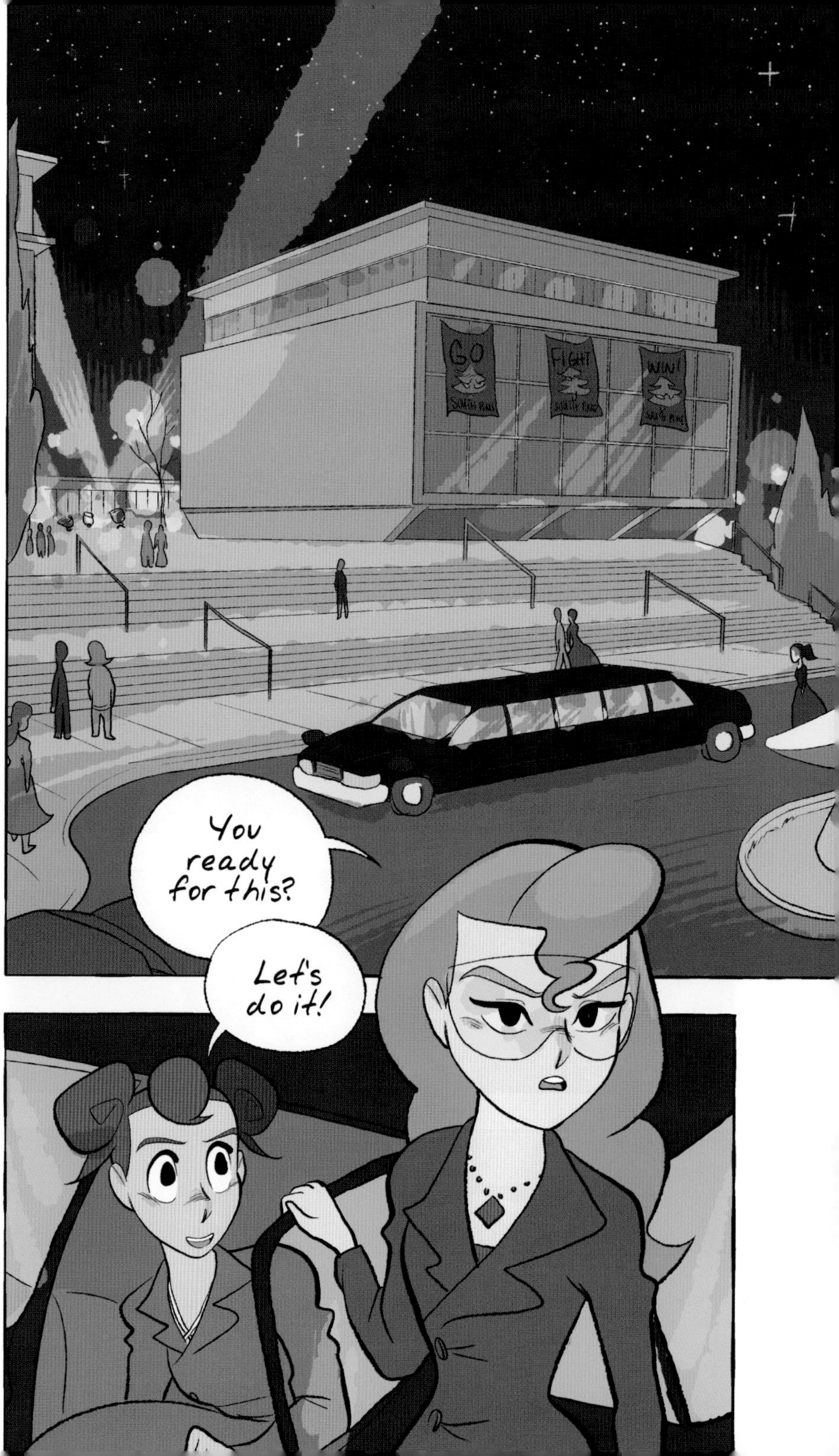
GO
FIGHT
WIN!
You ready for this?
Let's do it!

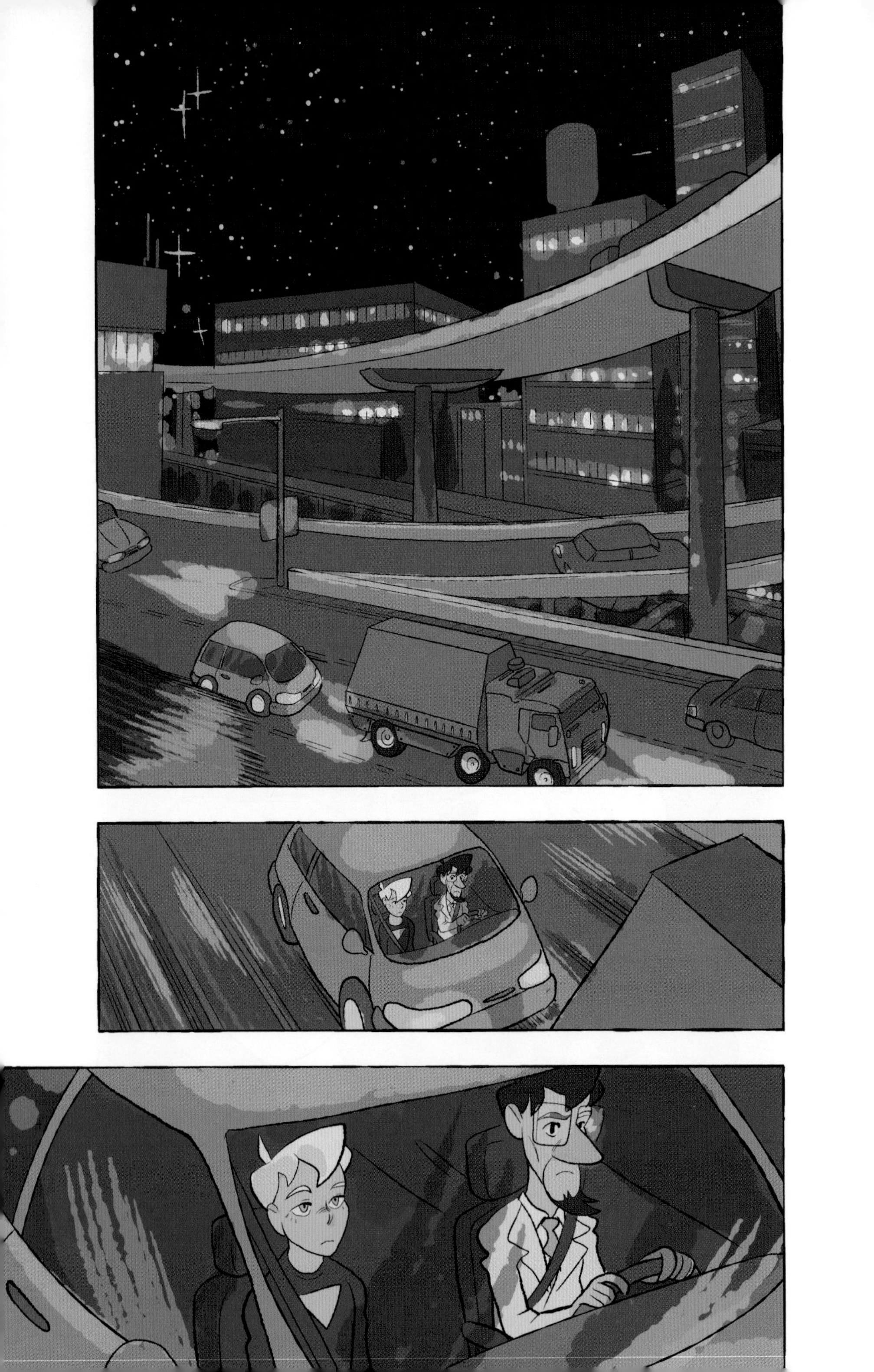

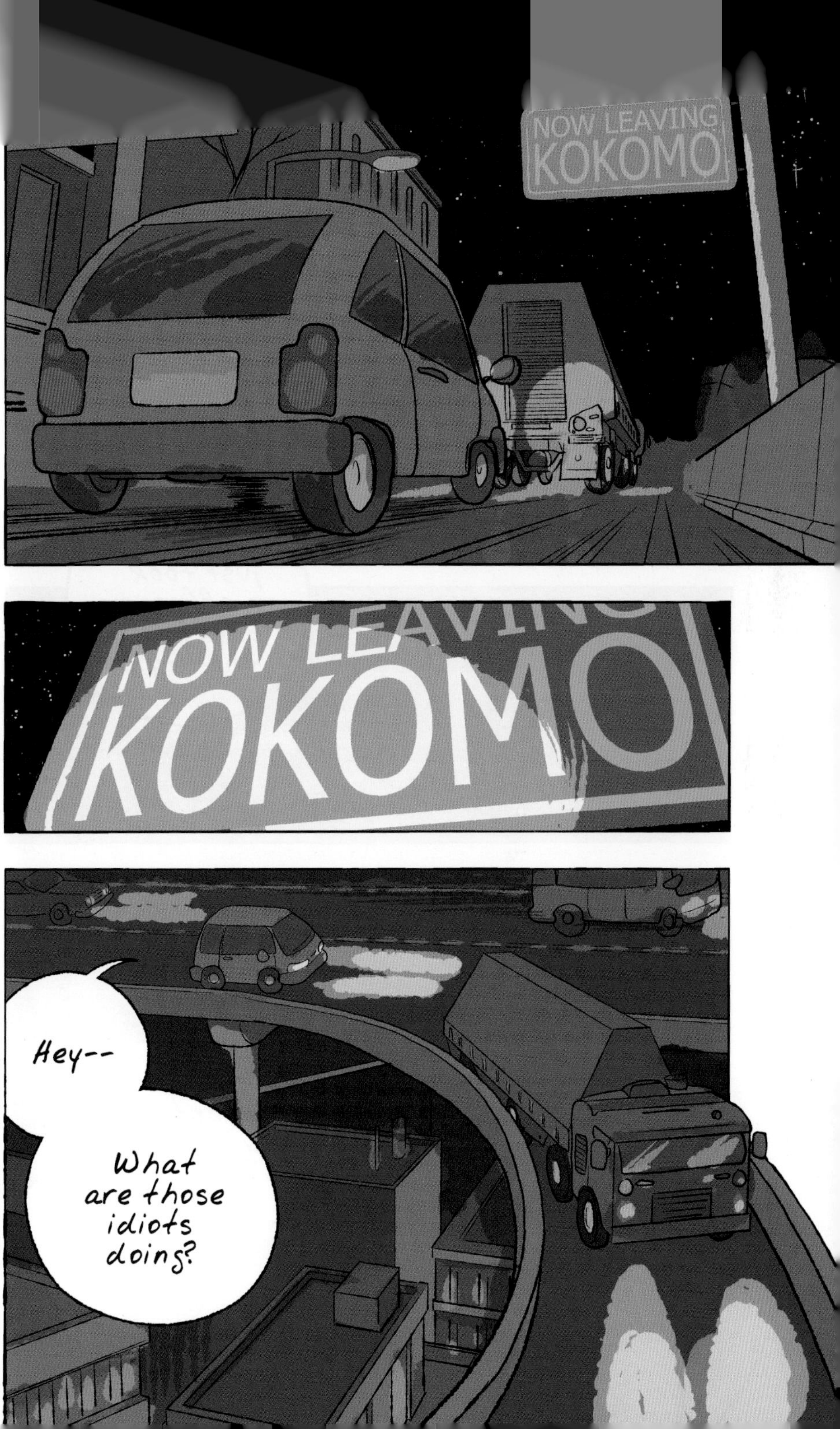
NOW LEAVING KOKOMO
NOW LEAVING KOKOMO
Hey--
What are those idiots doing?

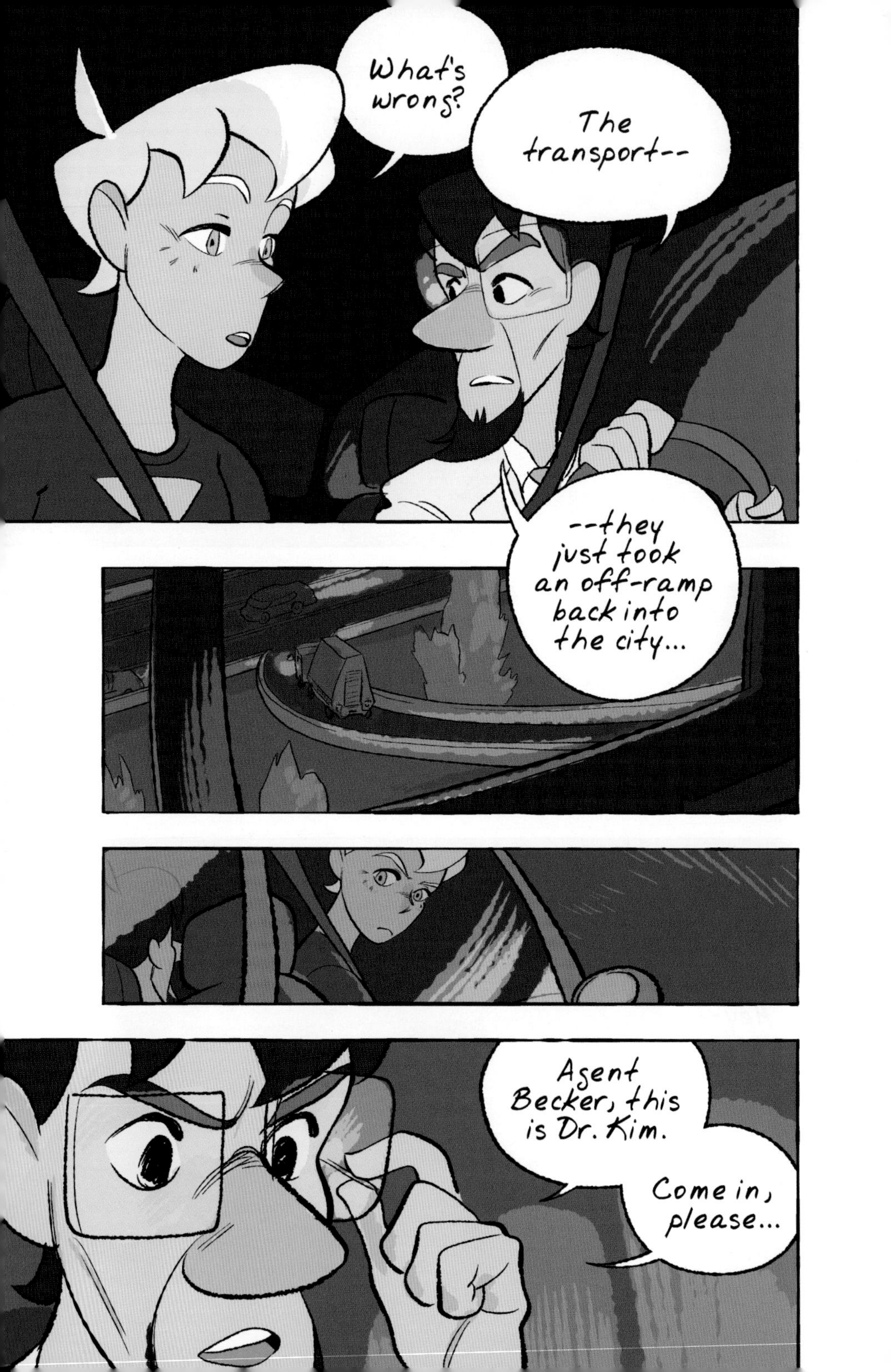
What's wrong?
The transport--
--they just took an off-ramp back into the city...
Agent Becker, this is Dr. Kim.
Come in, please...

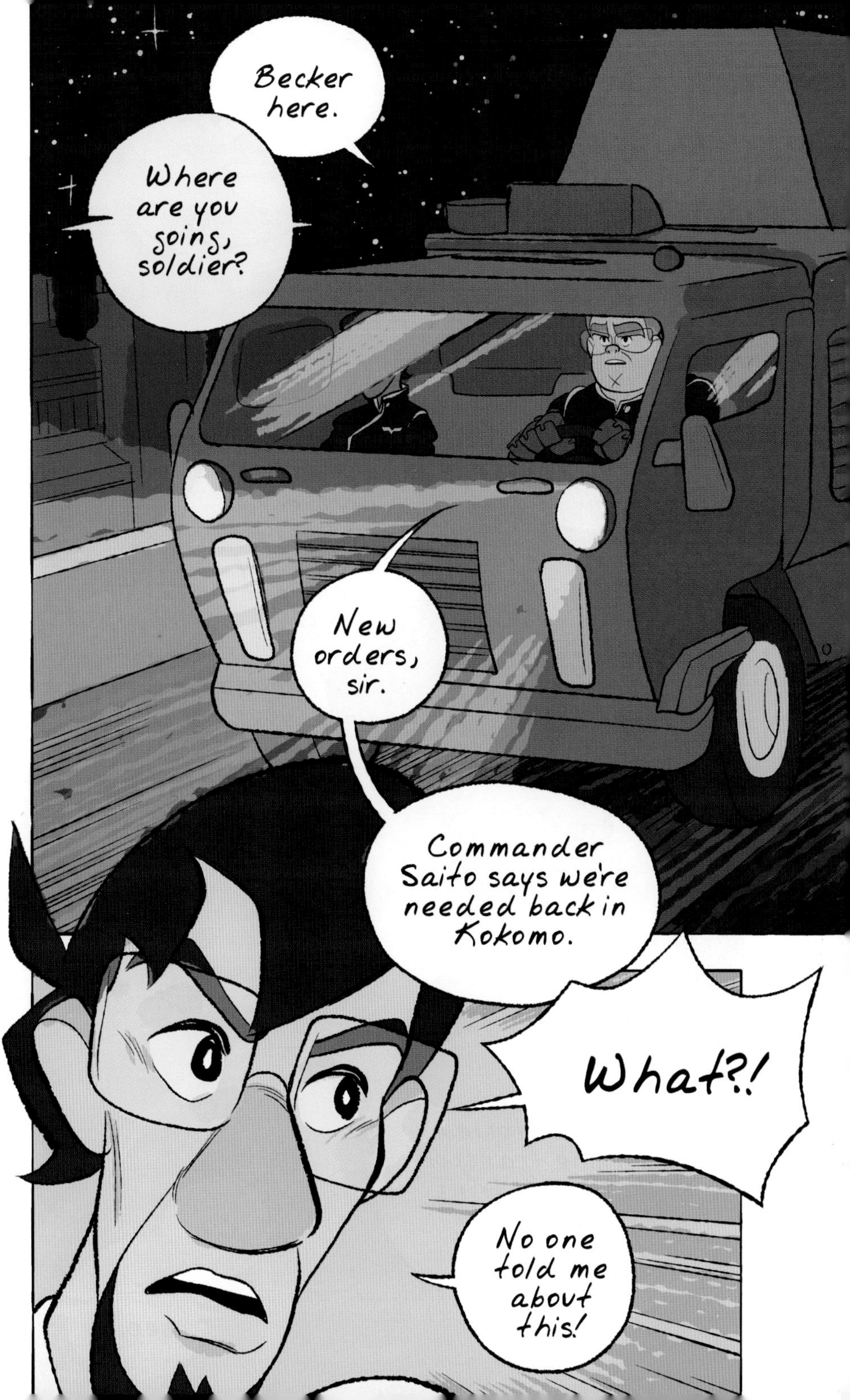
Becker here.
Where are you going, soldier?
New orders, sir.
Commander Saito says we're needed back in Kokomo.
What?!
No one told me about this!

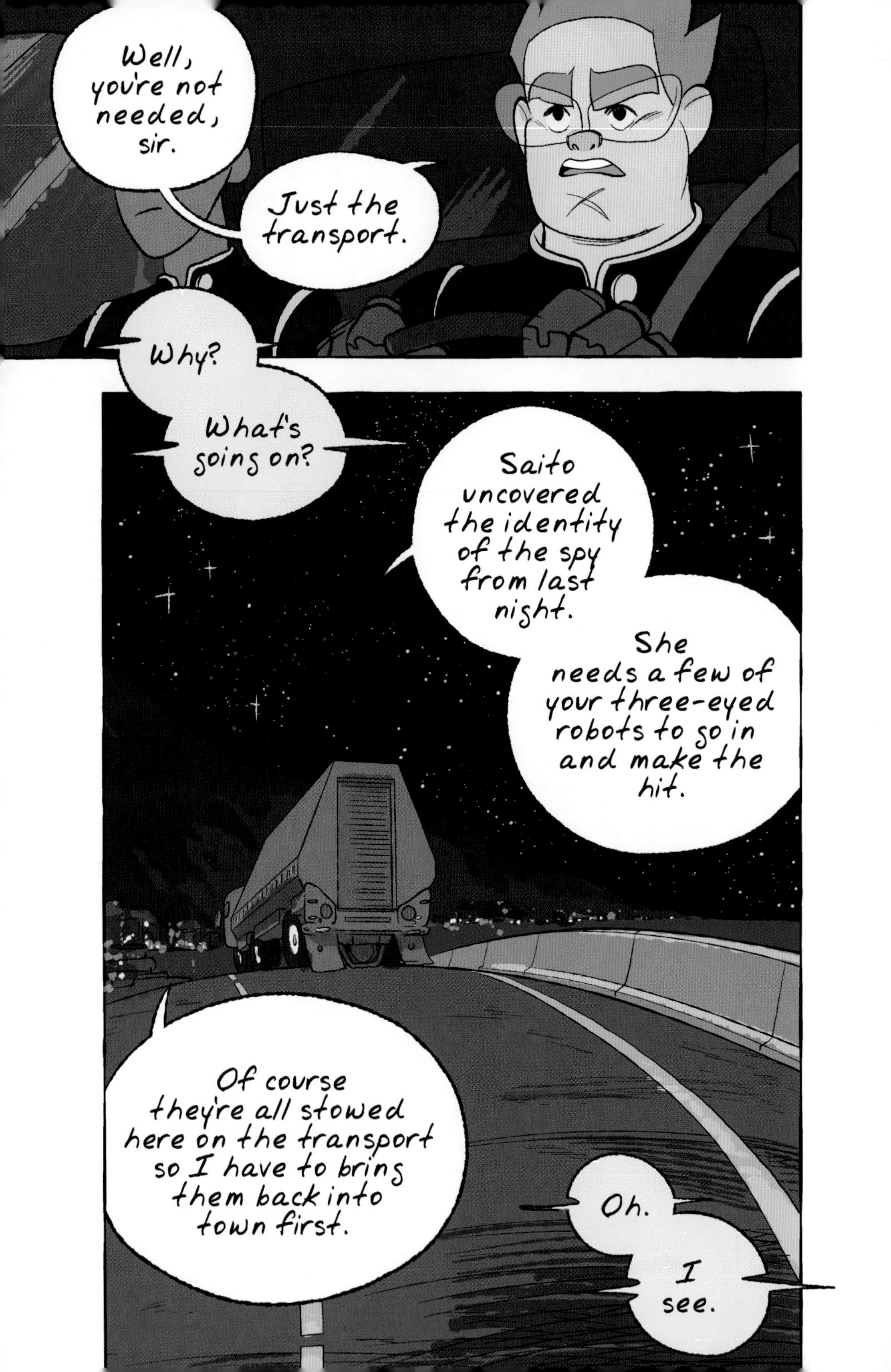
Well, you're not needed, sir.
Just the transport.
Why?
What's going on?
Saito uncovered the identity of the spy from last night.
She needs a few of your three-eyed robots to go in and make the hit.
Of course they're all stowed here on the transport so I have to bring them back into town first.
Oh.
I see.

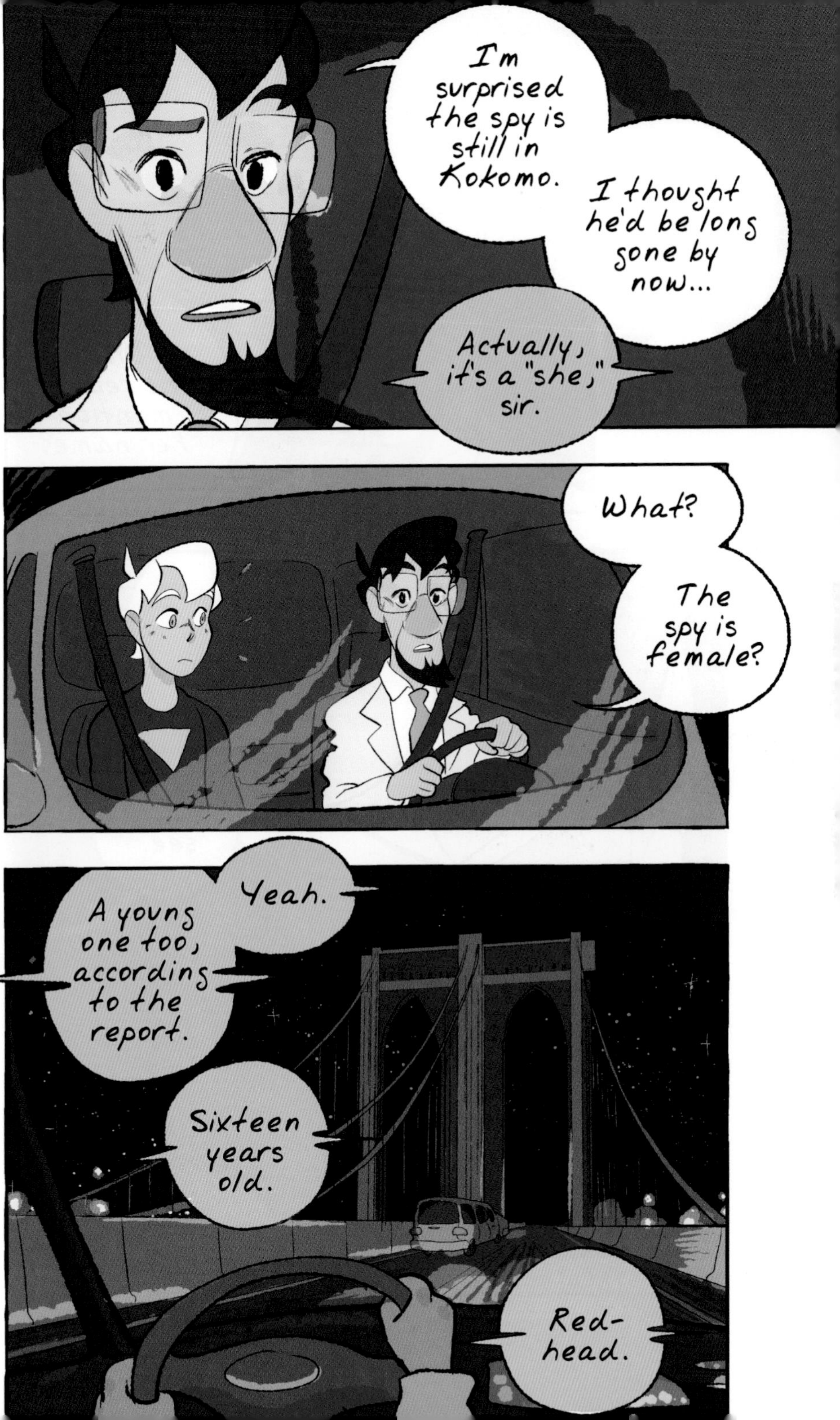
I'm surprised the spy is still in Kokomo.
I thought he'd be long gone by now...
Actually, it's a "she," sir.
What?
The spy is female?
Yeah.
A young one too, according to the report.
Sixteen years old.
Red-head.

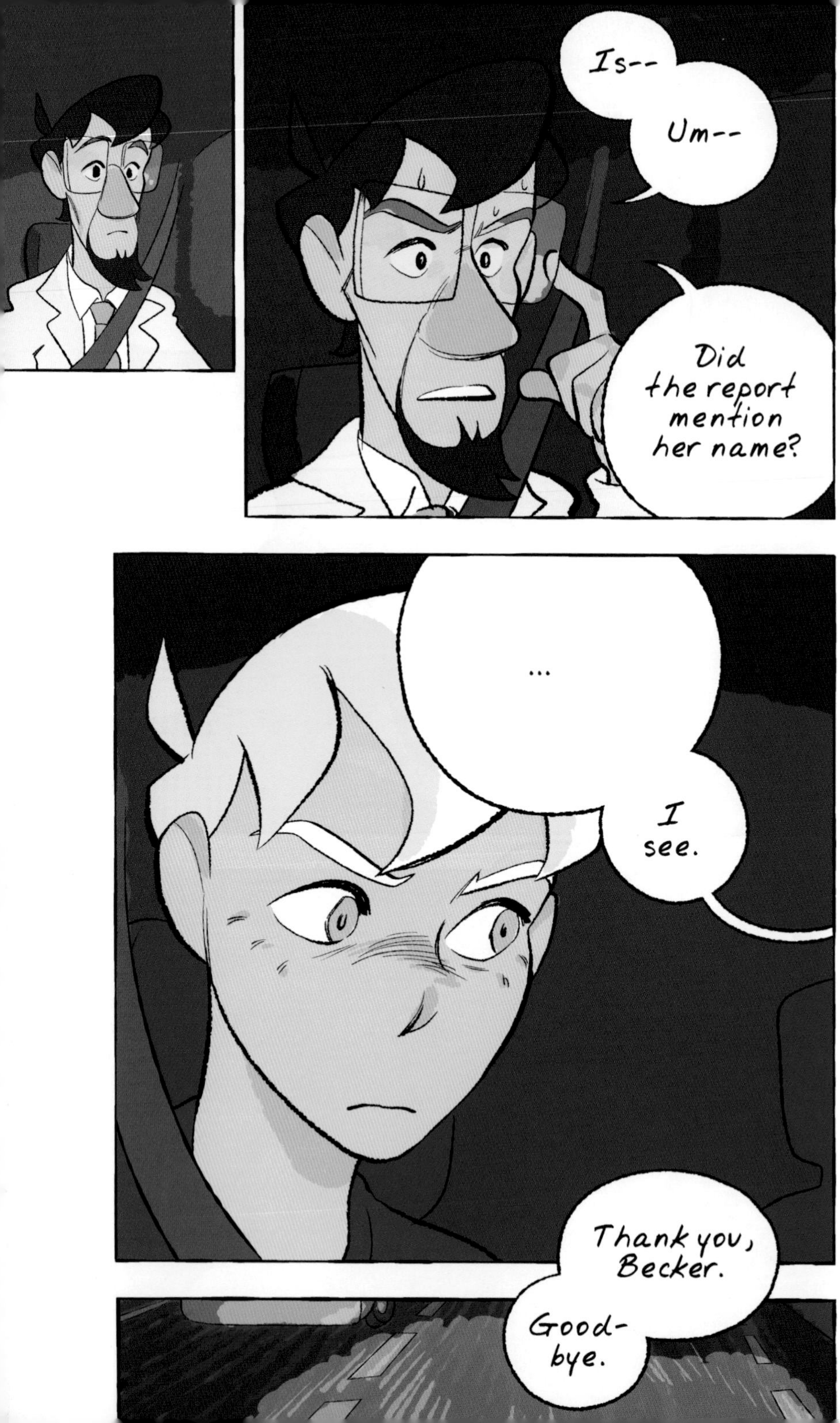

Is--
Um--
Did the report mention her name?
...
I see.
Thank you, Becker.
Good-bye.

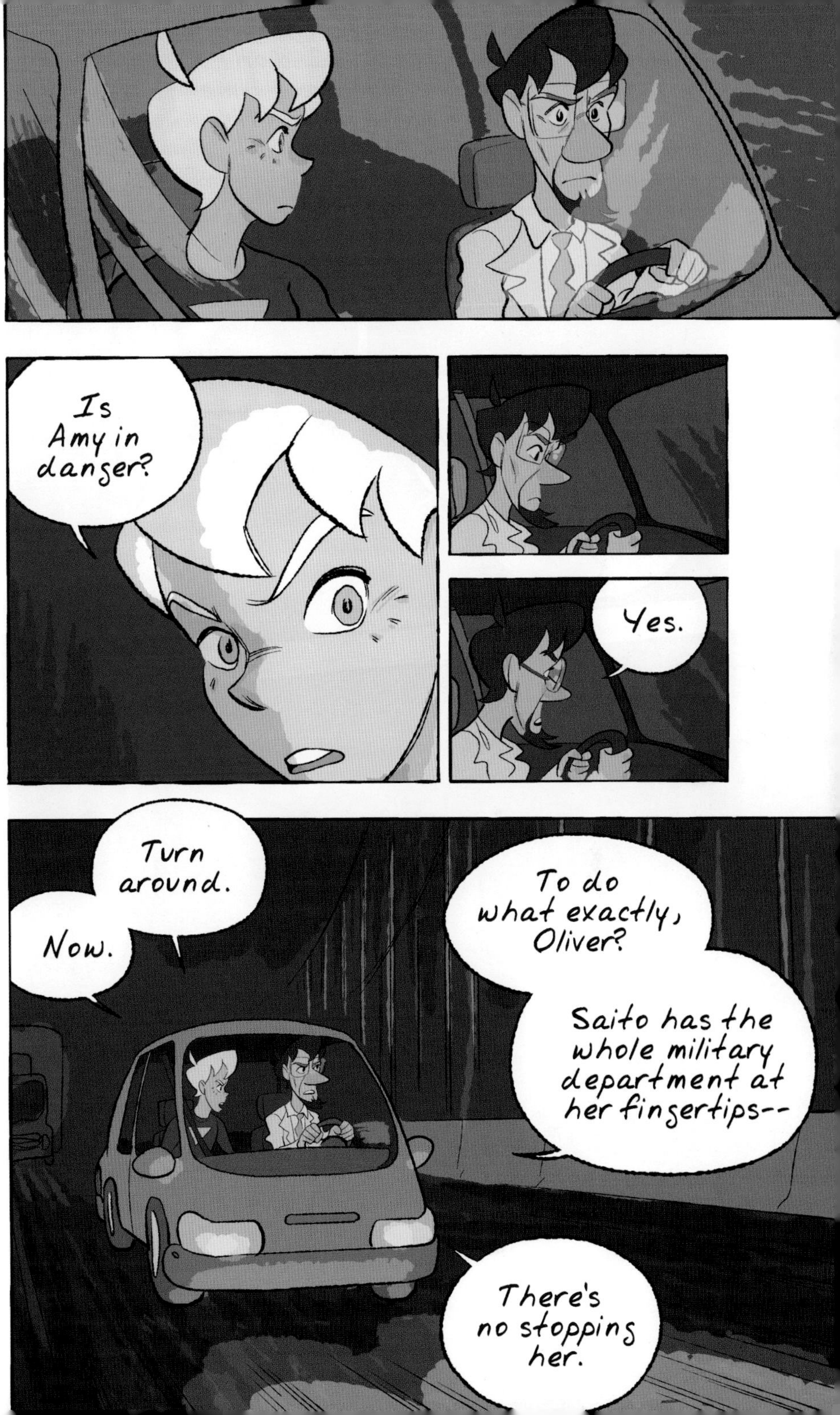
Is Amy in danger?
Yes.
Turn around.
Now.
To do what exactly, Oliver?
Saito has the whole military department at her fingertips--
There's no stopping her.

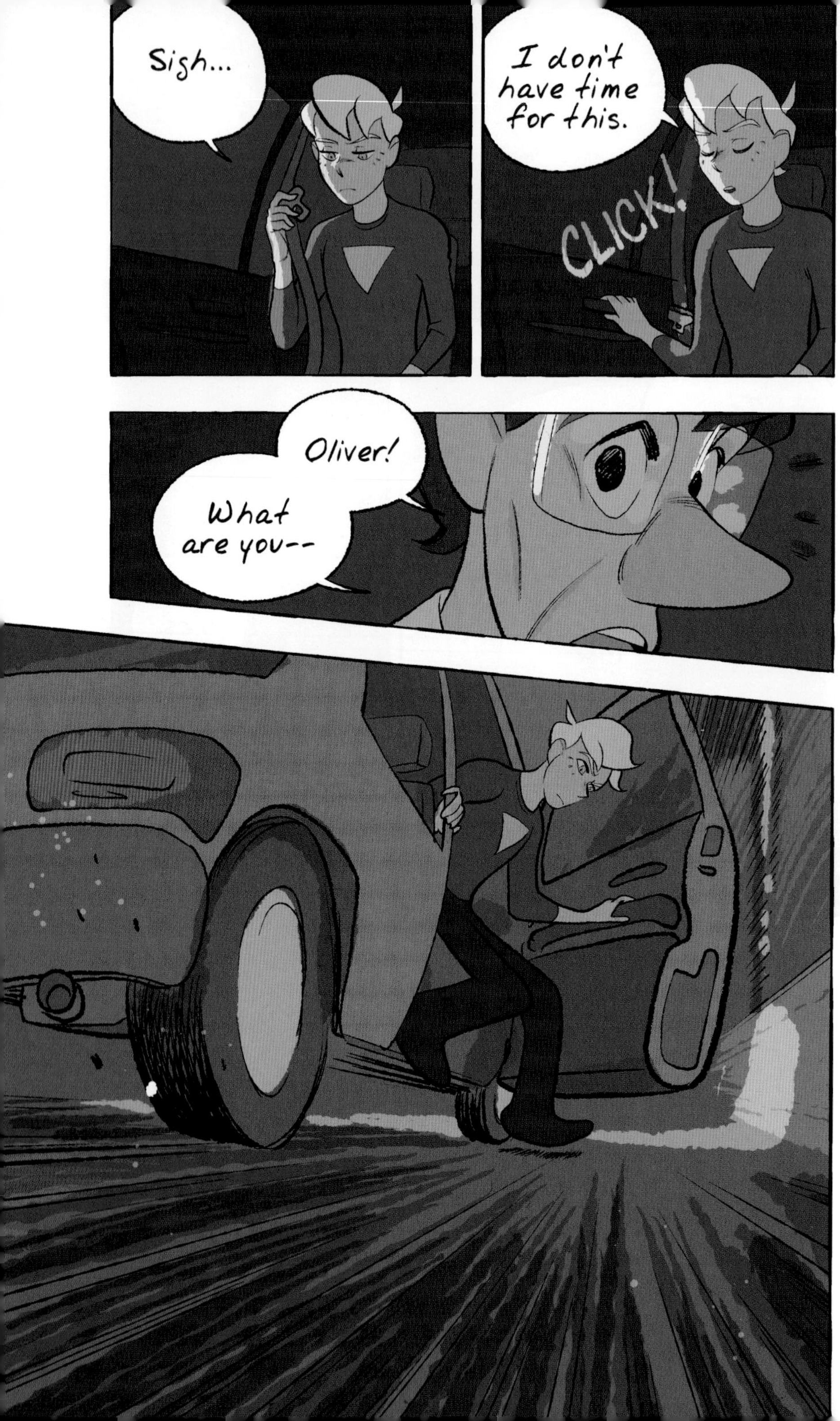
Sigh...
I don't have time for this.
CLICK!
Oliver!
What are you--

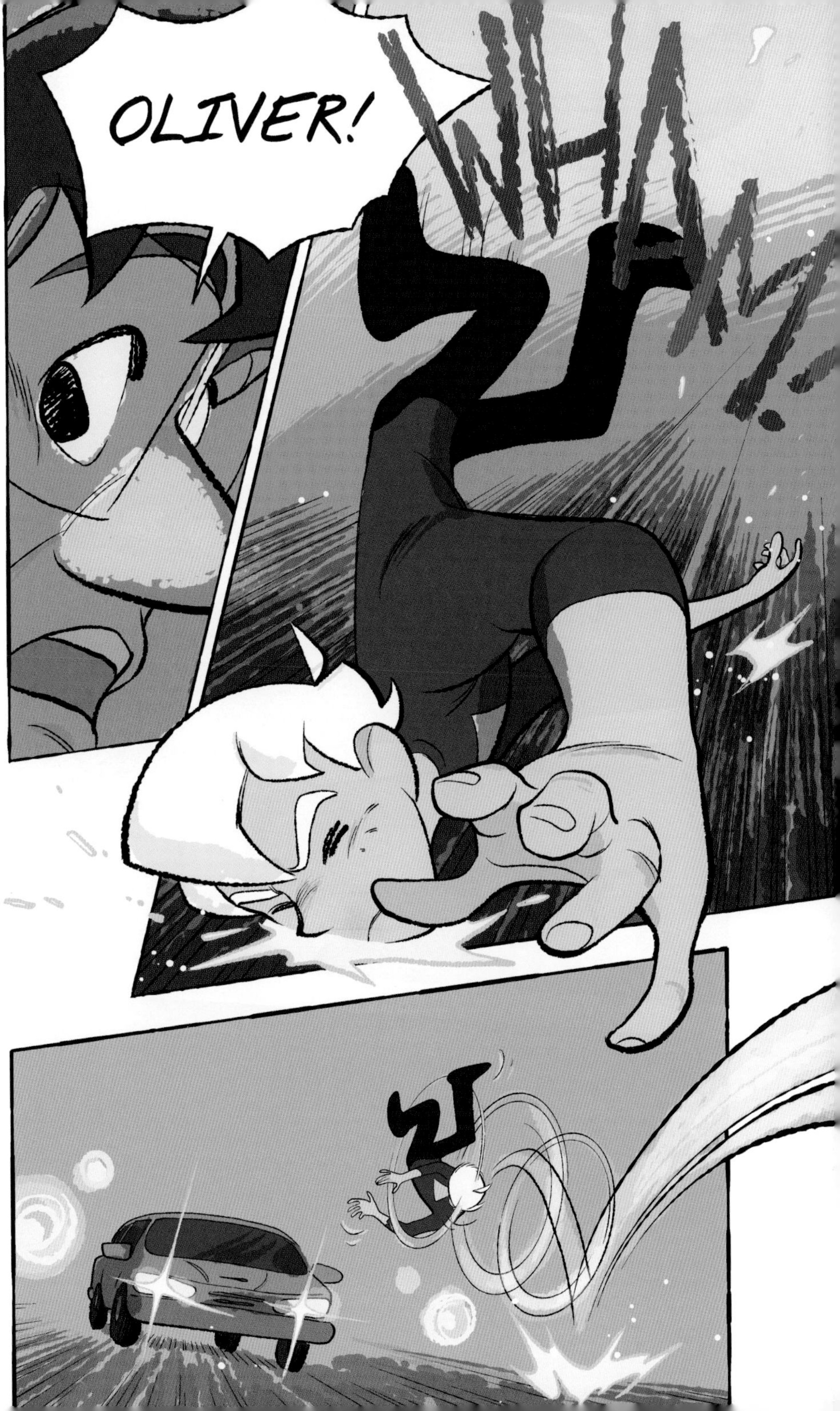
OLIVER!
WHAM!

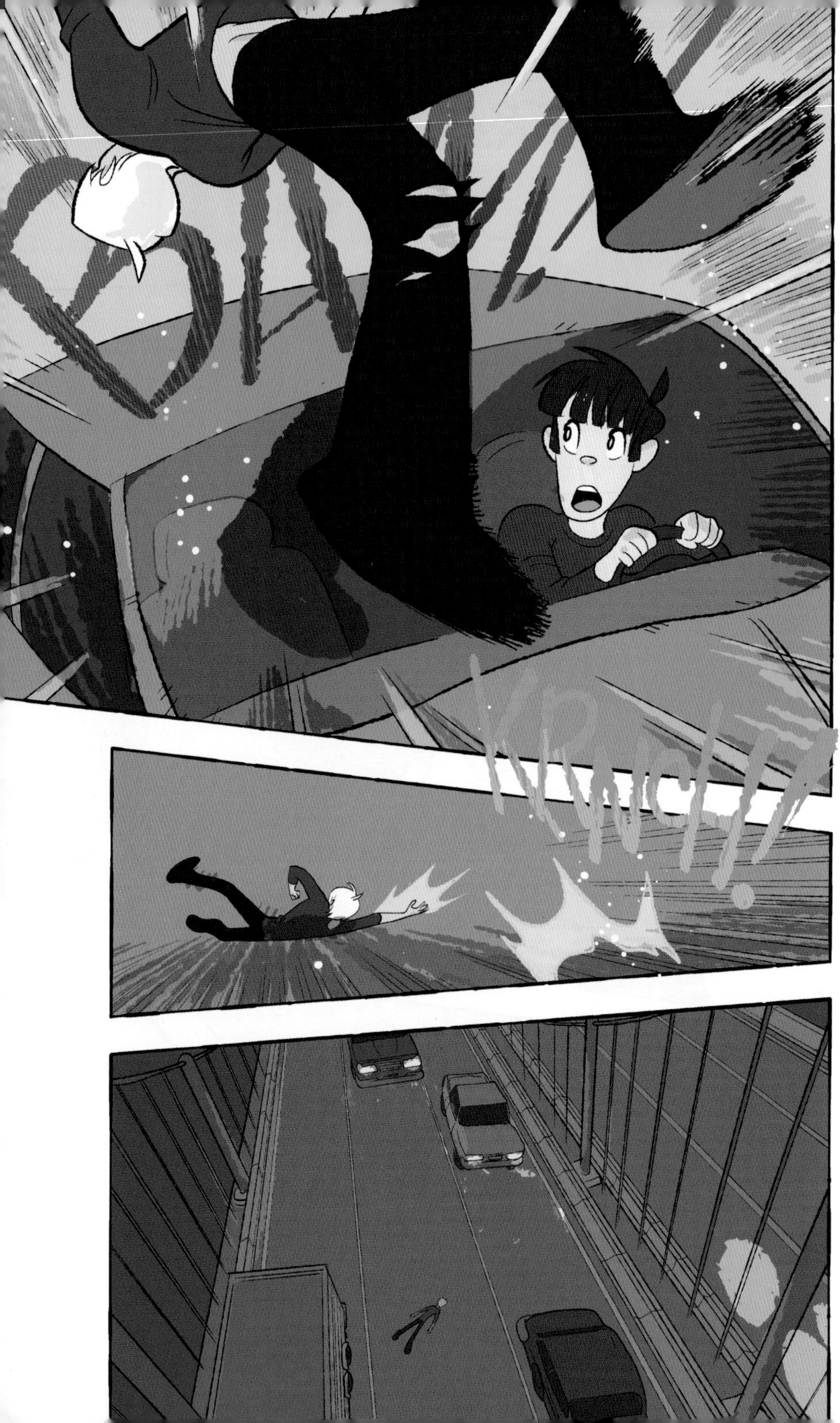

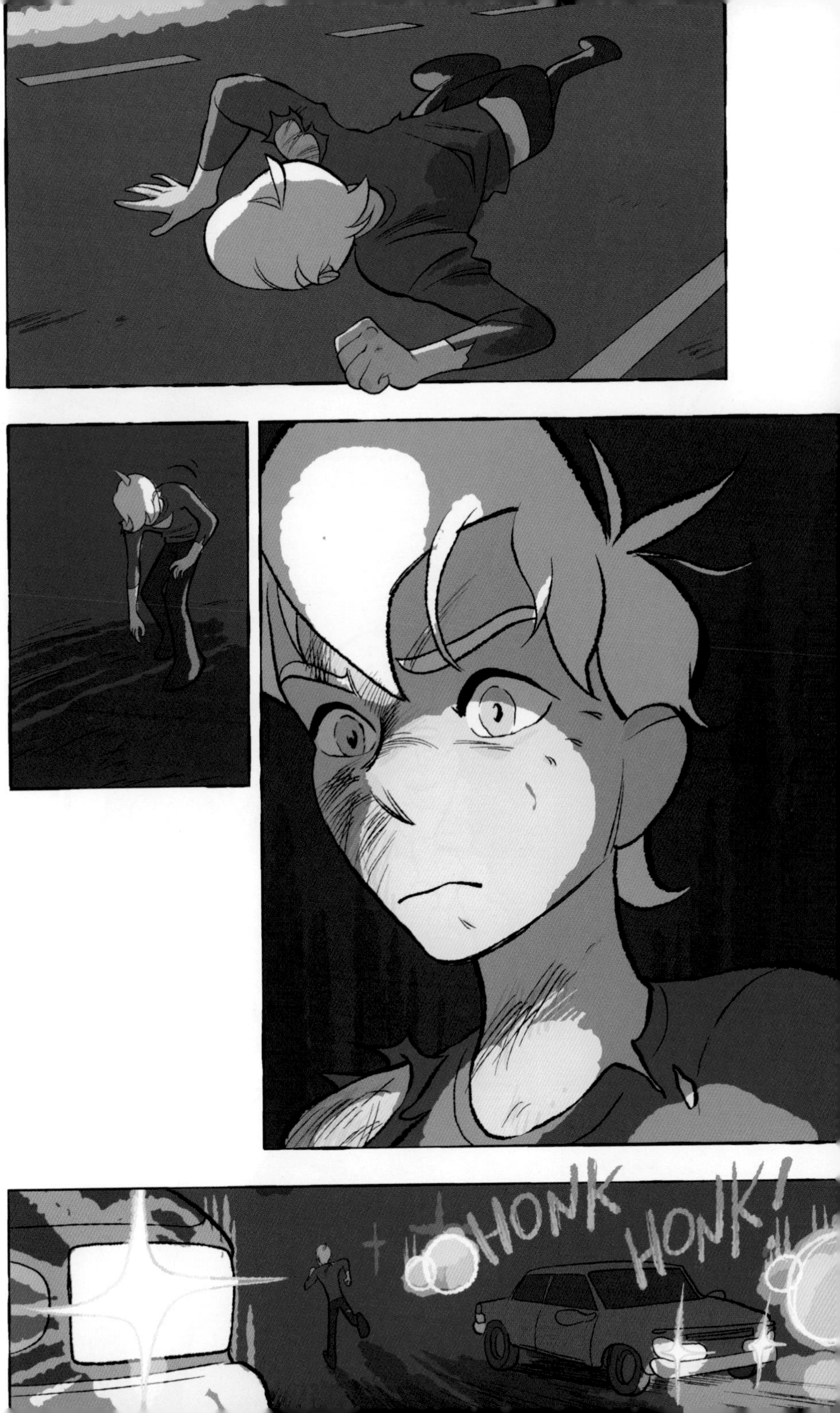
HONK HONK!

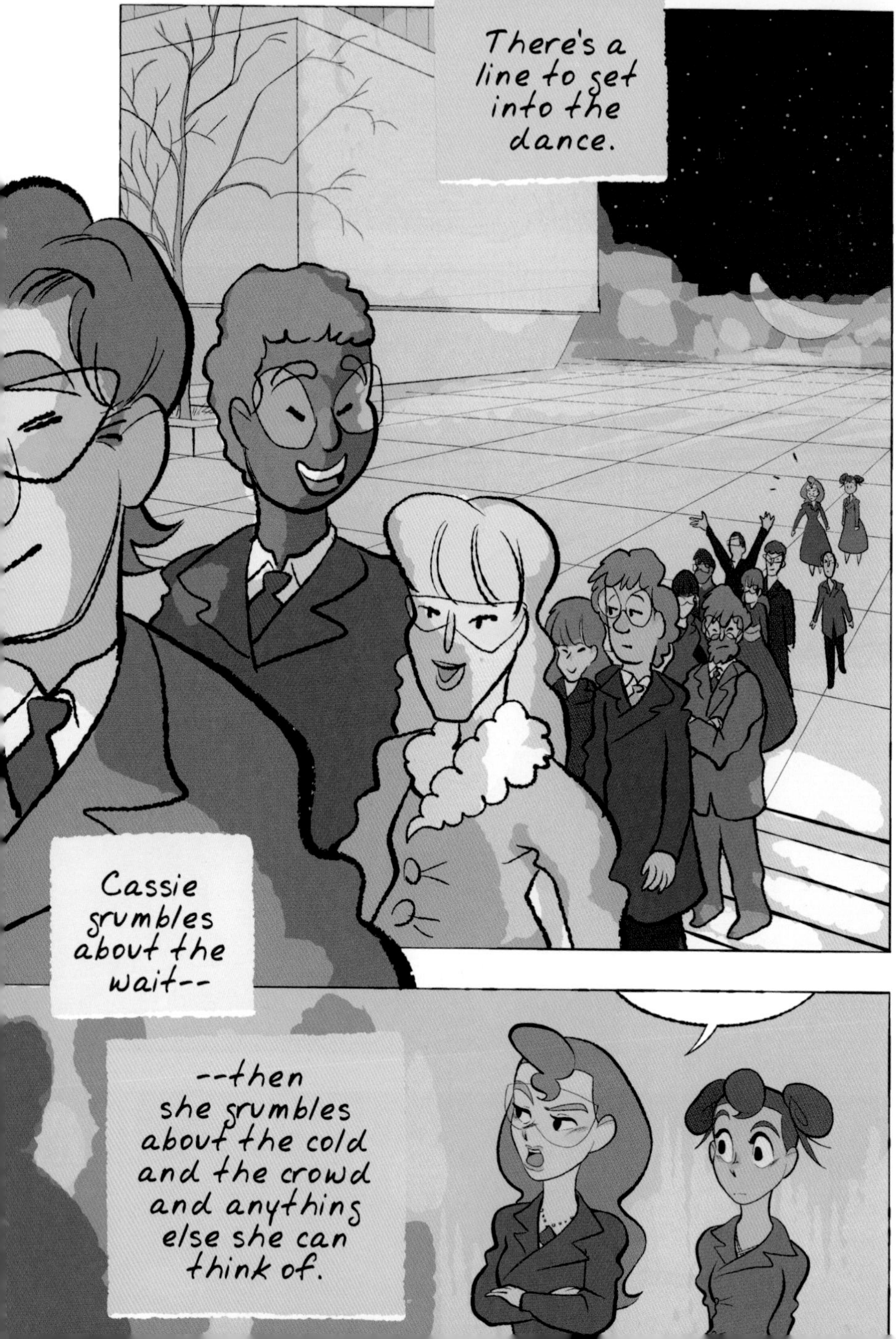
There's a line to get into the dance.
Cassie grumbles about the wait--
--then she grumbles about the cold and the crowd and anything else she can think of.

I ask her
if she's nervous
about talking to
David and she
says no.

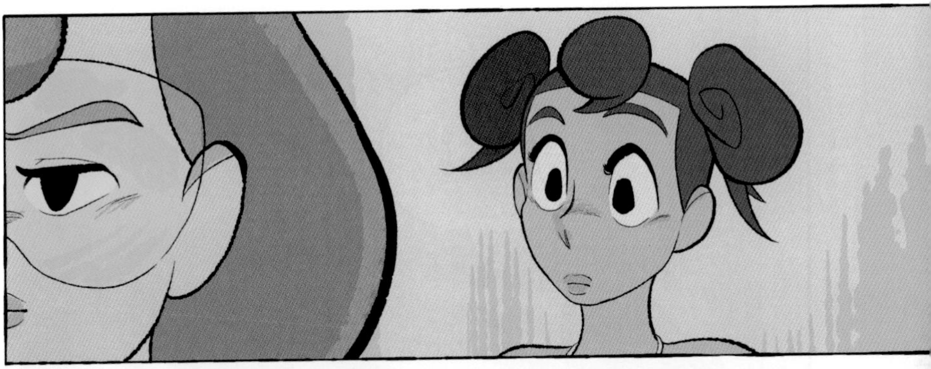

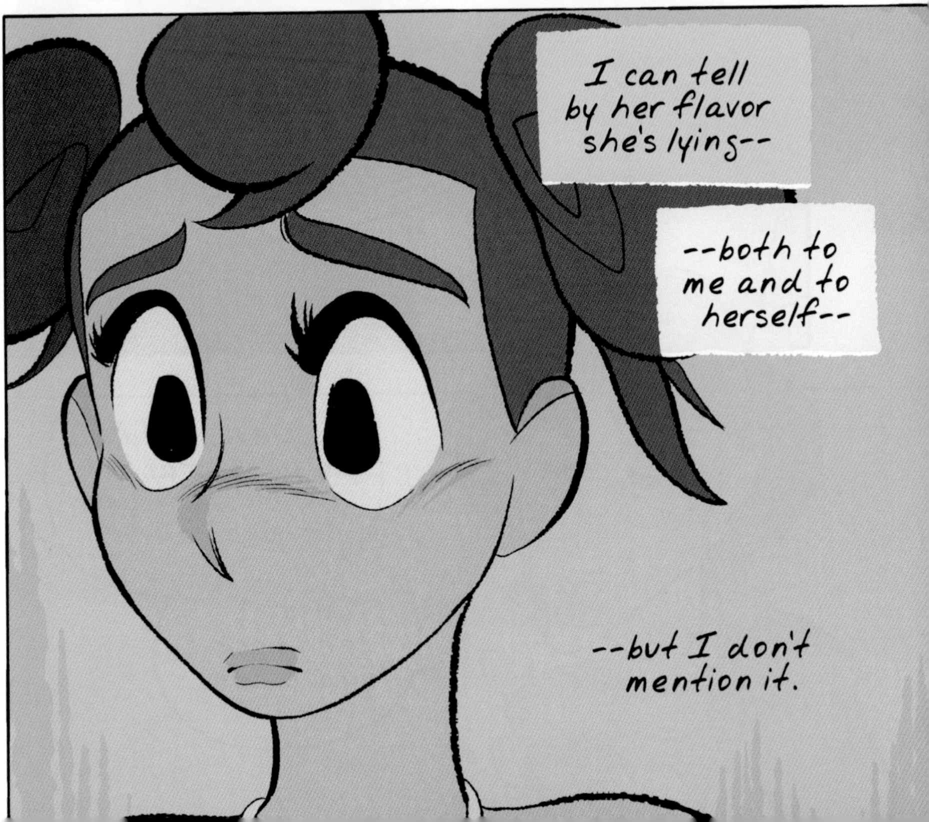
I can tell by her flavor she's lying--
--both to me and to herself--
--but I don't mention it.

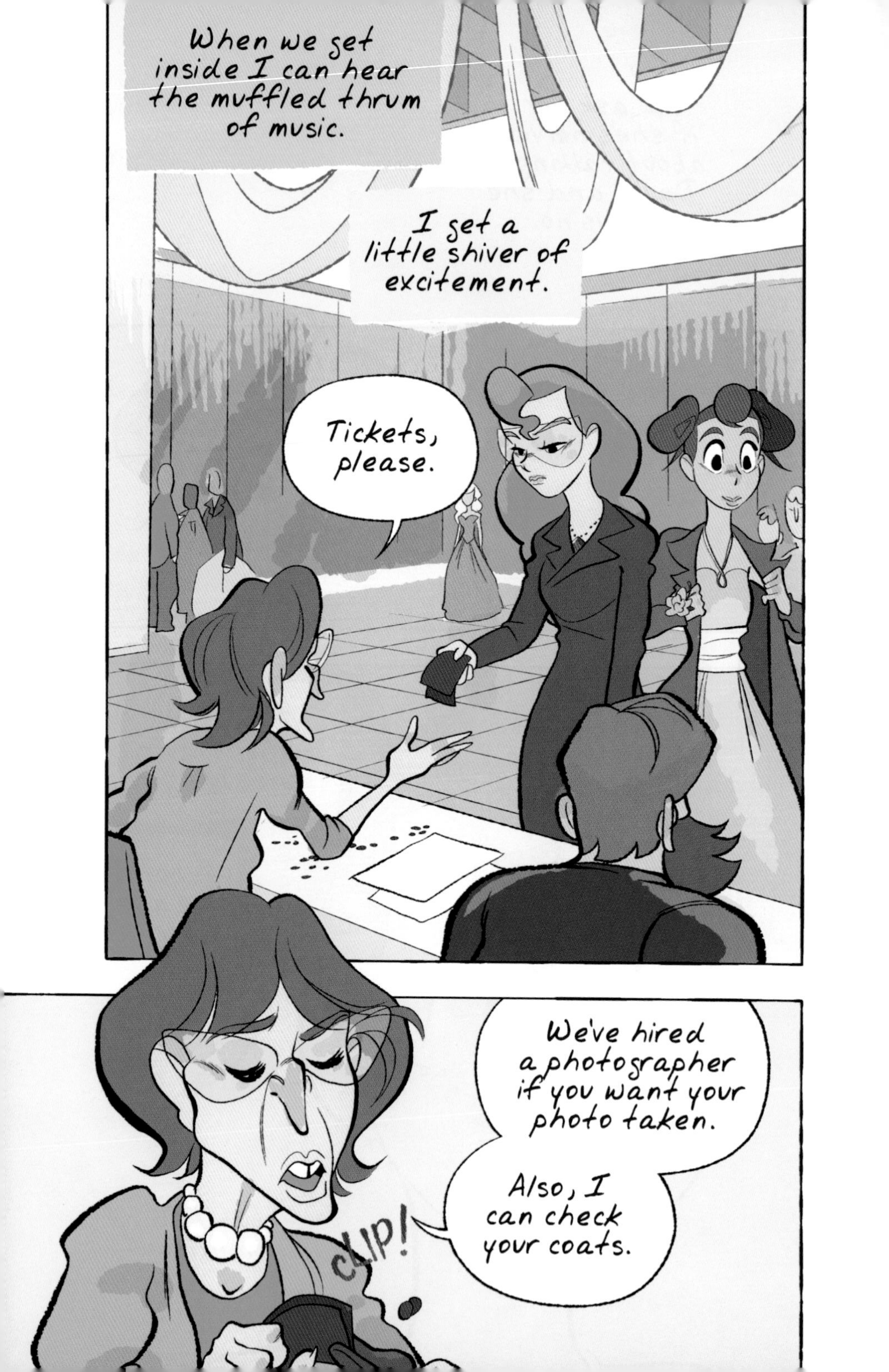
When we get inside I can hear the muffled thrum of music.
I get a little shiver of excitement.
Tickets, please.
We've hired a photographer if you want your photo taken.
Also, I can check your coats.
CLIP!

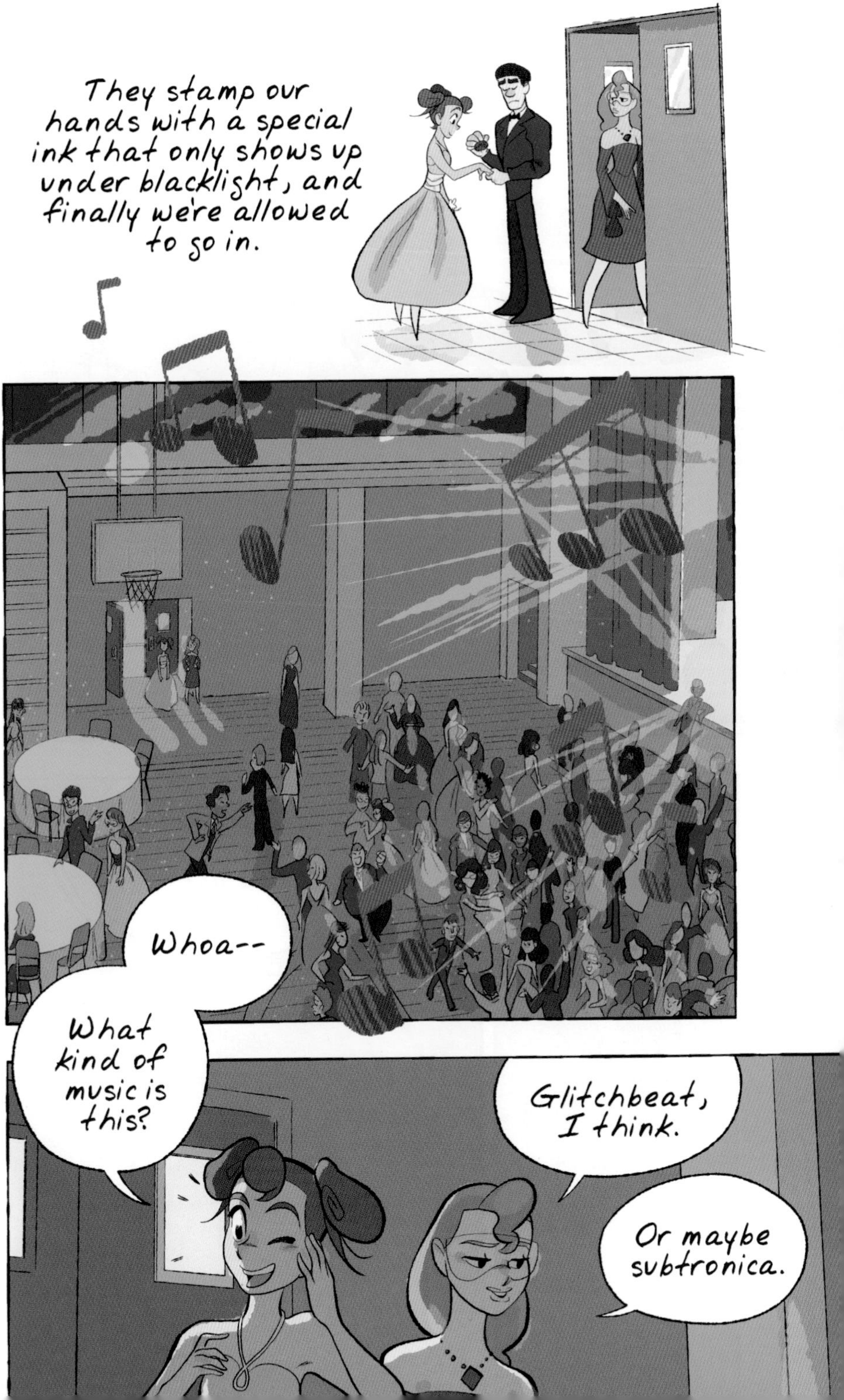
They stamp our hands with a special ink that only shows up under blacklight, and finally we're allowed to go in.
Whoa--
What kind of music is this?
Glitchbeat, I think.
Or maybe subtronica.

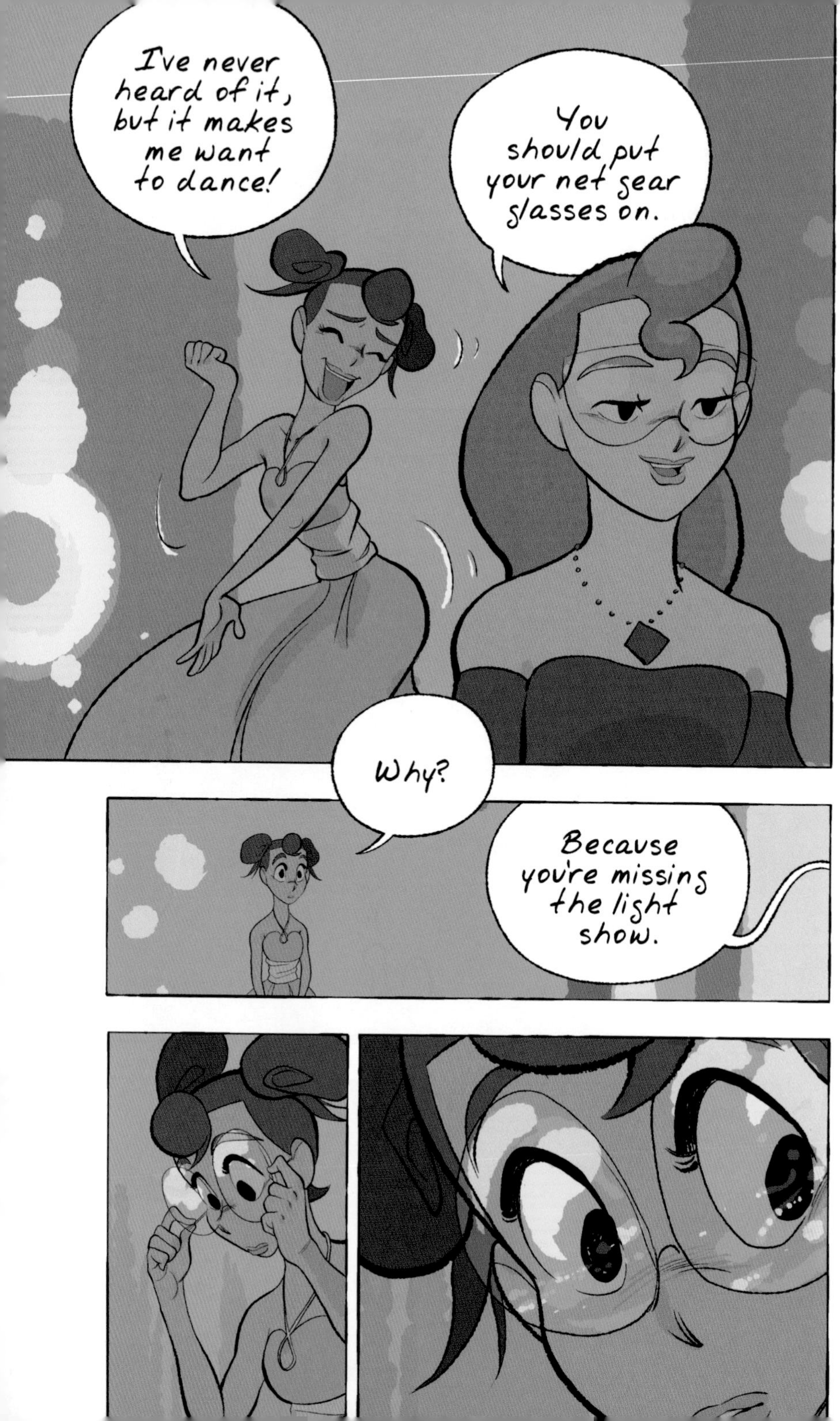
I've never heard of it, but it makes me want to dance!
You should put your net gear glasses on.
Why?
Because you're missing the light show.

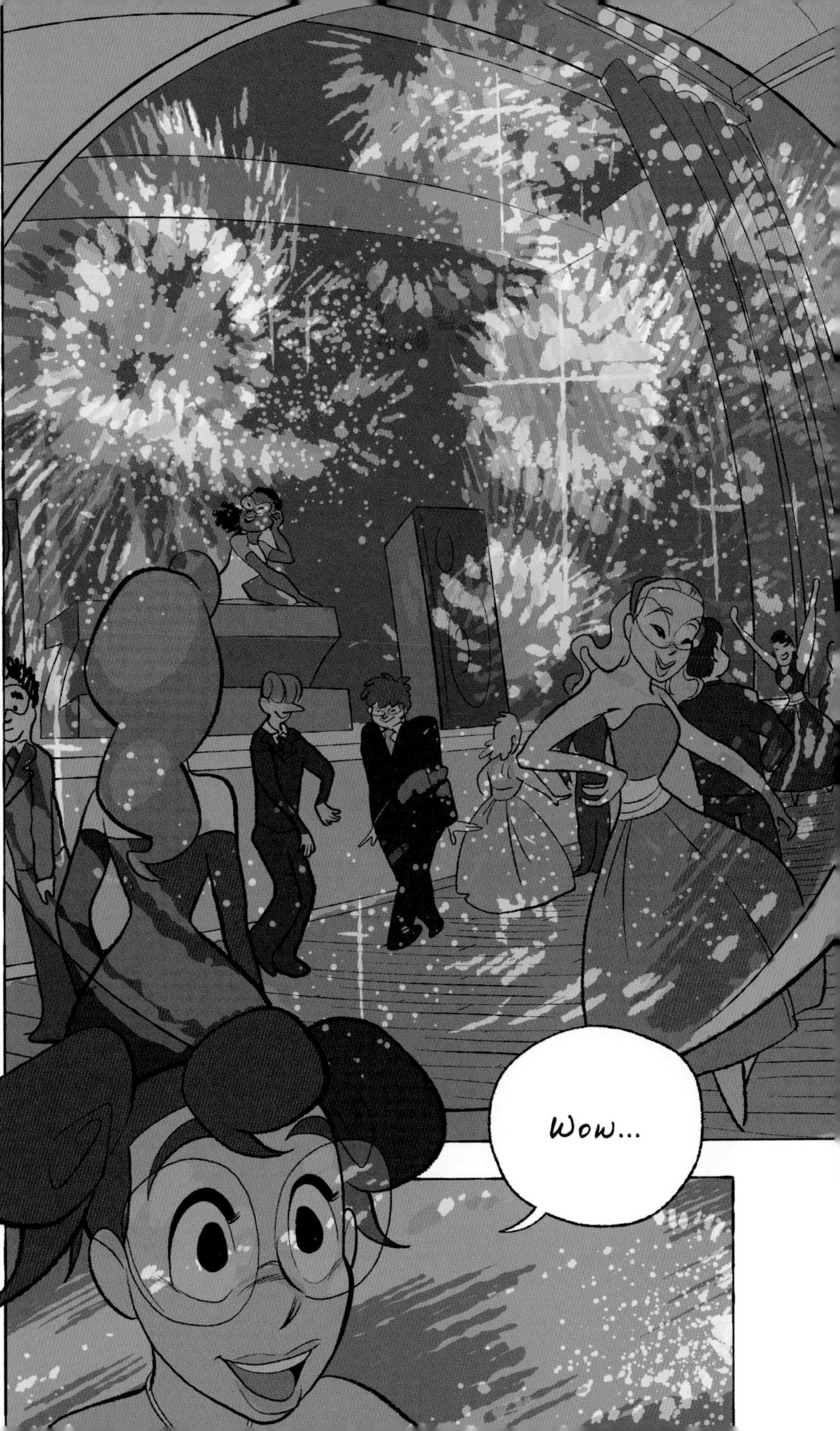
WOW...

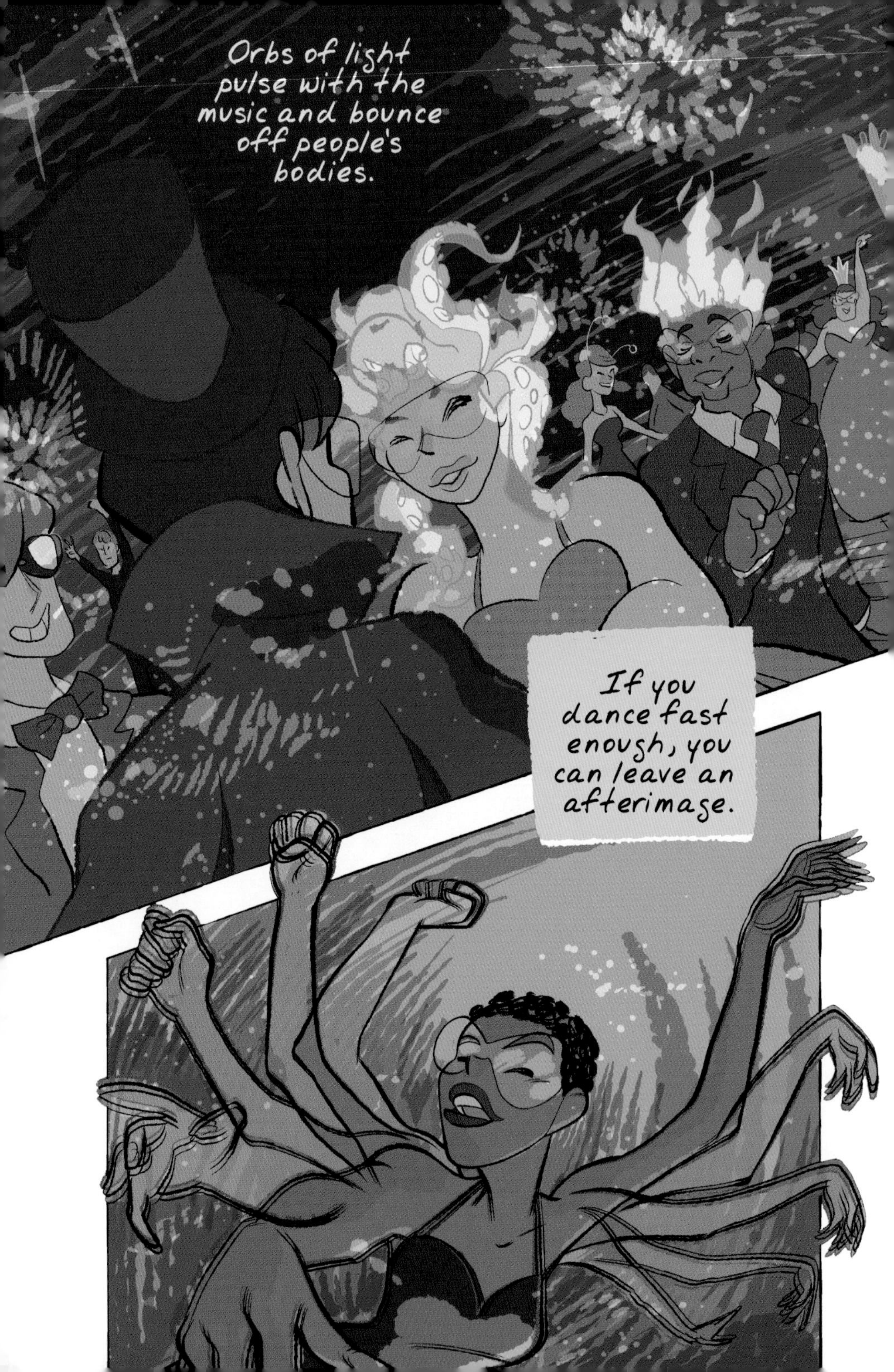
Orbs of light pulse with the music and bounce off people's bodies.
If you dance fast enough, you can leave an afterimage.

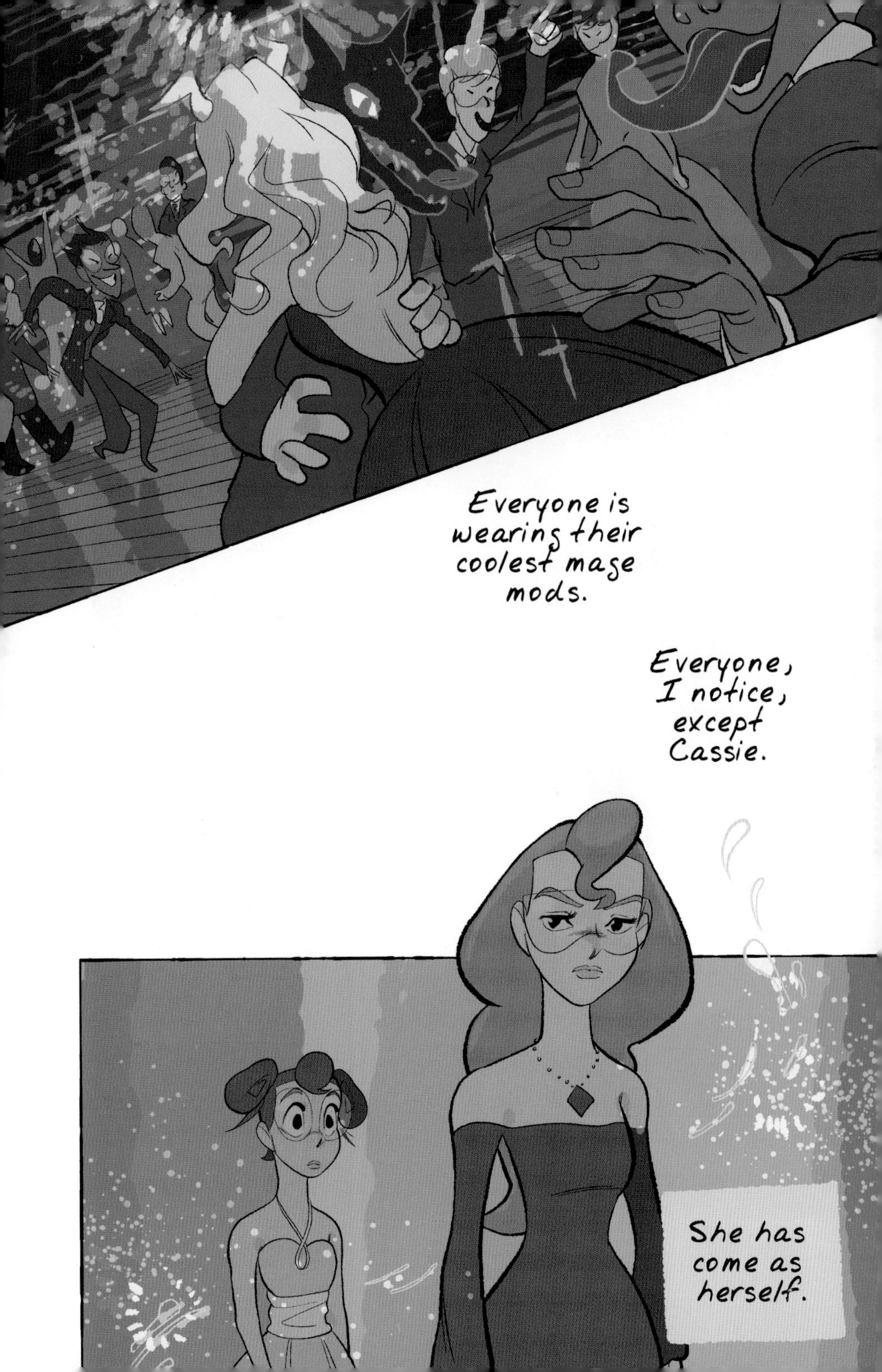
Everyone is wearing their coolest mage mods.
Everyone, I notice, except Cassie.
She has come as herself.

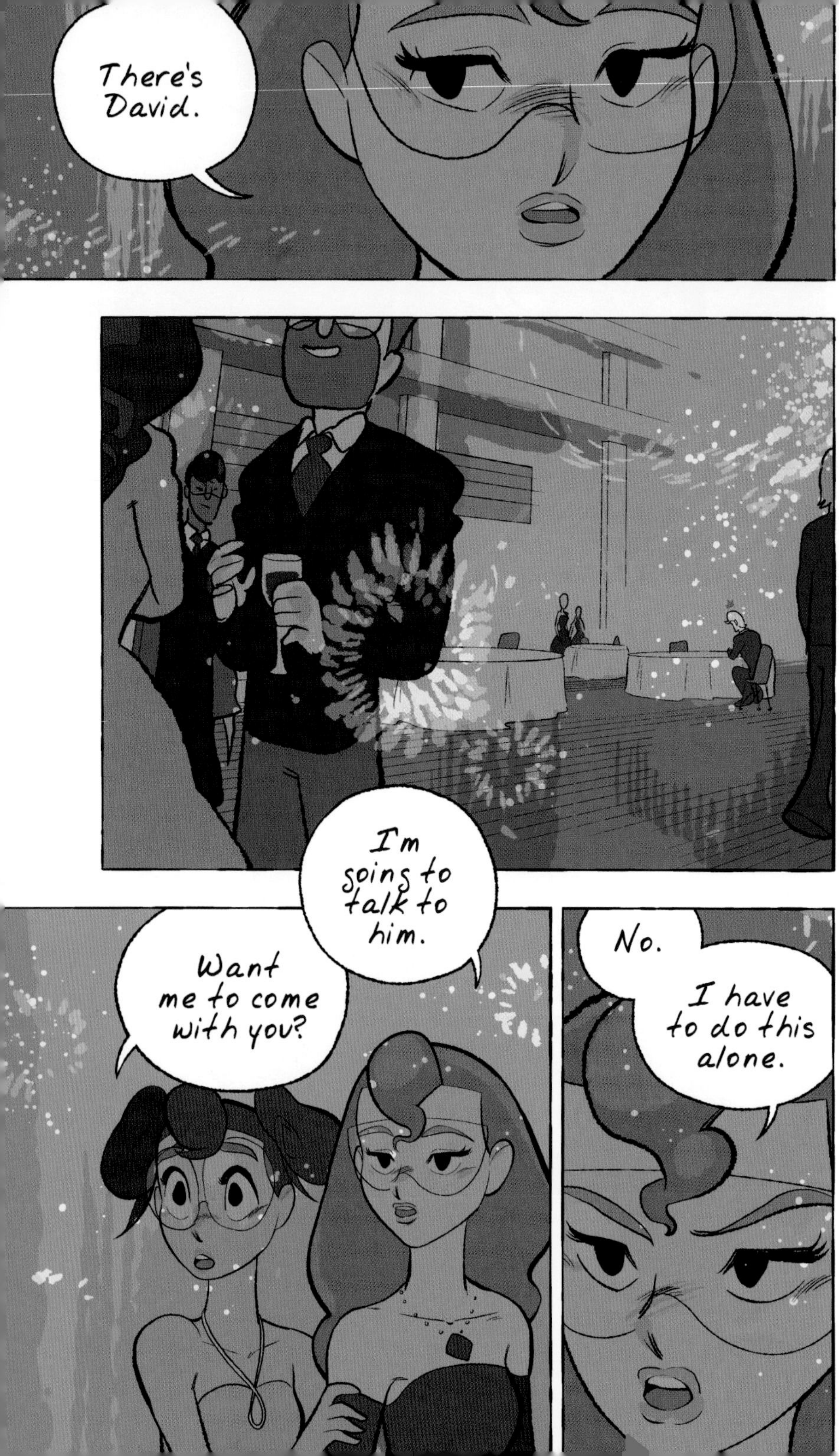
There's David.
I'm going to talk to him.
Want me to come with you?
No.
I have to do this alone.

Good luck.

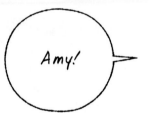

Amy!

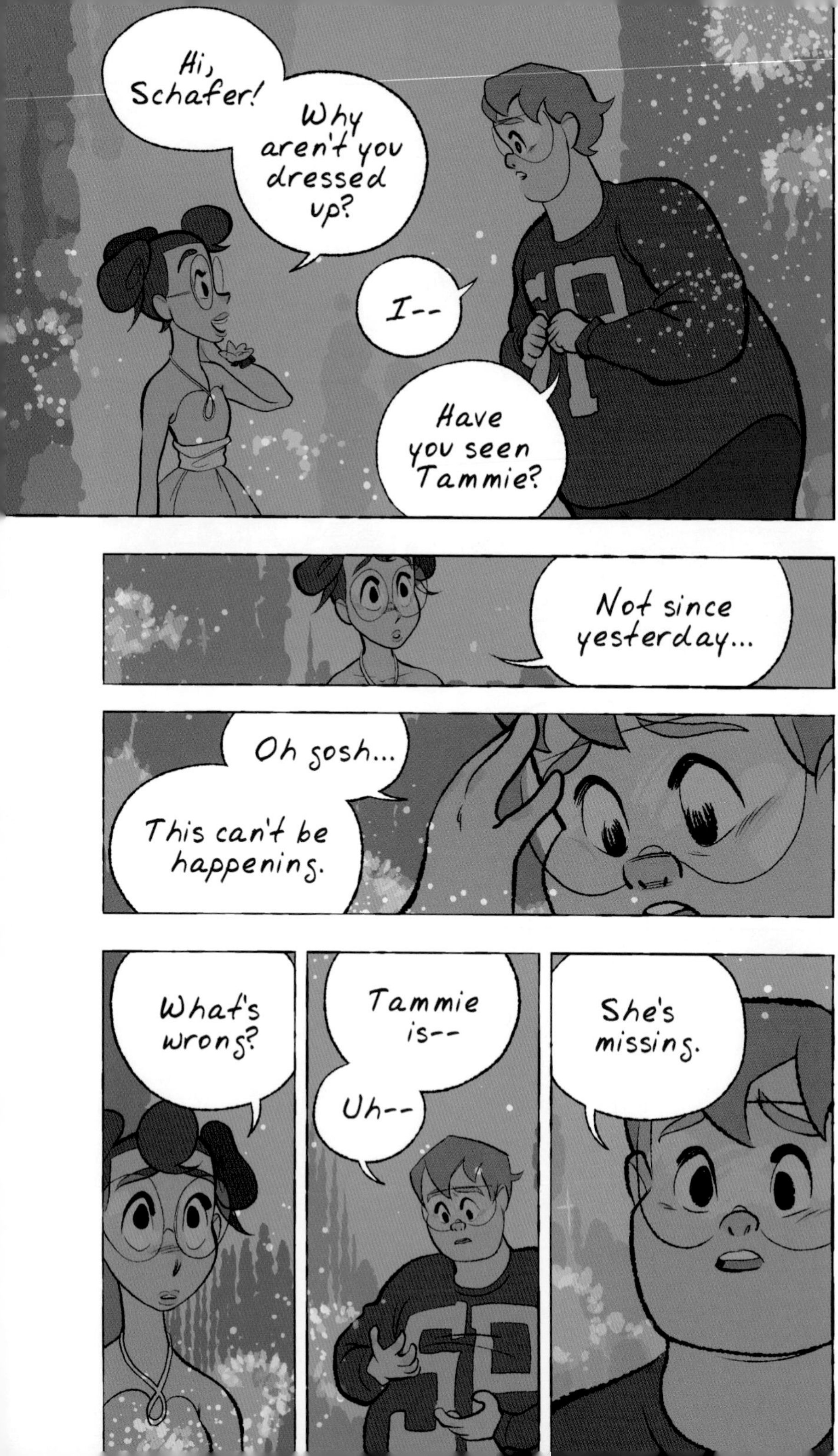
Hi, Schafer!
Why aren't you dressed up?
I--
Have you seen Tammie?
Not since yesterday...
Oh gosh...
This can't be happening.
What's wrong?
Tammie is--
Uh--
She's missing.

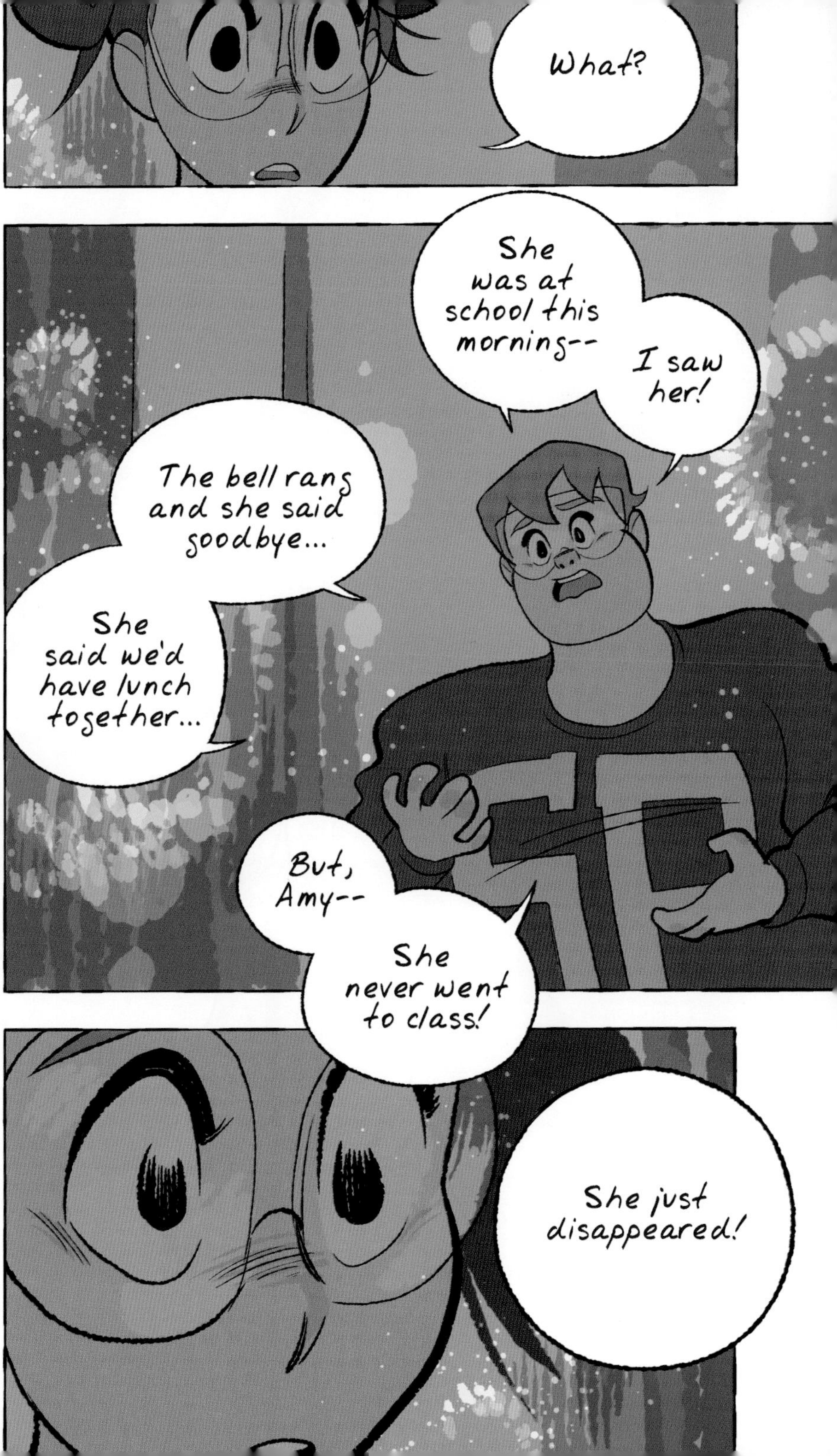
What?
She was at school this morning--
I saw her!
The bell rang and she said goodbye...
She said we'd have lunch together...
But, Amy--
She never went to class!
She just disappeared!

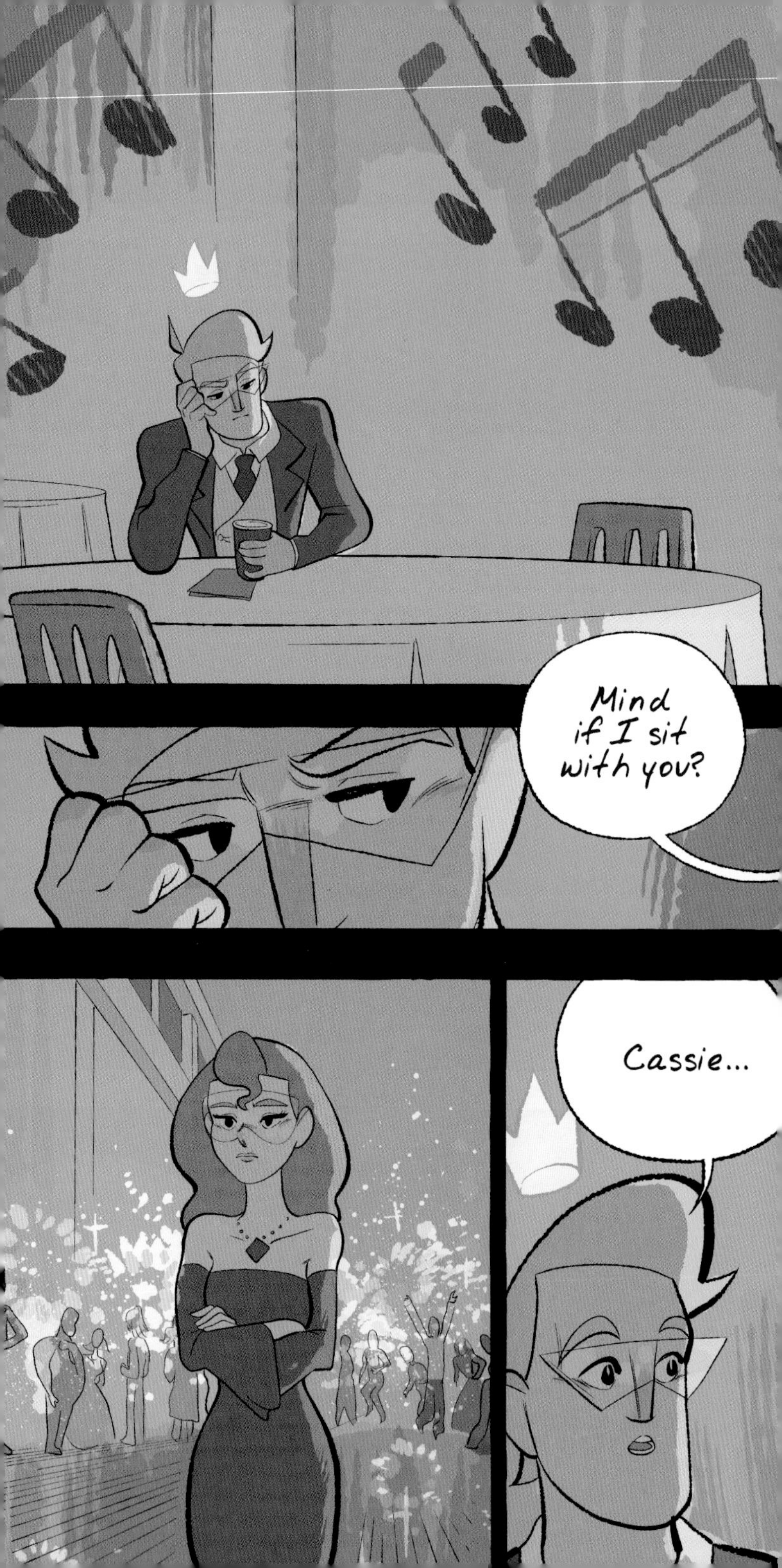
Mind if I sit with you?
Cassie...

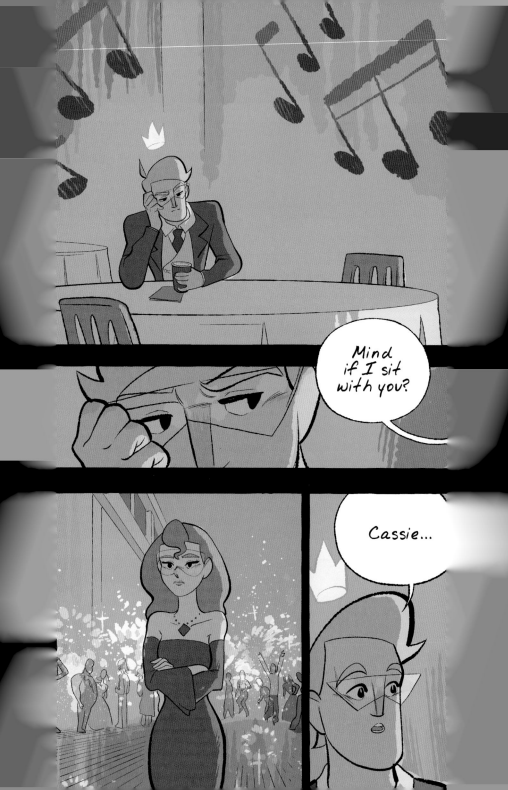

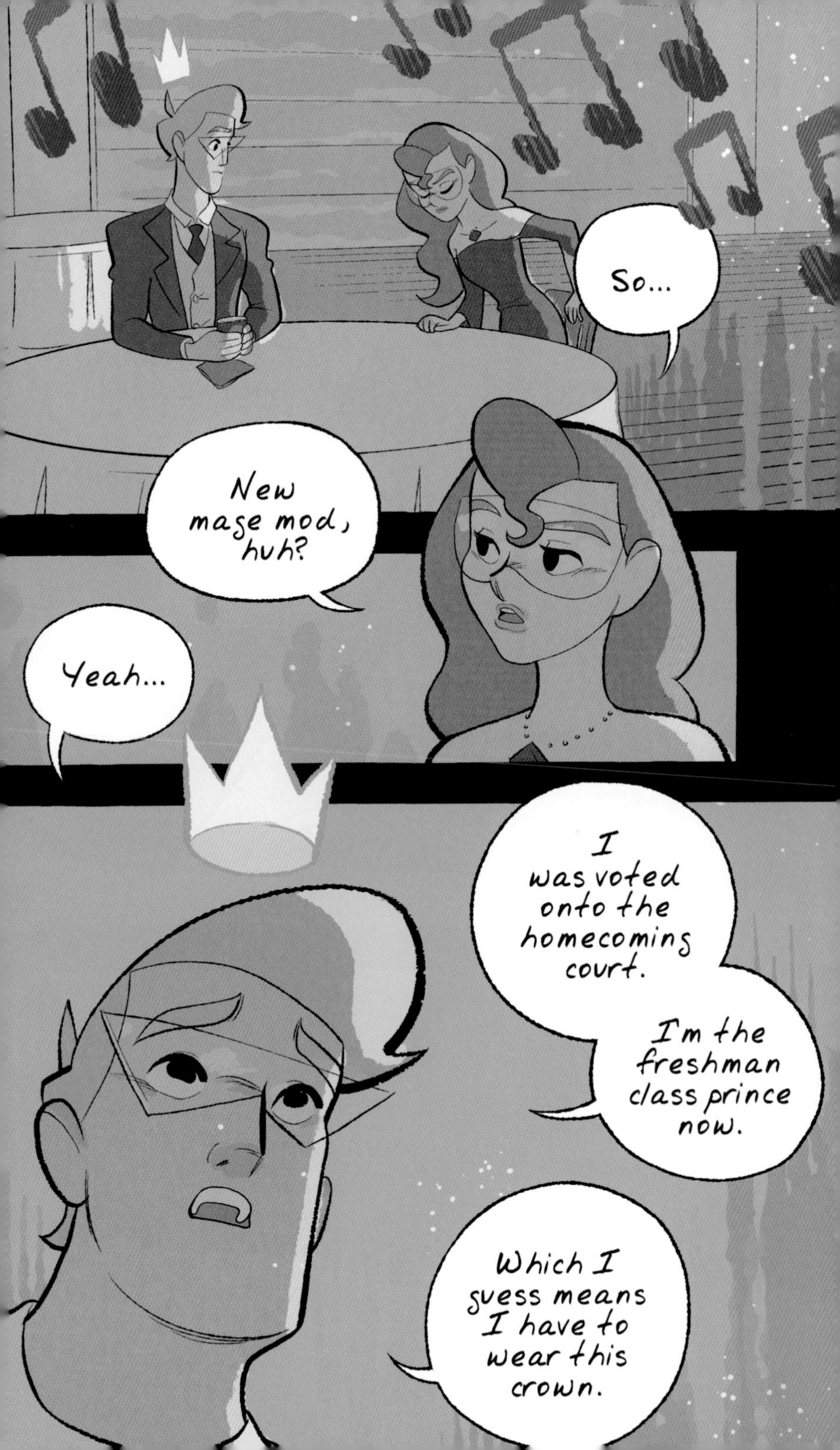
So...
New mage mod, huh?
Yeah...
I was voted onto the homecoming court.
I'm the freshman class prince now.
Which I guess means I have to wear this crown.

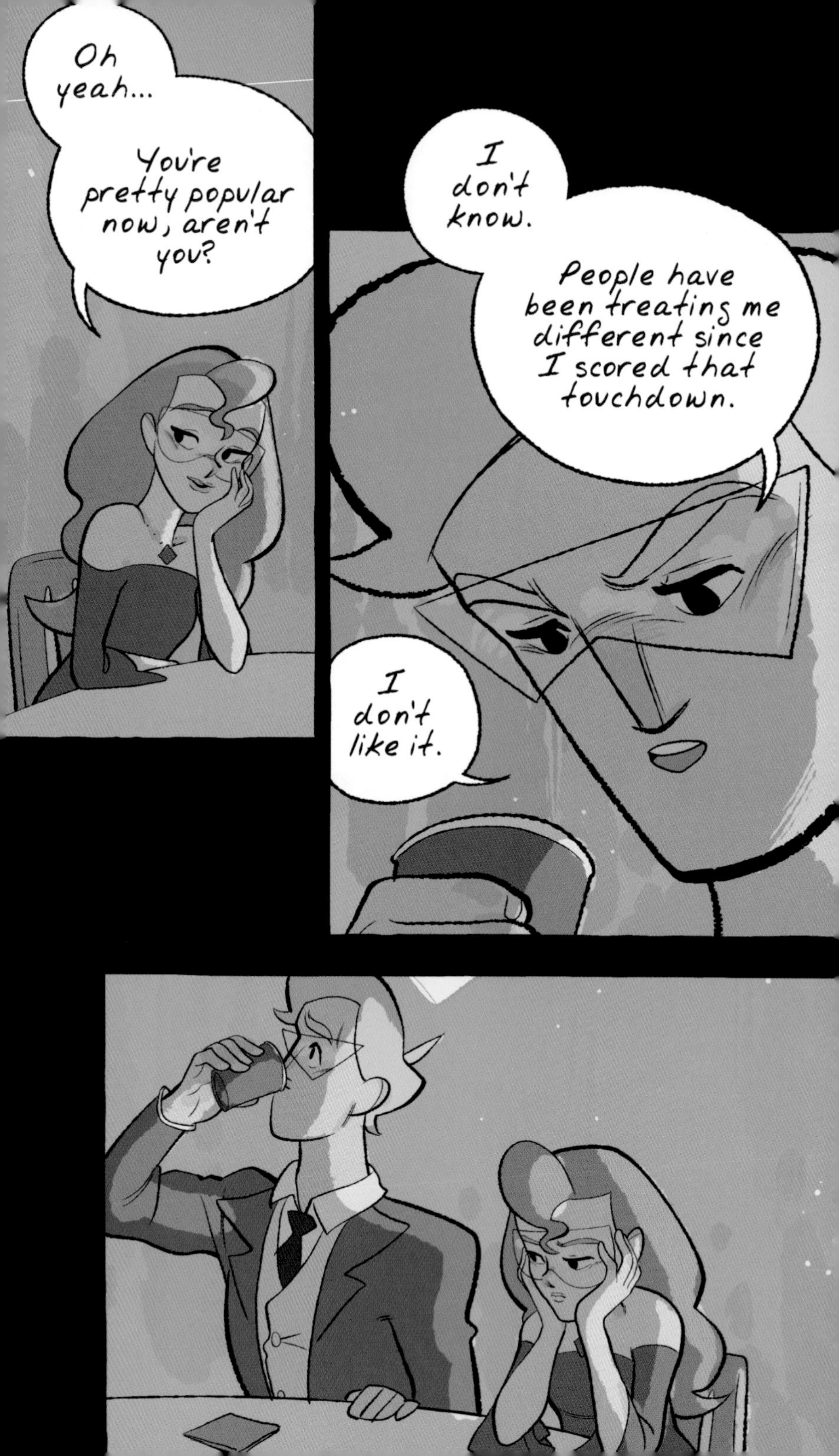
Oh yeah...
You're pretty popular now, aren't you?
I don't know.
People have been treating me different since I scored that touchdown.
I don't like it.

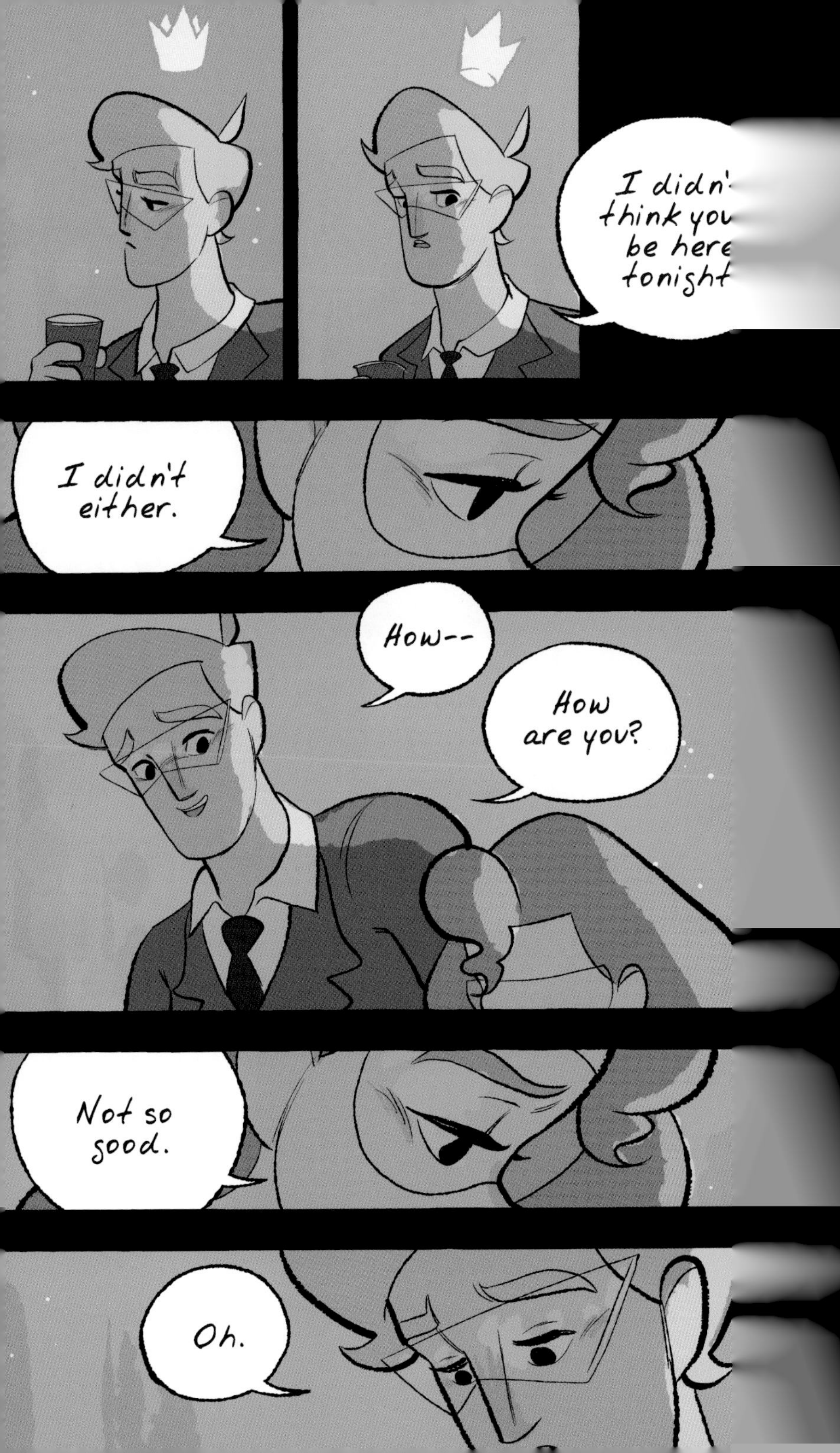
I didn
think you
be here
tonight
I didn't either.
How--
How are you?
Not so good.
Oh.

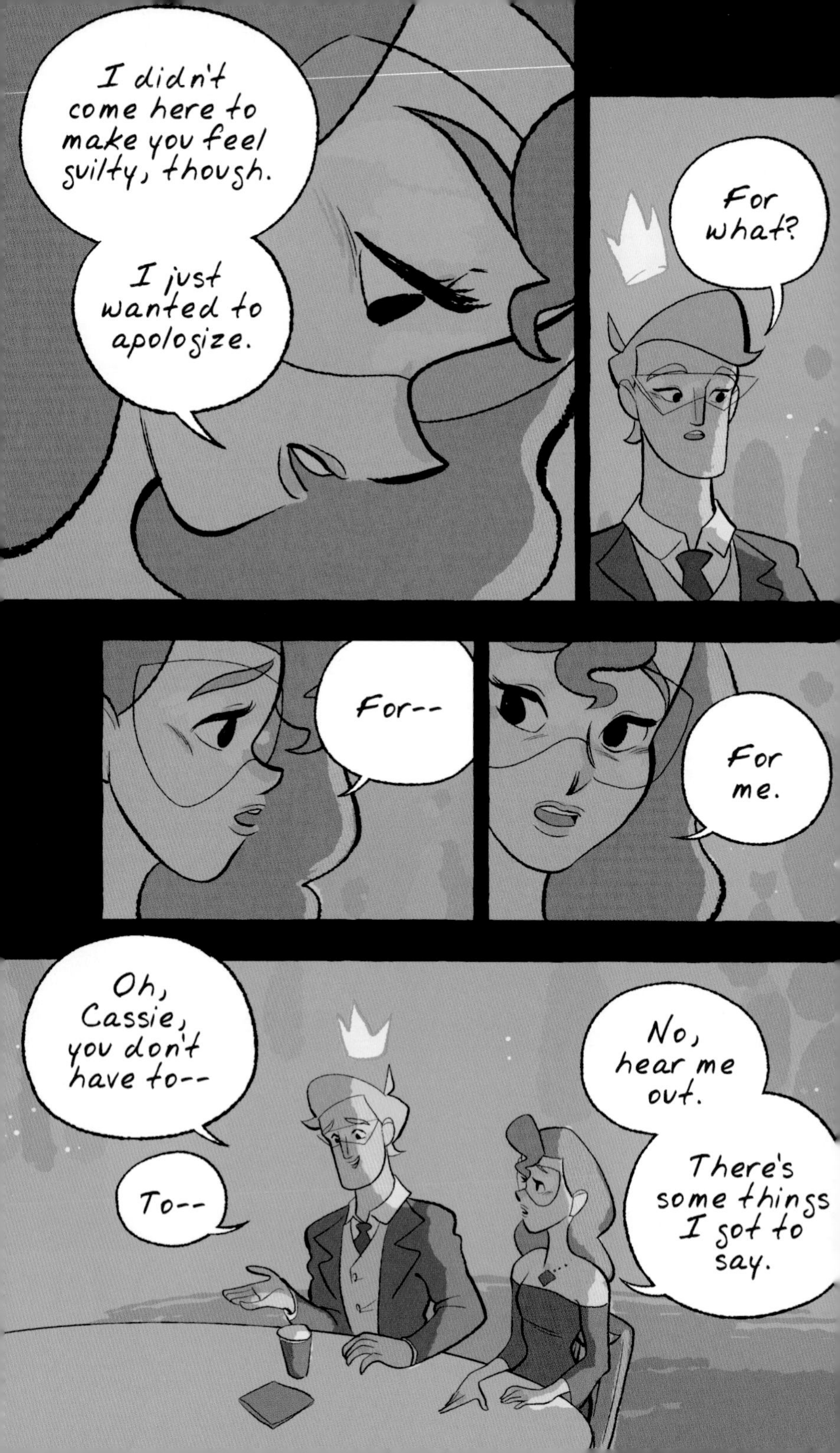
I didn't come here to make you feel guilty, though.
I just wanted to apologize.
For what?
For--
For me.
Oh, Cassie, you don't have to--
To--
No, hear me out.
There's some things I got to say.

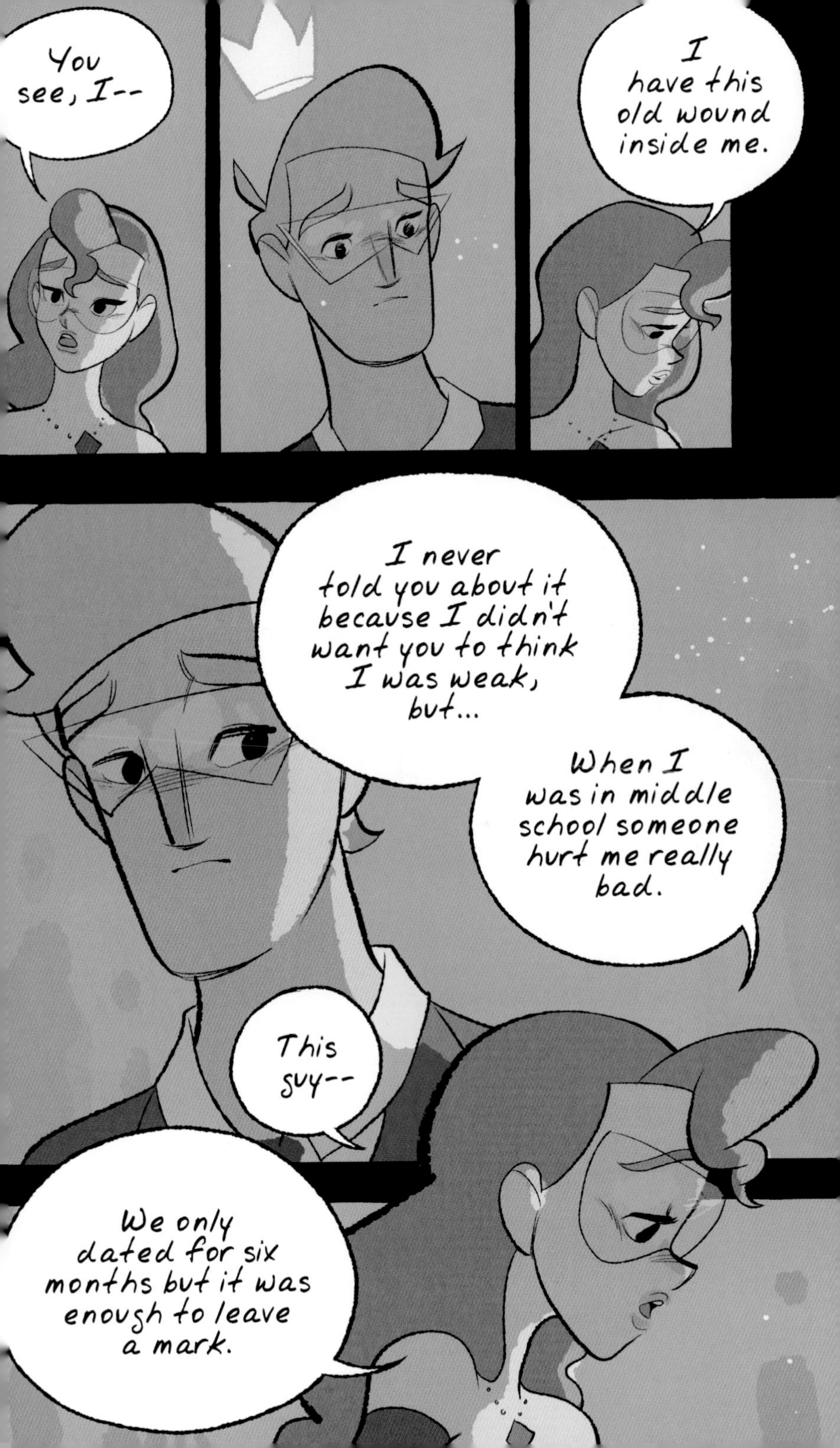
You see, I--
I have this old wound inside me.
I never told you about it because I didn't want you to think I was weak, but...
When I was in middle school someone hurt me really bad.
This guy--
We only dated for six months but it was enough to leave a mark.

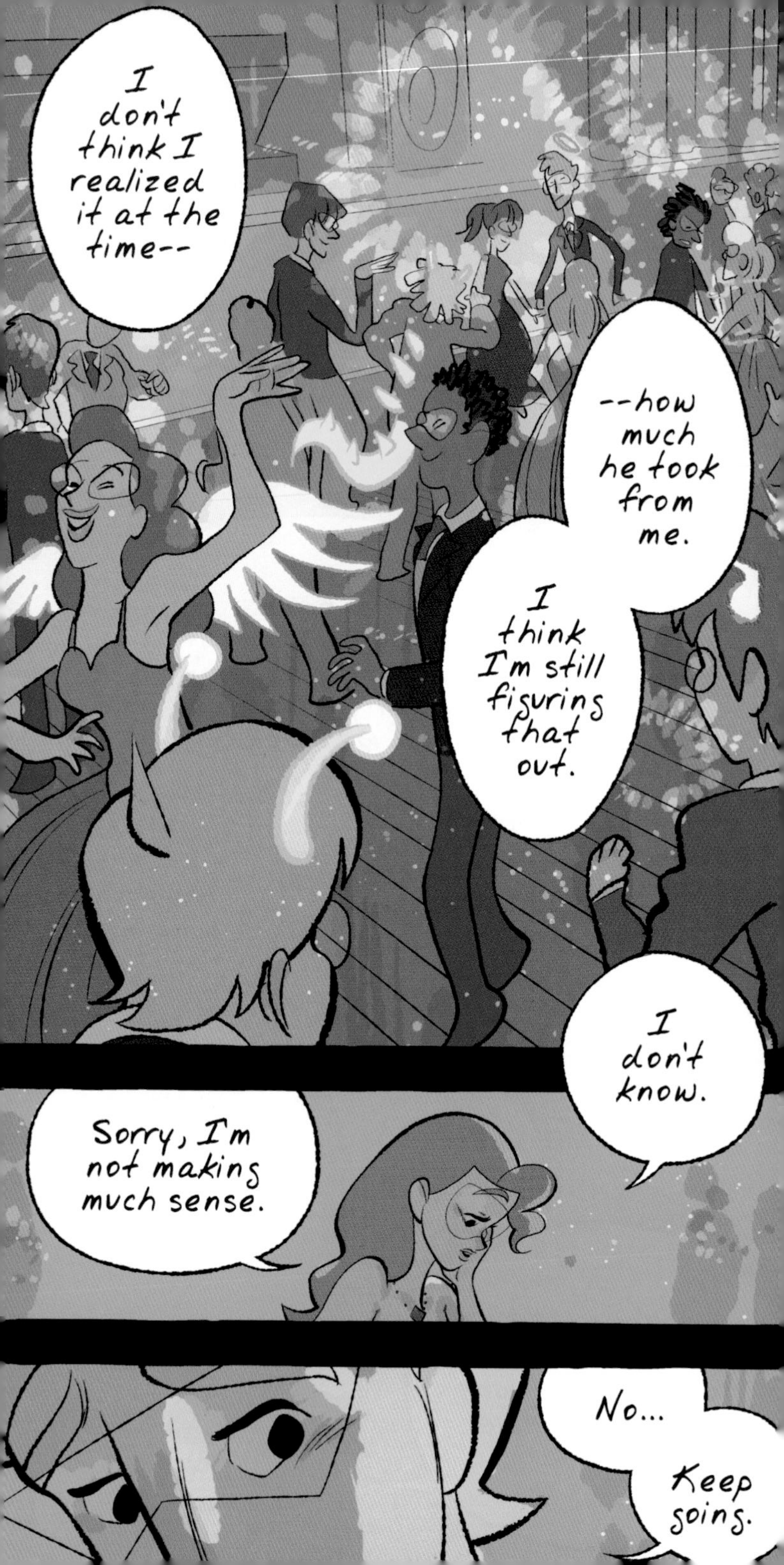
I don't think I realized it at the time--
--how much he took from me.
I think I'm still figuring that out.
I don't know.
Sorry, I'm not making much sense.
No...
Keep going.

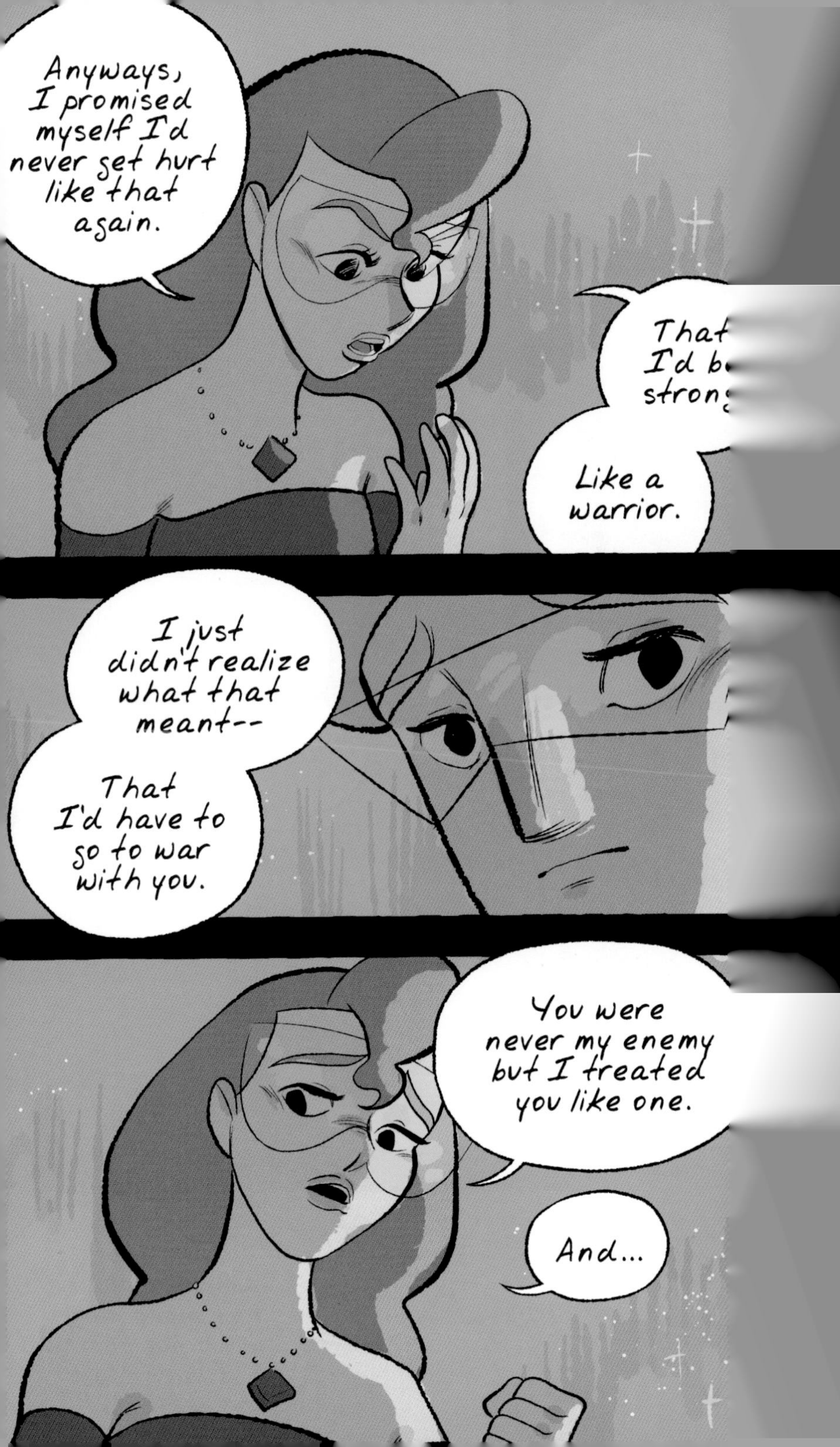
Anyways, I promised myself I'd never get hurt like that again.
That I'd b stron
Like a warrior.
I just didn't realize what that meant--
That I'd have to go to war with you.
You were never my enemy but I treated you like one.
And...

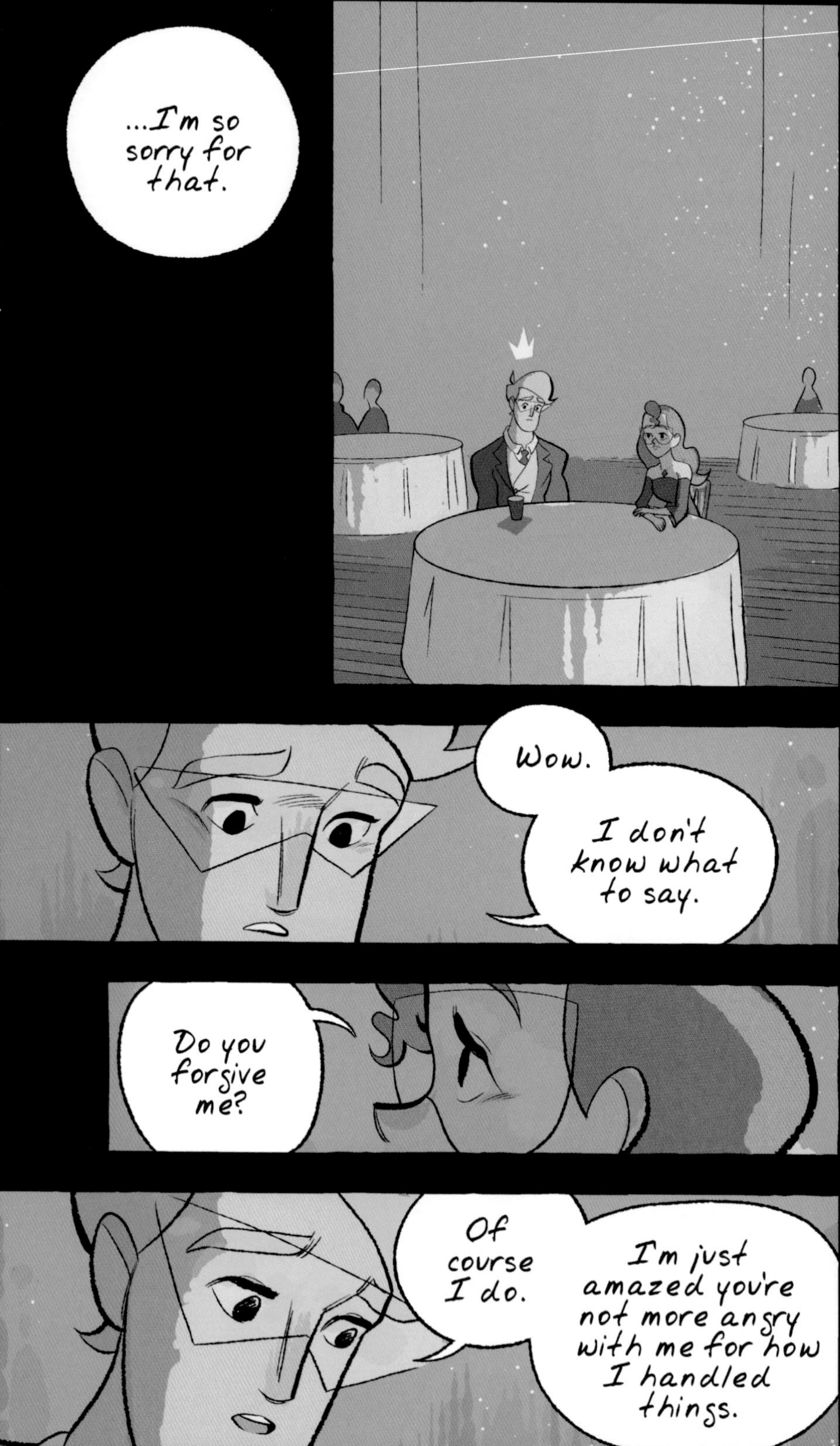
...I'm so sorry for that.
Wow.
I don't know what to say.
Do you forgive me?
Of course I do.
I'm just amazed you're not more angry with me for how I handled things.

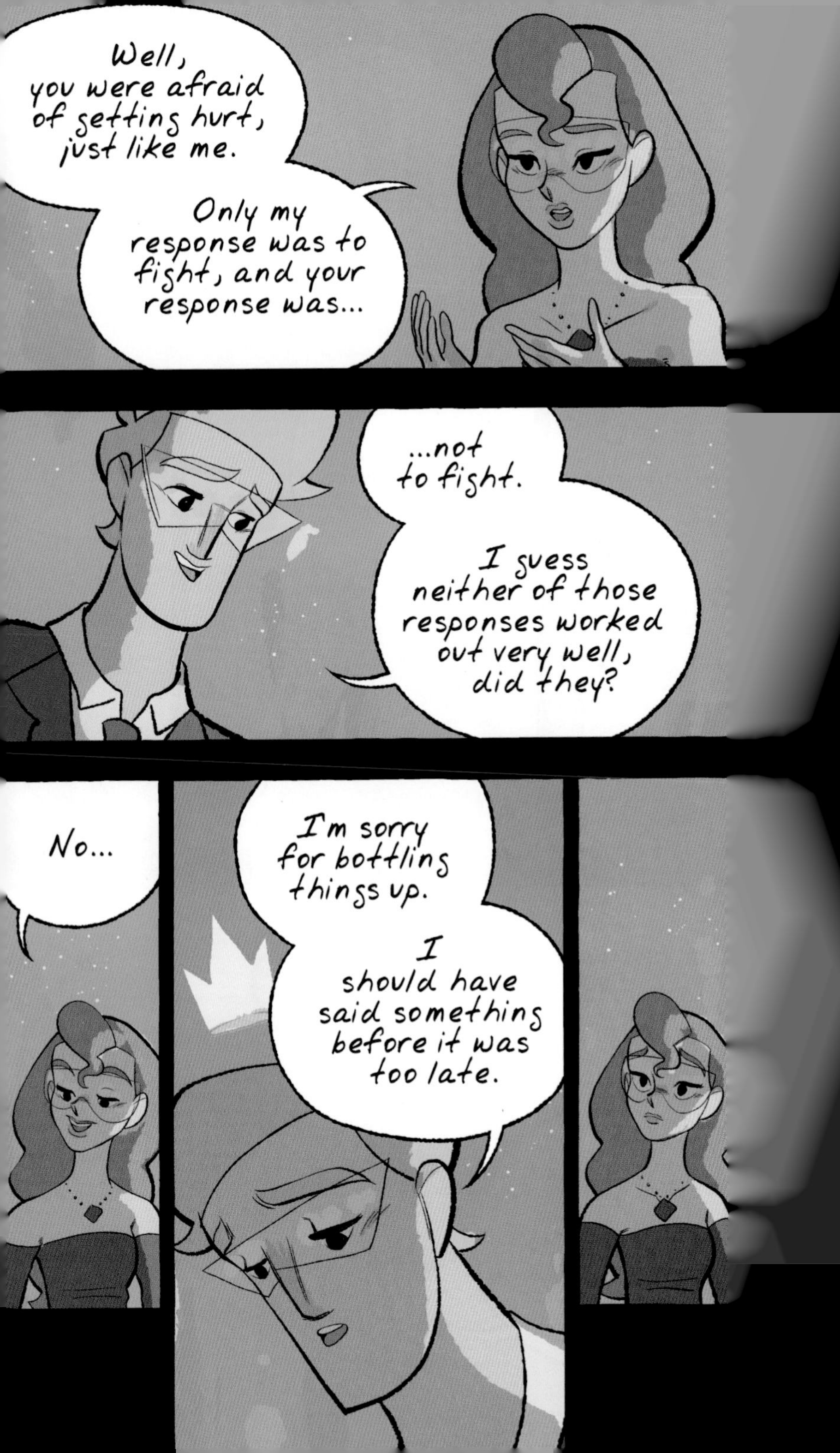
Well, you were afraid of getting hurt, just like me.
Only my response was to fight, and your response was...
...not to fight.
I guess neither of those responses worked out very well, did they?
No...
I'm sorry for bottling things up.
I should have said something before it was too late.

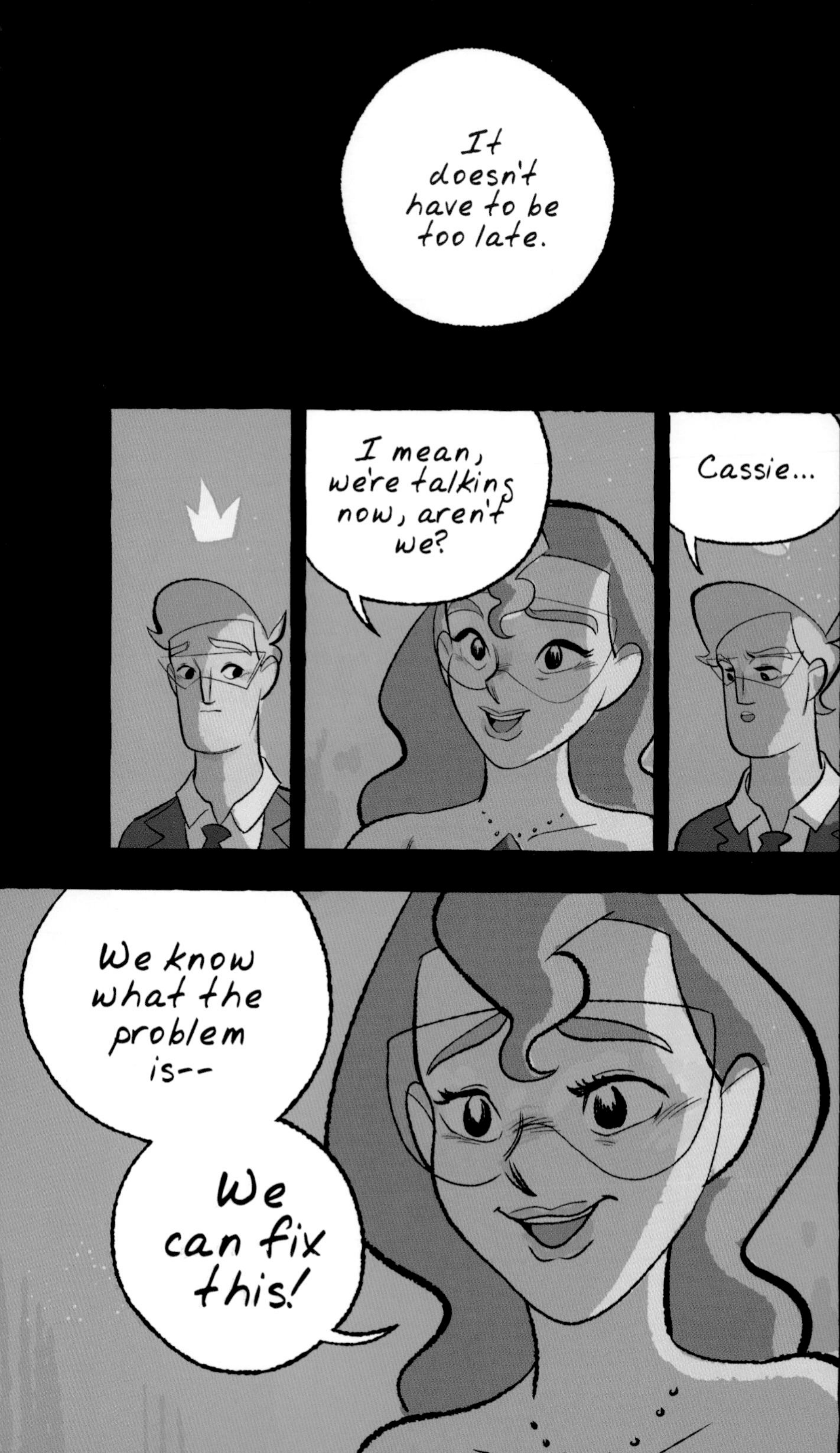
It doesn't have to be too late.
I mean, we're talking now, aren't we?
Cassie...
We know what the problem is--
We can fix this!

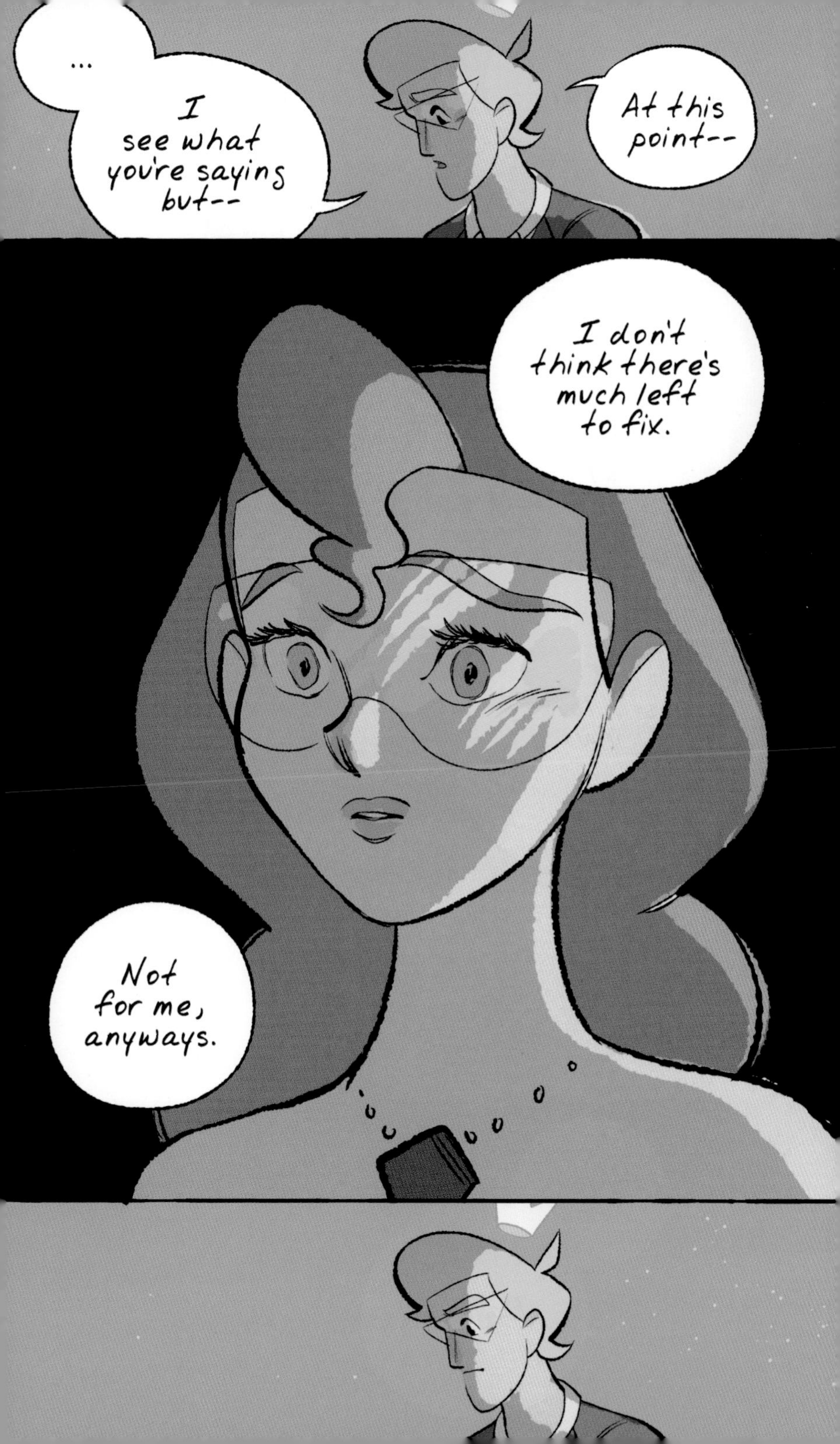
...
I see what you're sayins but--
At this point--
I don't think there's much left to fix.
Not for me, anyways.

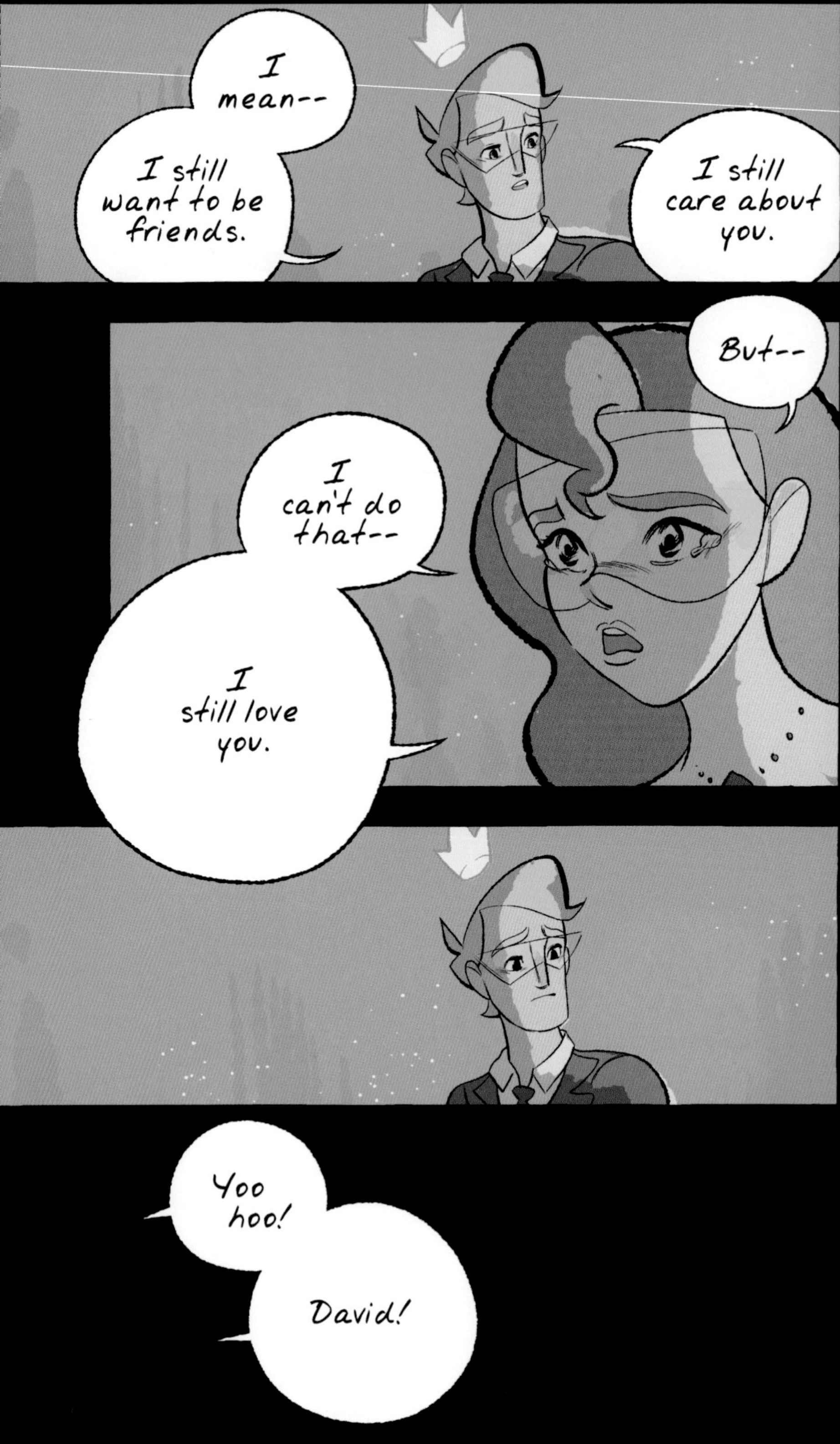
I mean--
I still want to be friends.
I still care about you.
But--
I can't do that--
I still love you.
Yoo hoo!
David!

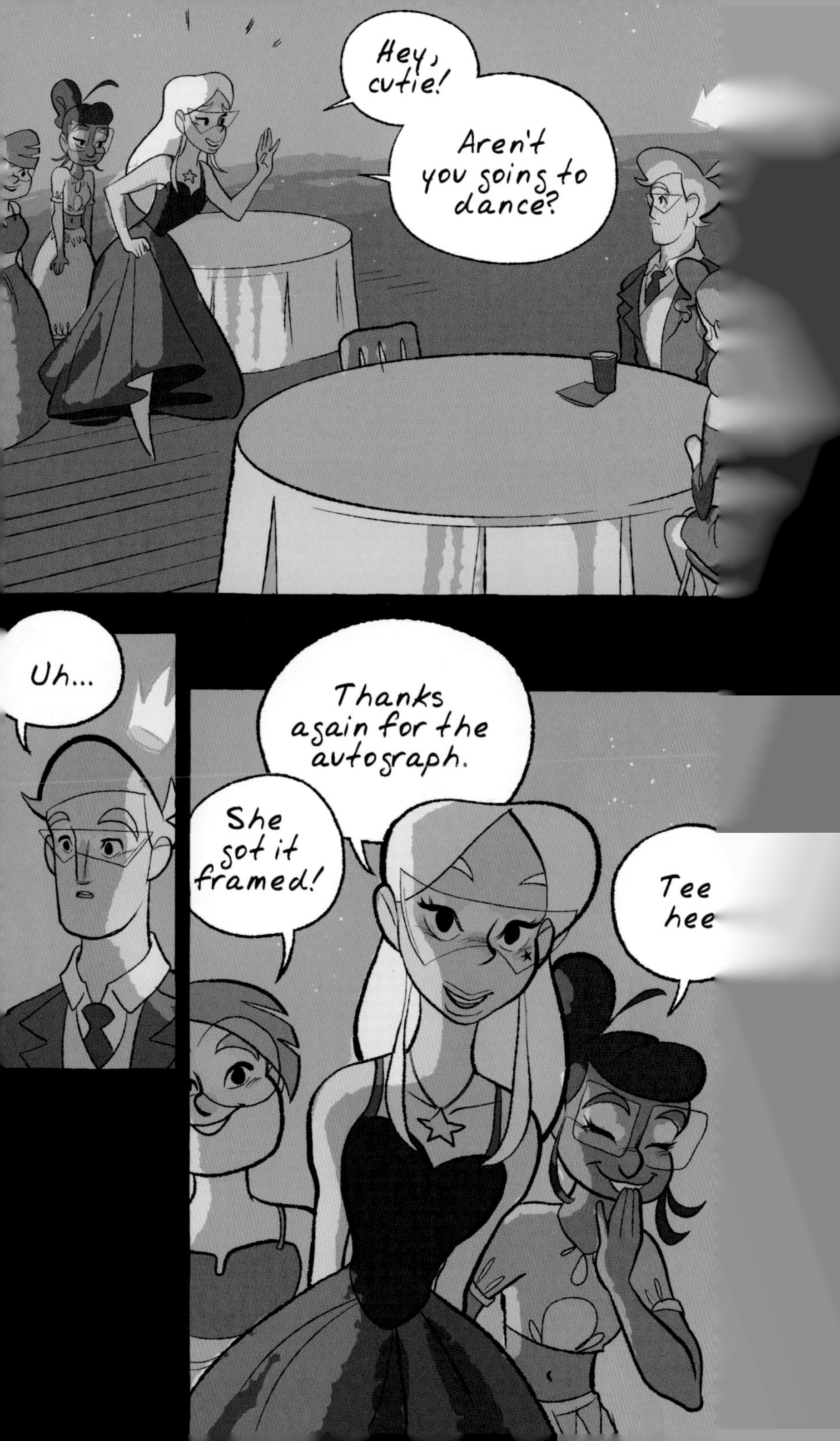
Hey, cutie!
Aren't you going to dance?
Uh...
Thanks again for the autograph.
She got it framed!
Tee hee

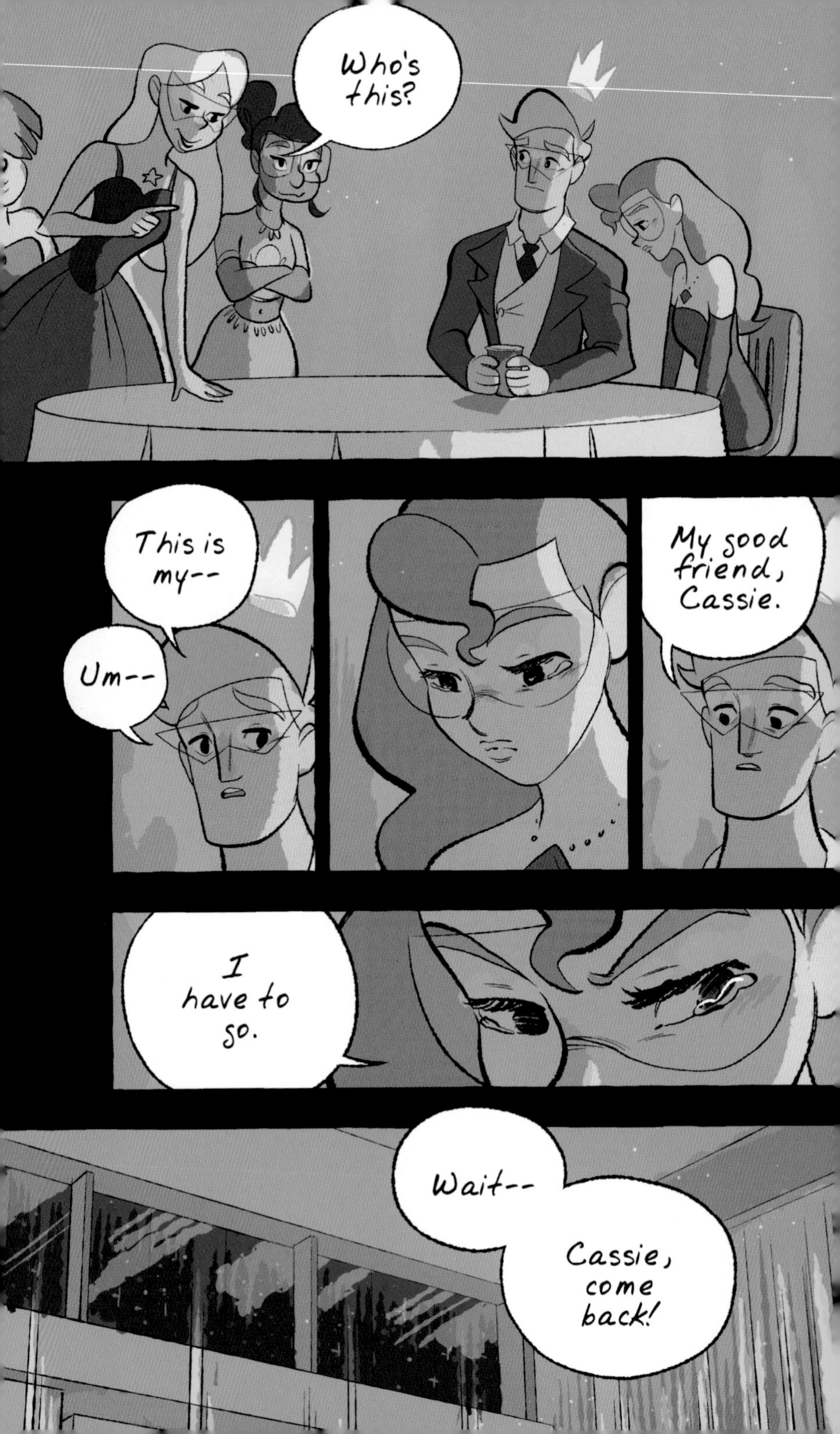
Who's this?
This is my--
Um--
My good friend, Cassie.
I have to go.
Wait--
Cassie, come back!

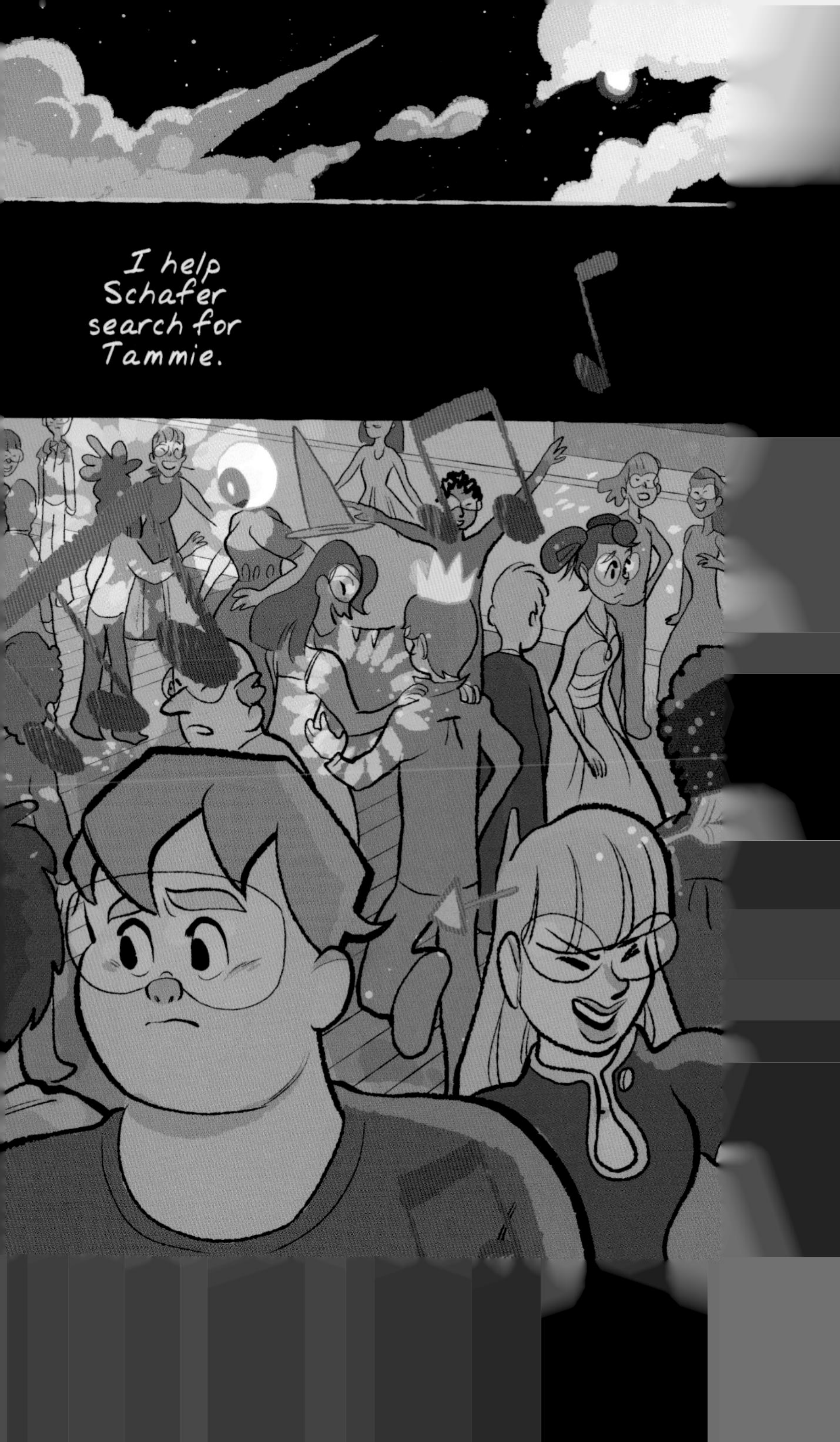
I help Schafer search for Tammie.

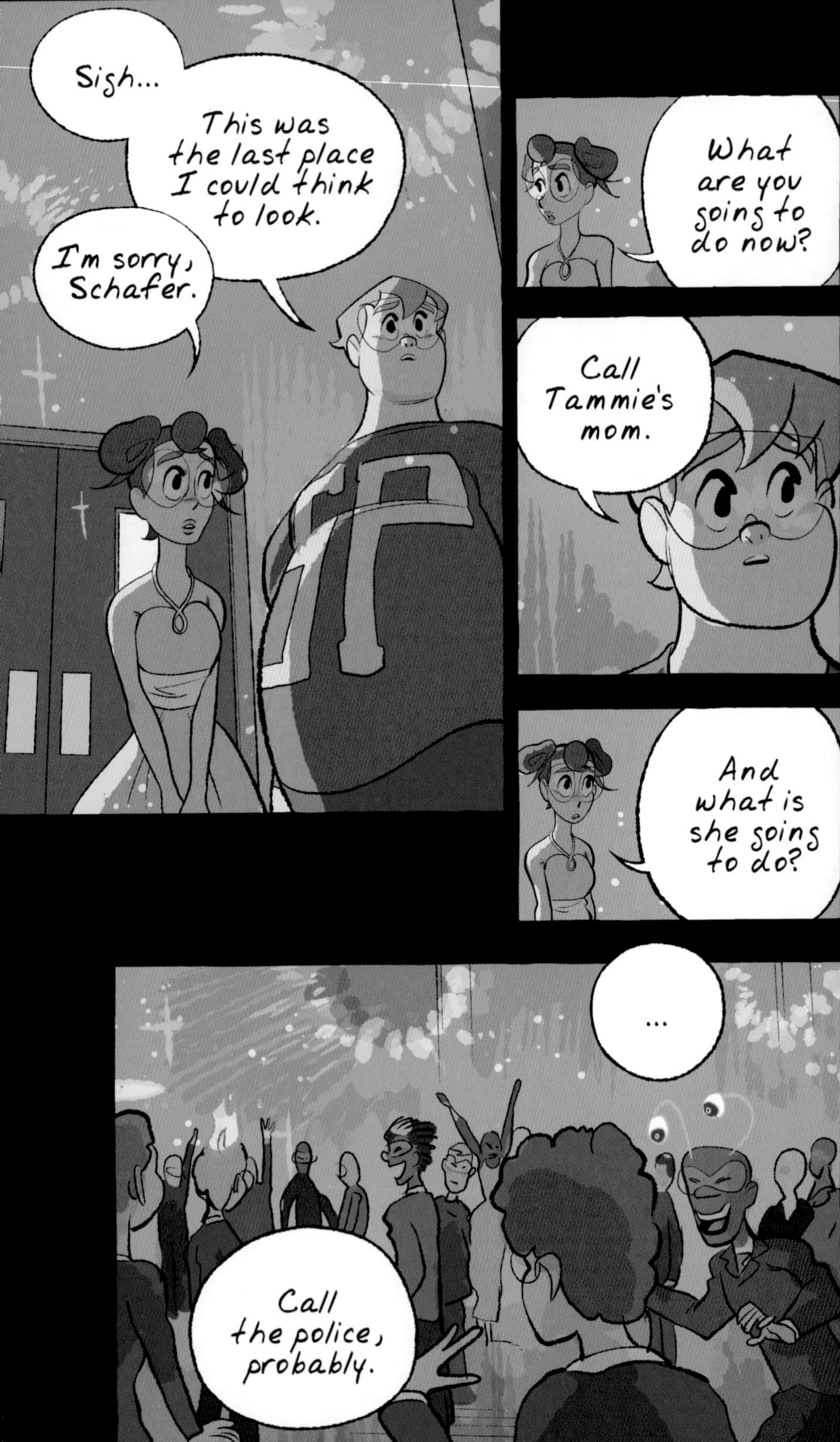
Sigh...
This was the last place I could think to look.
I'm sorry, Schafer.
What are you going to do now?
Call Tammie's mom.
And what is she going to do?
...
Call the police, probably.

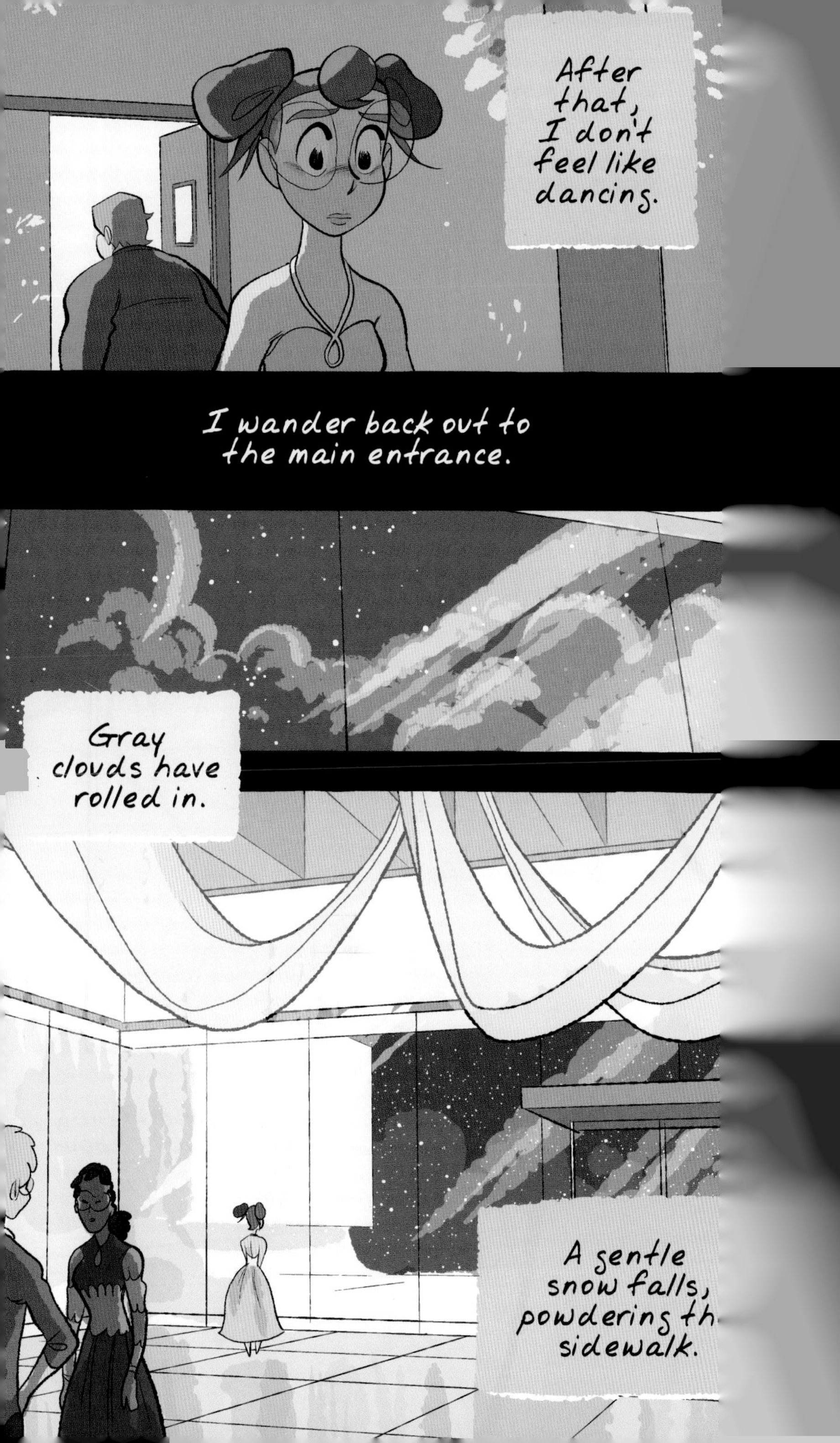
After that, I don't feel like dancing.
I wander back out to the main entrance.
Gray clouds have rolled in.
A gentle snow falls, powdering th
sidewalk.

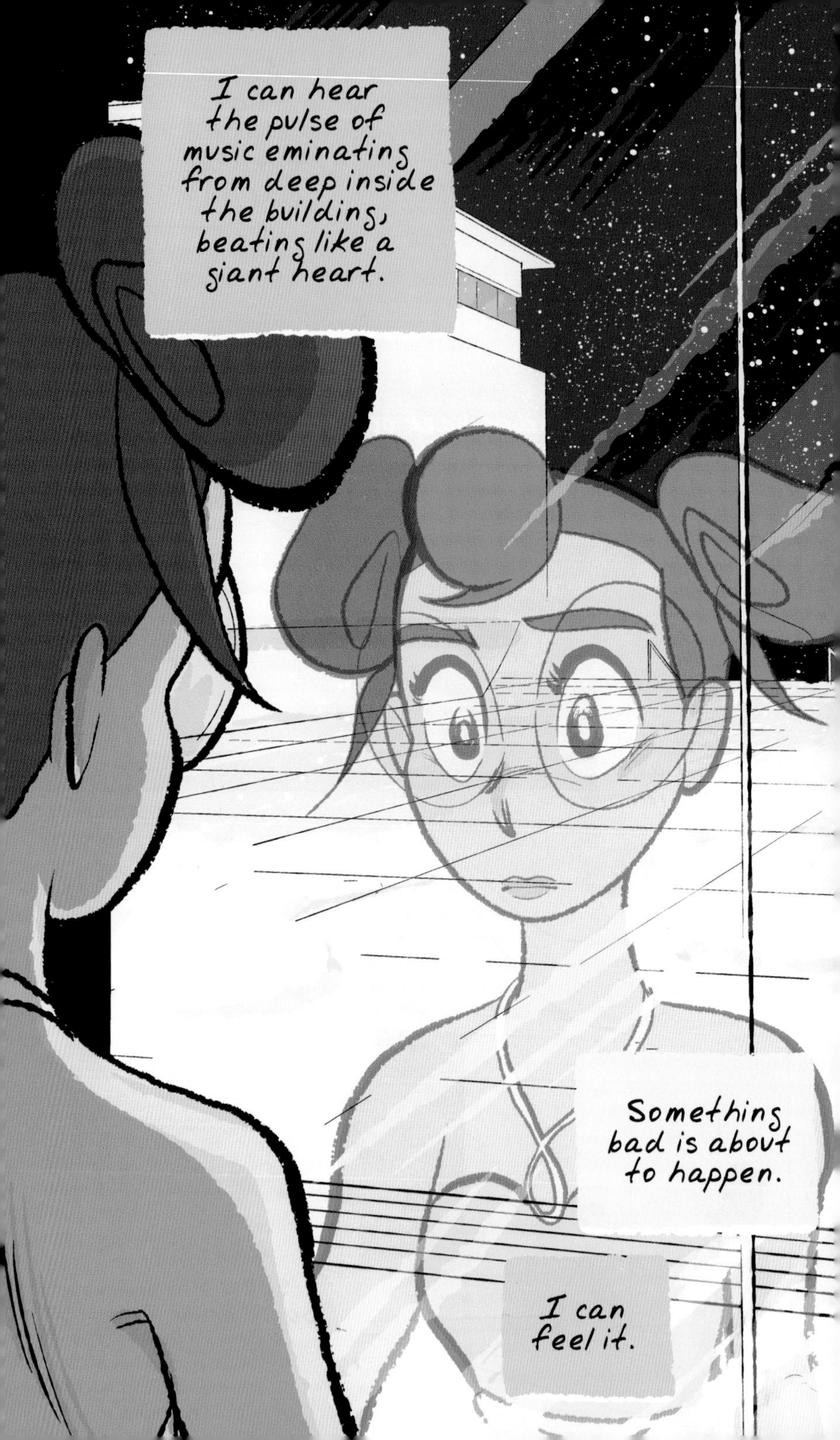
I can hear the pulse of music eminating from deep inside the buildings, beating like a giant heart.
Somethins bad is about to happen.
I can feel it.

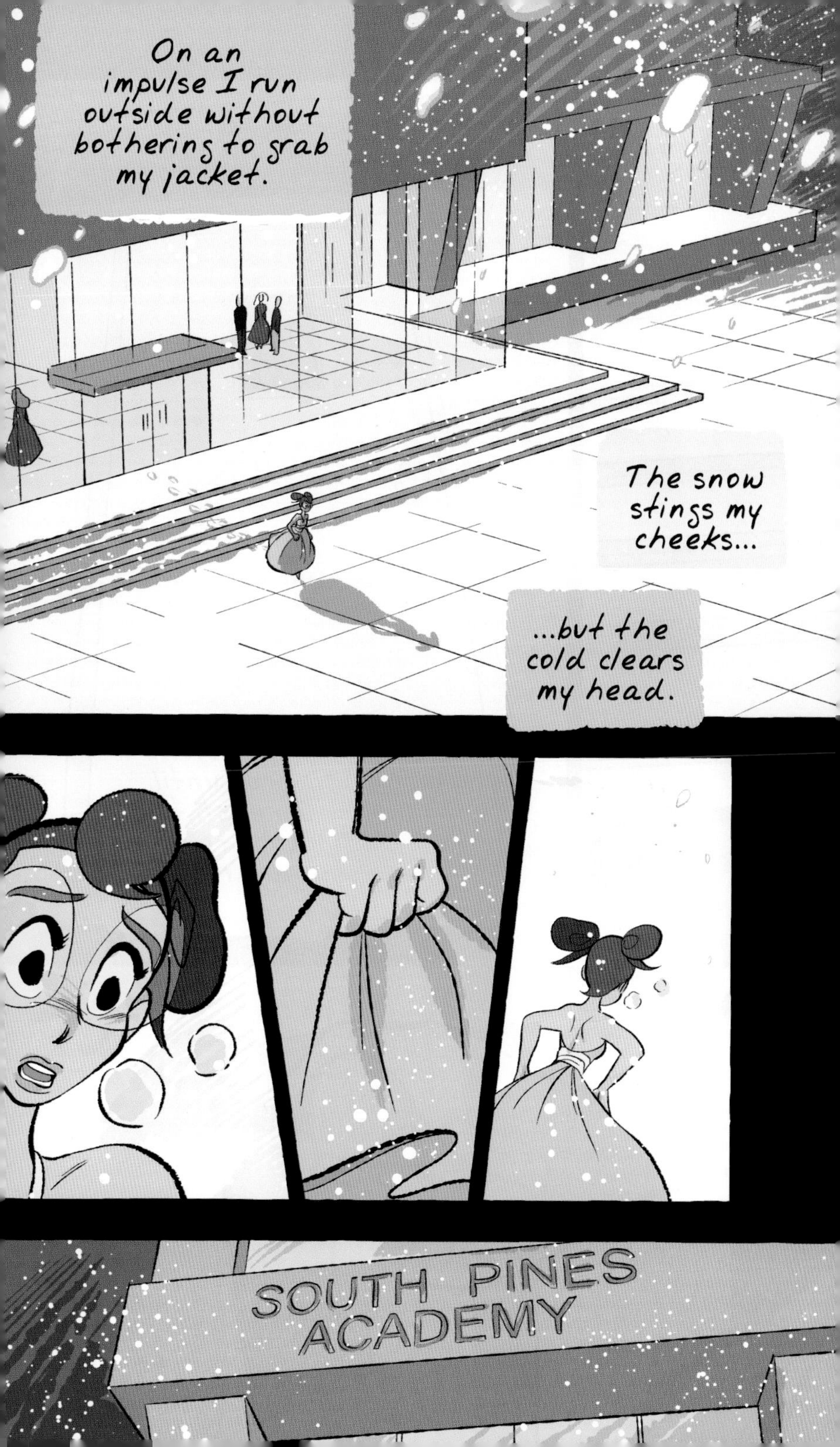
On an impulse I run outside without botherins to grab my jacket.
The snow stings my cheeks...
...but the cold clears my head.
SOUTH PINES ACADEMY

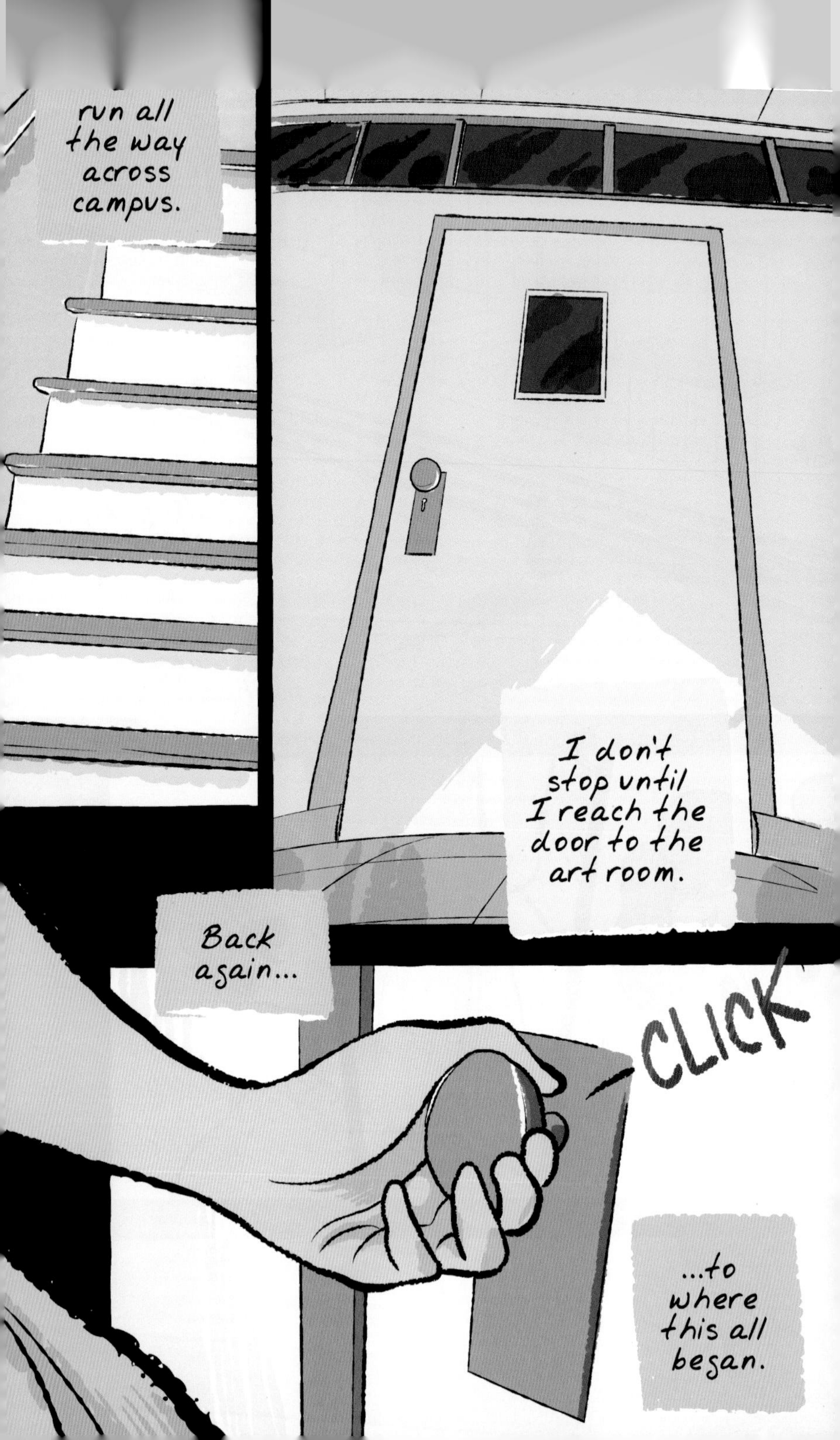
run all the way across campus.
I don't stop until I reach the door to the art room.
Back again...
CLICK
...to where this all began.

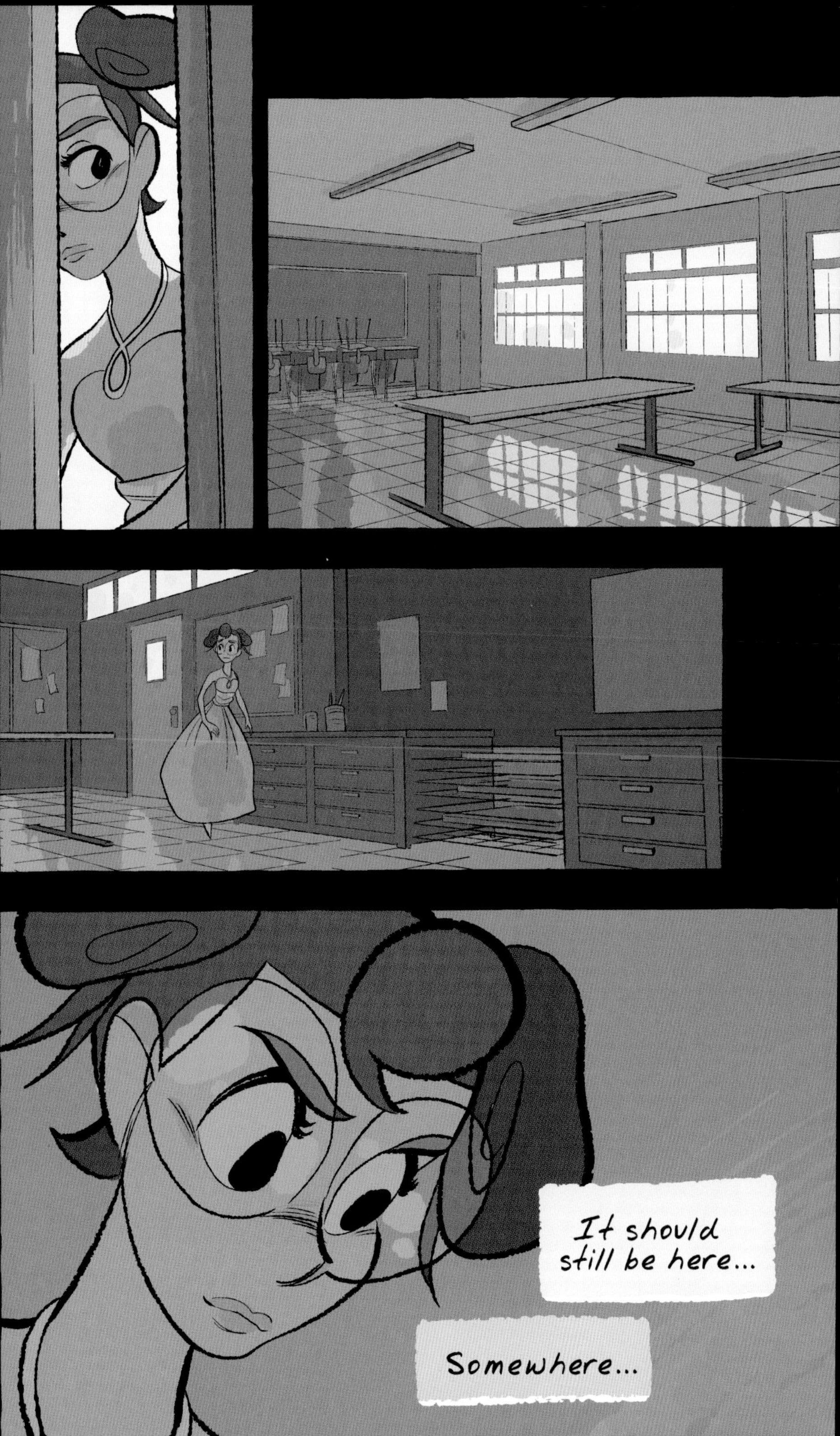
It should still be here...
Somewhere...

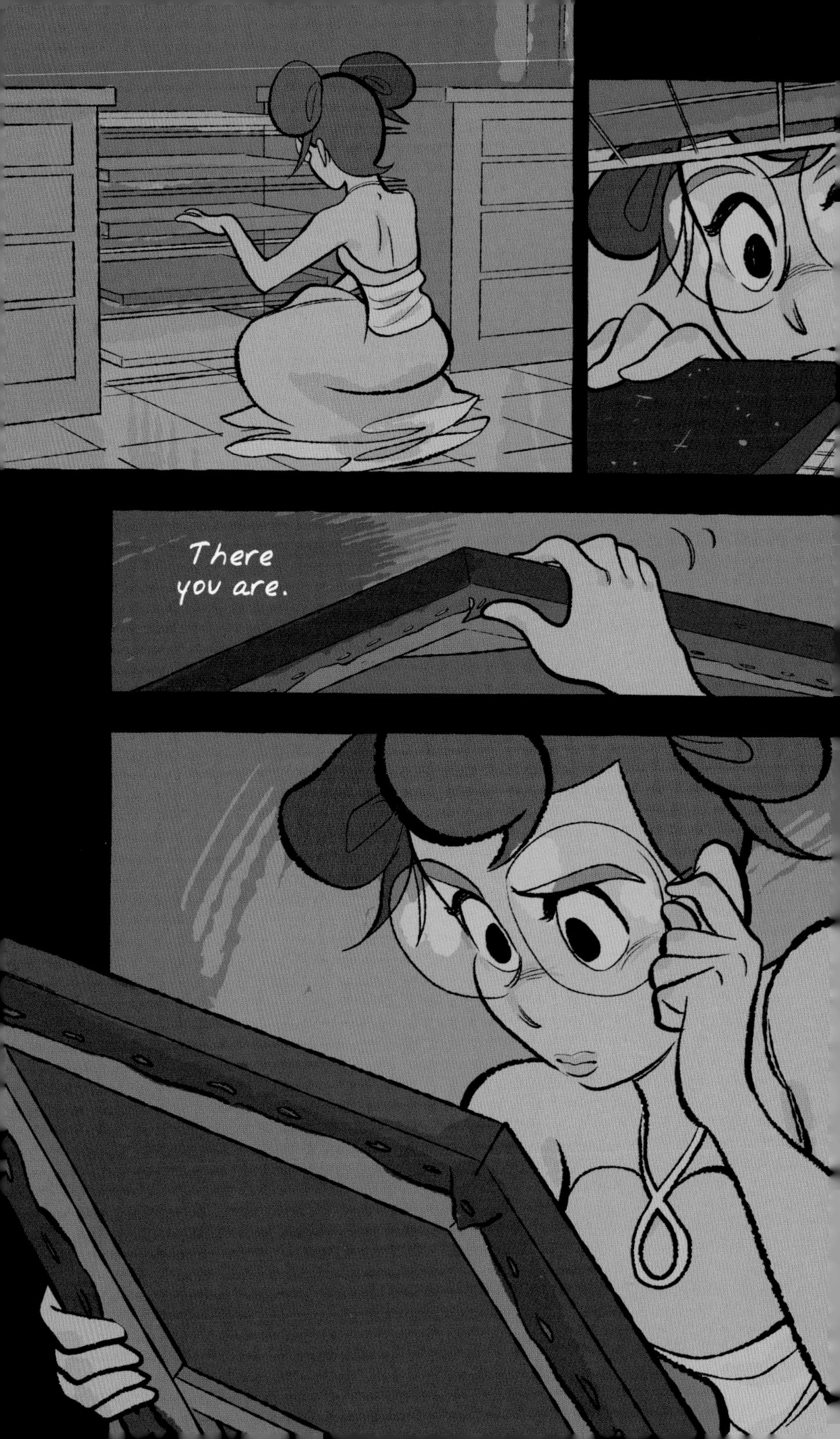
There you are.

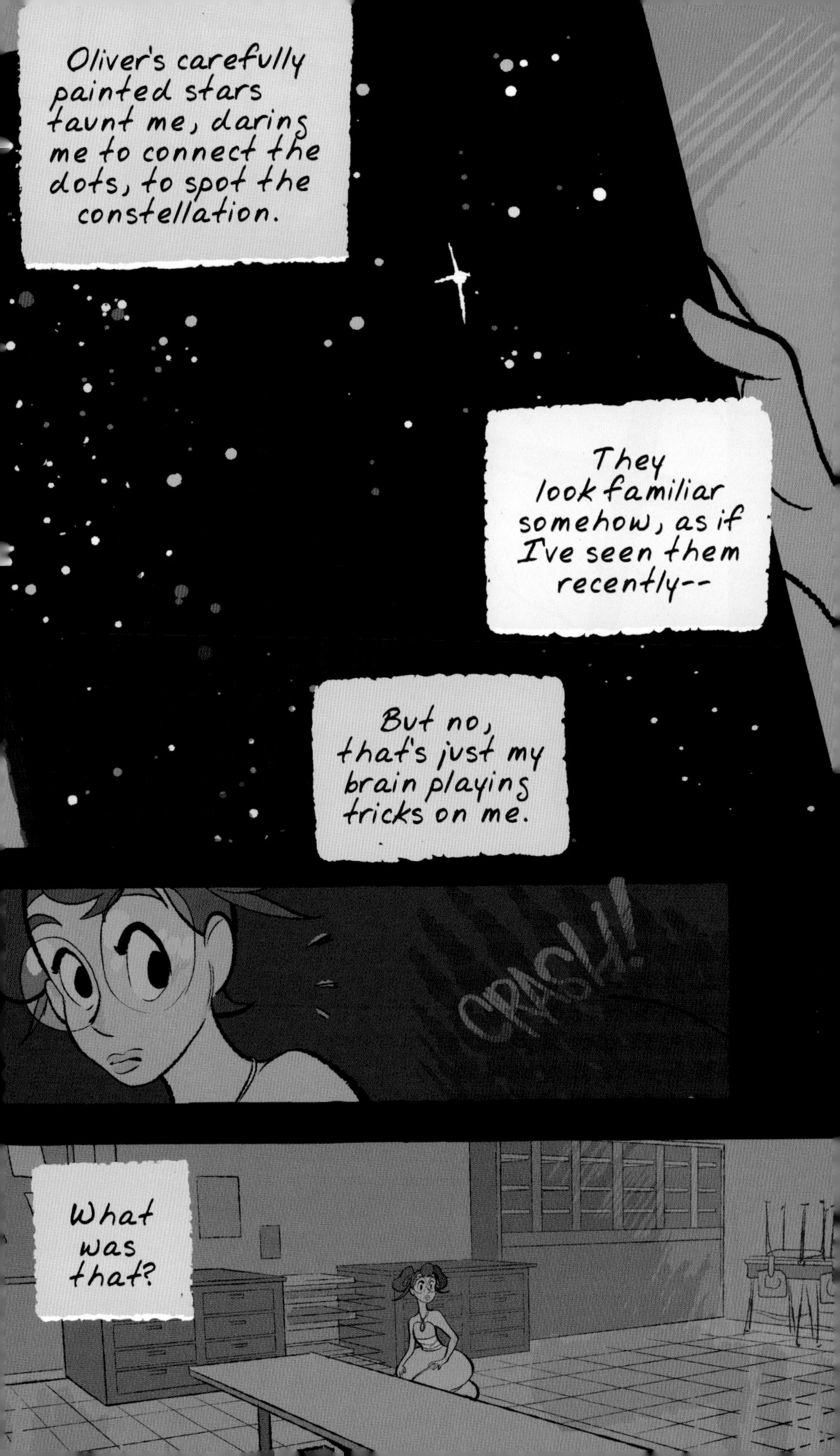
Oliver's carefully painted stars taunt me, daring me to connect the dots, to spot the constellation.
They look familiar somehow, as if I've seen them recently--
But no, that's just my brain playing tricks on me.
CRASH!
What was that?

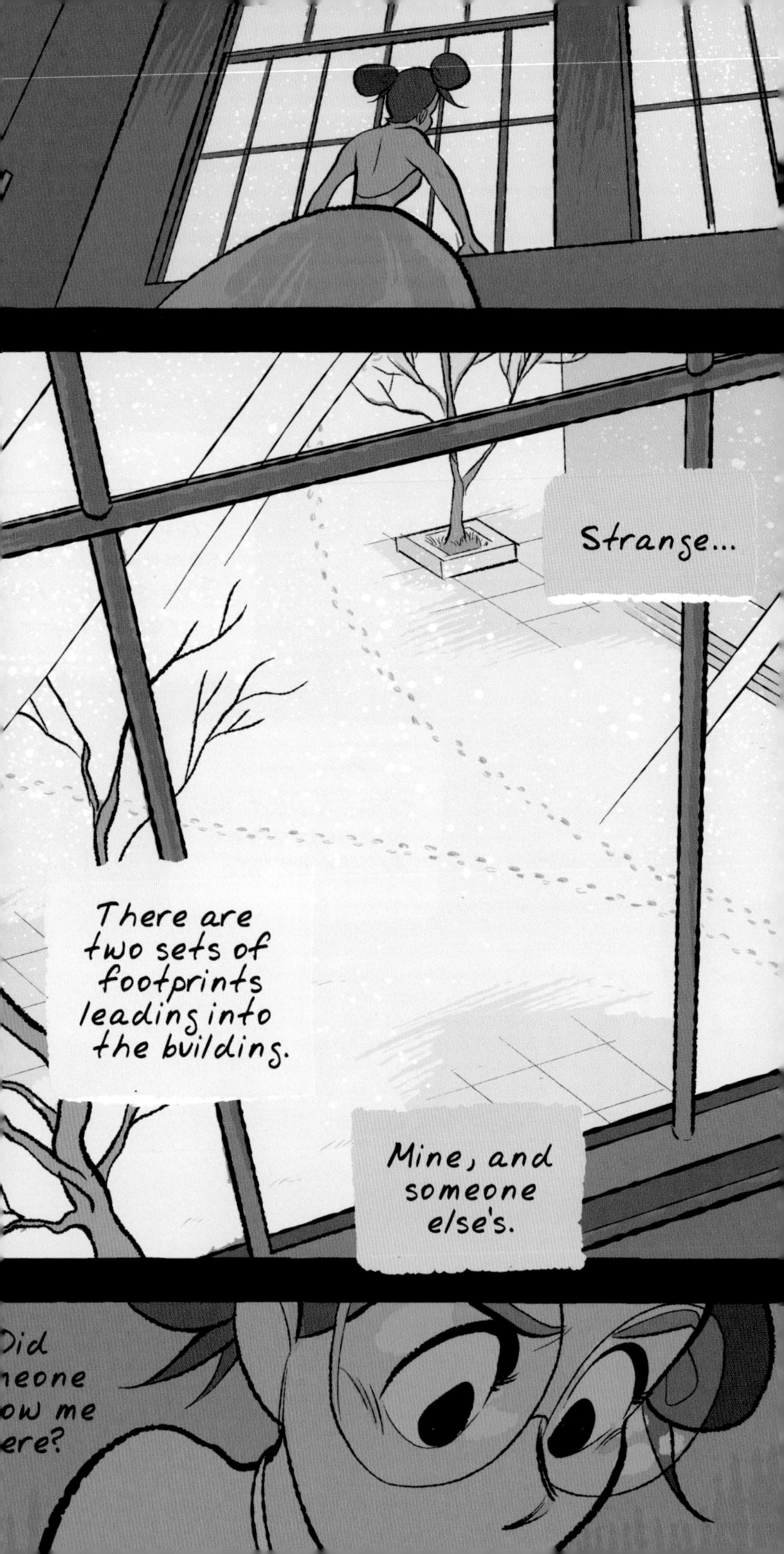
Strange...
There are two sets of footprints leading into the building.
Mine, and someone else's.

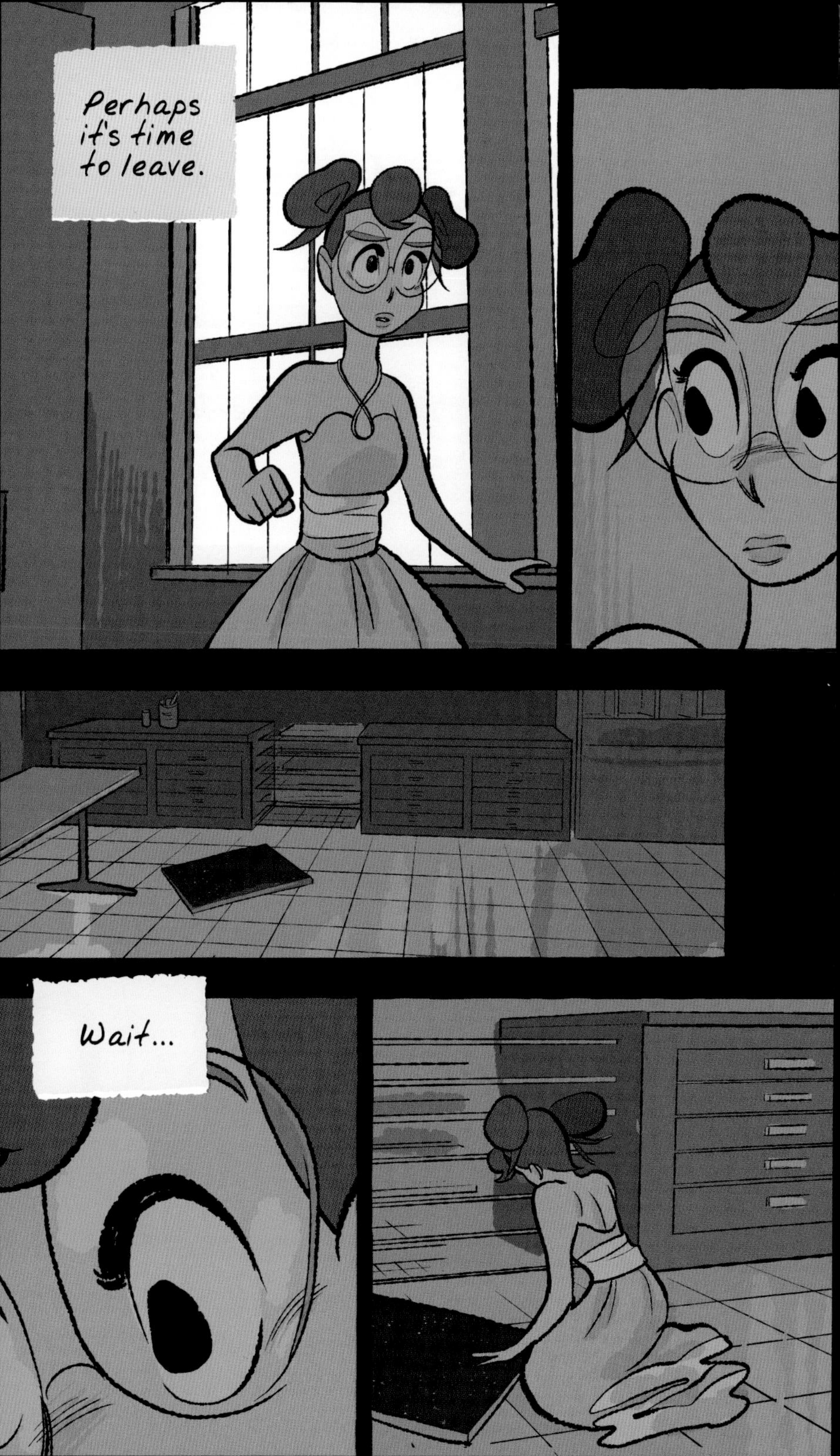
Perhaps it's time to leave.
Wait...

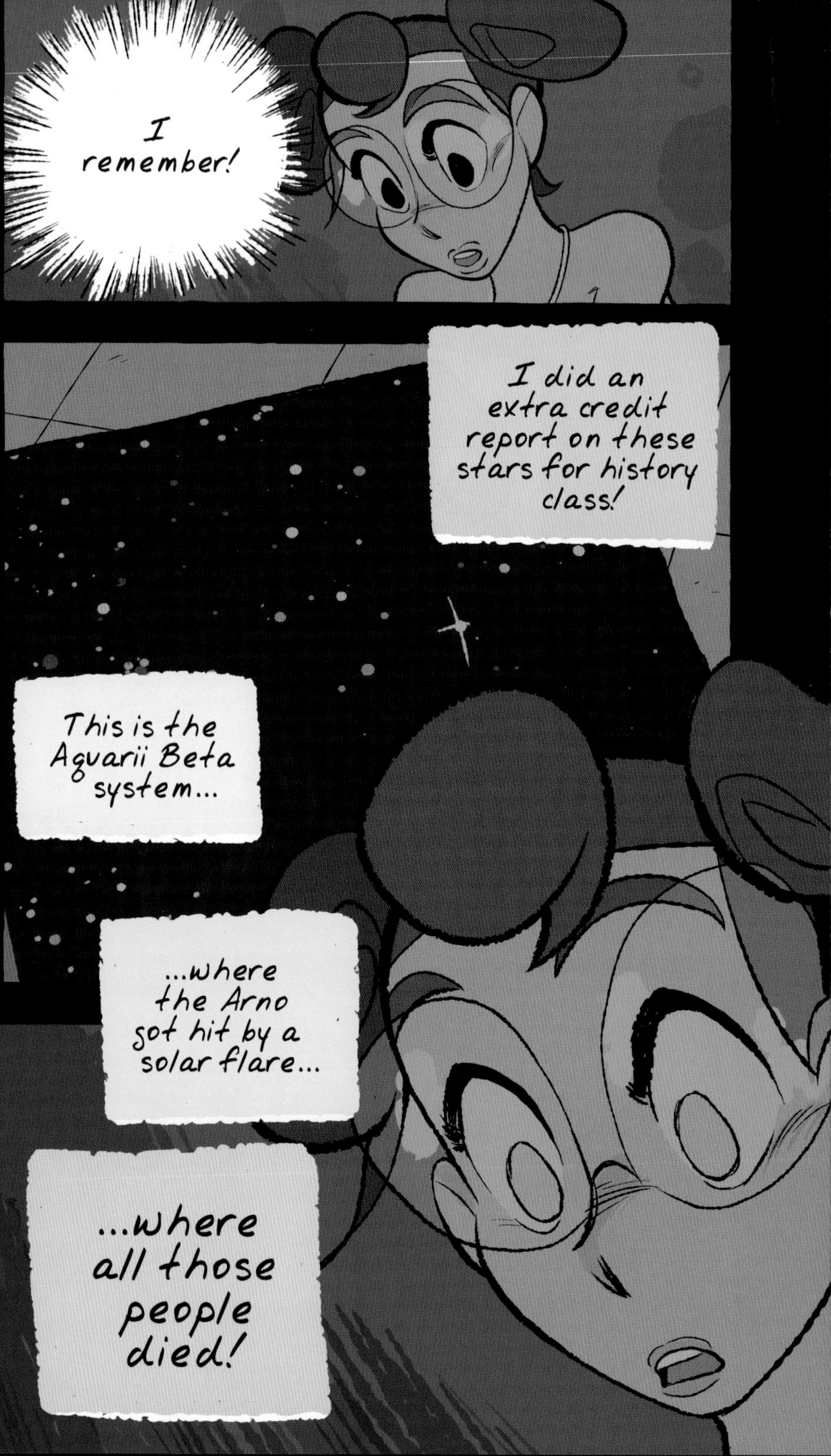
I remember!
I did an extra credit report on these stars for history class!
This is the Aquarii Beta system...
...where the Arno got hit by a solar flare...
...where all those people died!

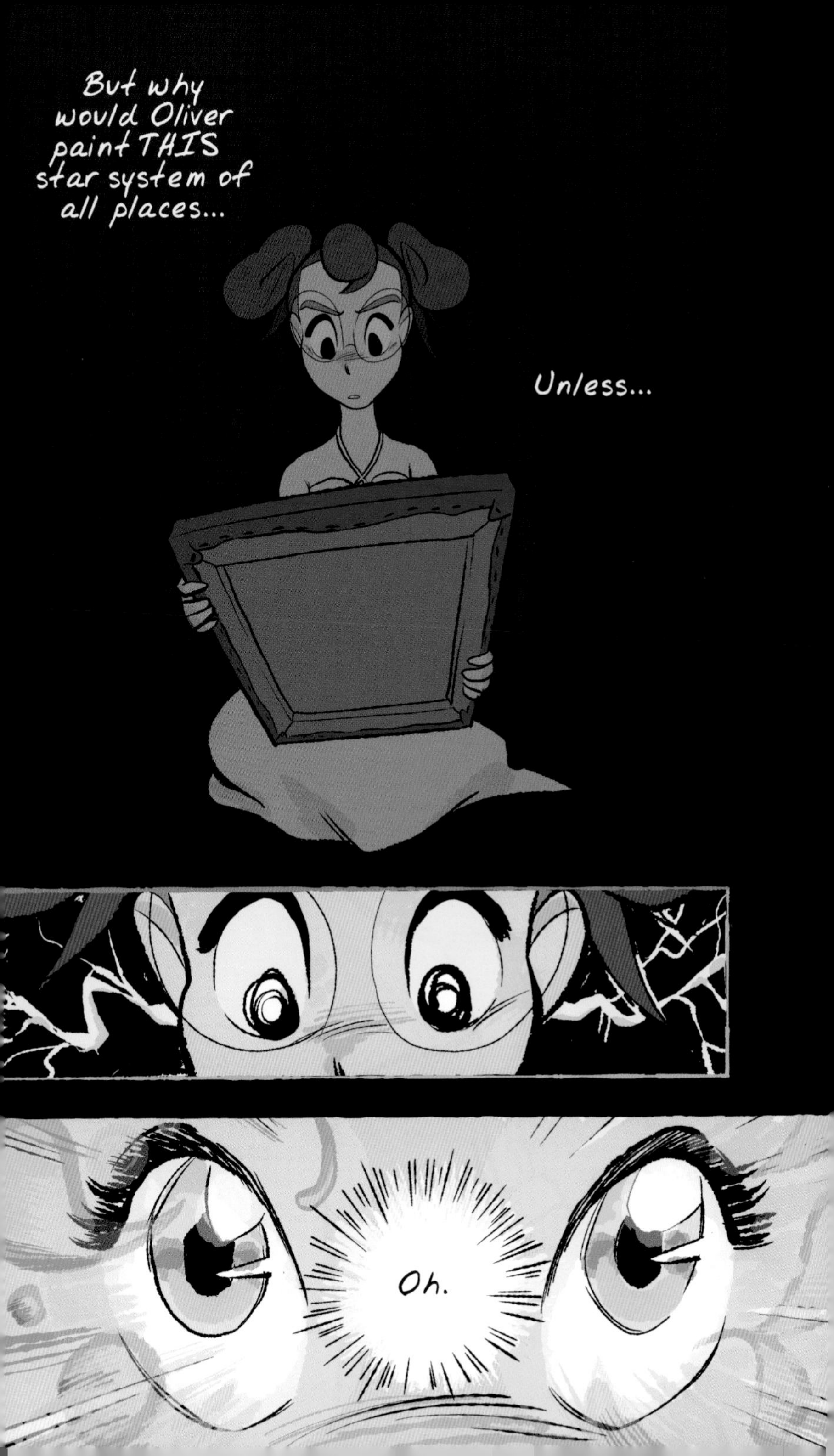
But why would Oliver paint THIS star system of all places...
Unless...
Oh.

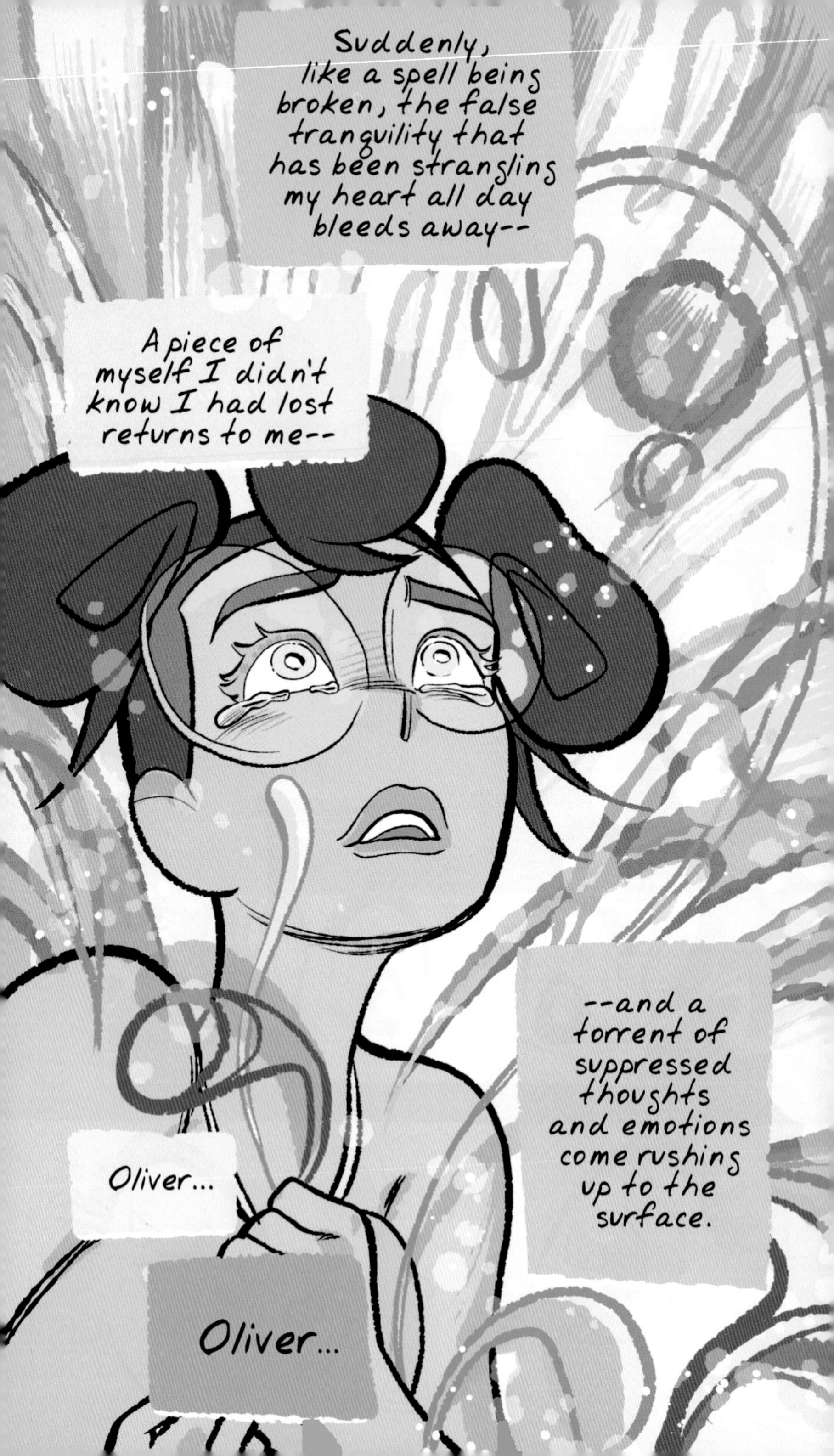
Suddenly, like a spell being broken, the false tranquility that has been strangling my heart all day bleeds away--
A piece of myself I didn't know I had lost returns to me--
--and a torrent of suppressed thoughts and emotions come rushing up to the surface.
Oliver...
Oliver...

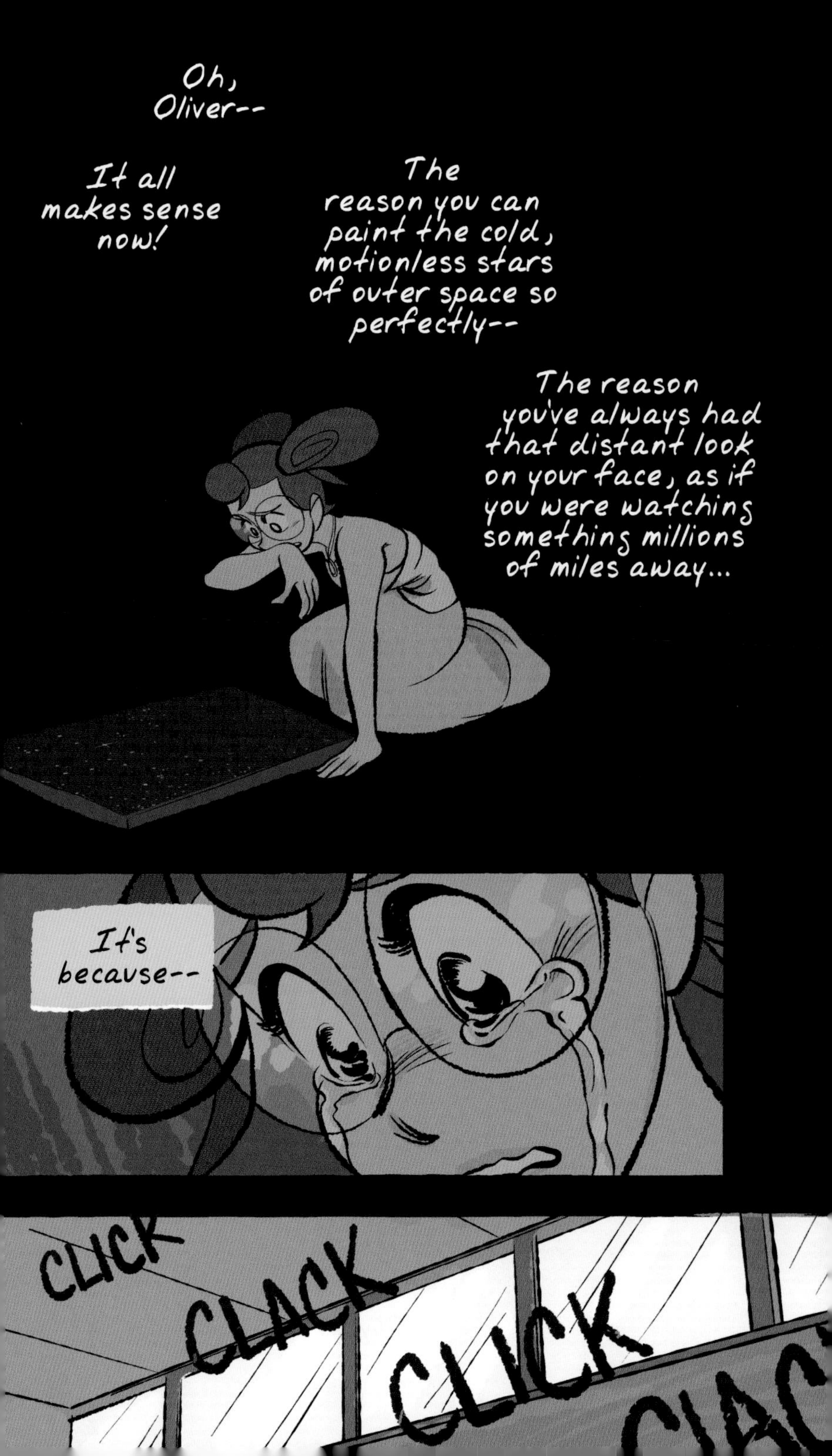

Oh, Oliver--
It all makes sense now!
The reason you can paint the cold, motionless stars of outer space so perfectly--
The reason you've always had that distant look on your face, as if you were watching something millions of miles away...
It's because--
CLICK
CLACK
CLICK

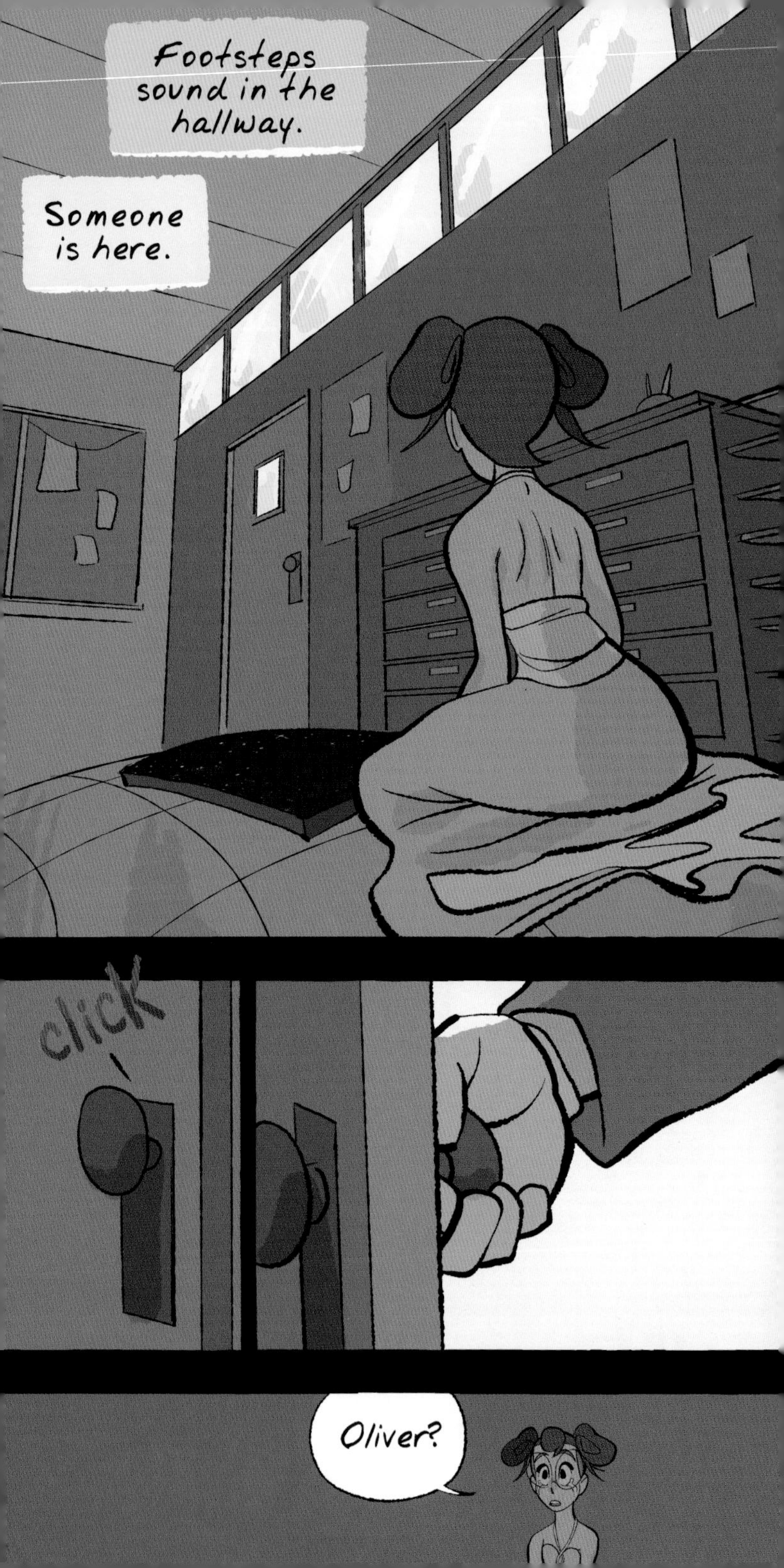
Footsteps sound in the hallway.
Someone is here.
click
Oliver?

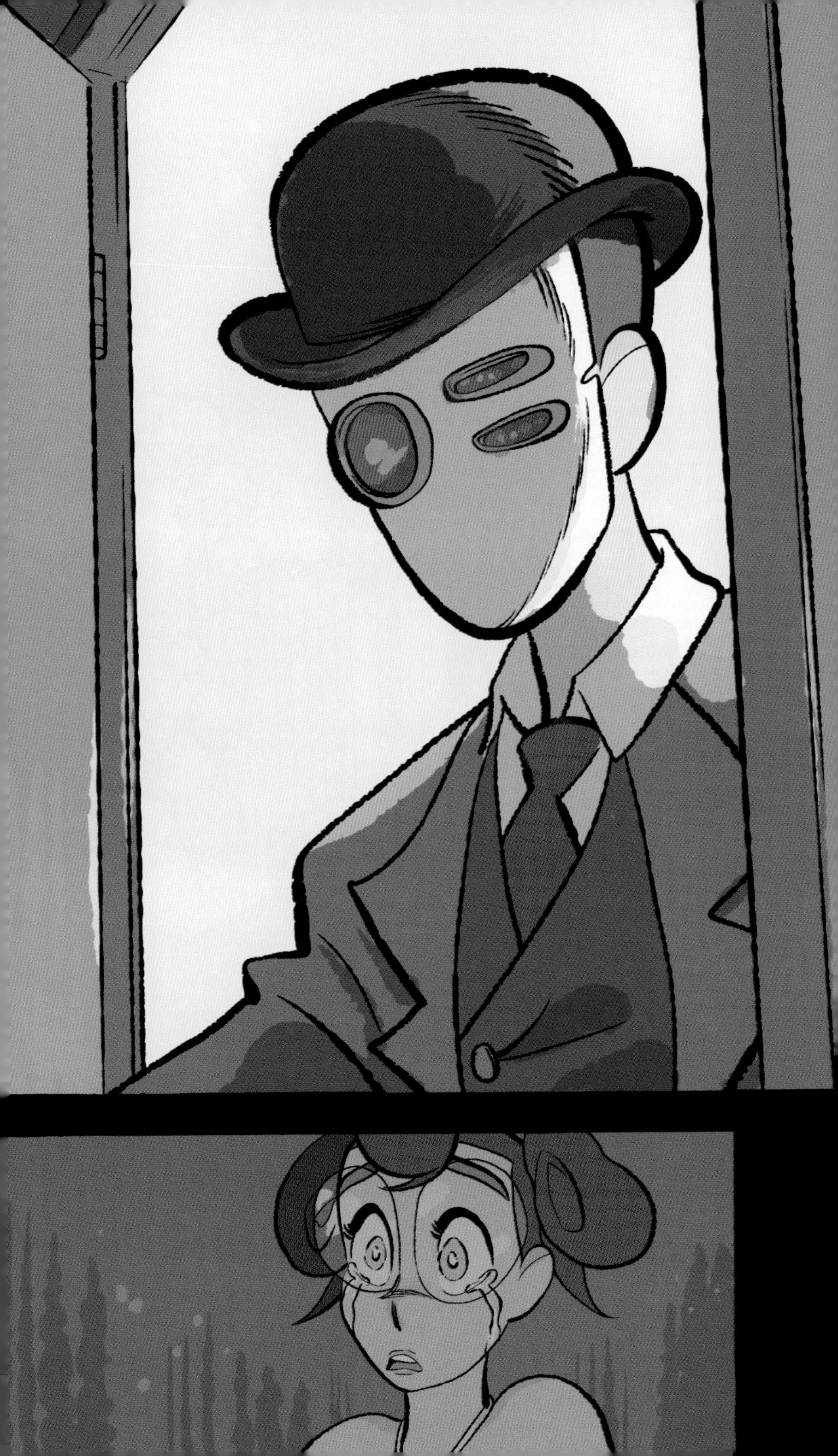

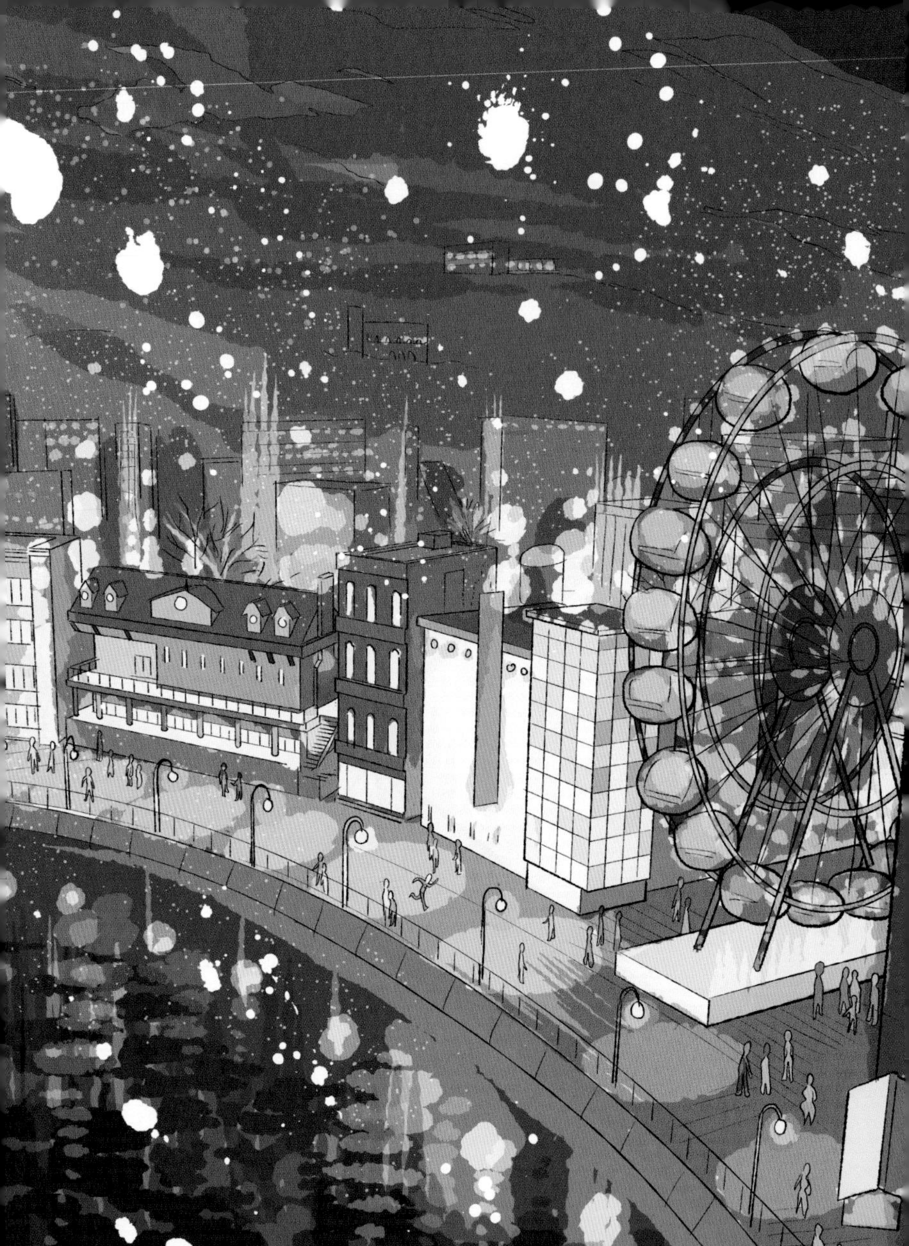

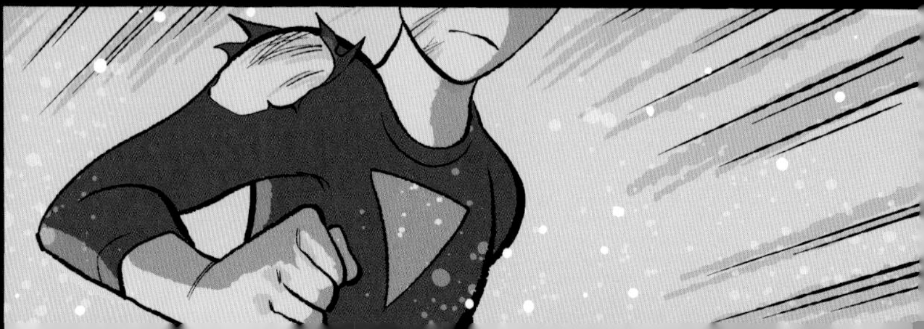

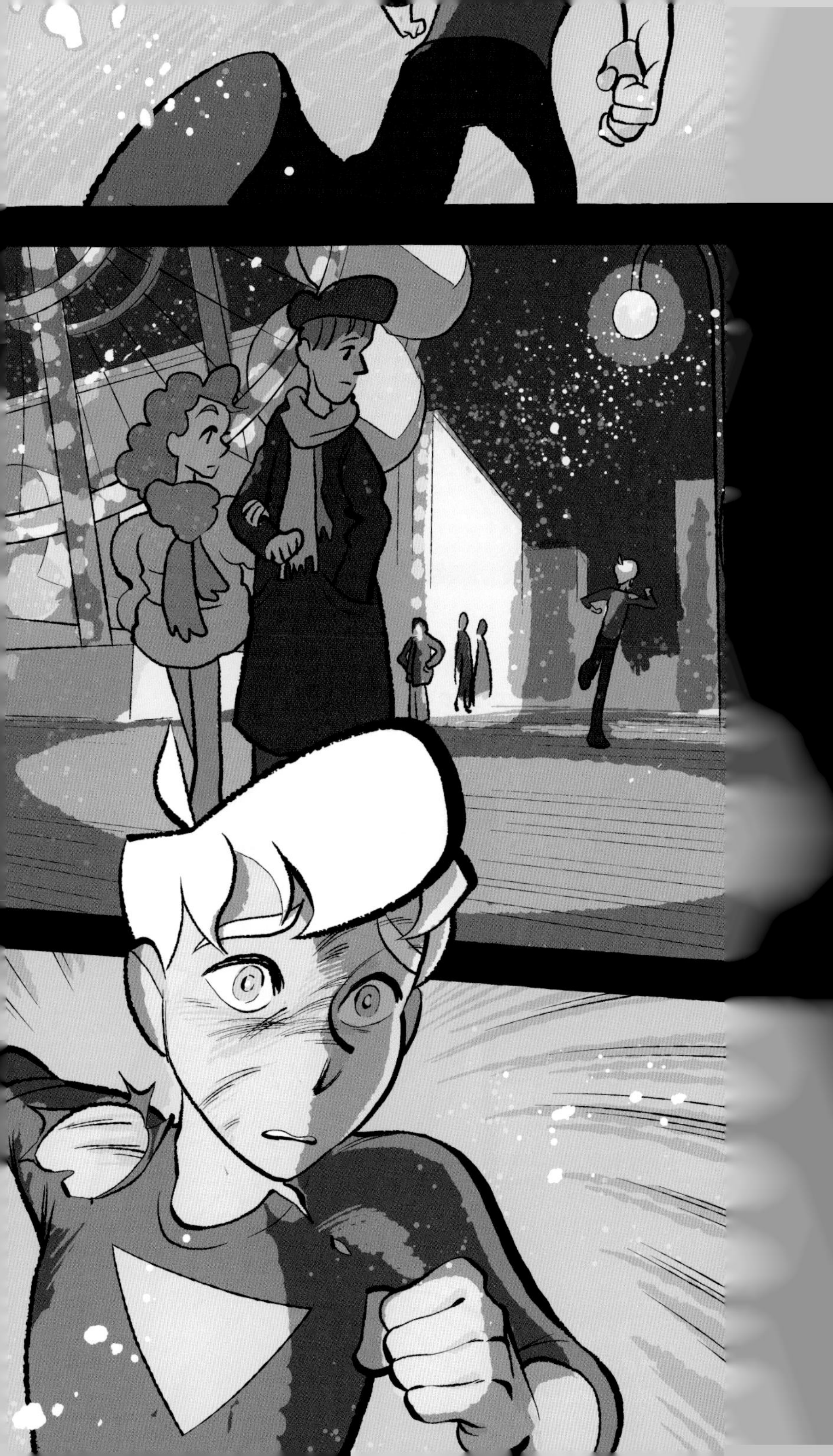

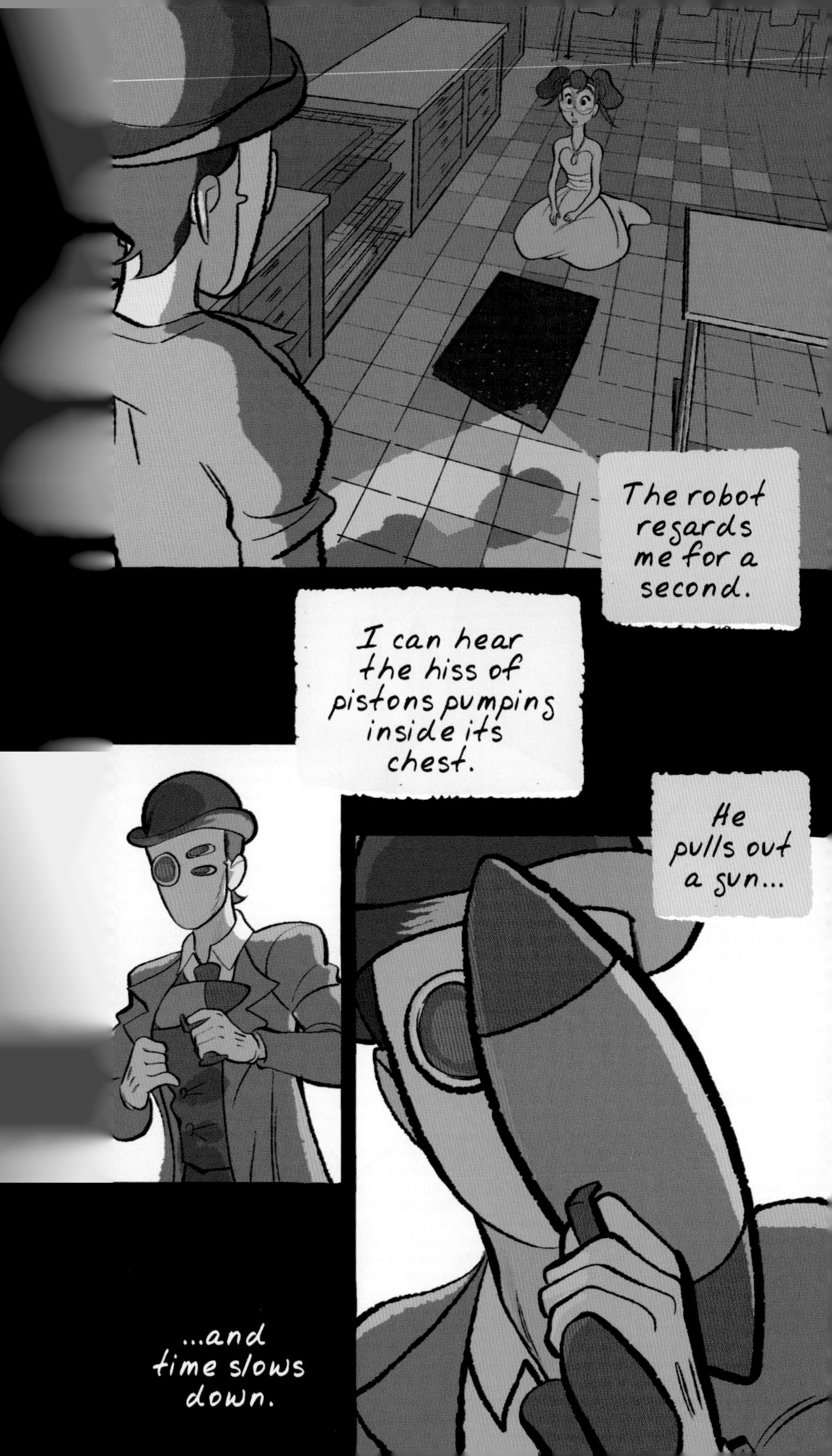
The robot regards me for a second.
I can hear the hiss of pistons pumping inside its chest.
He pulls out a gun...
...and time slows down.

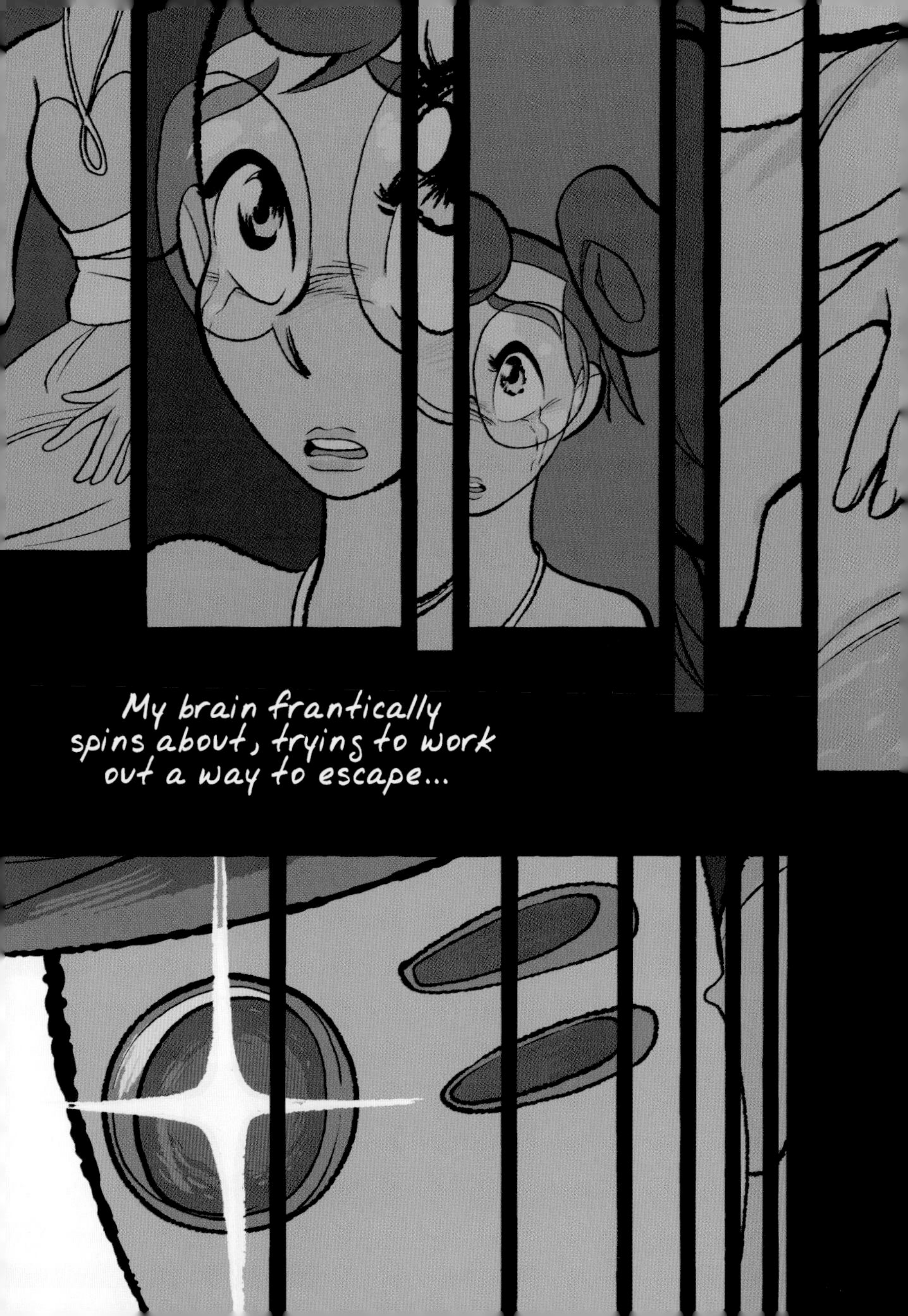
My brain frantically spins about, trying to work out a way to escape...

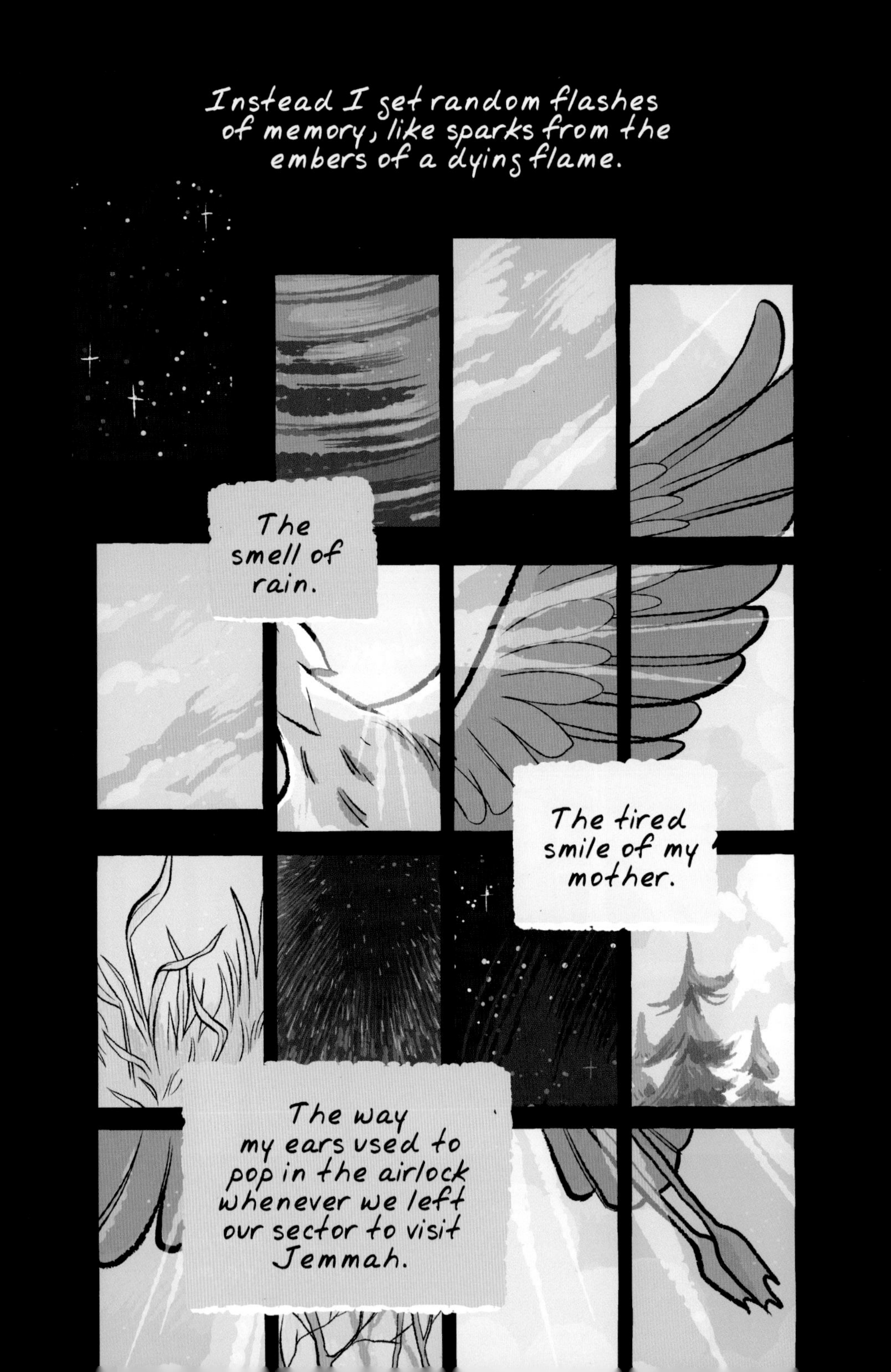
Instead I get random flashes of memory, like sparks from the embers of a dying flame.
The smell of rain.
The tired smile of my mother.
The way my ears used to pop in the airlock whenever we left our sector to visit Jemmah.

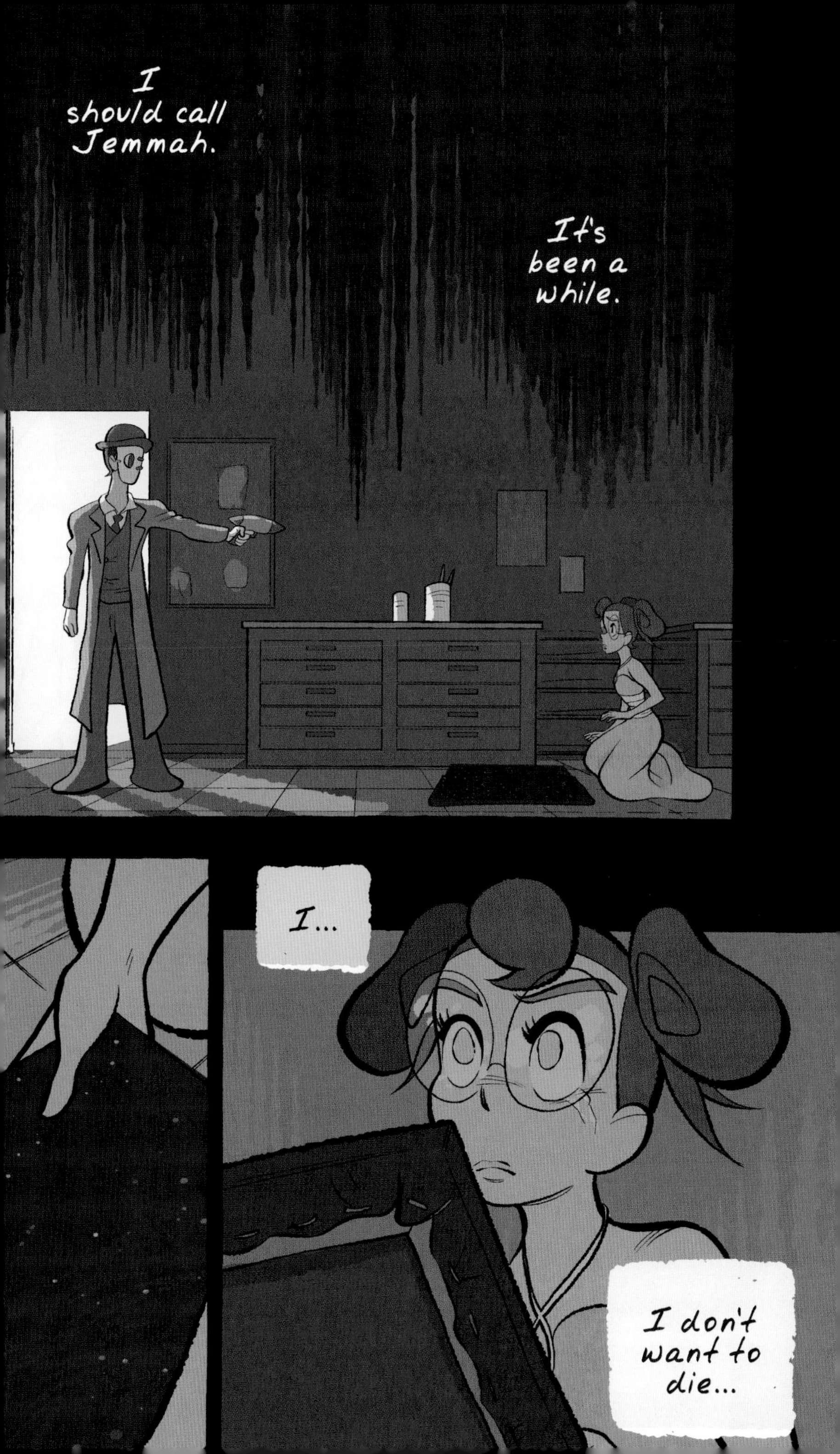
I should call Jemmah.
It's been a while.
I...
I don't want to die...

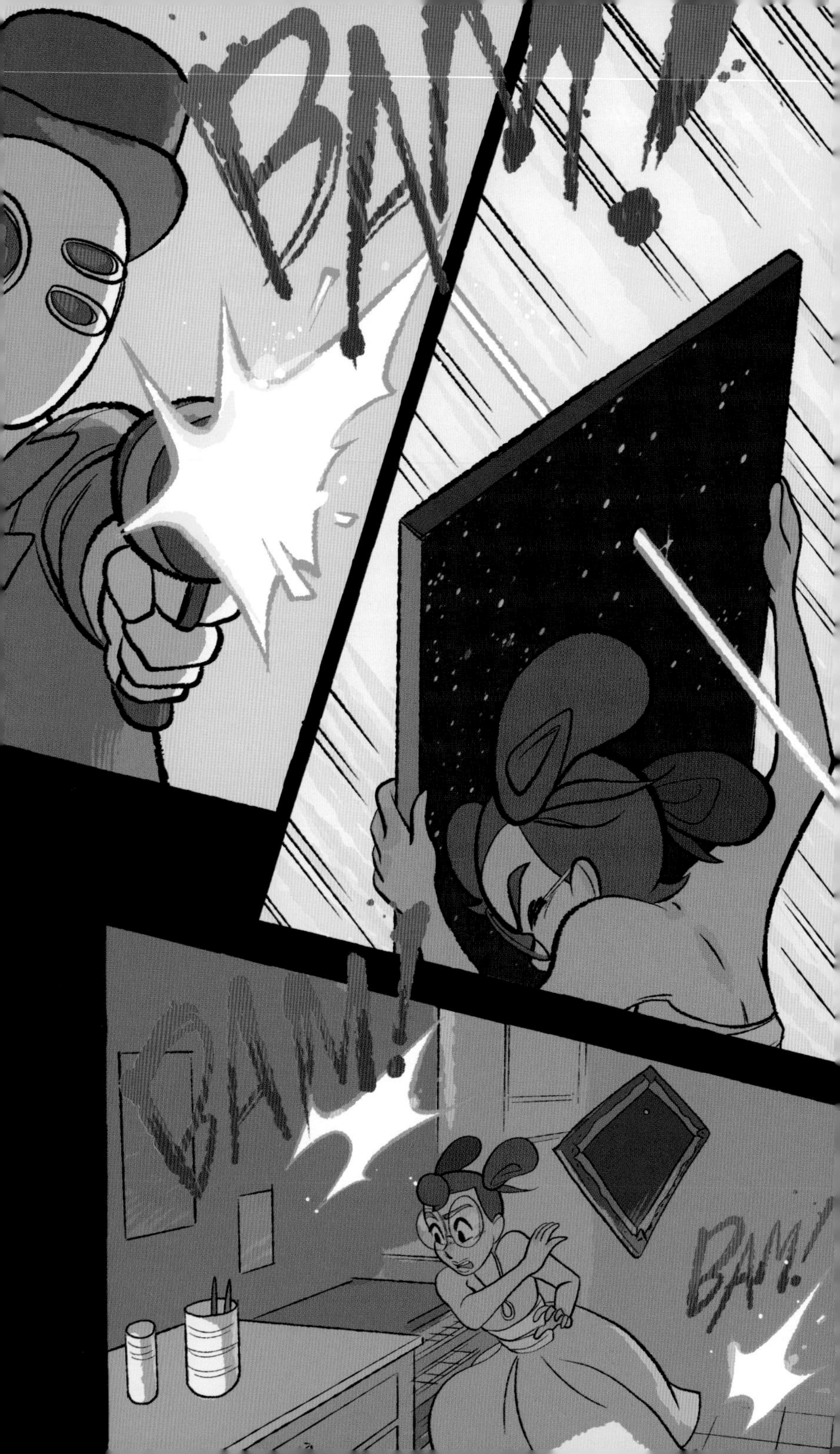
BAM!
BAM!
BAM!

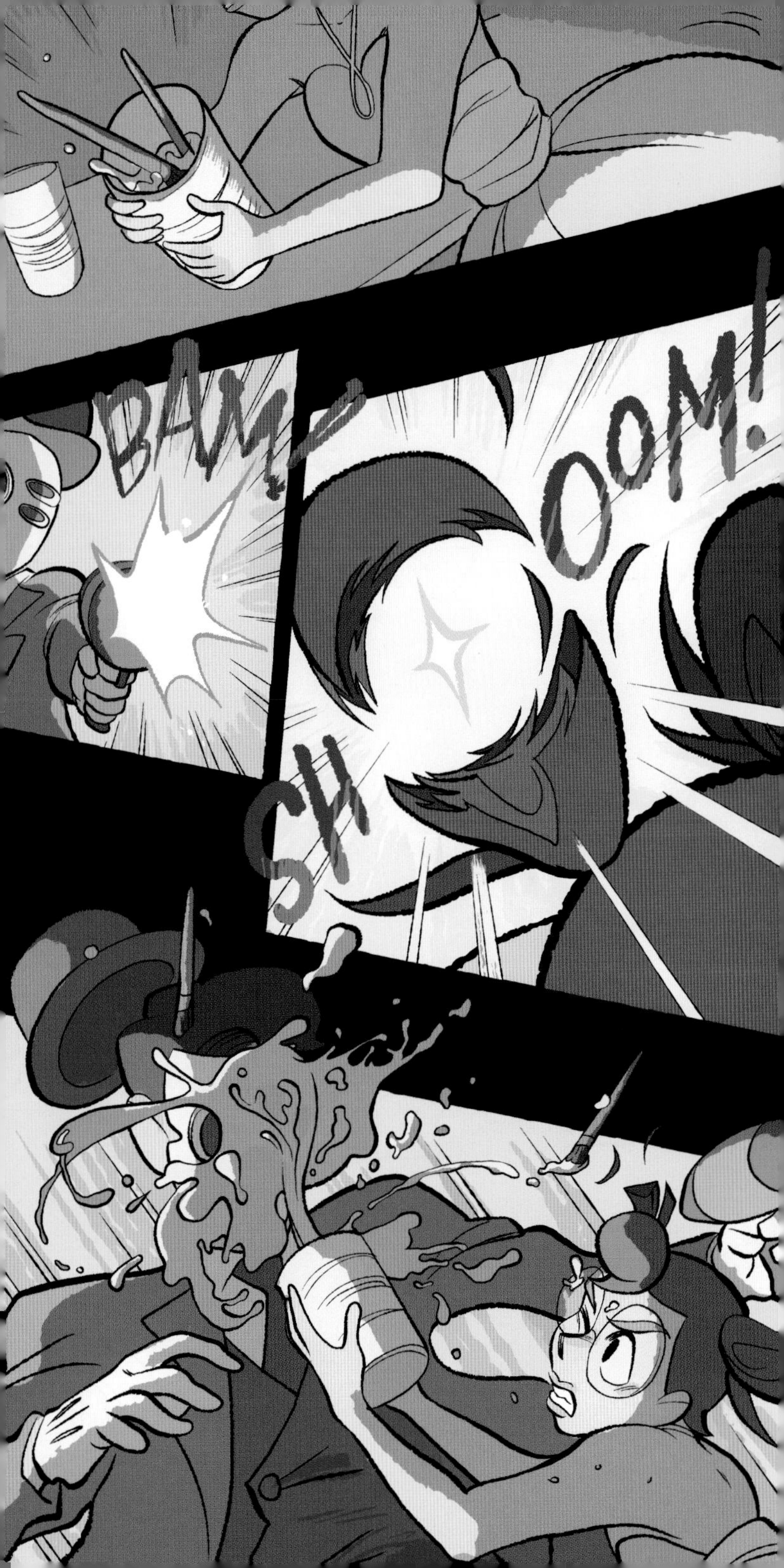
BAM
SHOOM!

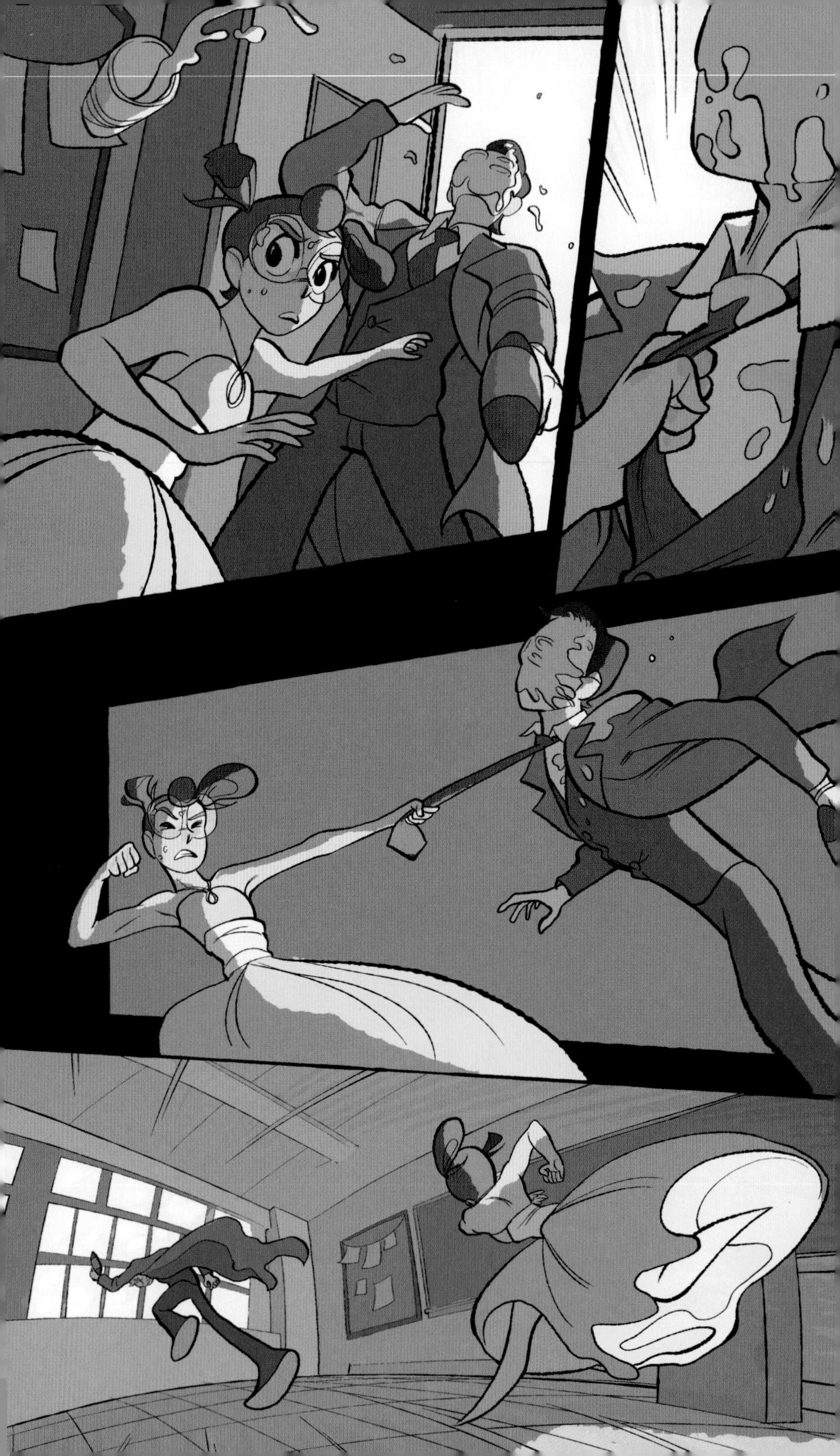

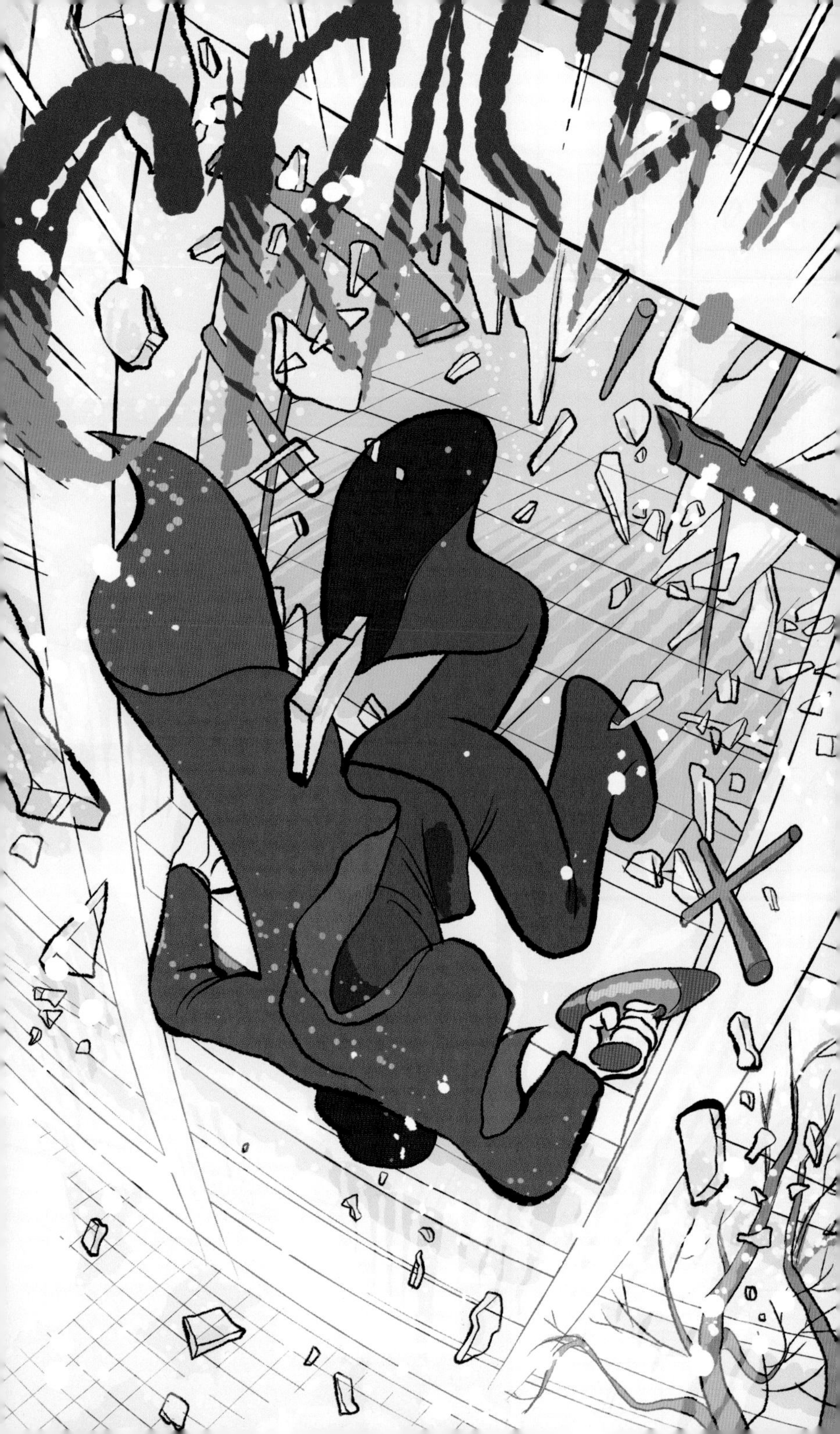
CRASH

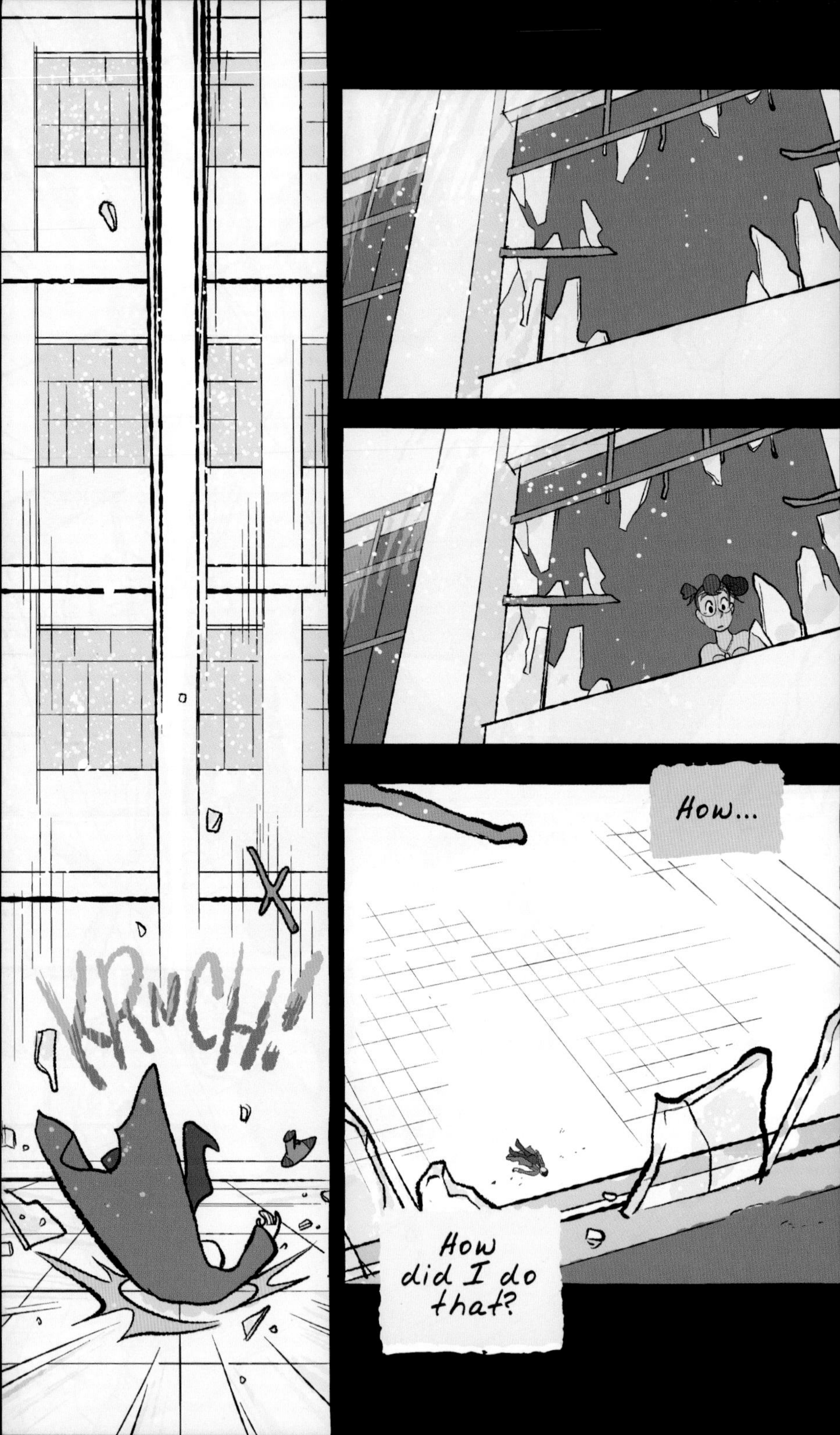
KRNCH!
How...
How did I do that?

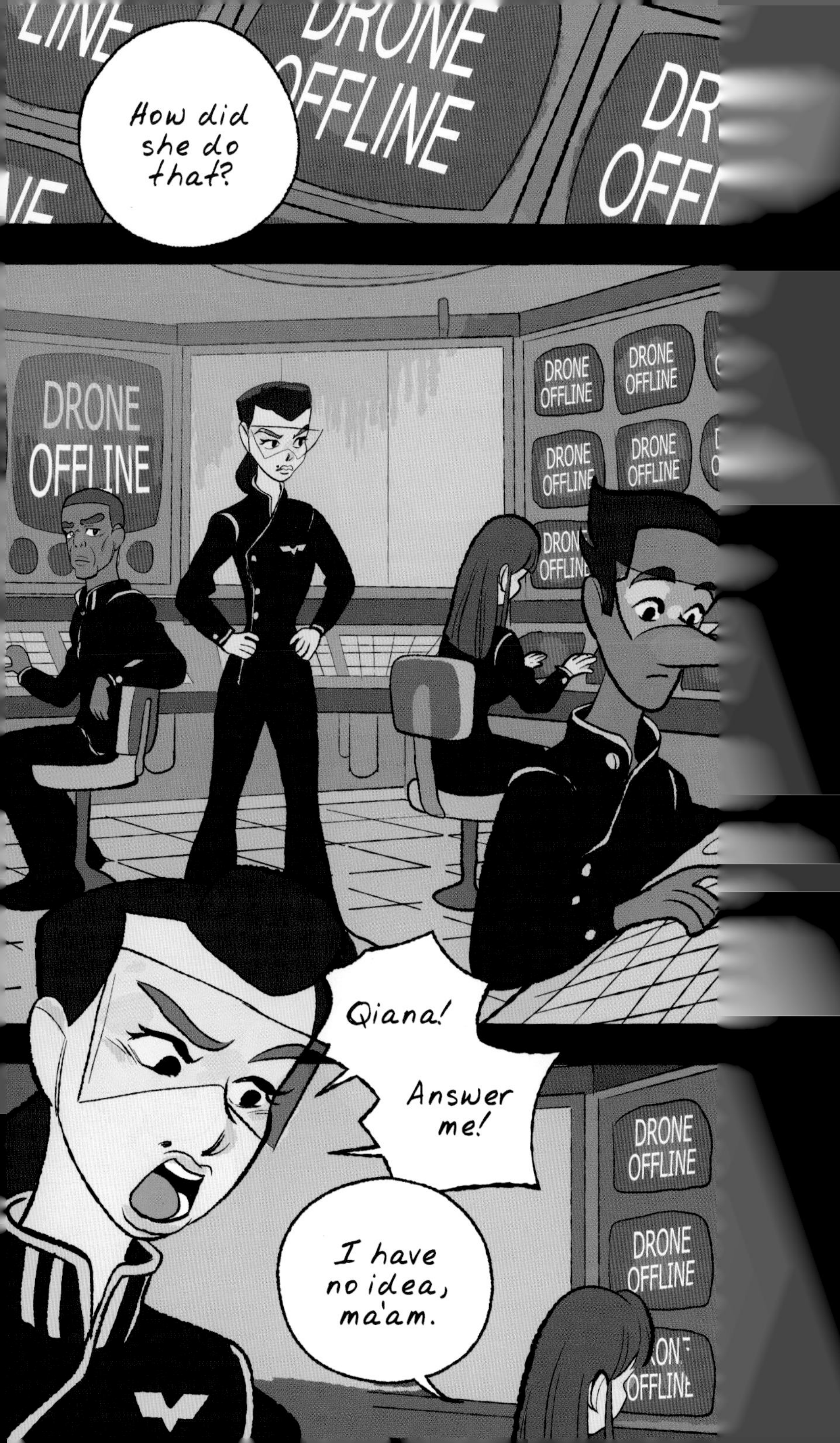

LINE
DRONE OFFLINE
How did she do that?
DRONE OFFLINE
DRONE OFFLINE
DRONE OFFLINE
DRONE OFFLINE
DRONE OFFLINE
DRONE OFFLINE
DRONE OFFLINE
Qiana!
Answer me!
DRONE OFFLINE
DRONE OFFLINE
I have no idea, ma'am.
OFFLINE

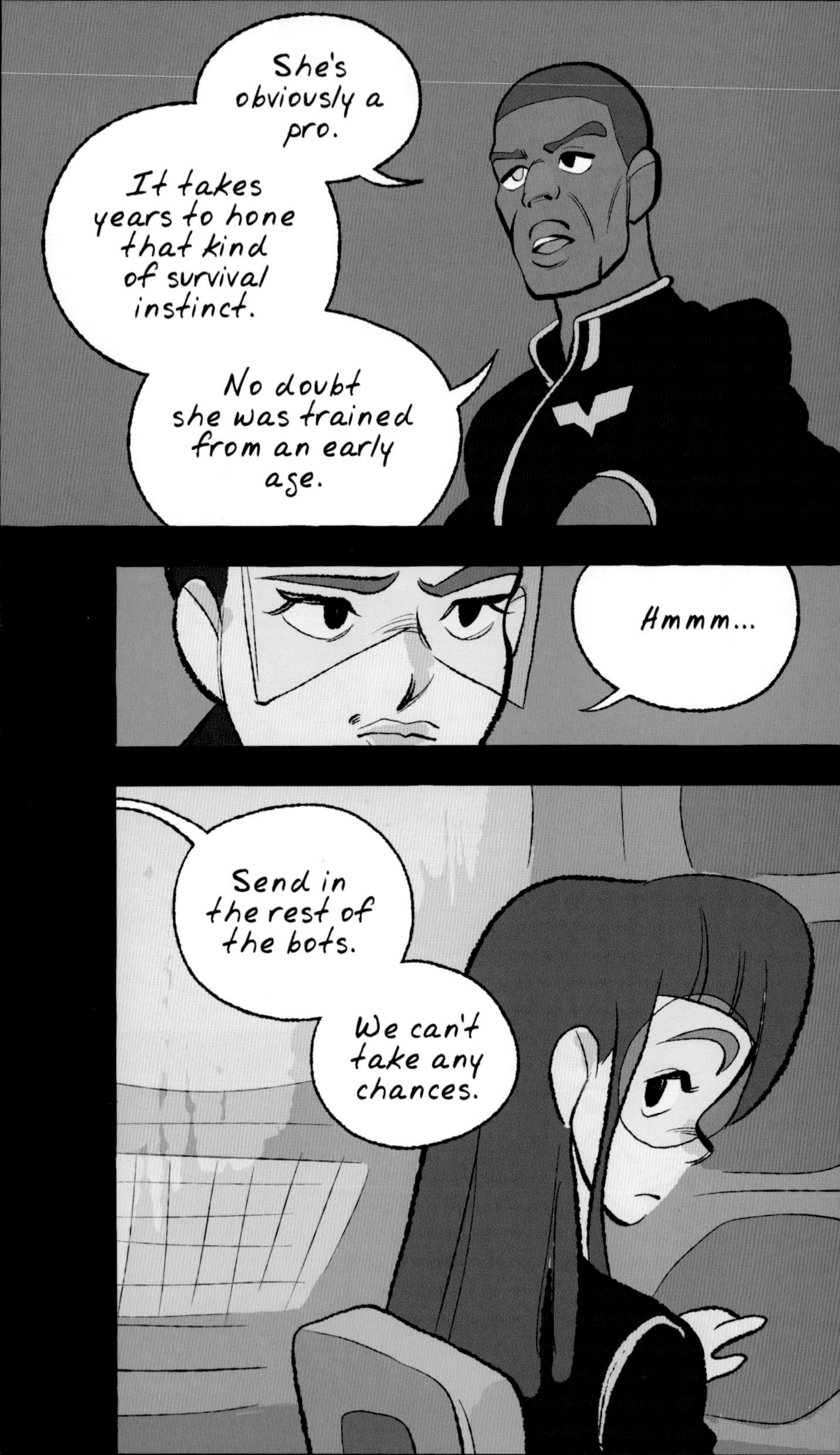
She's obviously a pro.
It takes years to hone that kind of survival instinct.
No doubt she was trained from an early age.
Hmmm...
Send in the rest of the bots.
We can't take any chances.

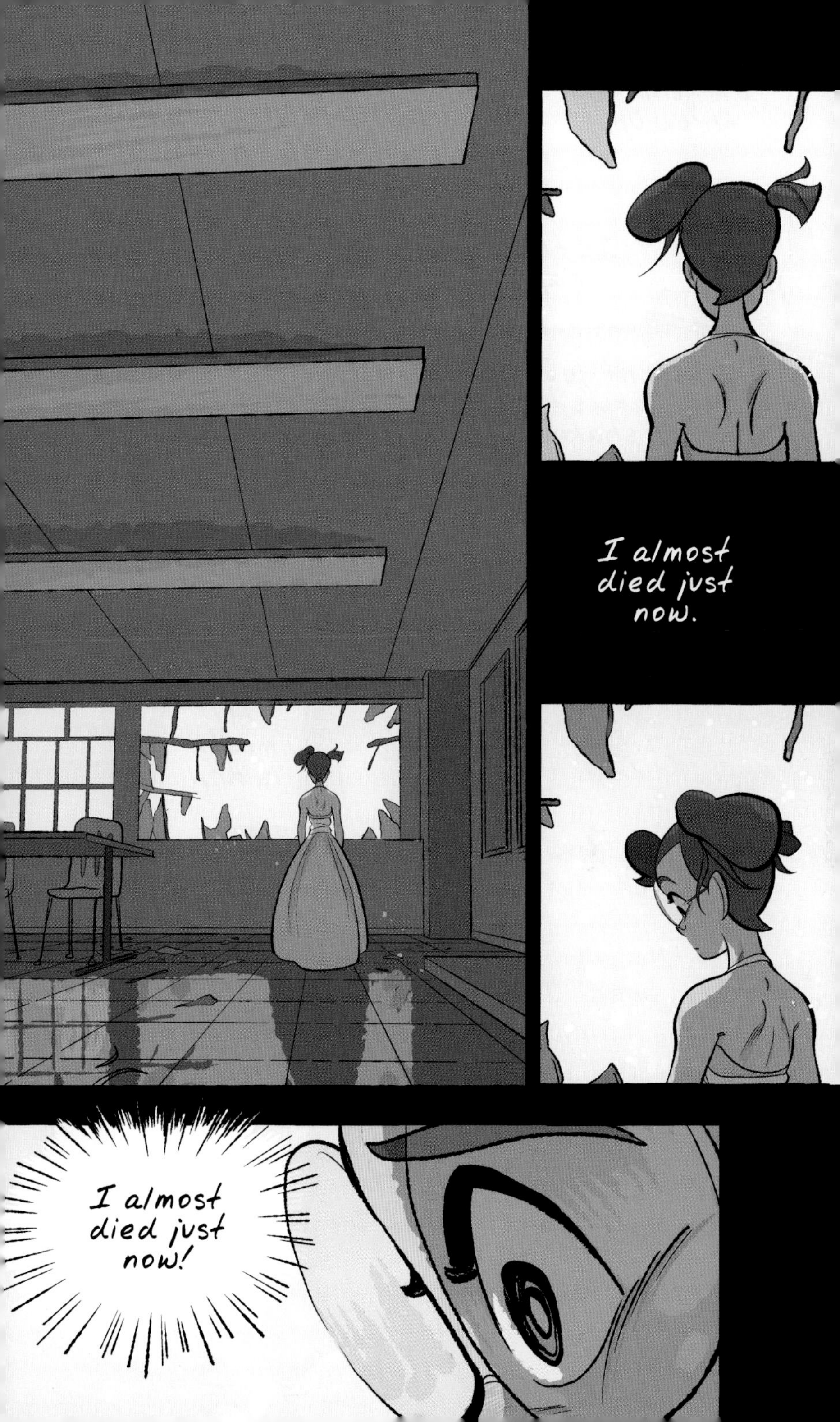
I almost died just now.
I almost died just now!

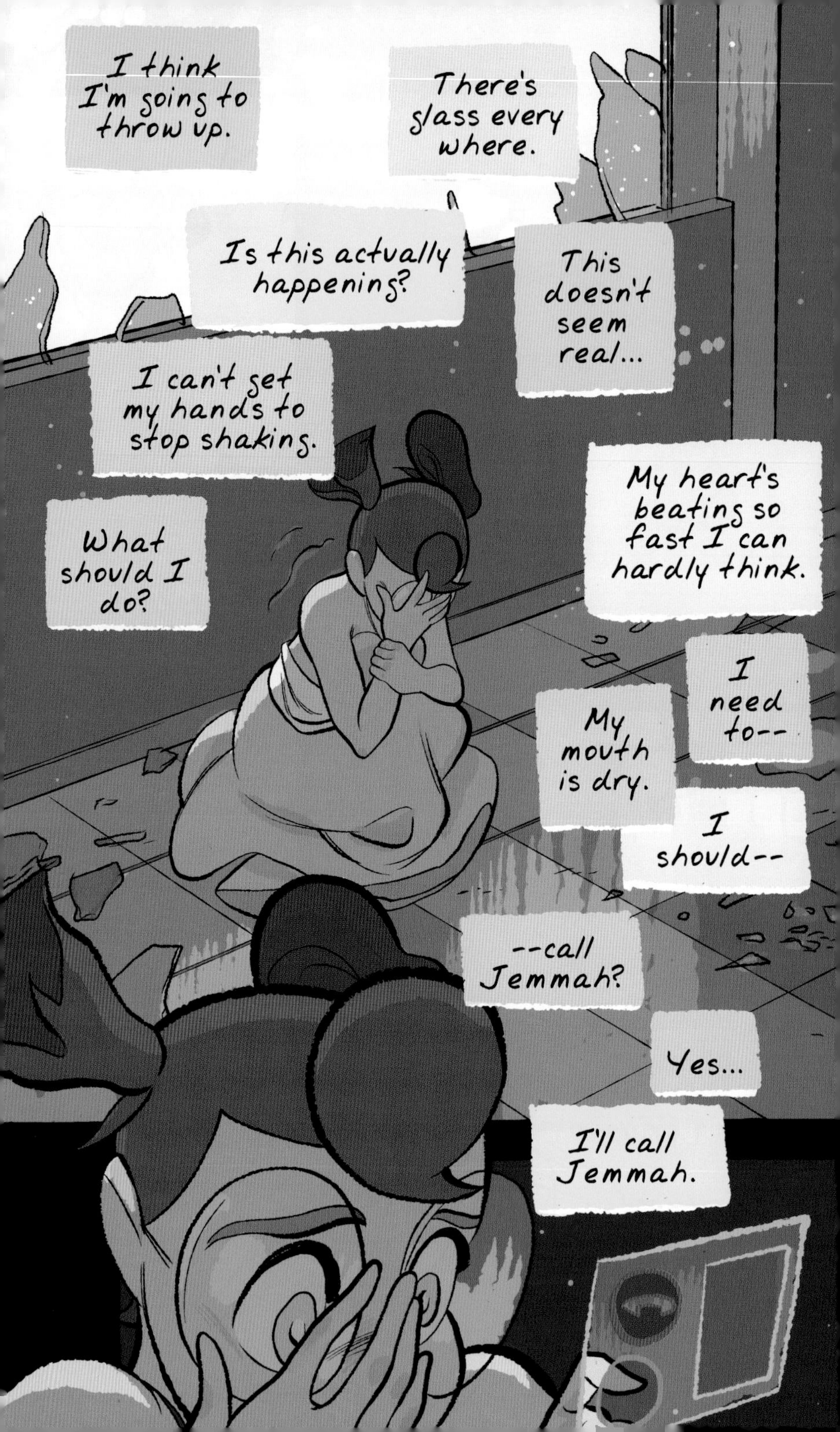
I think I'm going to throw up.
There's glass every where.
Is this actually happening?
This doesn't seem real...
I can't get my hands to stop shaking.
What should I do?
My heart's beating so fast I can hardly think.
I need to--
My mouth is dry.
I should--
--call Jemmah?
Yes...
I'll call Jemmah.

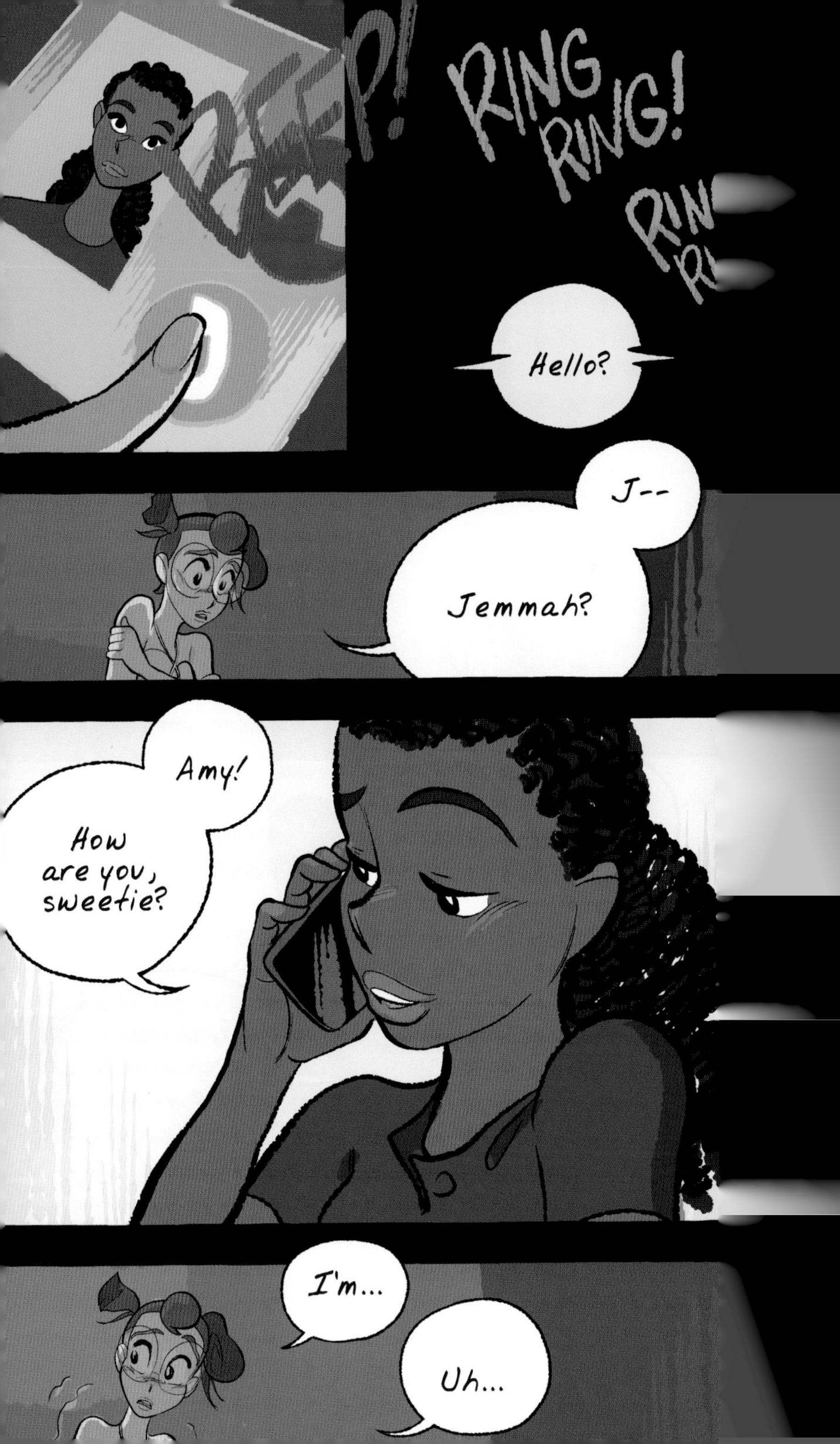
BEEP!
RING RING!
RING RI
Hello?
J--
Jemmah?
Amy!
How are you, sweetie?
I'm...
Uh...

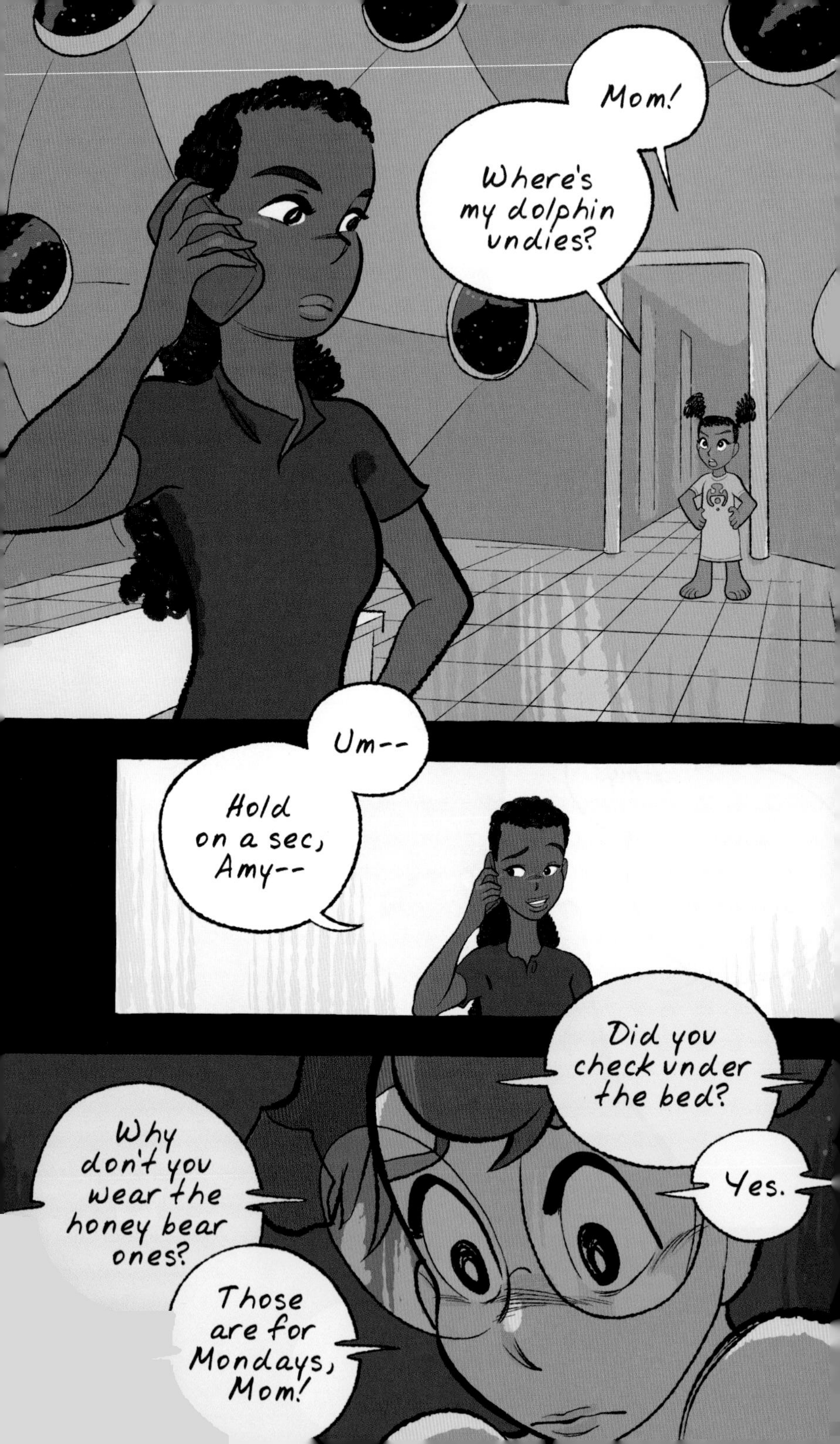
Mom!
Where's my dolphin undies?
Um--
Hold on a sec, Amy--
Did you check under the bed?
Yes.
Why don't you wear the honey bear ones?
Those are for Mondays, Mom!

Well, so ask your father then.

Okay...

Sorry, Amy, sometimes the girls--

BEEP!!

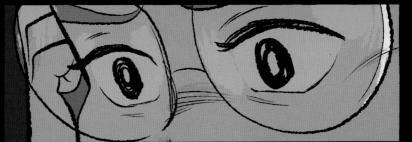

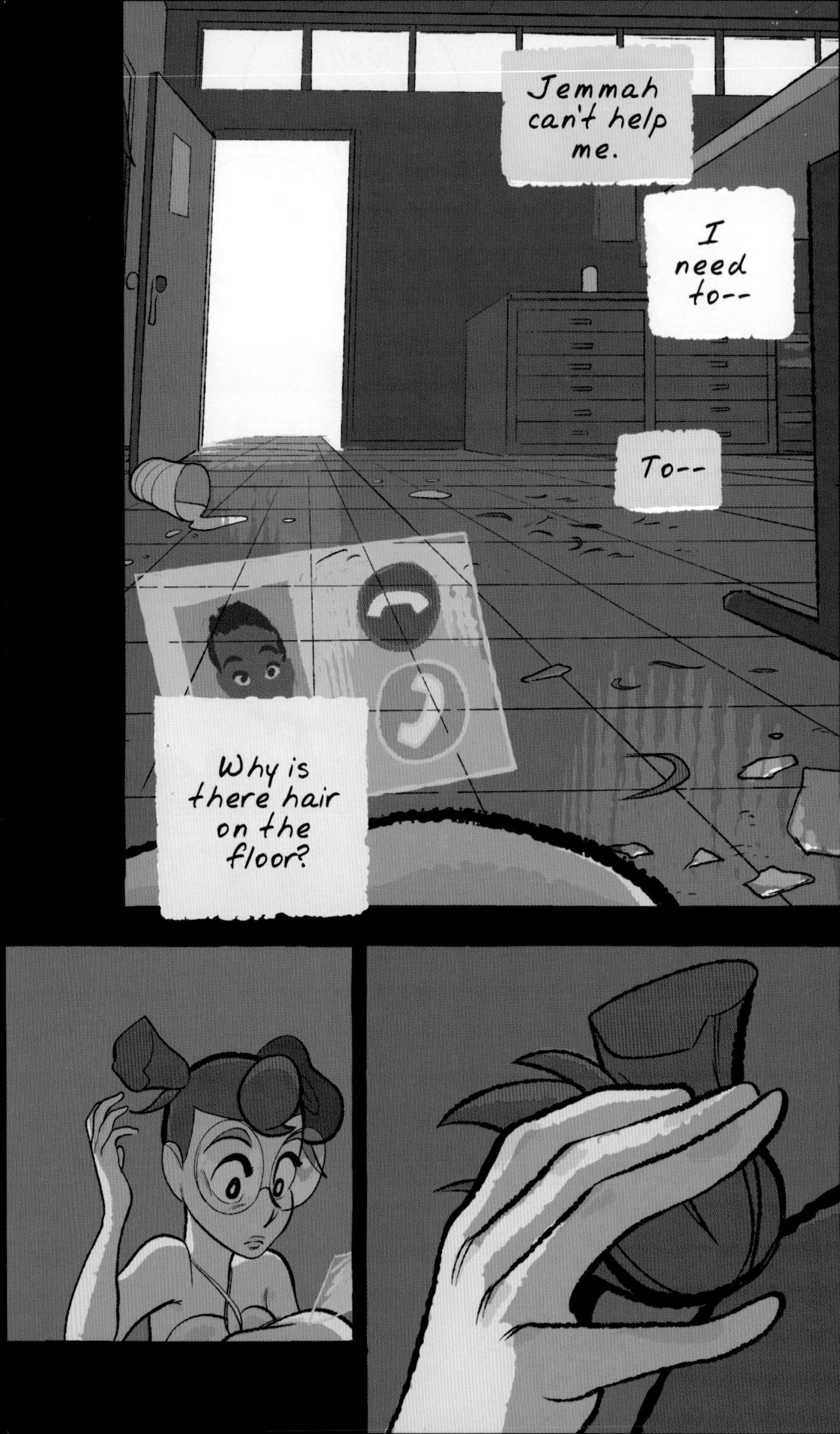
Jemmah can't help me.
I need to--
To--
Why is there hair on the floor?

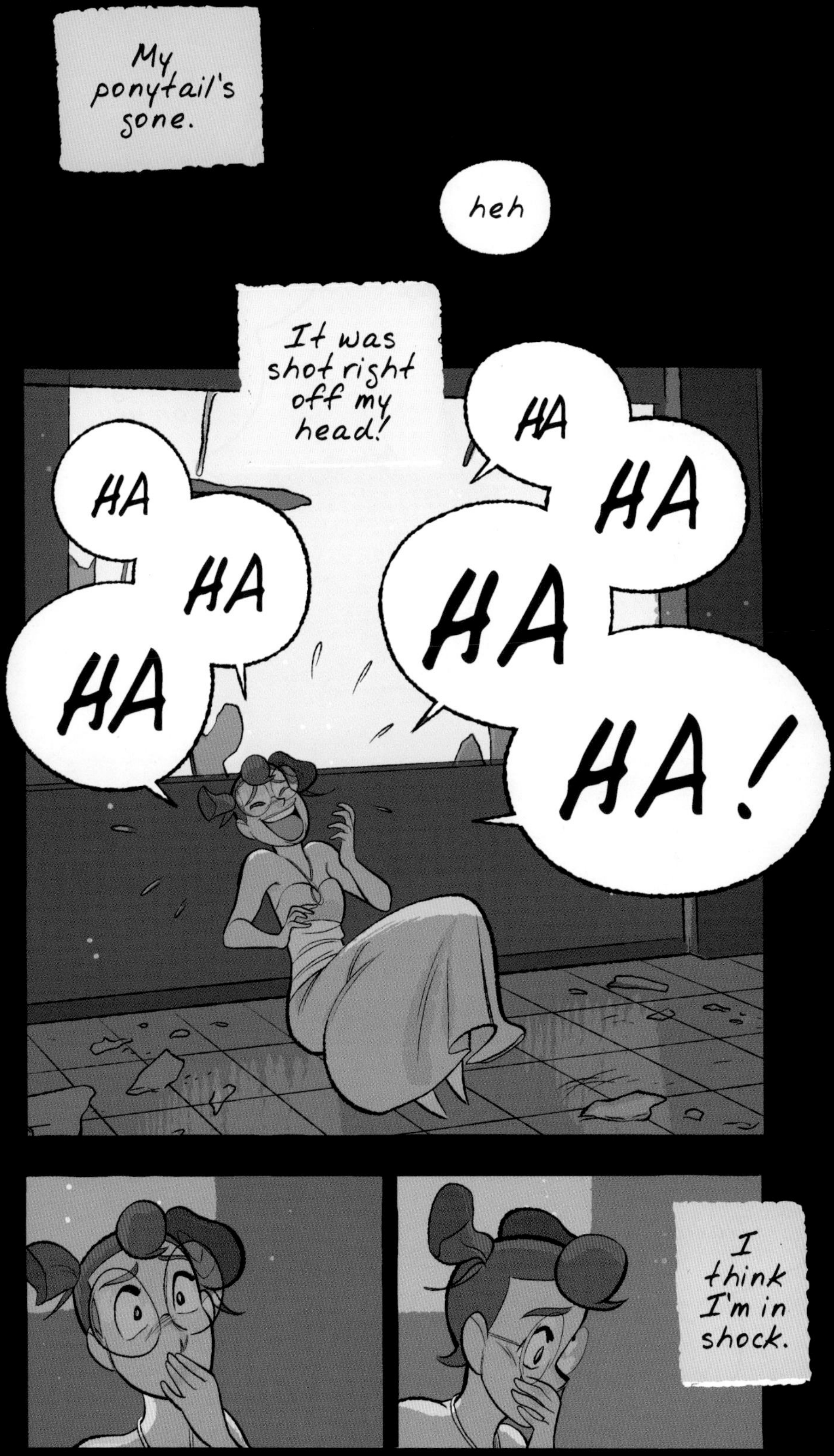
My ponytail's gone.
heh
It was shot right off my head!
HA HA HA
HA HA HA HA!
I think I'm in shock.

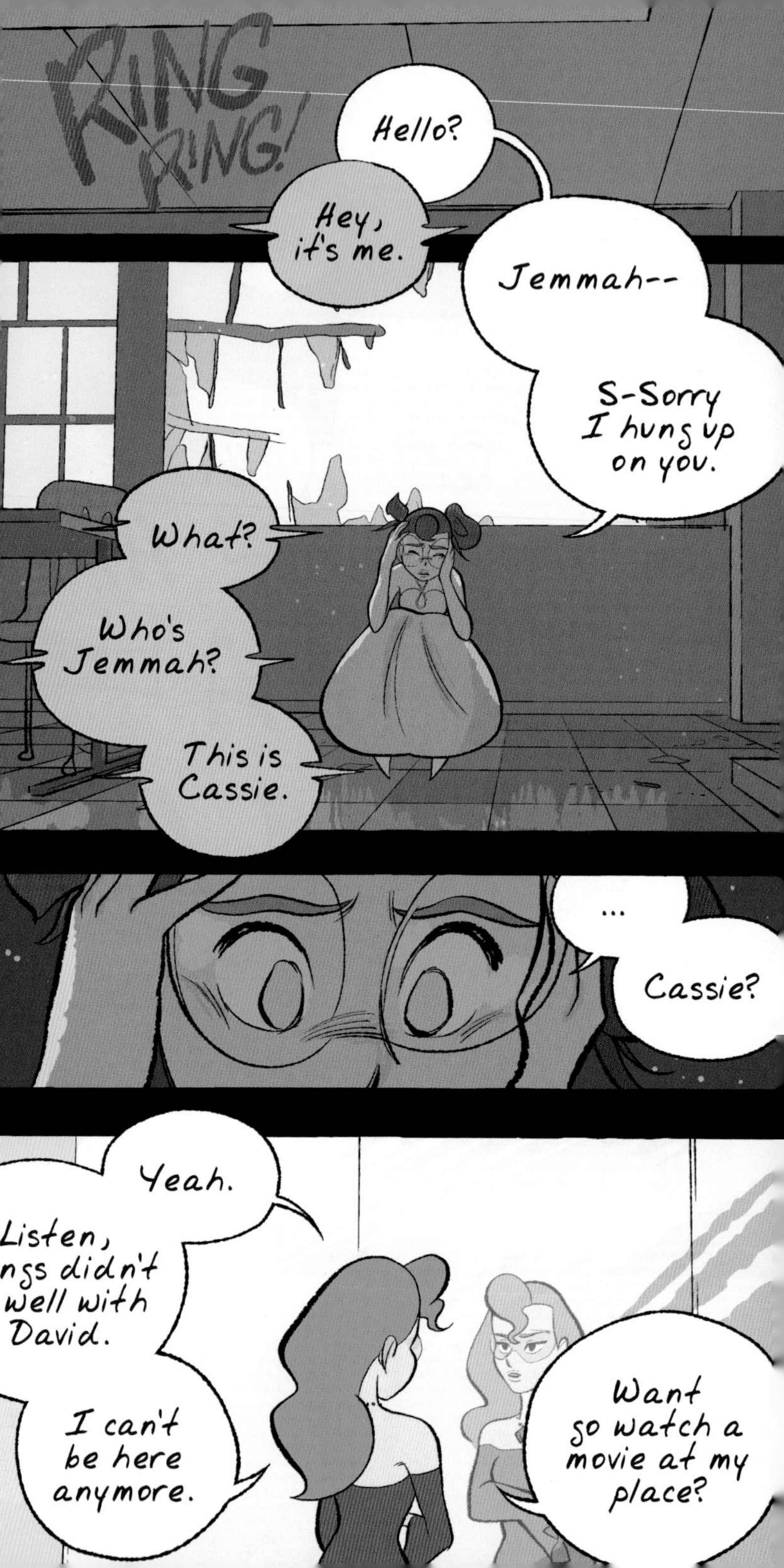
RING RING!
Hello?
Hey, it's me.
Jemmah--
S-Sorry I hung up on you.
What?
Who's Jemmah?
This is Cassie.
...
Cassie?
Yeah.
Listen, ngs didn't well with David.
I can't be here anymore.
Want go watch a movie at my place?

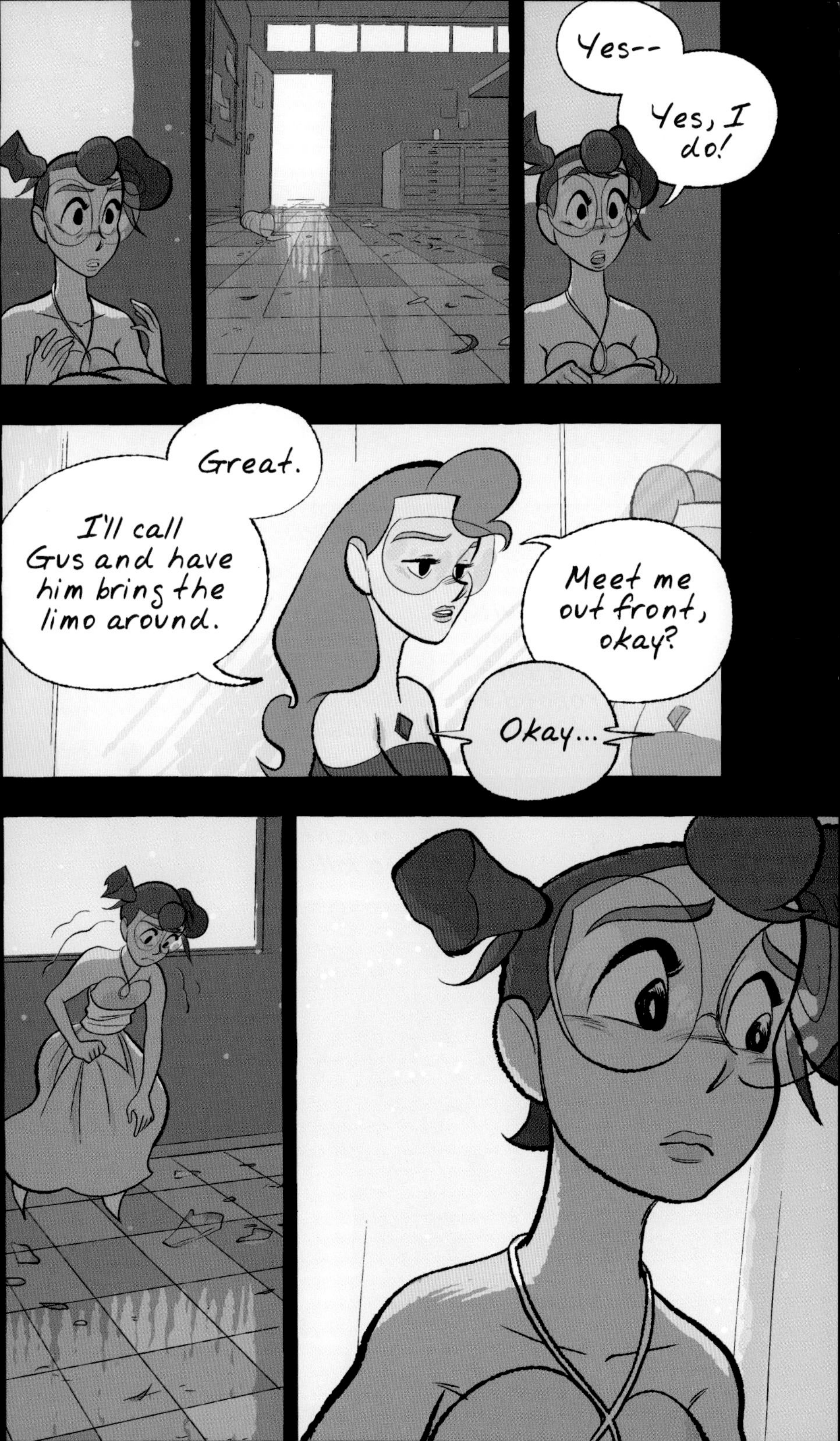
Yes--
Yes, I do!
Great.
I'll call Gus and have him bring the limo around.
Meet me out front, okay?
Okay...

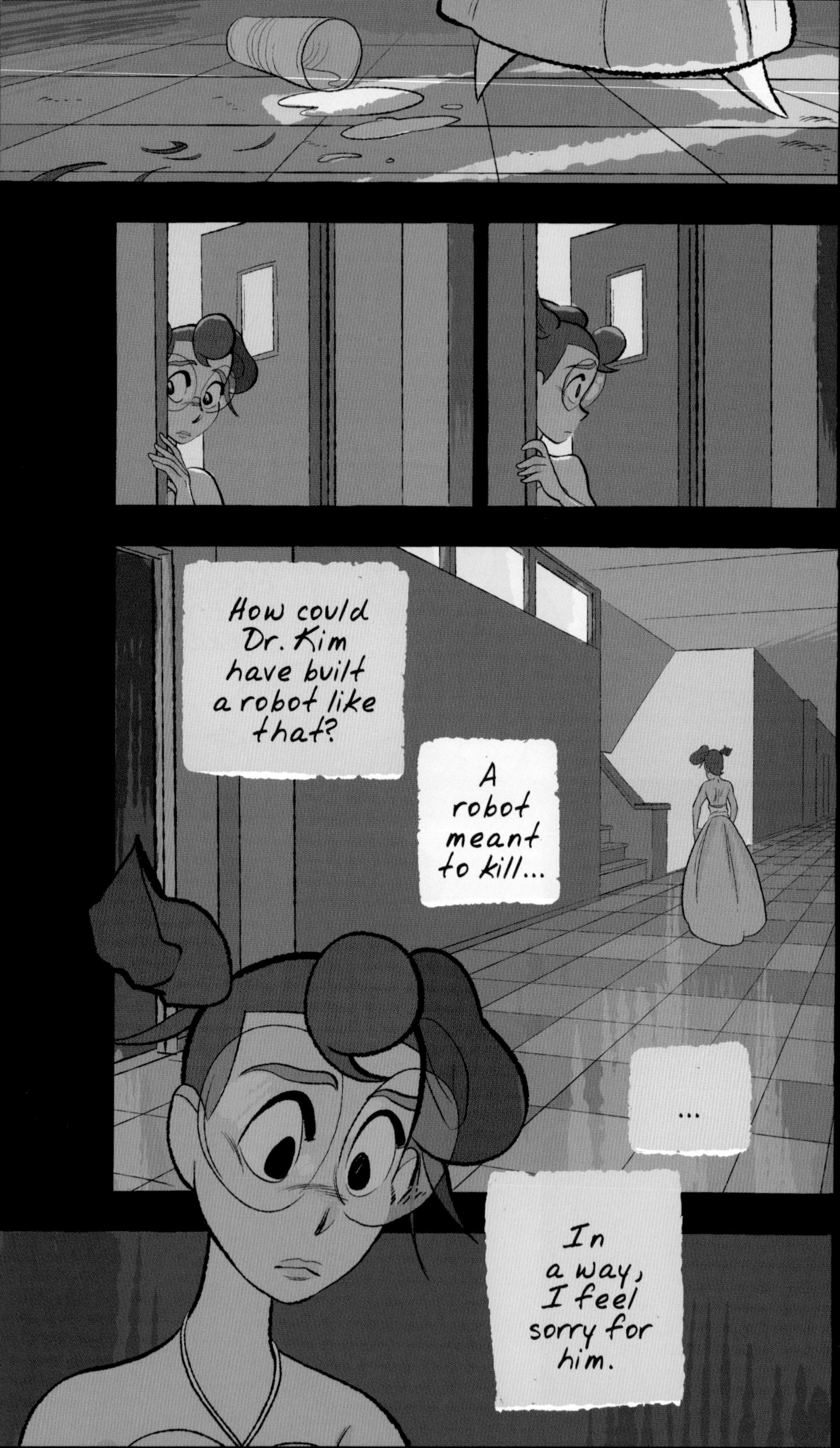

How could Dr. Kim have built a robot like that?
A robot meant to kill...
...
In a way, I feel sorry for him.

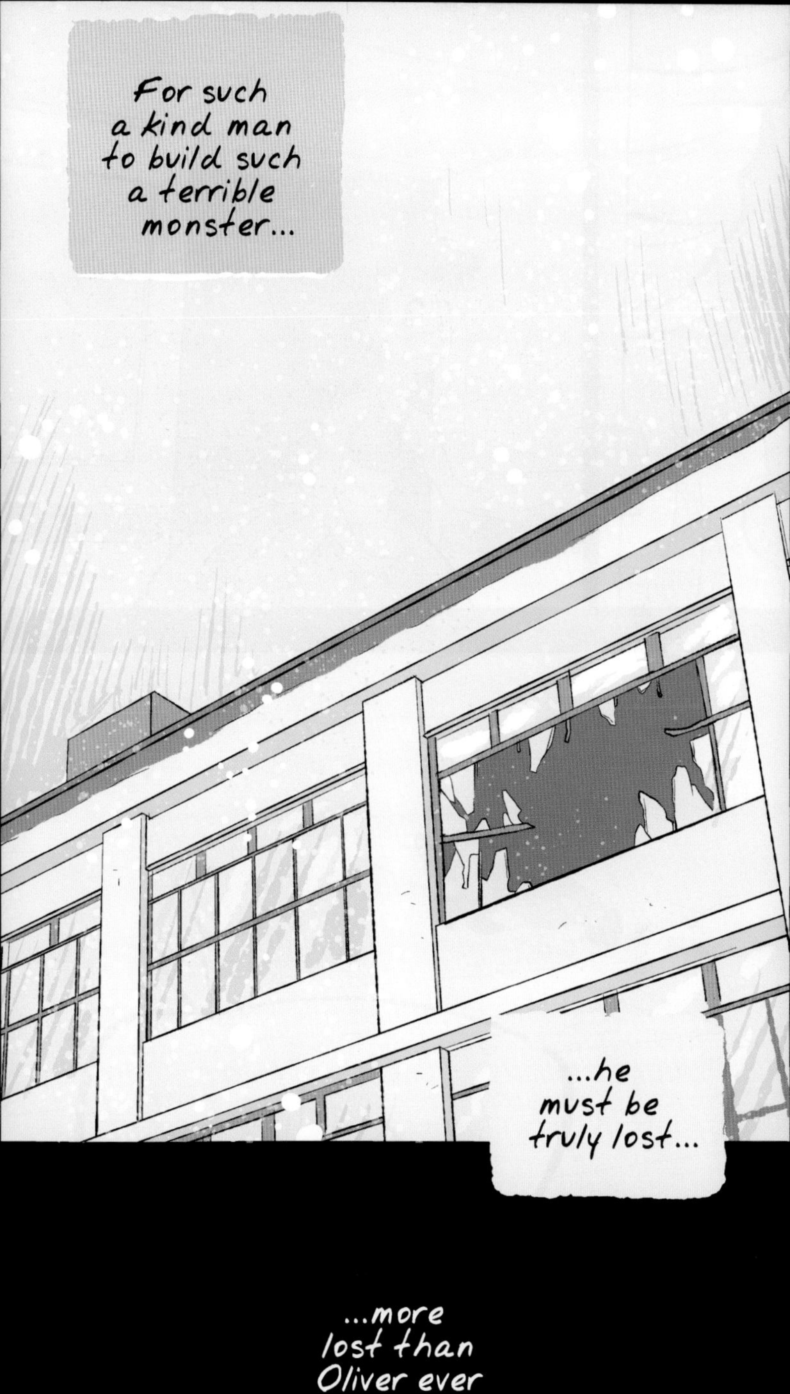
For such a kind man to build such a terrible monster...
...he must be truly lost...
...more lost than Oliver ever

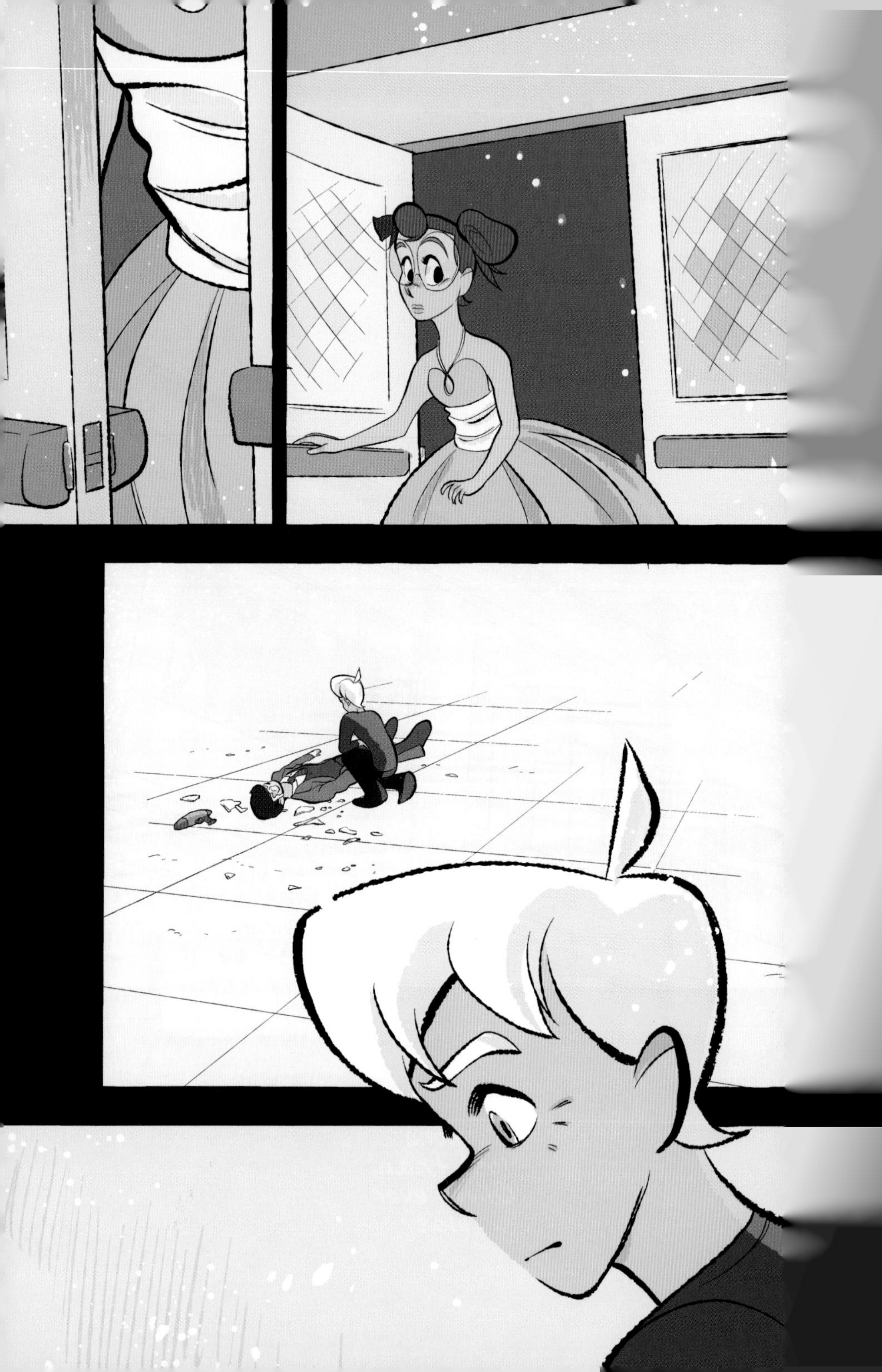

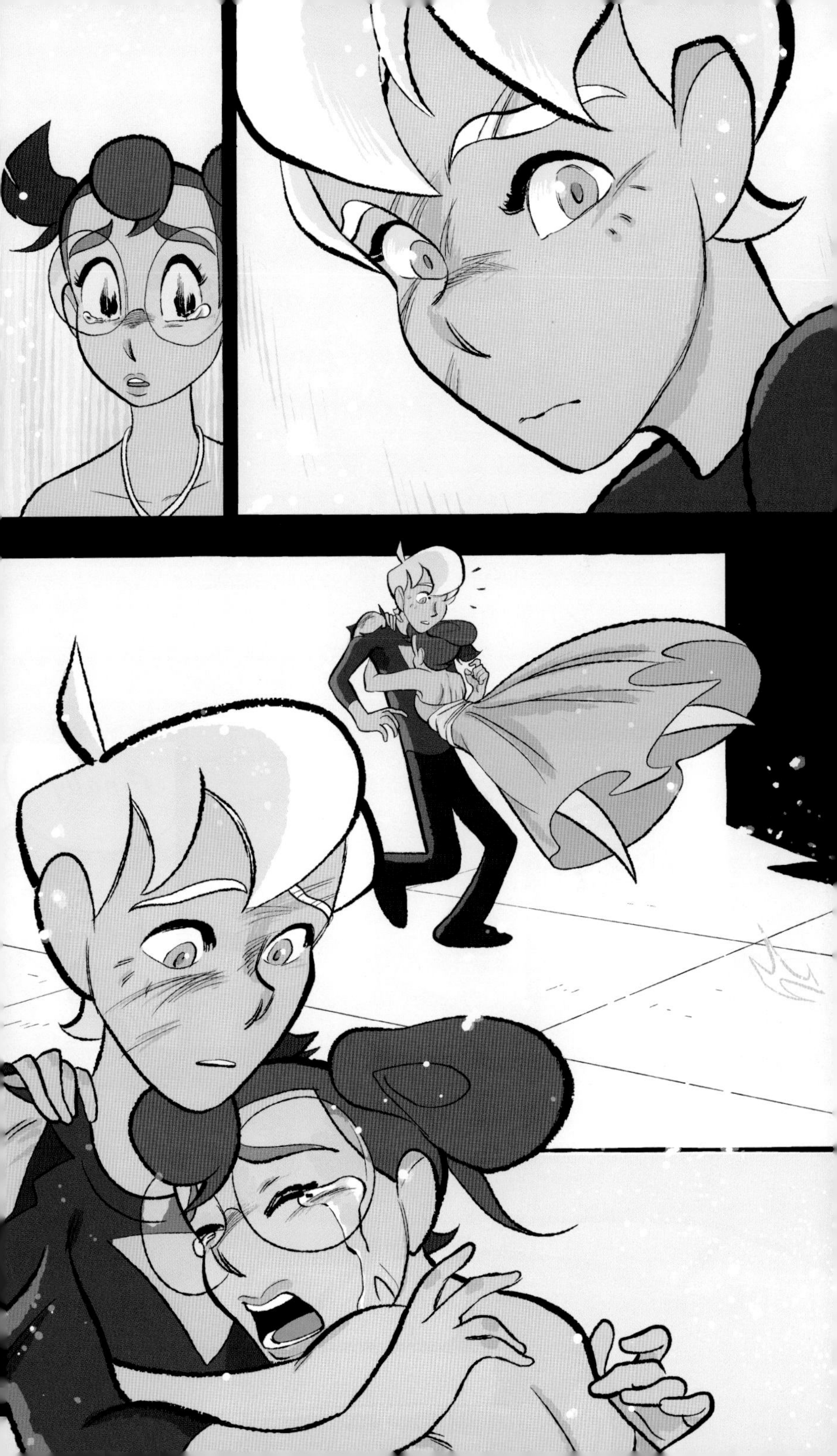

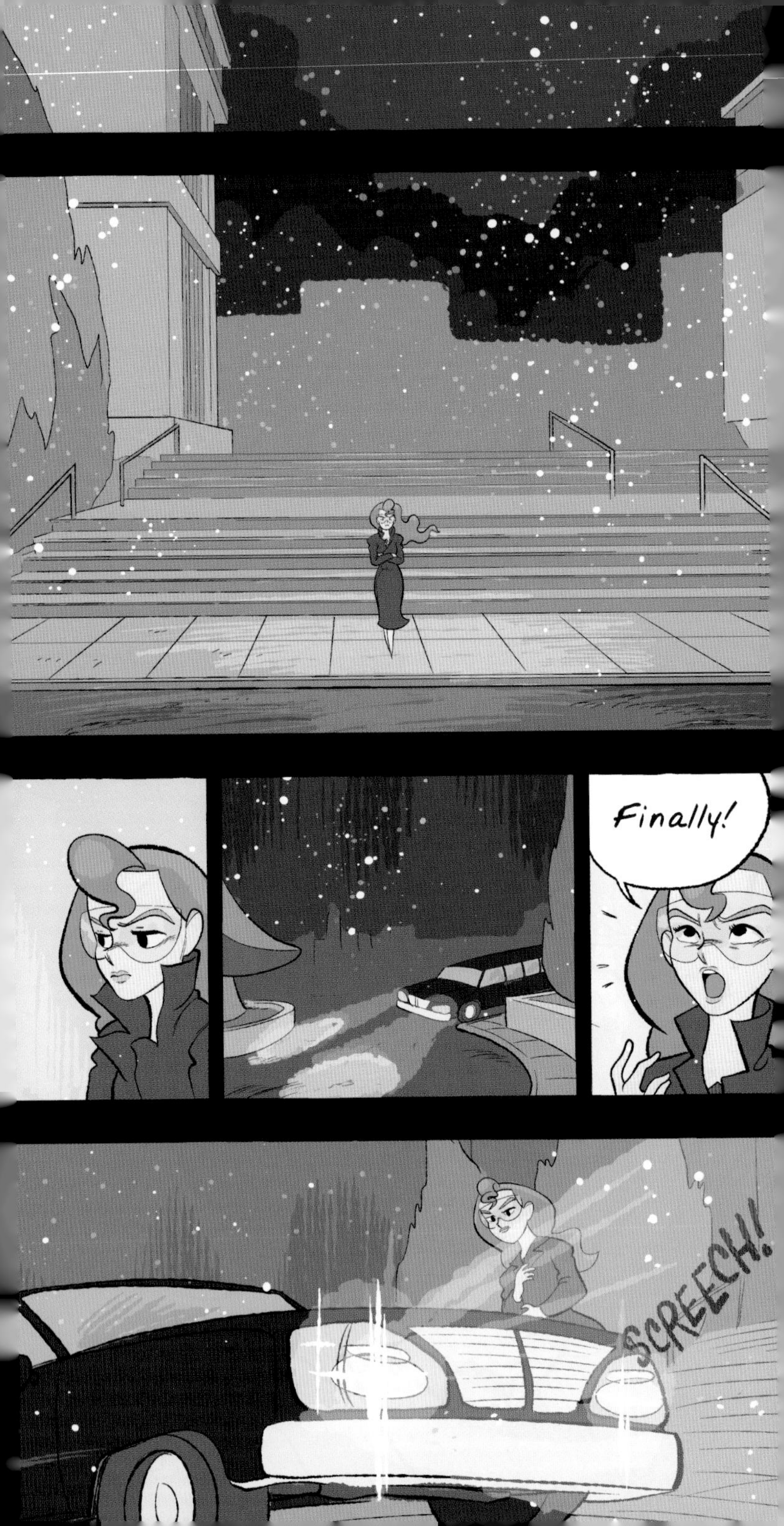
Finally!
SCREECH!

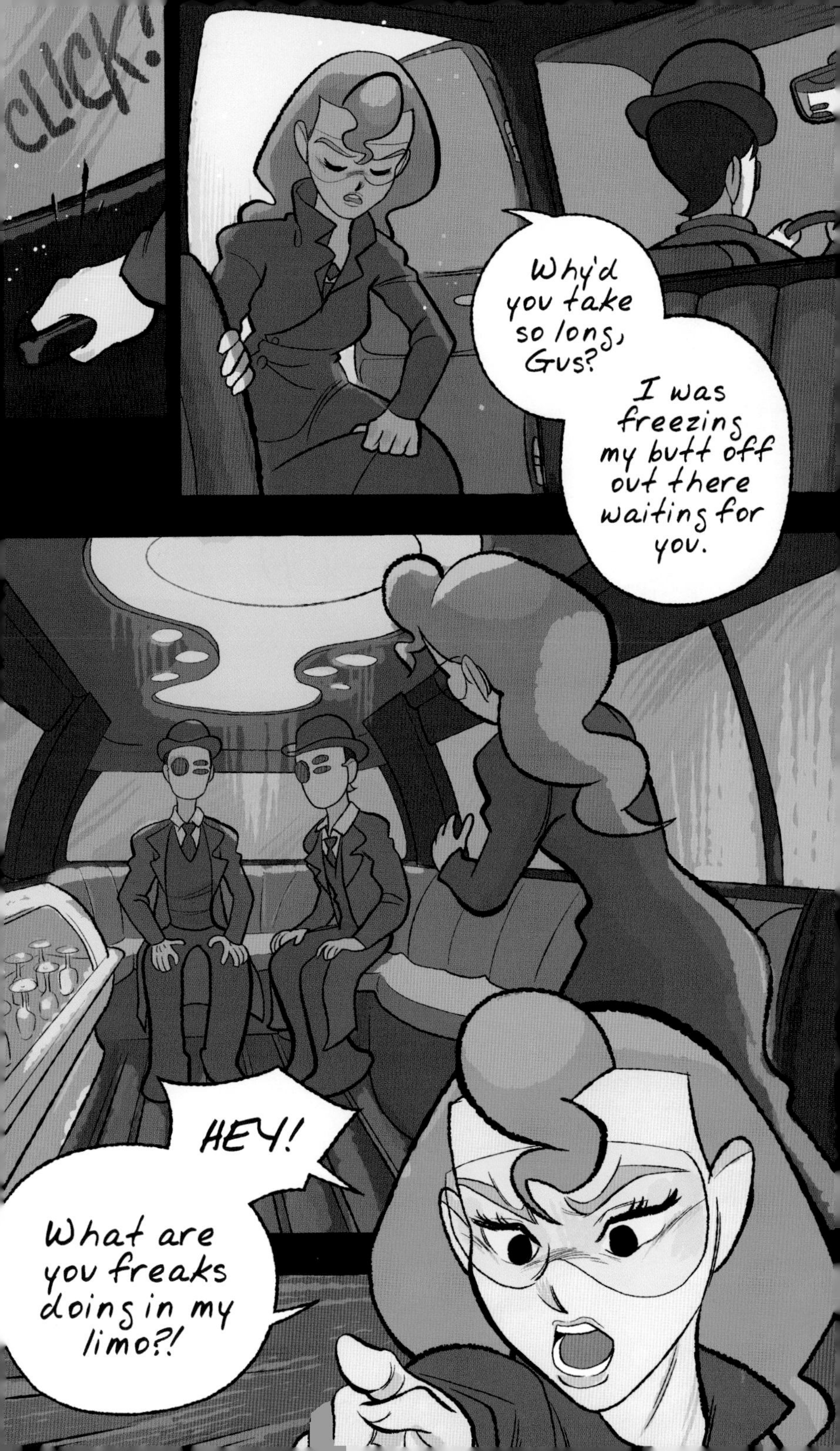
CLICK!
Why'd you take so long, Gus?
I was freezing my butt off out there waiting for you.
HEY!
What are you freaks doing in my limo?!

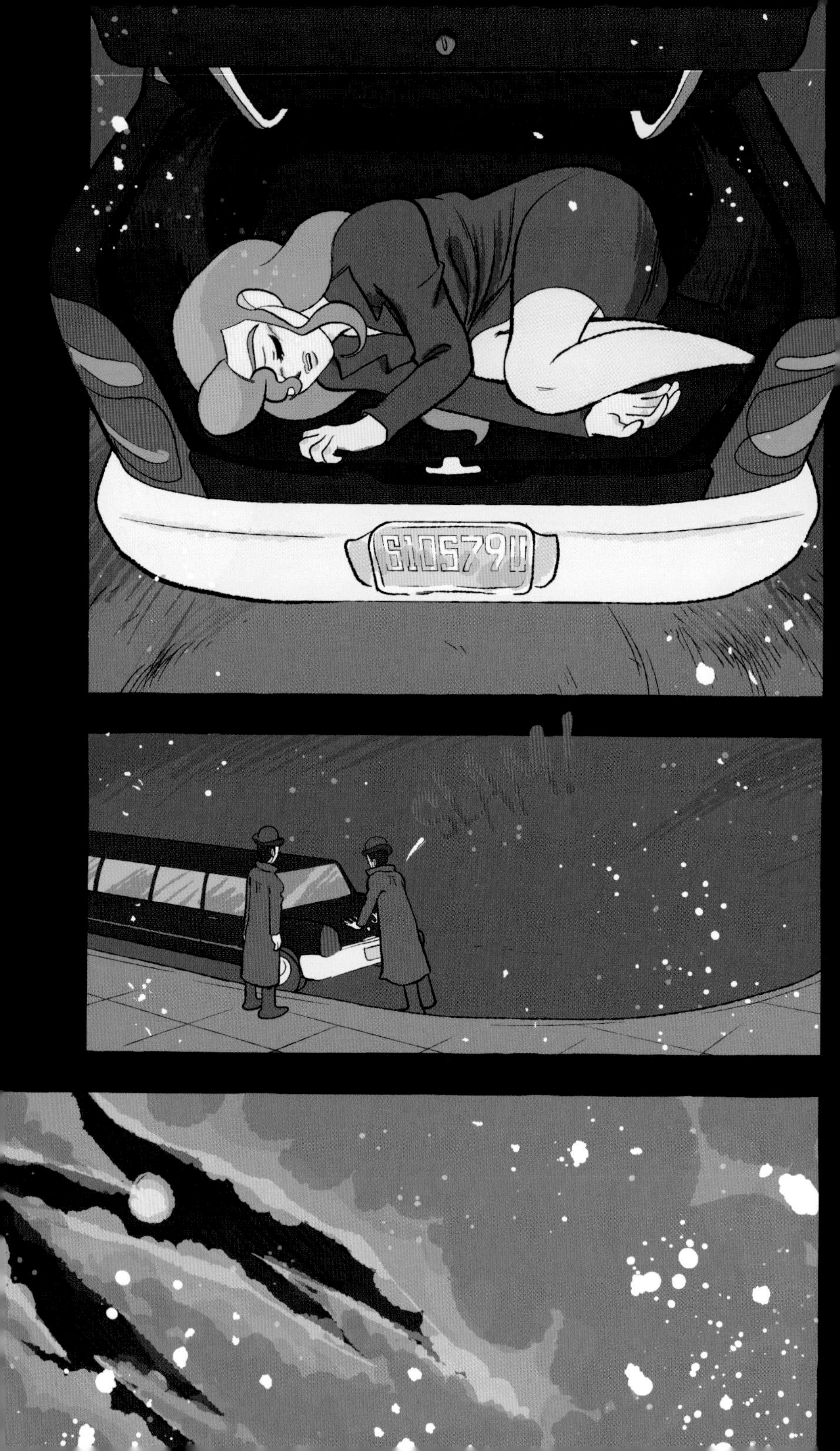
SLAM!!

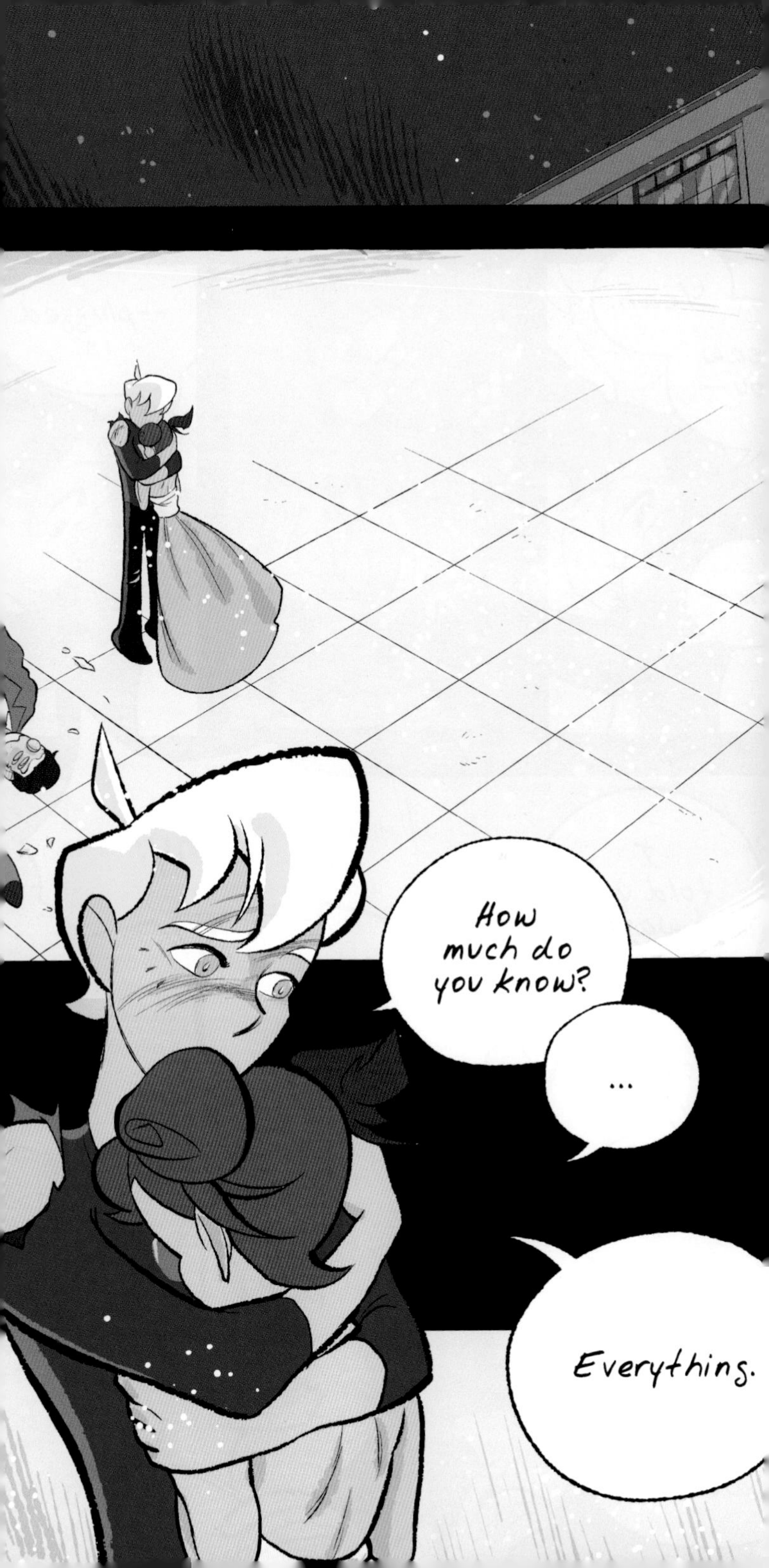
How much do you know?
...
Everything.

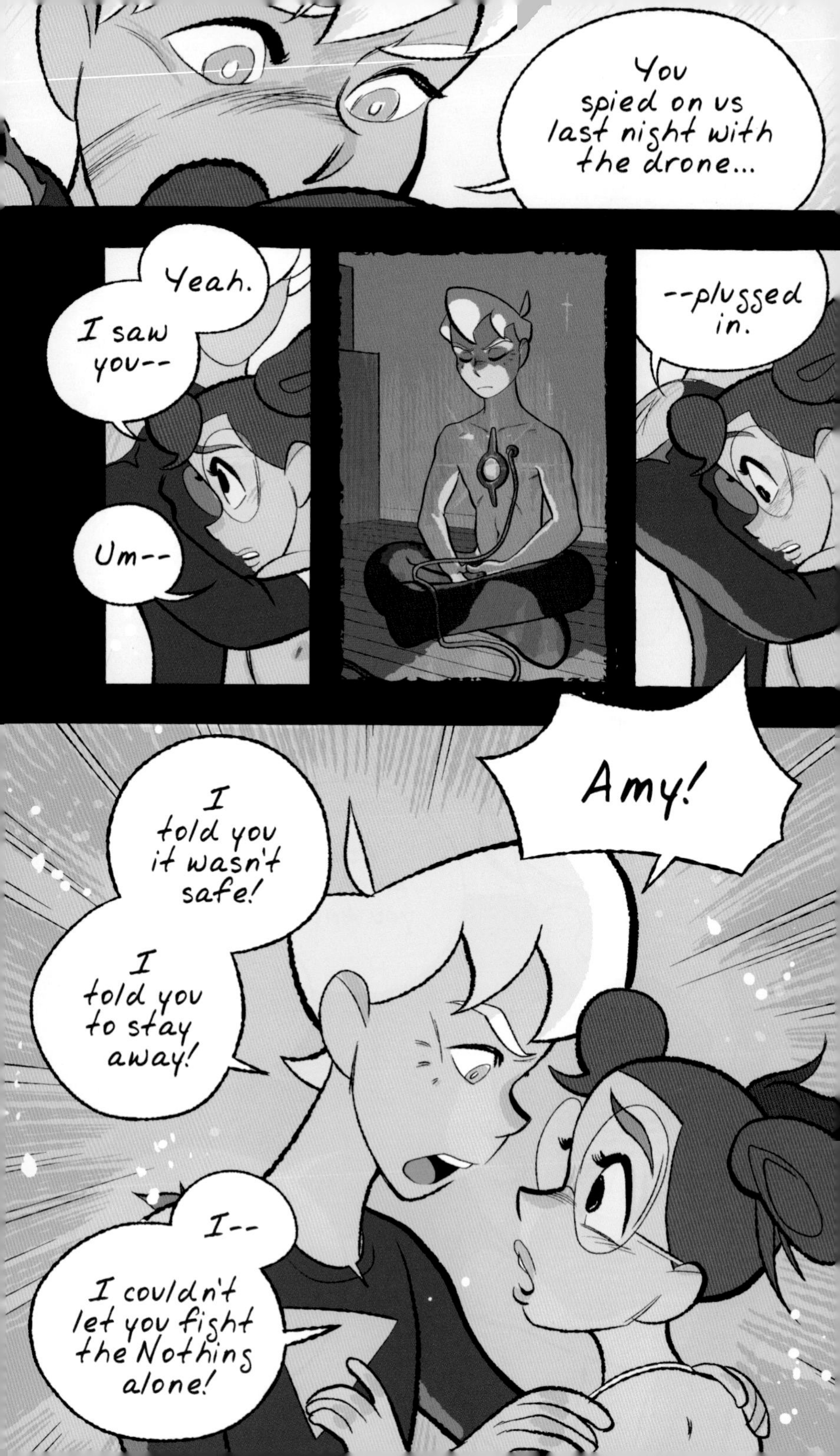
You spied on us last night with the drone...
Yeah.
I saw you--
Um--
--plugged in.
Amy!
I told you it wasn't safe!
I told you to stay away!
I--
I couldn't let you fight the Nothing alone!

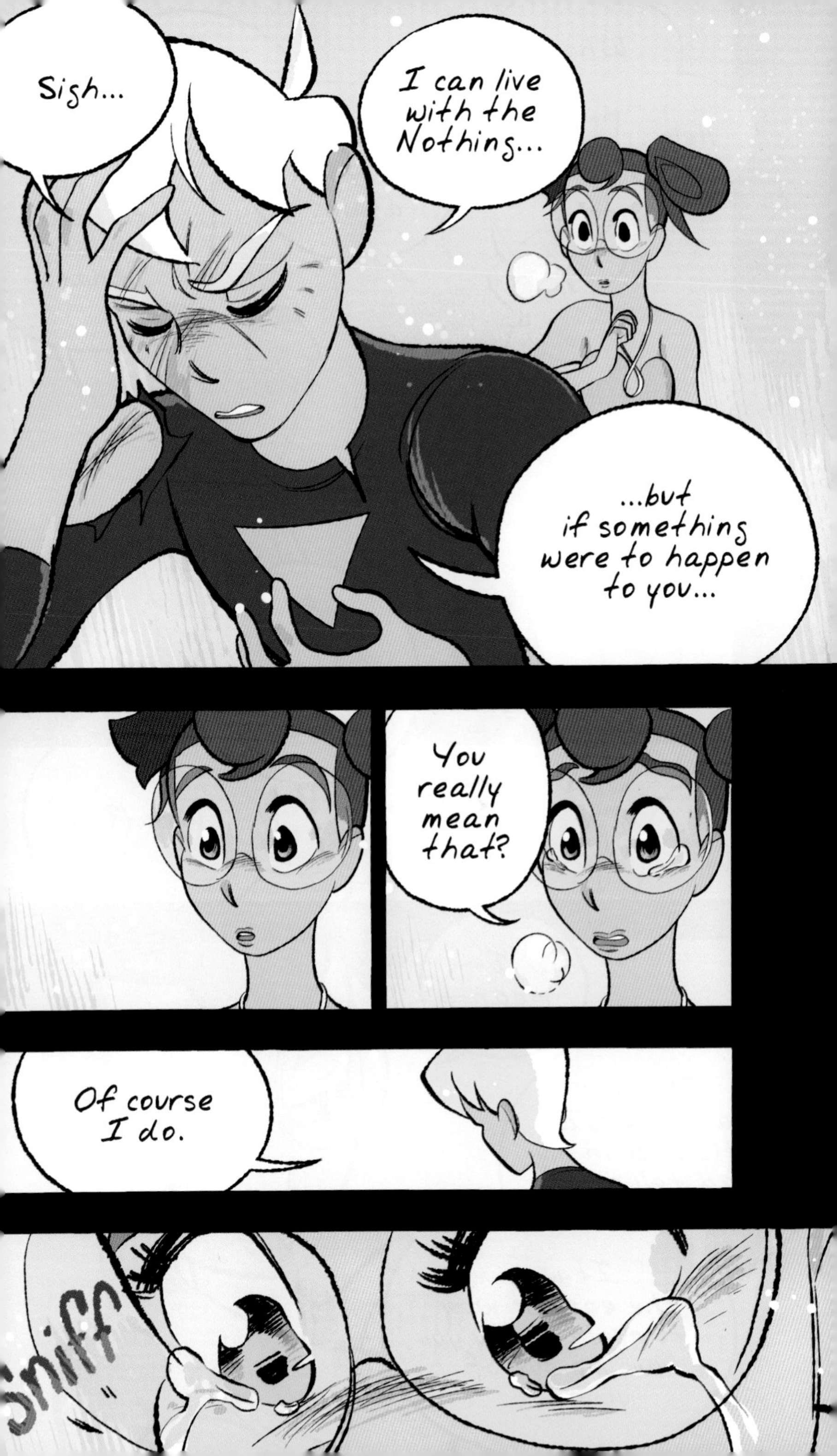
Sigh...
I can live with the Nothing...
...but if something were to happen to you...
You really mean that?
Of course I do.
Sniff

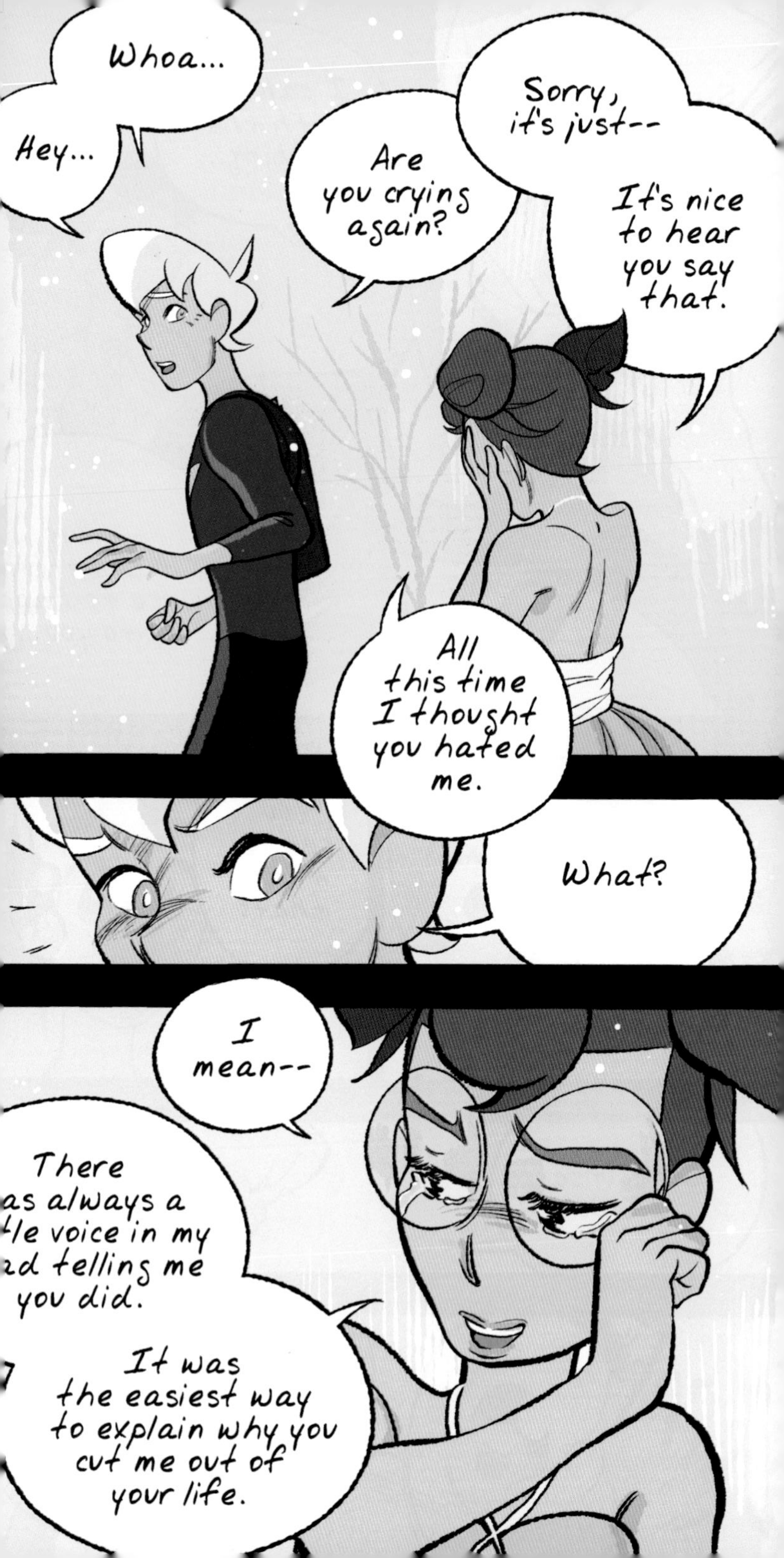
Whoa...
Hey...
Are you crying again?
Sorry, it's just--
It's nice to hear you say that.
All this time I thought you hated me.
What?
I mean--
There as always a le voice in my ad telling me you did.
It was the easiest way to explain why you cut me out of your life.

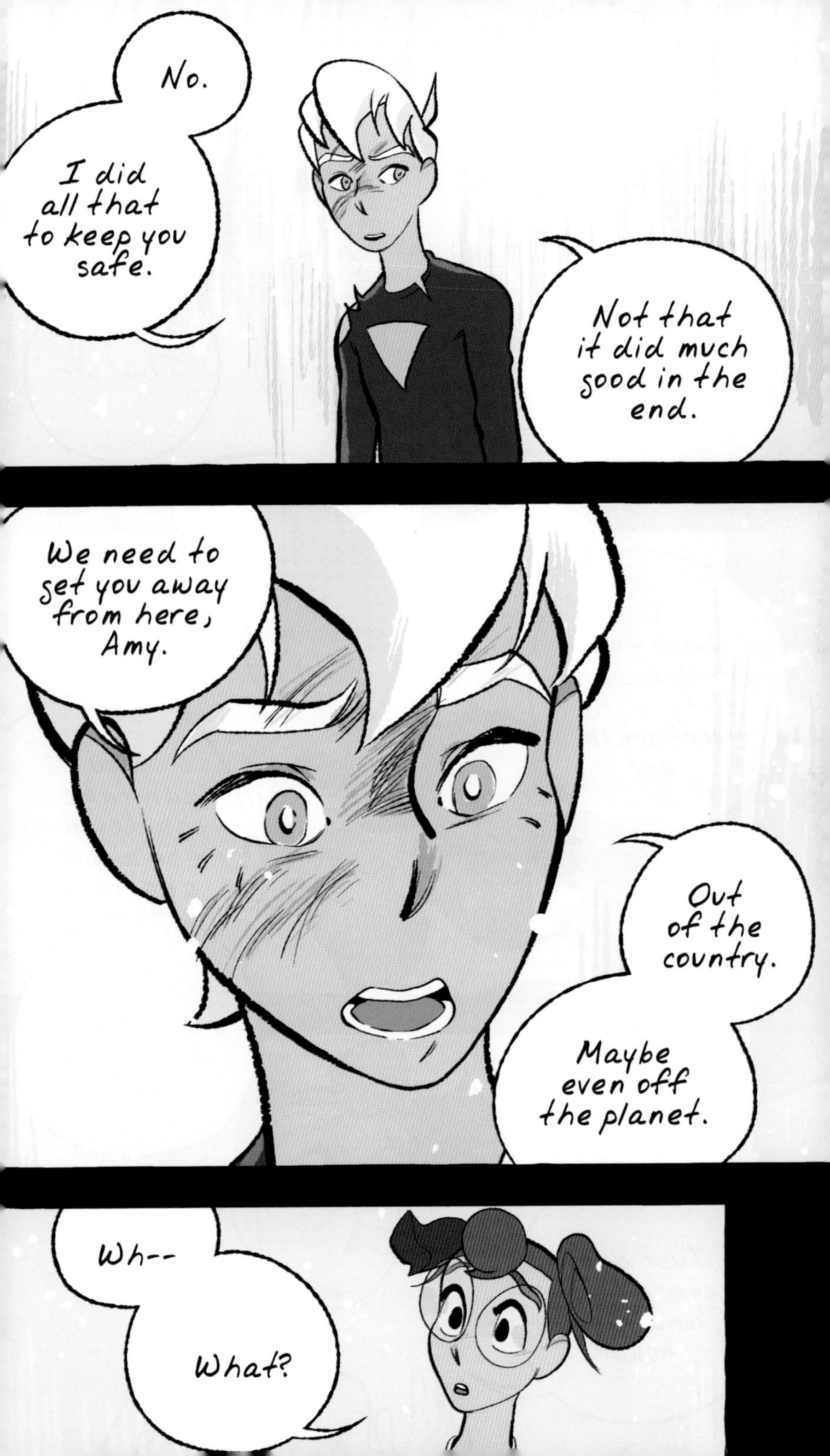
No.
I did all that to keep you safe.
Not that it did much good in the end.
We need to get you away from here, Amy.
Out of the country.
Maybe even off the planet.
Wh--
What?

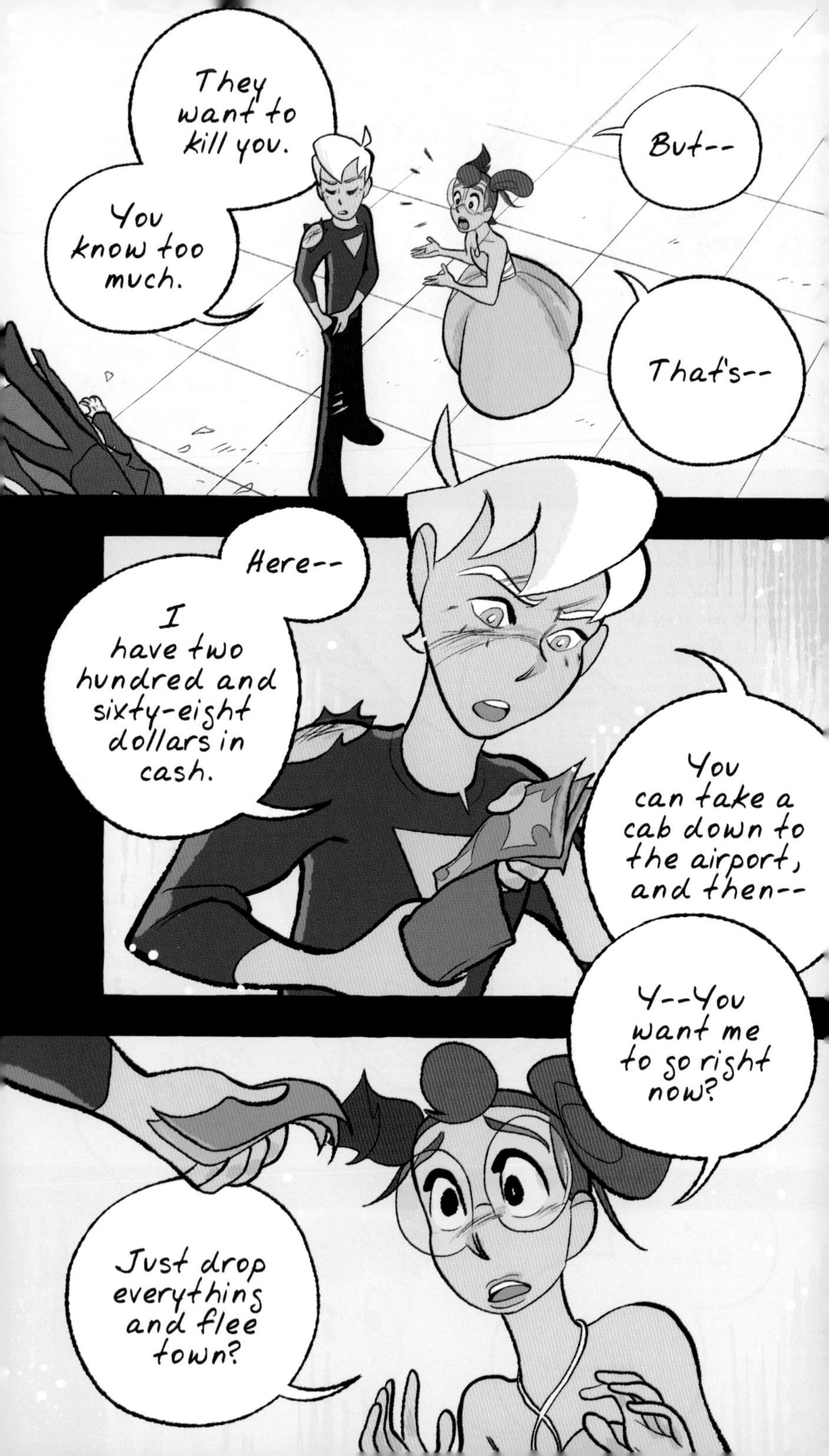
They want to kill you.
You know too much.
But--
That's--
Here--
I have two hundred and sixty-eight dollars in cash.
You can take a cab down to the airport, and then--
Y--You want me to go right now?
Just drop everything and flee town?

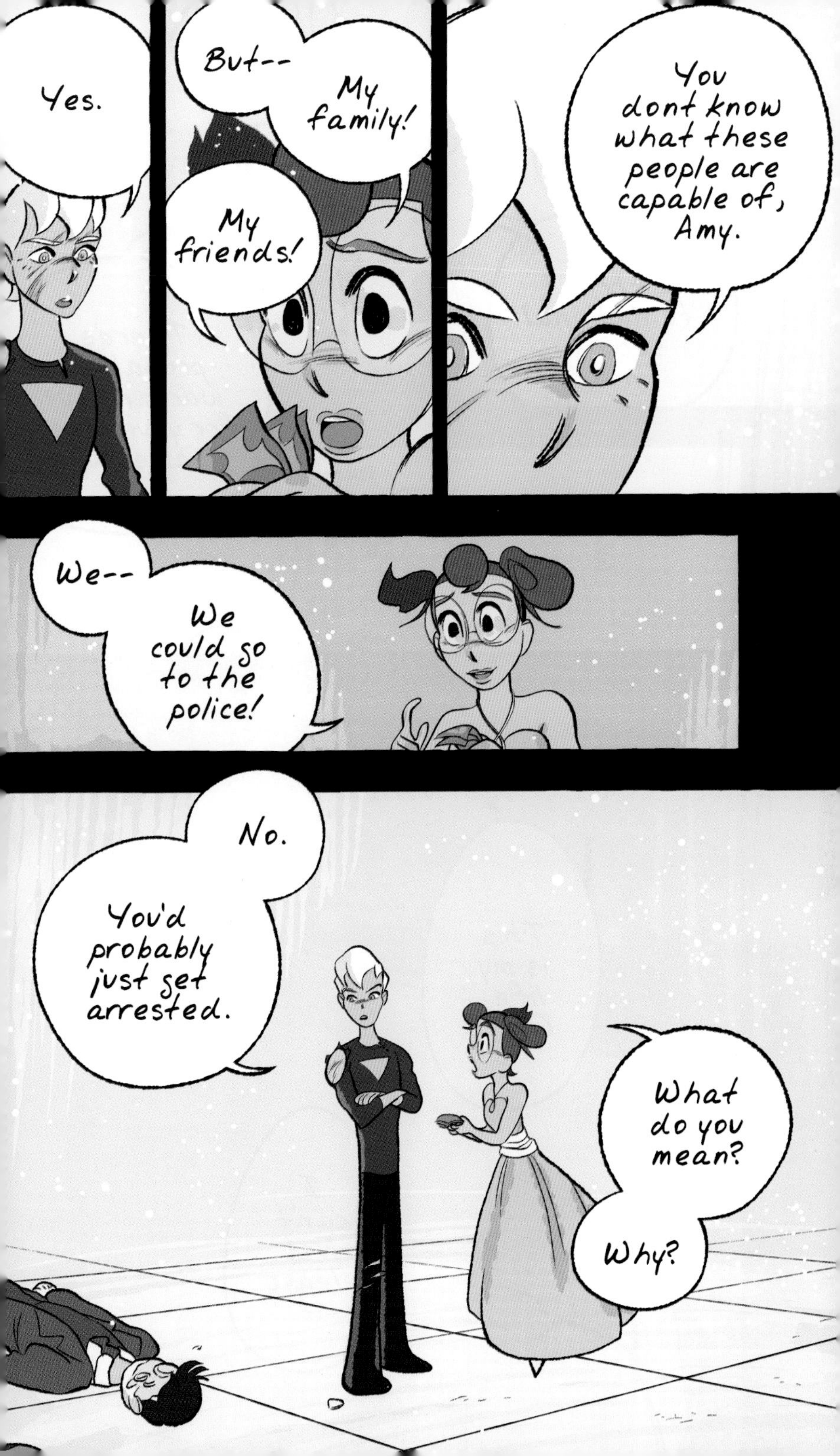
Yes.
But--
My family!
My friends!
You dont know what these people are capable of, Amy.
We--
We could go to the police!
No.
You'd probably just get arrested.
What do you mean?
Why?

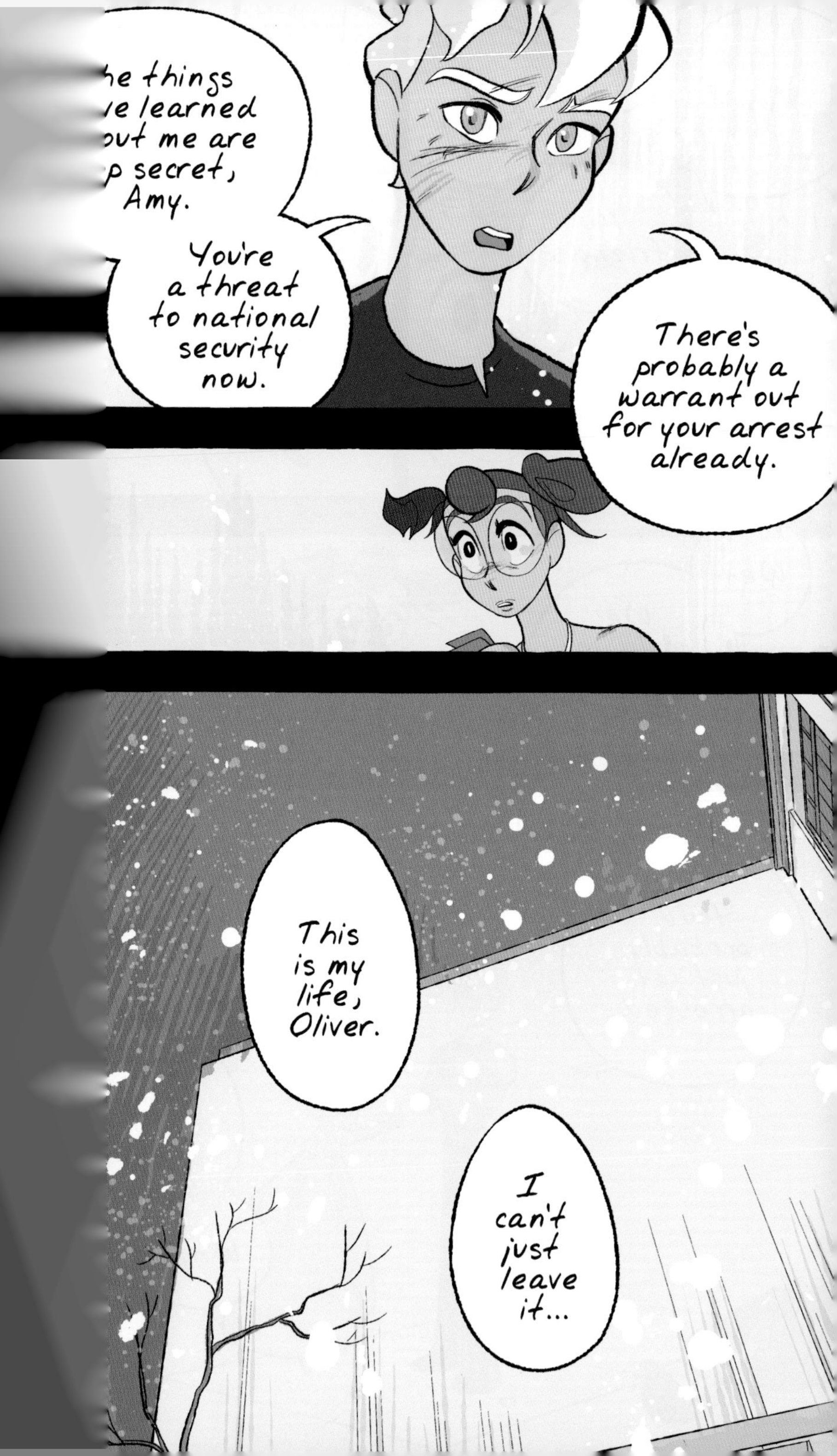

he things ve learned out me are p secret, Amy.
You're a threat to national security now.
There's probably a warrant out for your arrest already.
This is my life, Oliver.
I can't just leave it...

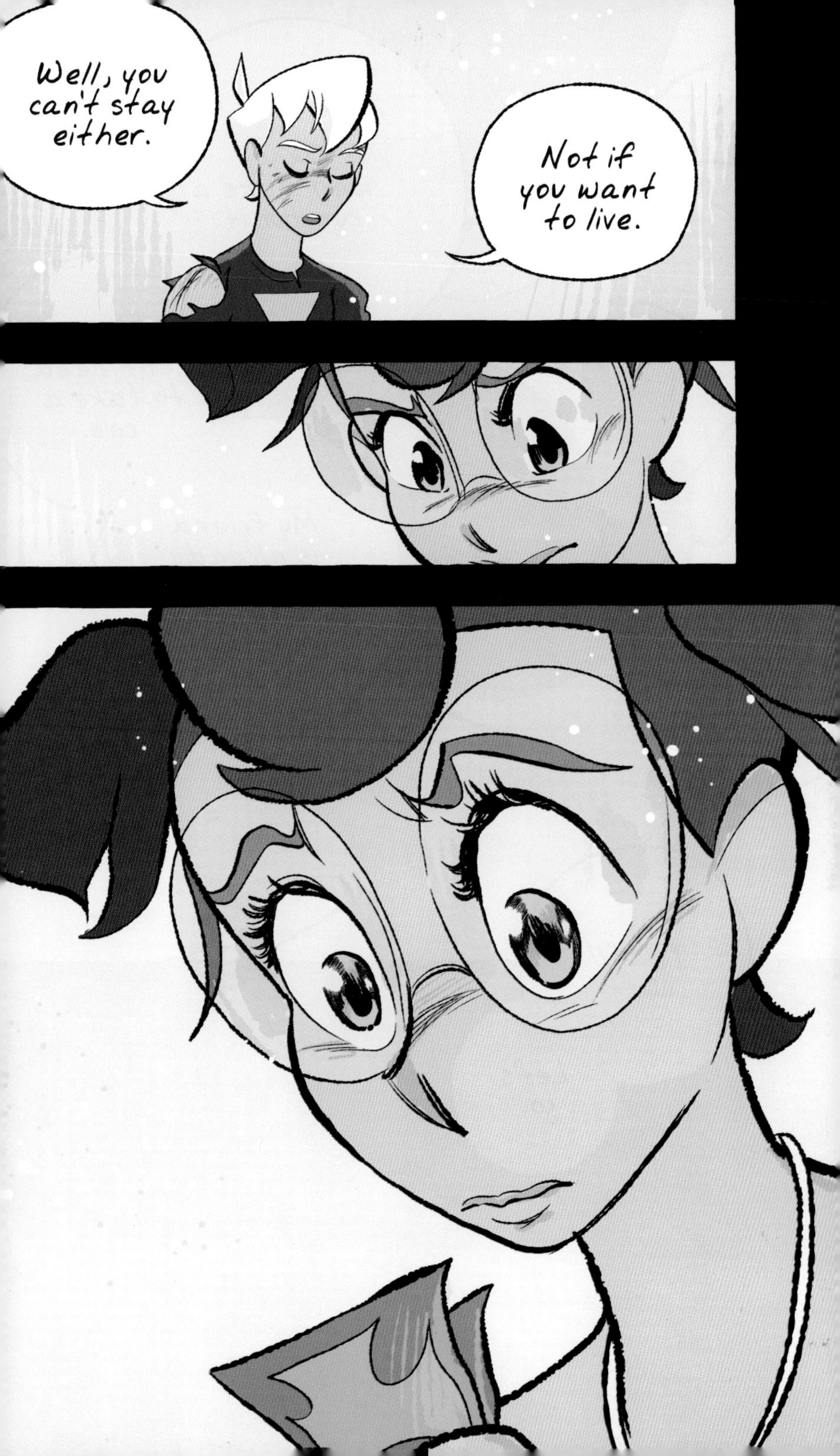
Well, you can't stay either.
Not if you want to live.

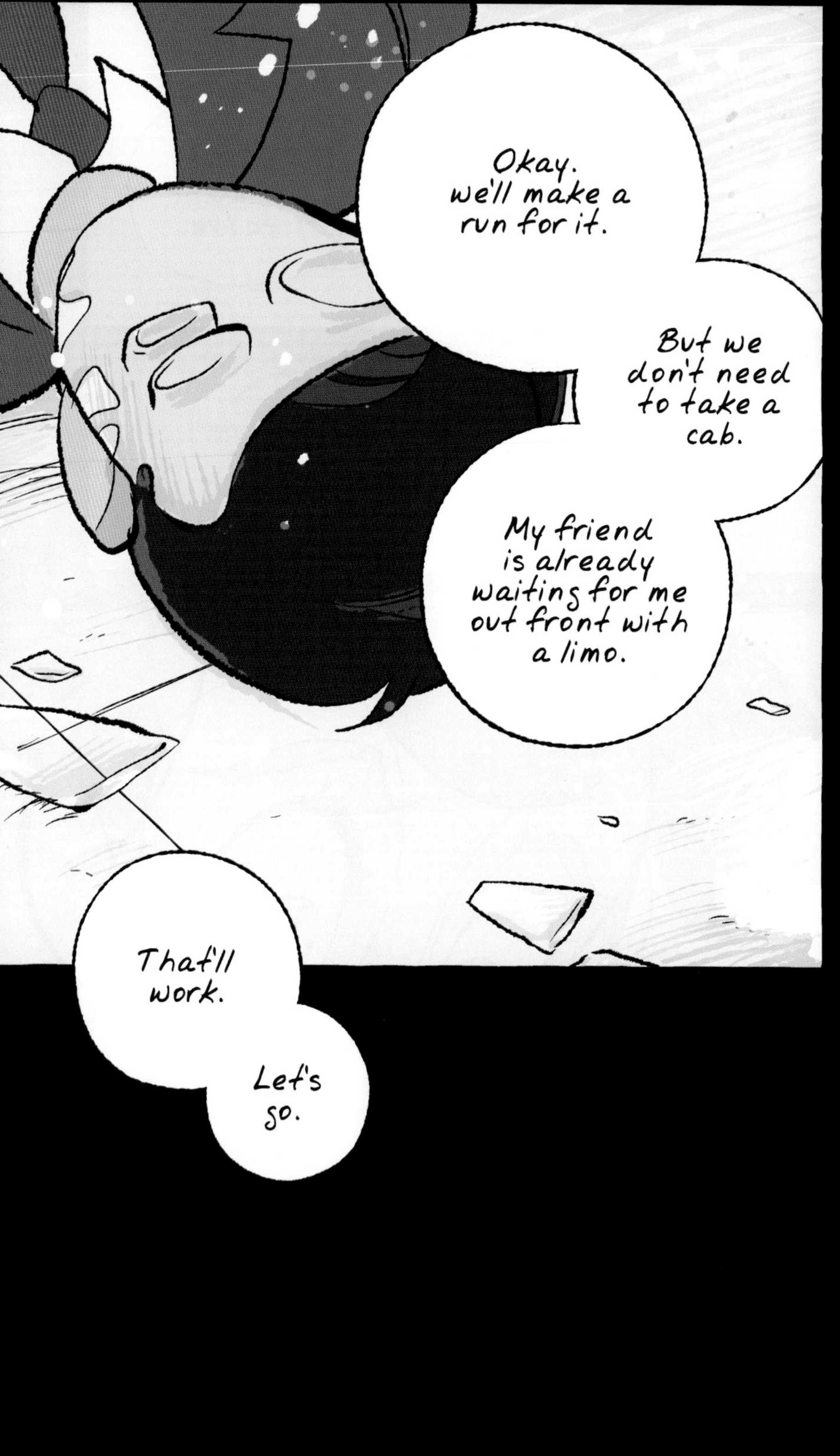
Okay. we'll make a run for it.
But we don't need to take a cab.
My friend is already waiting for me out front with a limo.
That'll work.
Let's go.

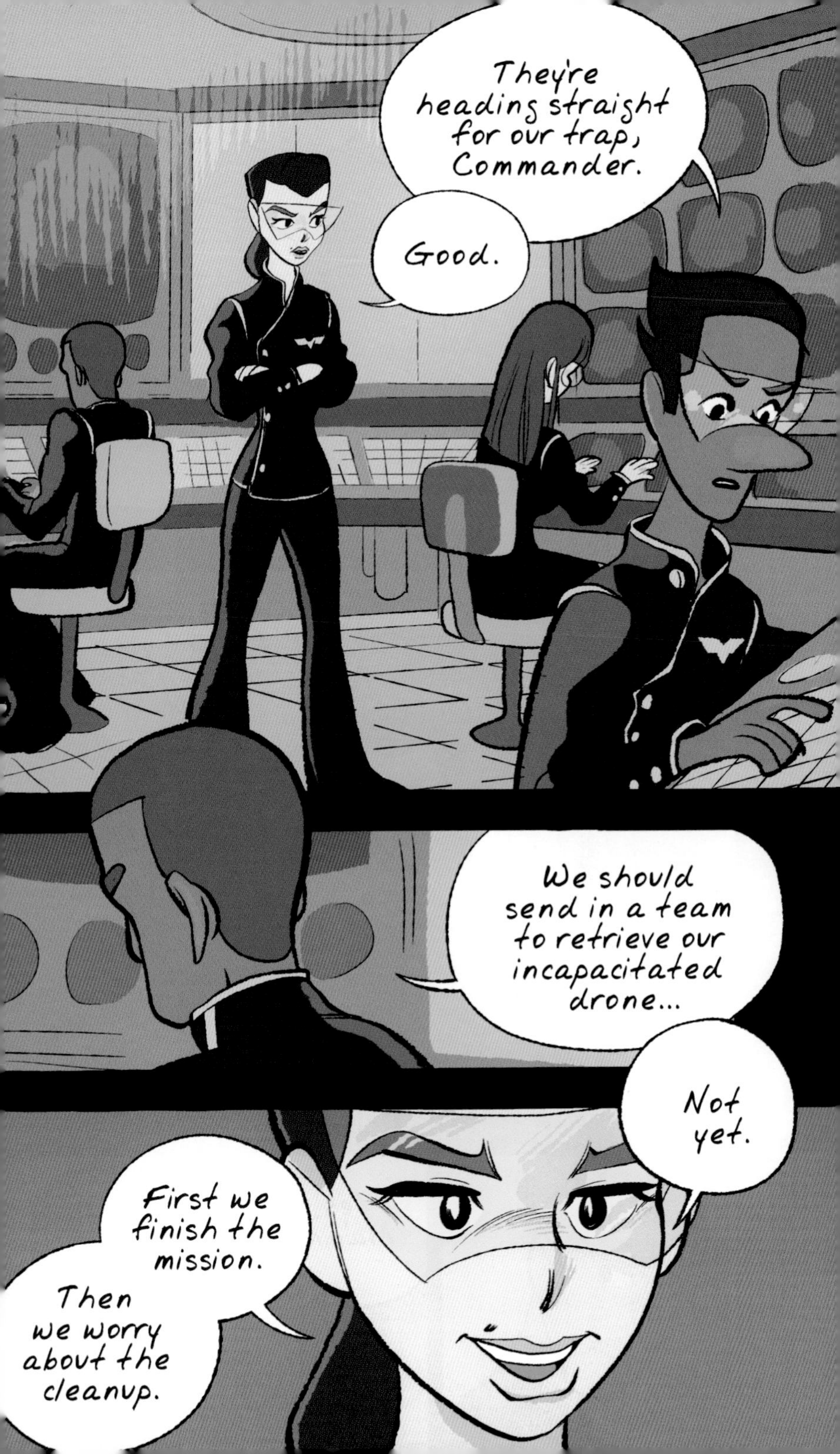
They're heading straight for our trap, Commander.
Good.
We should send in a team to retrieve our incapacitated drone...
Not yet.
First we finish the mission.
Then we worry about the cleanup.

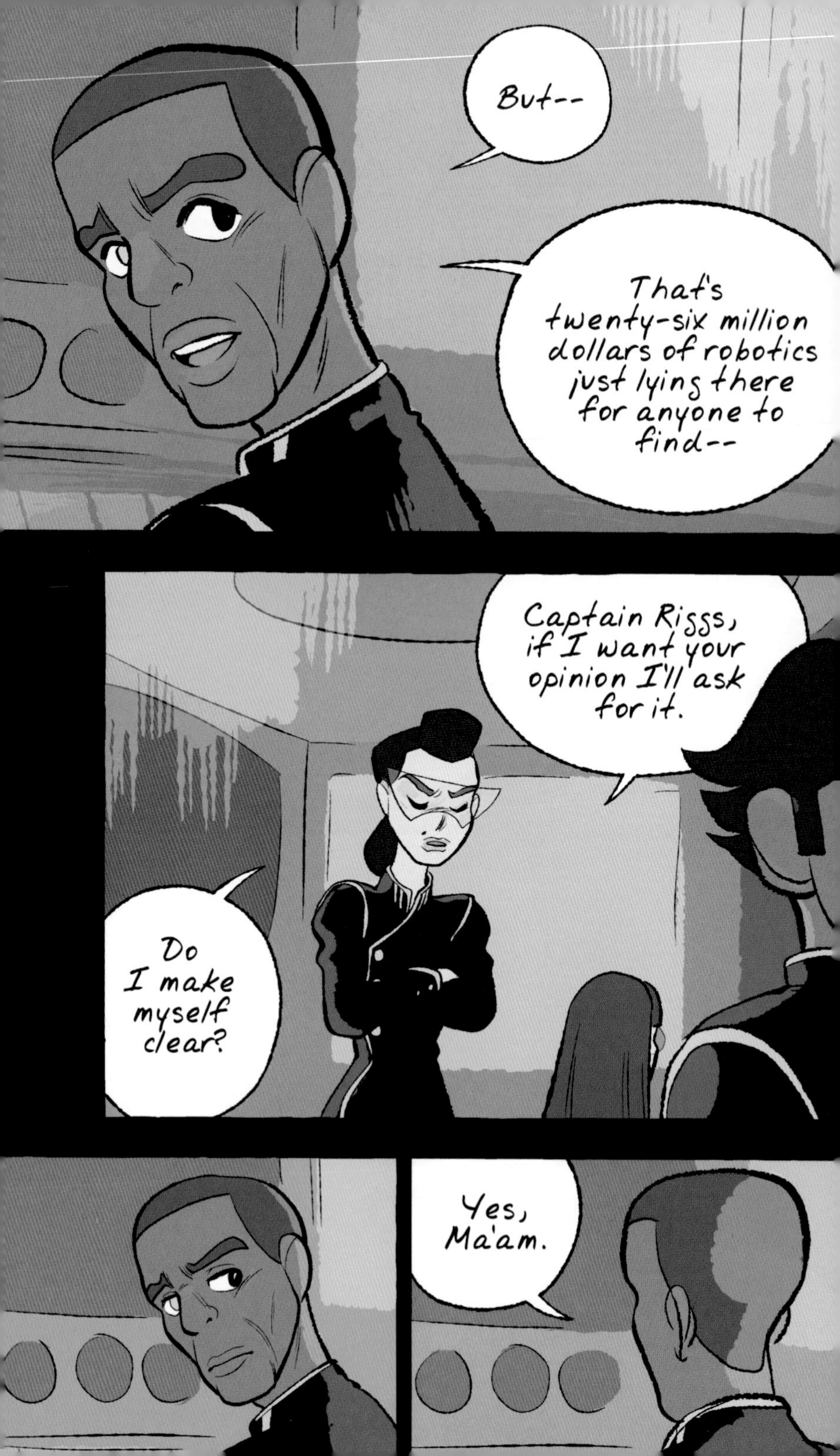
But--
That's twenty-six million dollars of robotics just lying there for anyone to find--
Captain Risgs, if I want your opinion I'll ask for it.
Do I make myself clear?
Yes, Ma'am.

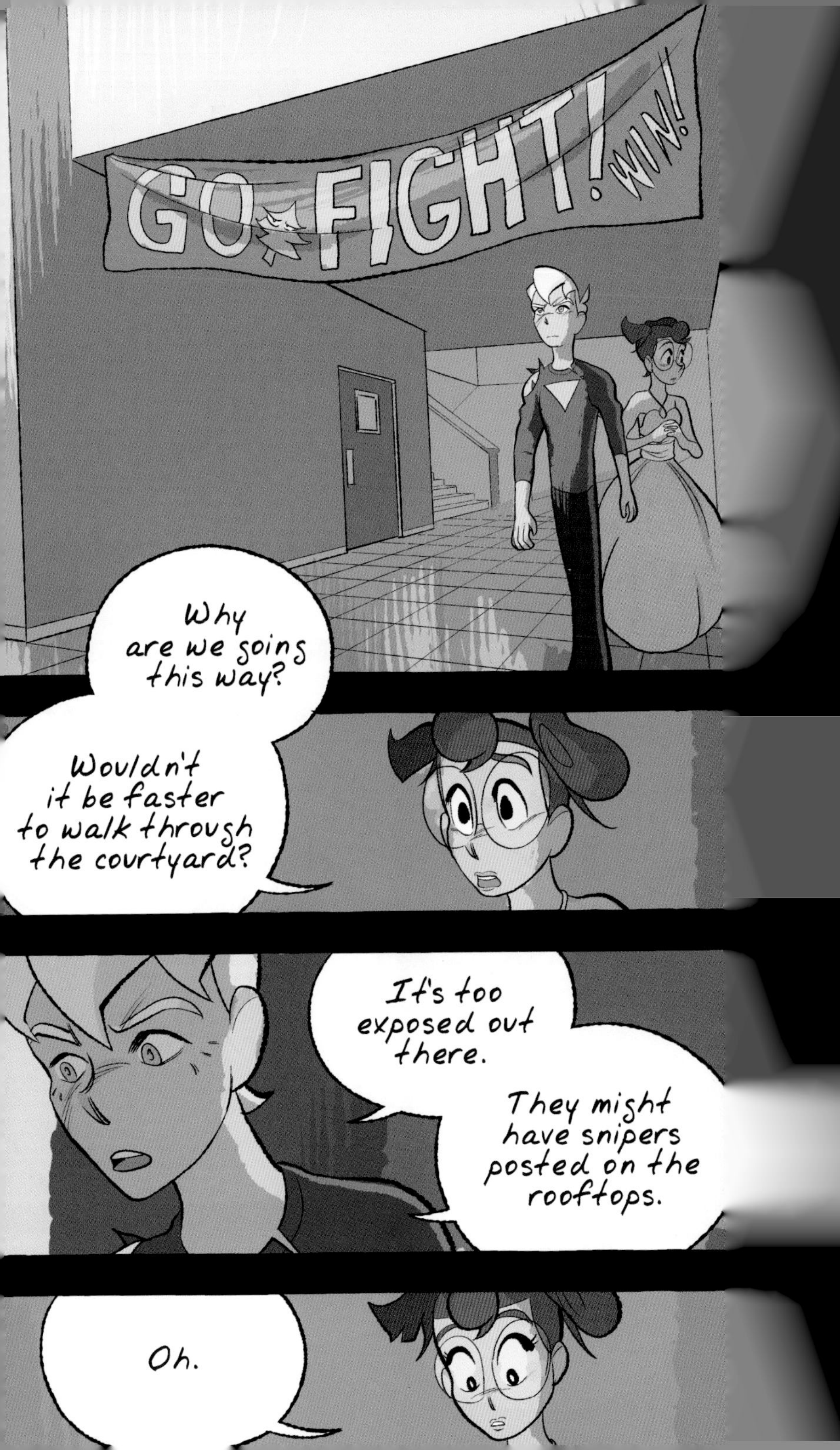
GO FIGHT! WIN!
Why are we going this way?
Wouldn't it be faster to walk through the courtyard?
It's too exposed out there.
They might have snipers posted on the rooftops.
Oh.

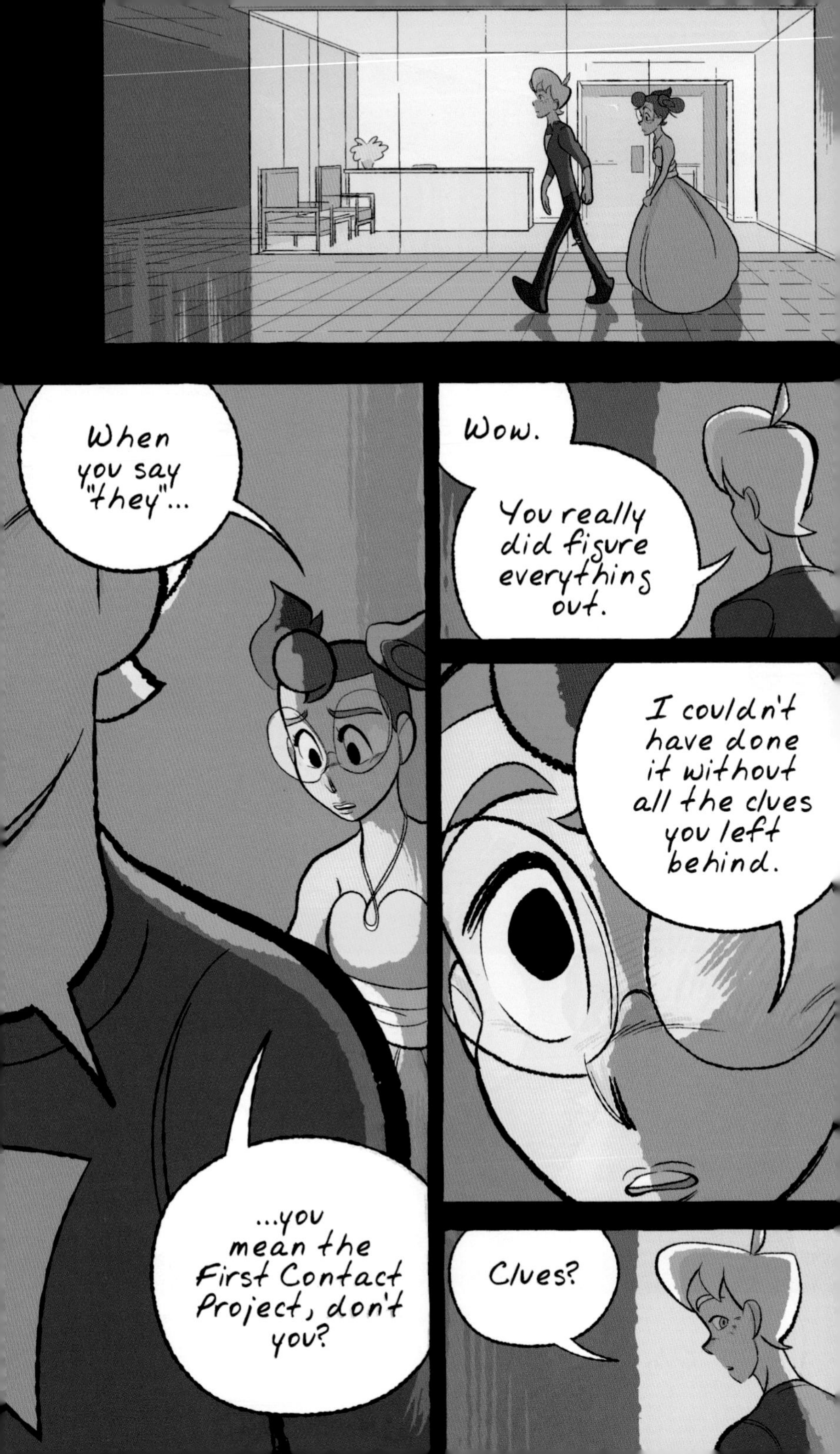
When you say "they"...
...you mean the First Contact Project, don't you?
Wow.
You really did figure everything out.
I couldn't have done it without all the clues you left behind.
Clues?

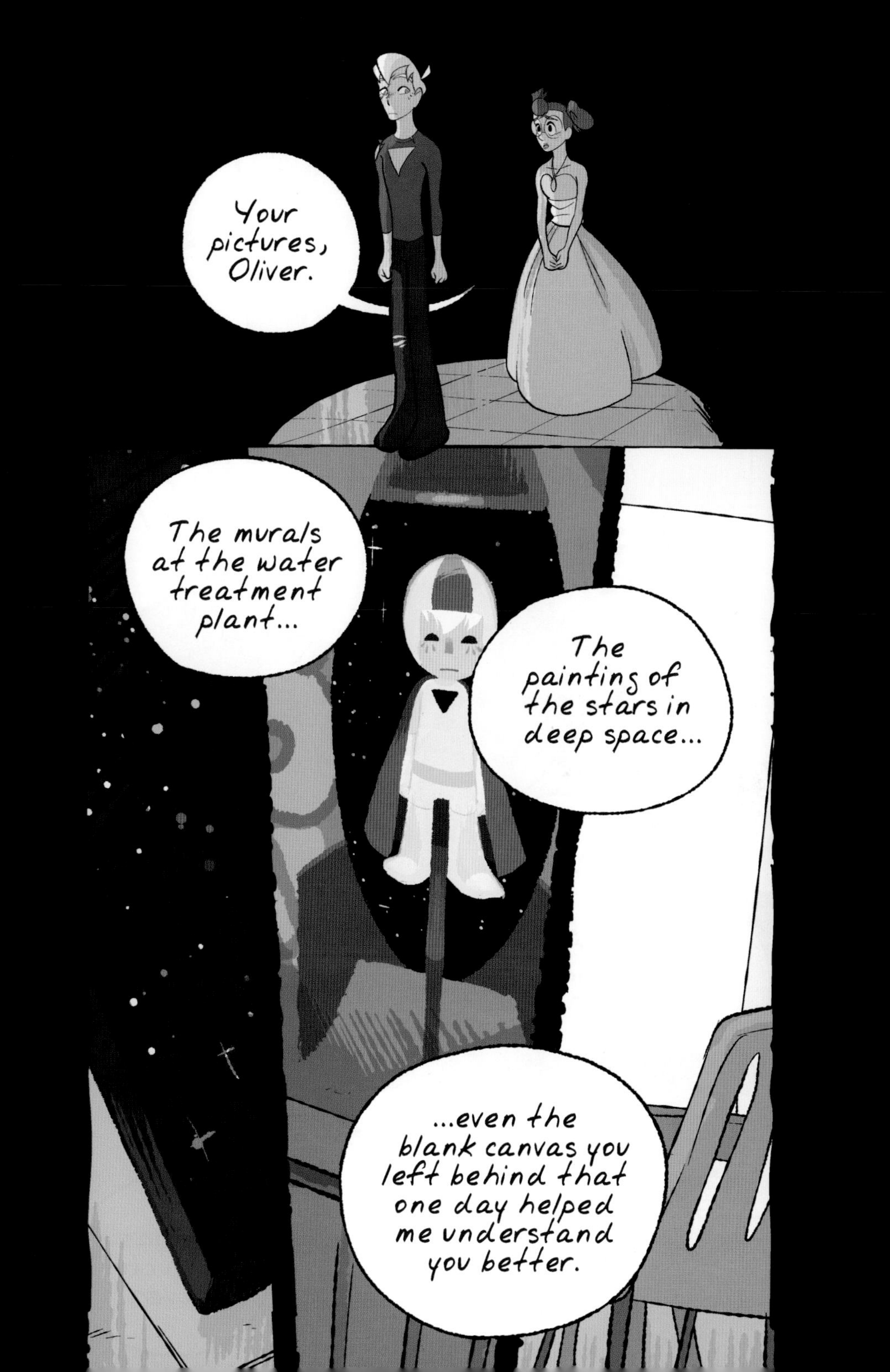
Your pictures, Oliver.
The murals at the water treatment plant...
The painting of the stars in deep space...
...even the blank canvas you left behind that one day helped me understand you better.

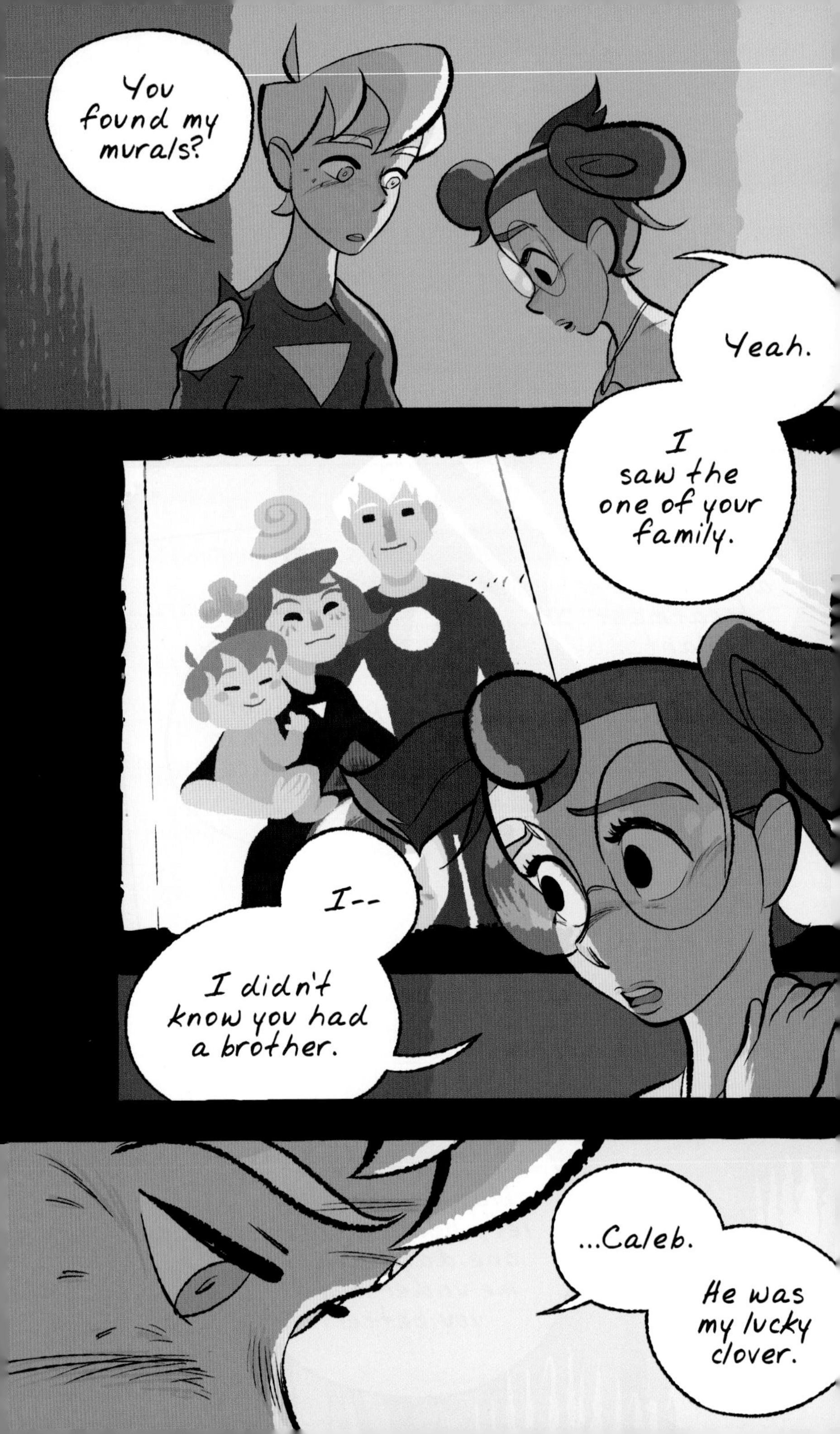
You found my murals?
Yeah.
I saw the one of your family.
I--
I didn't know you had a brother.
...Caleb.
He was my lucky clover.

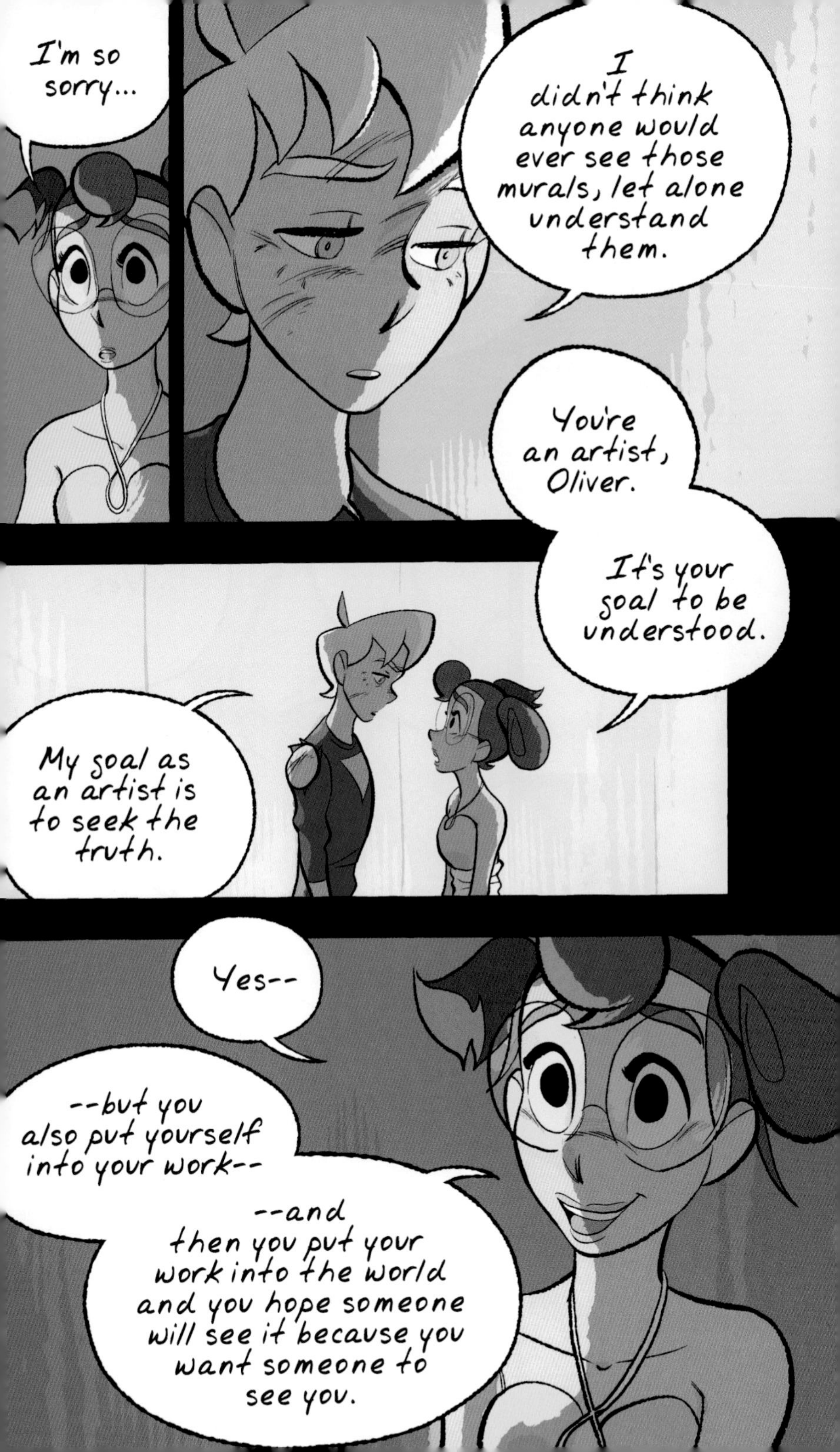
I'm so sorry...
I didn't think anyone would ever see those murals, let alone understand them.
You're an artist, Oliver.
It's your goal to be understood.
My goal as an artist is to seek the truth.
Yes--
--but you also put yourself into your work--
--and then you put your work into the world and you hope someone will see it because you want someone to see you.

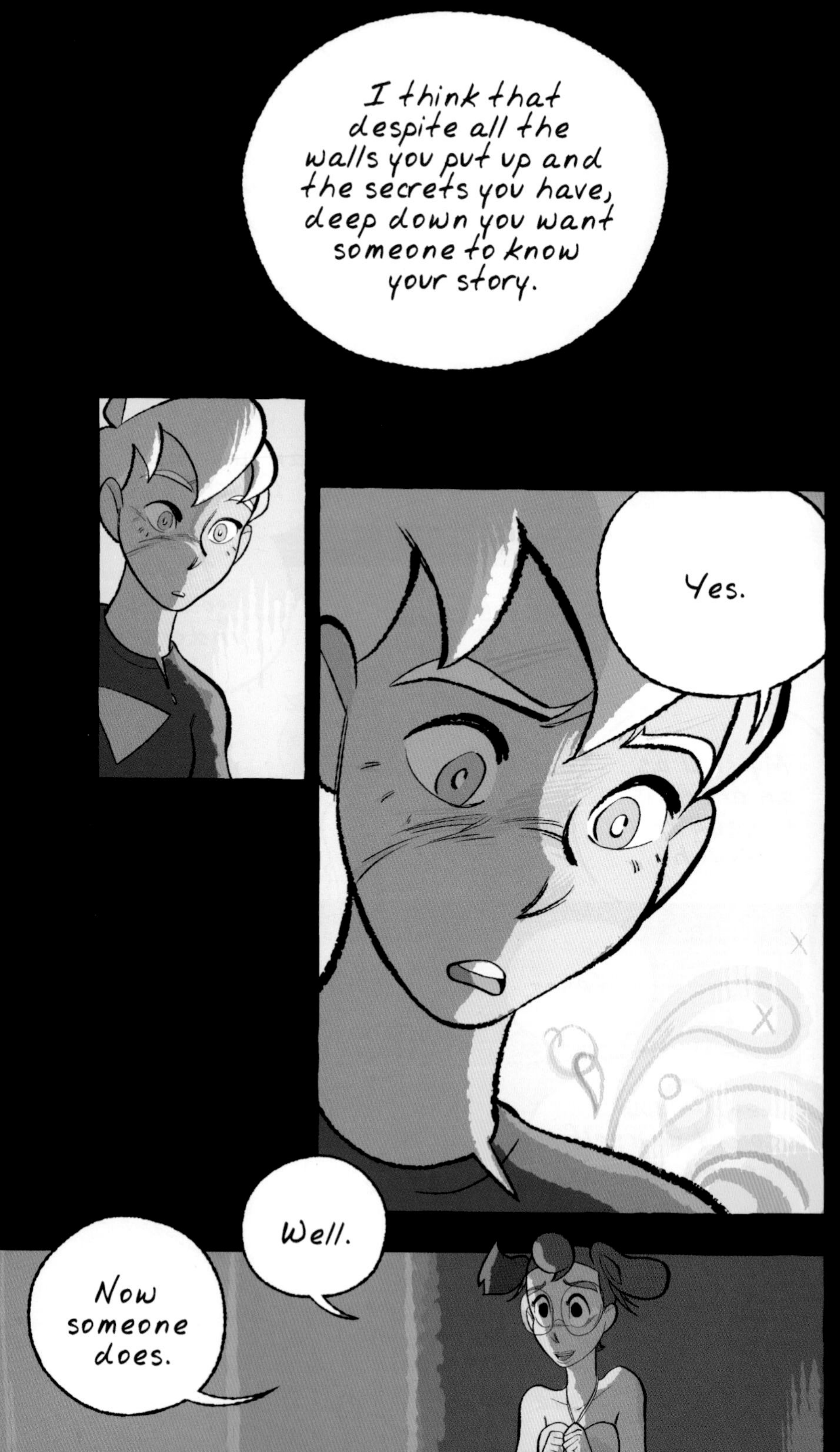
I think that despite all the walls you put up and the secrets you have, deep down you want someone to know your story.
Yes.
Well.
Now someone does.

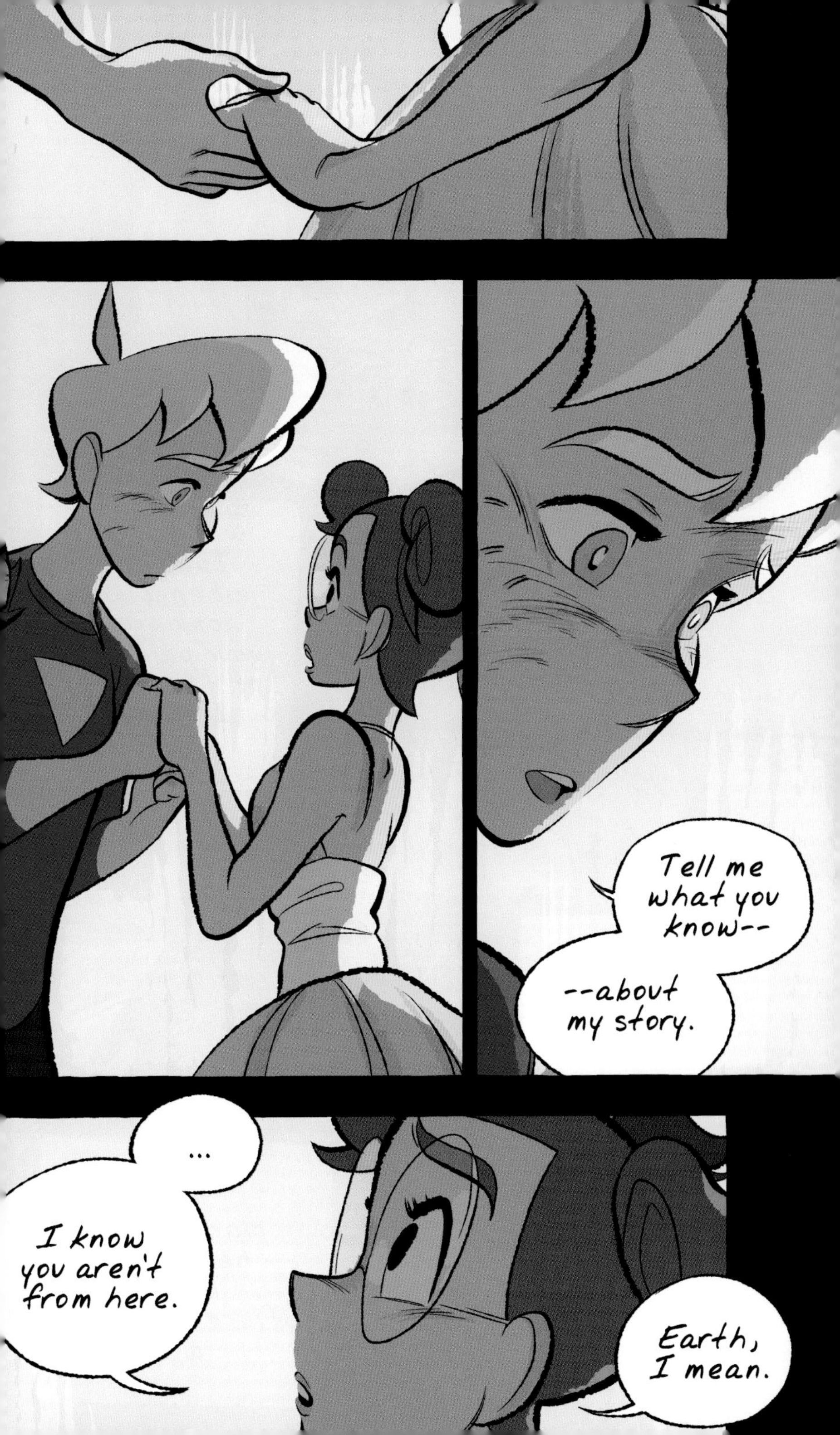
Tell me what you know--
--about my story.
...
I know you aren't from here.
Earth, I mean.

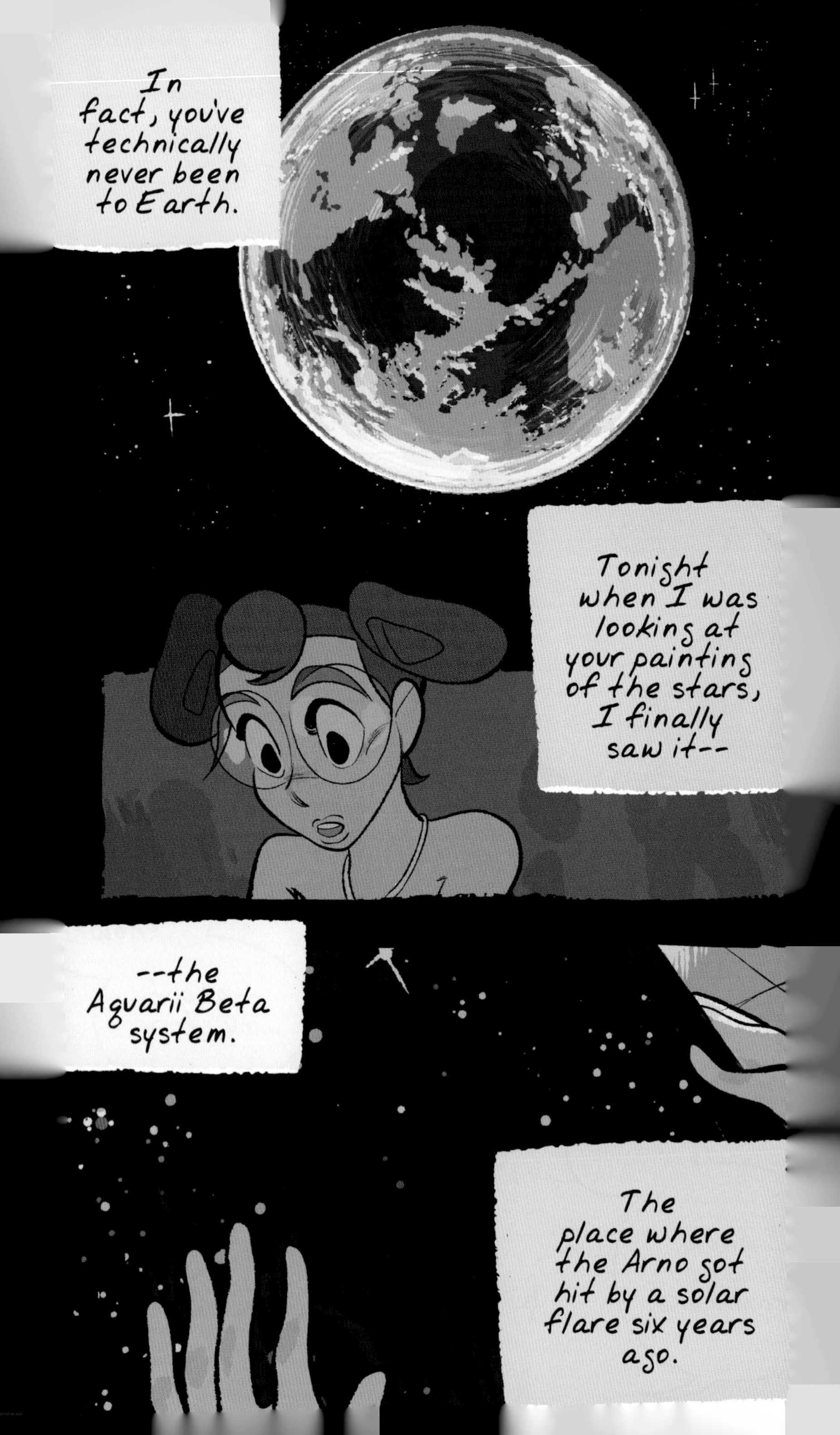
In fact, you've technically never been to Earth.
Tonight when I was looking at your paintings of the stars, I finally saw it--
--the Aquarii Beta system.
The place where the Arno got hit by a solar flare six years ago.

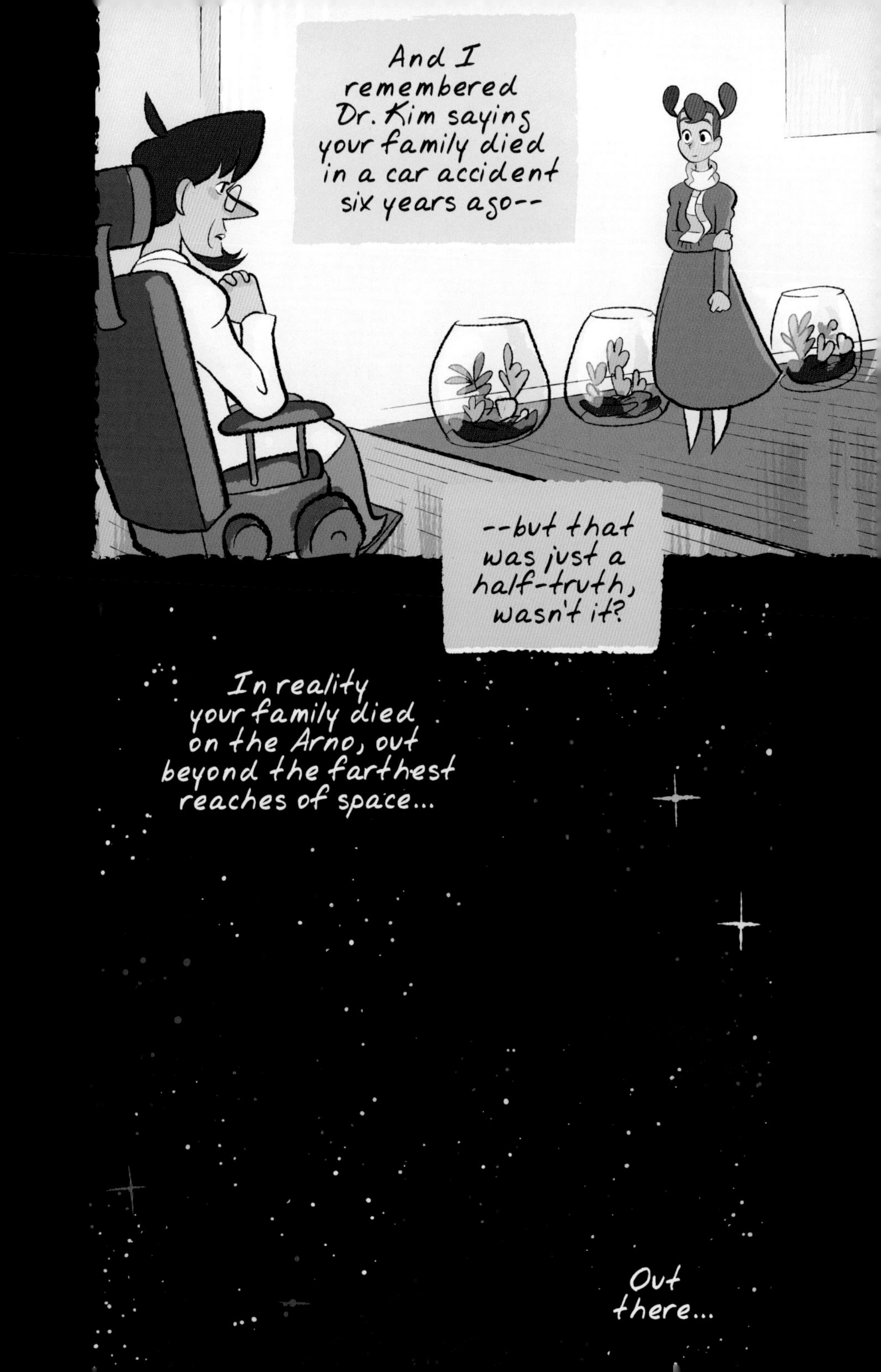
And I remembered Dr. Kim saying your family died in a car accident six years ago--
--but that was just a half-truth, wasn't it?
In reality your family died on the Arno, out beyond the farthest reaches of space...
Out there...

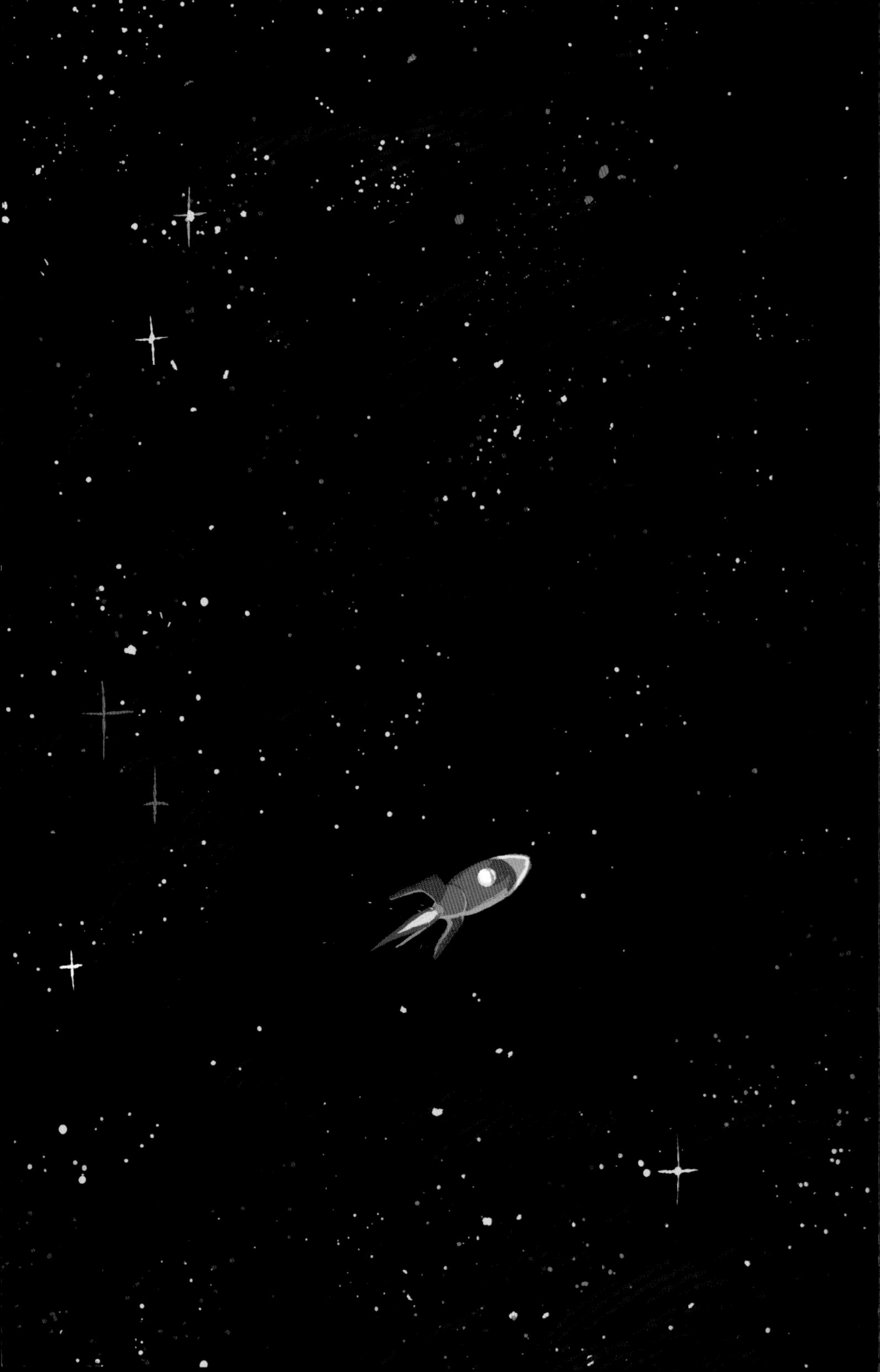

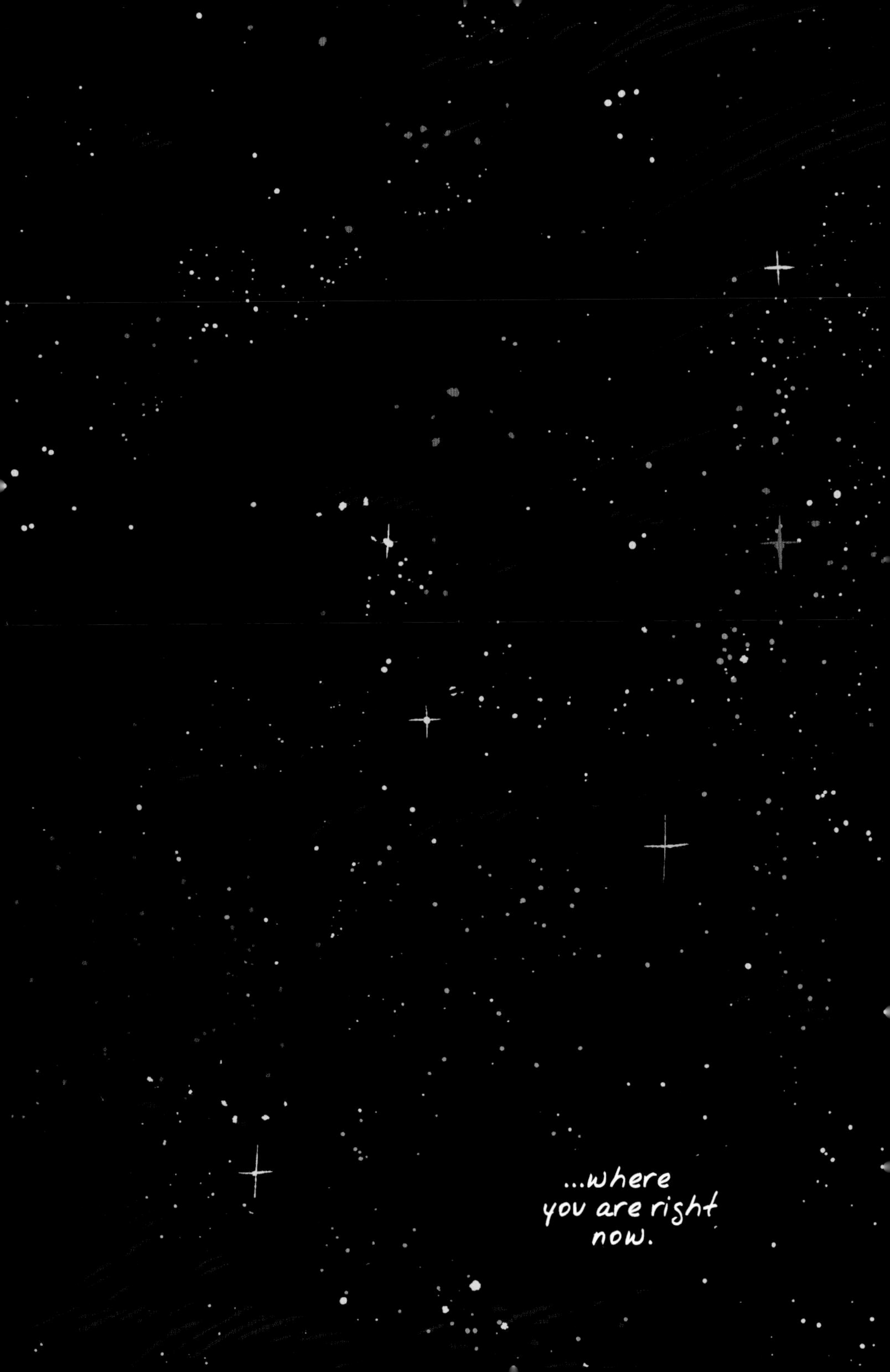
...where
you are right
now.

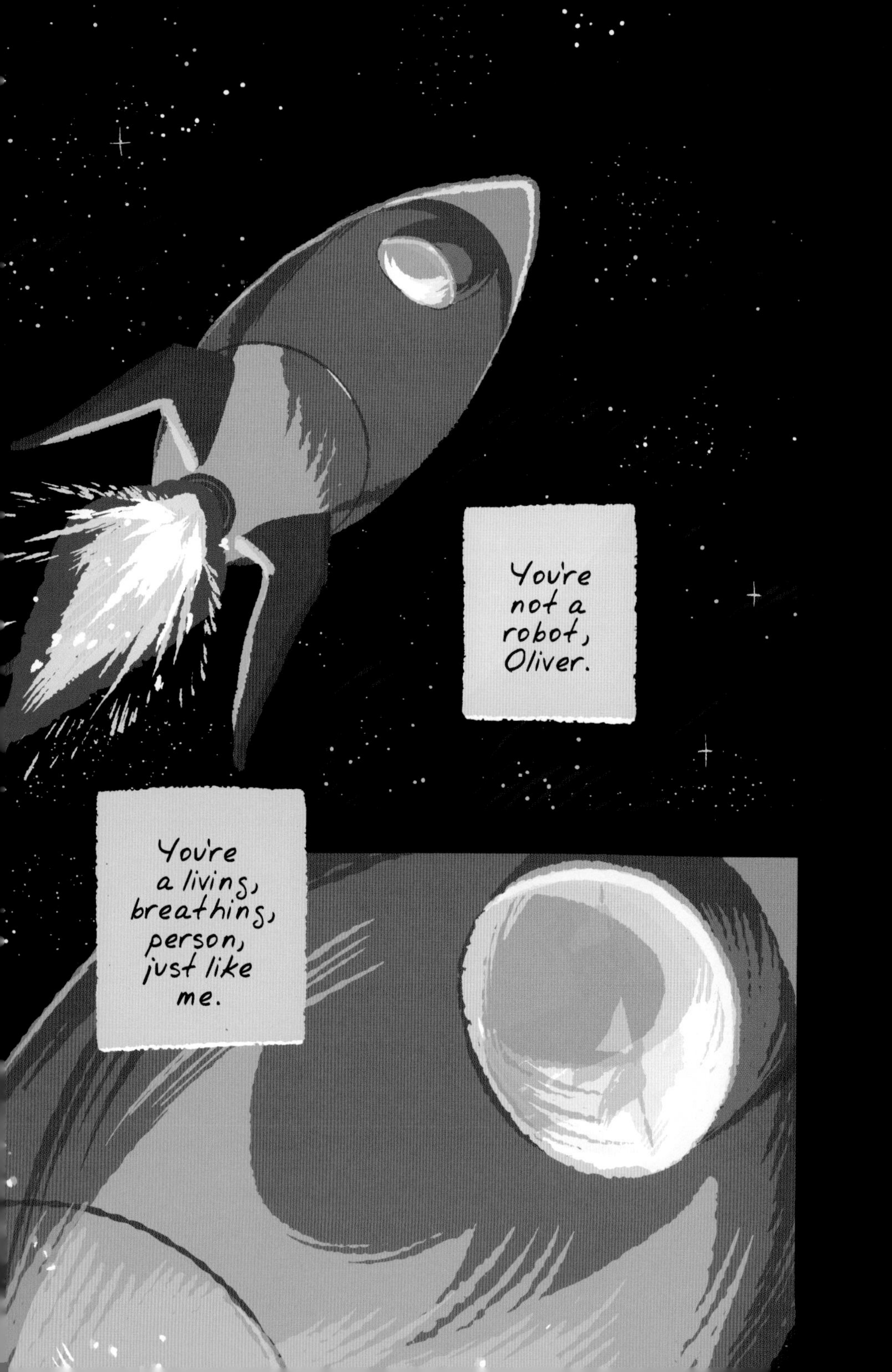
You're not a robot, Oliver.
You're a living, breathing, person, just like me.

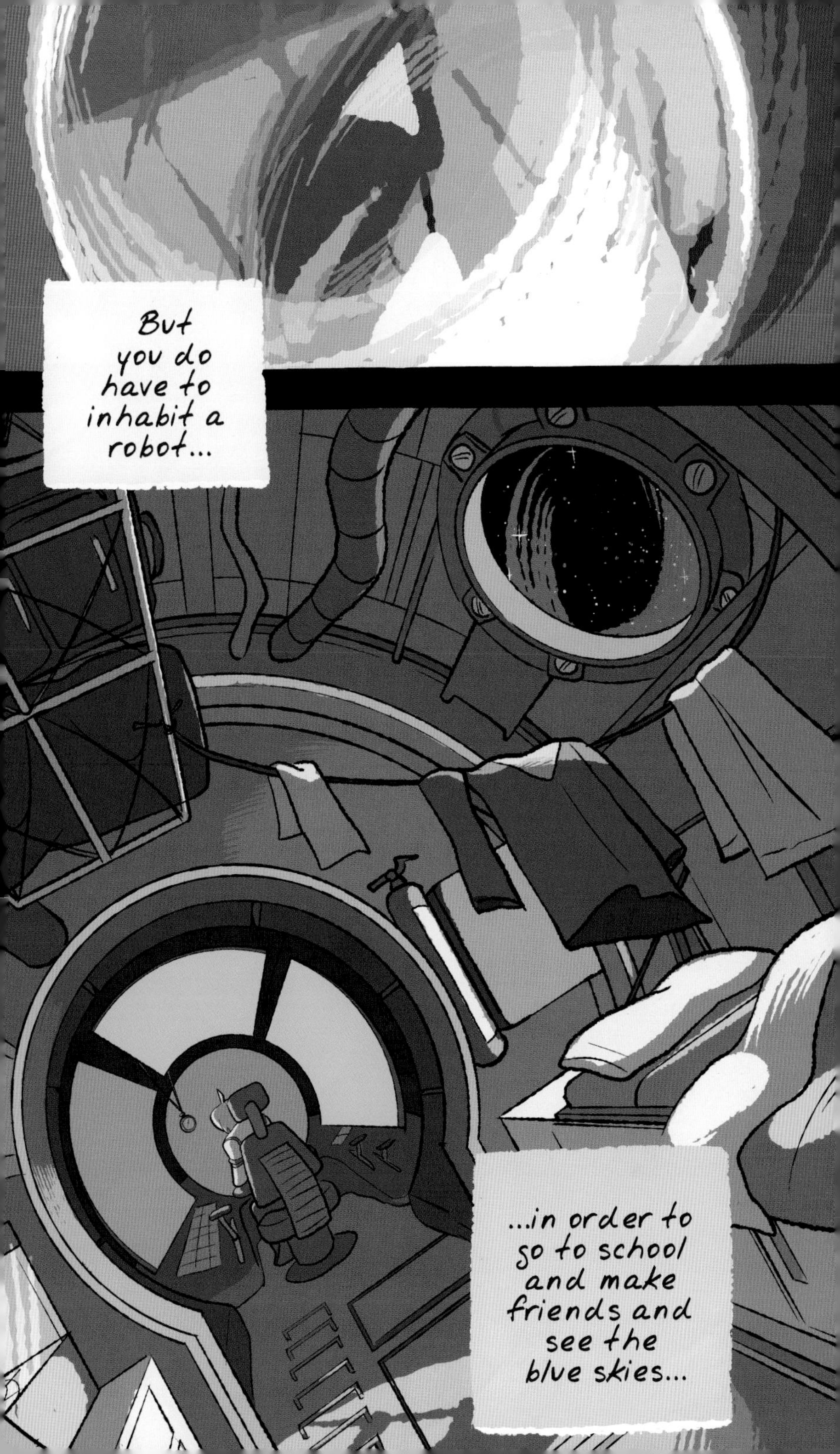
But you do have to inhabit a robot...
...in order to go to school and make friends and see the blue skies...

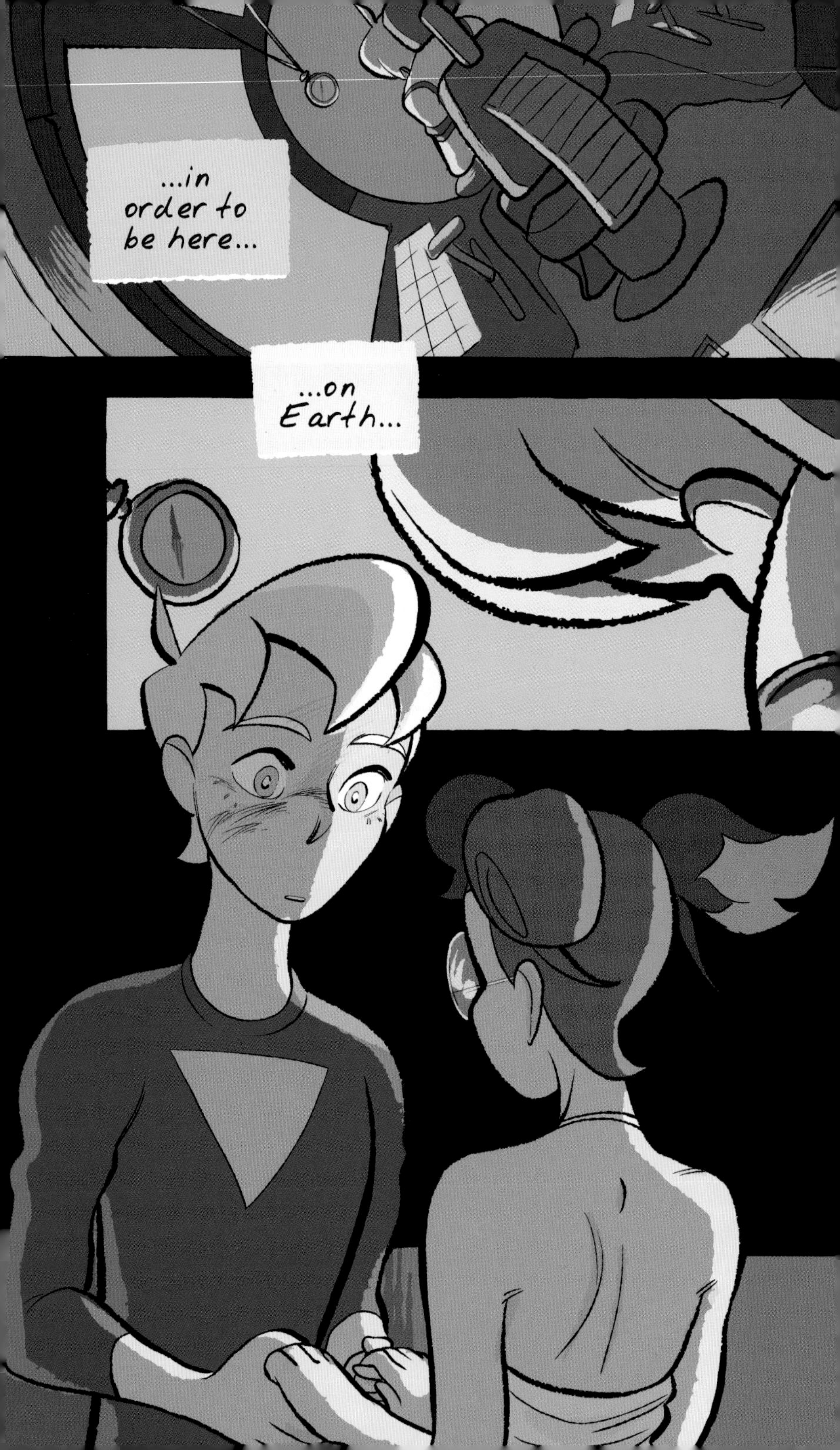
...in order to be here...
...on Earth...

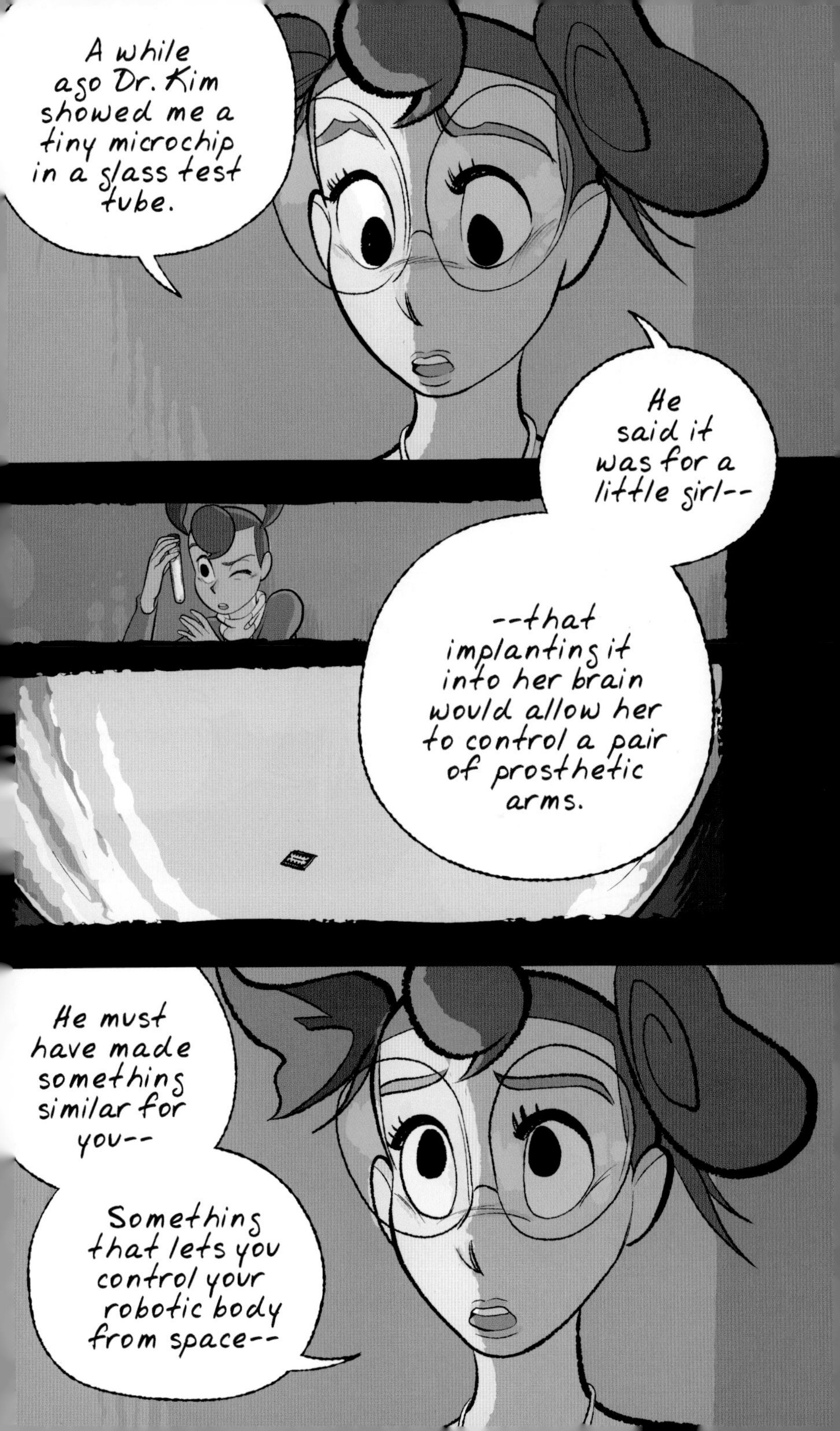
A while ago Dr. Kim showed me a tiny microchip in a glass test tube.
He said it was for a little girl--
--that implanting it into her brain would allow her to control a pair of prosthetic arms.
He must have made something similar for you--
Something that lets you control your robotic body from space--

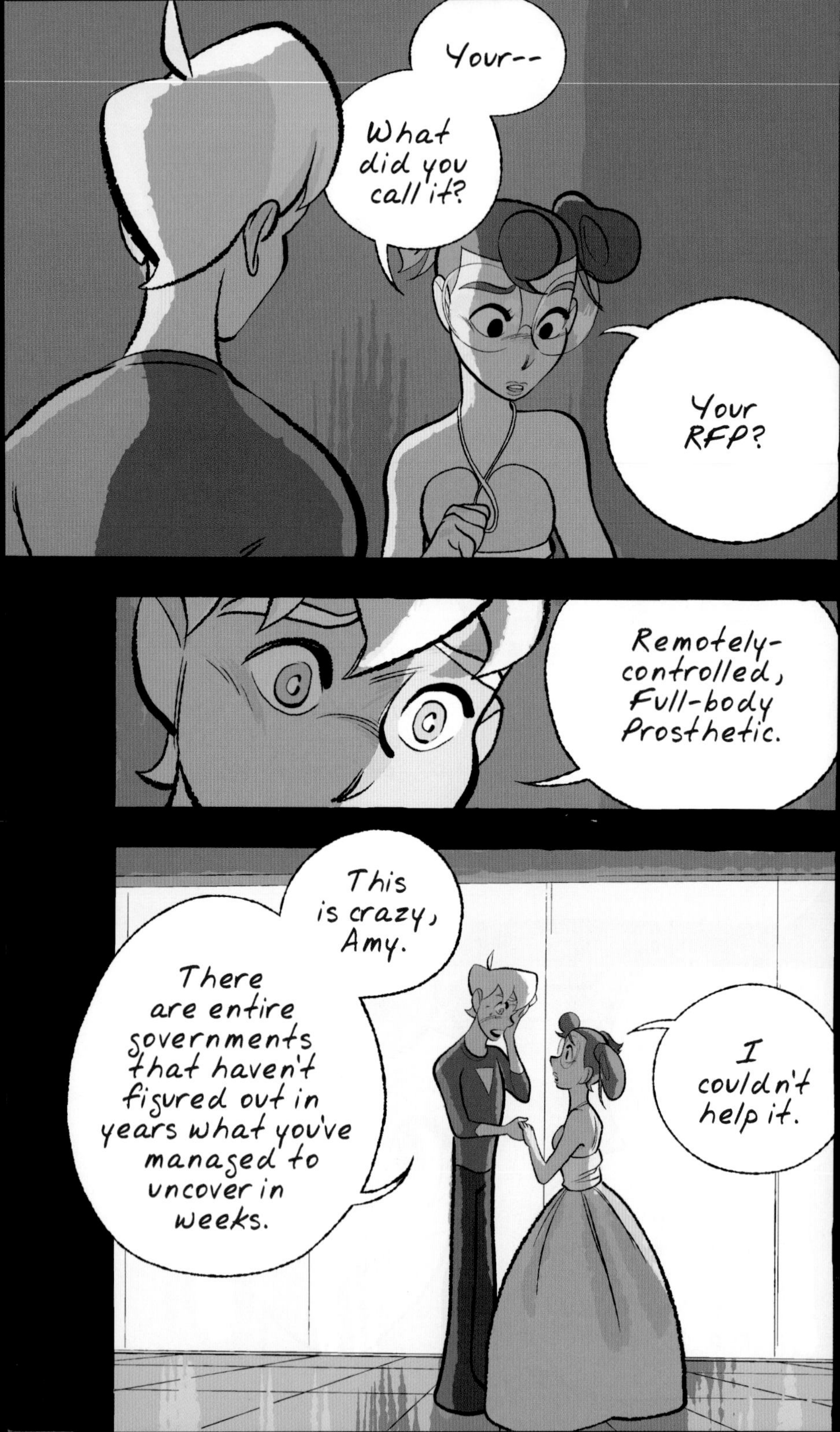
Your--
What did you call it?
Your RFP?
Remotely-controlled, Full-body Prosthetic.
This is crazy, Amy.
There are entire governments that haven't figured out in years what you've managed to uncover in weeks.
I couldn't help it.

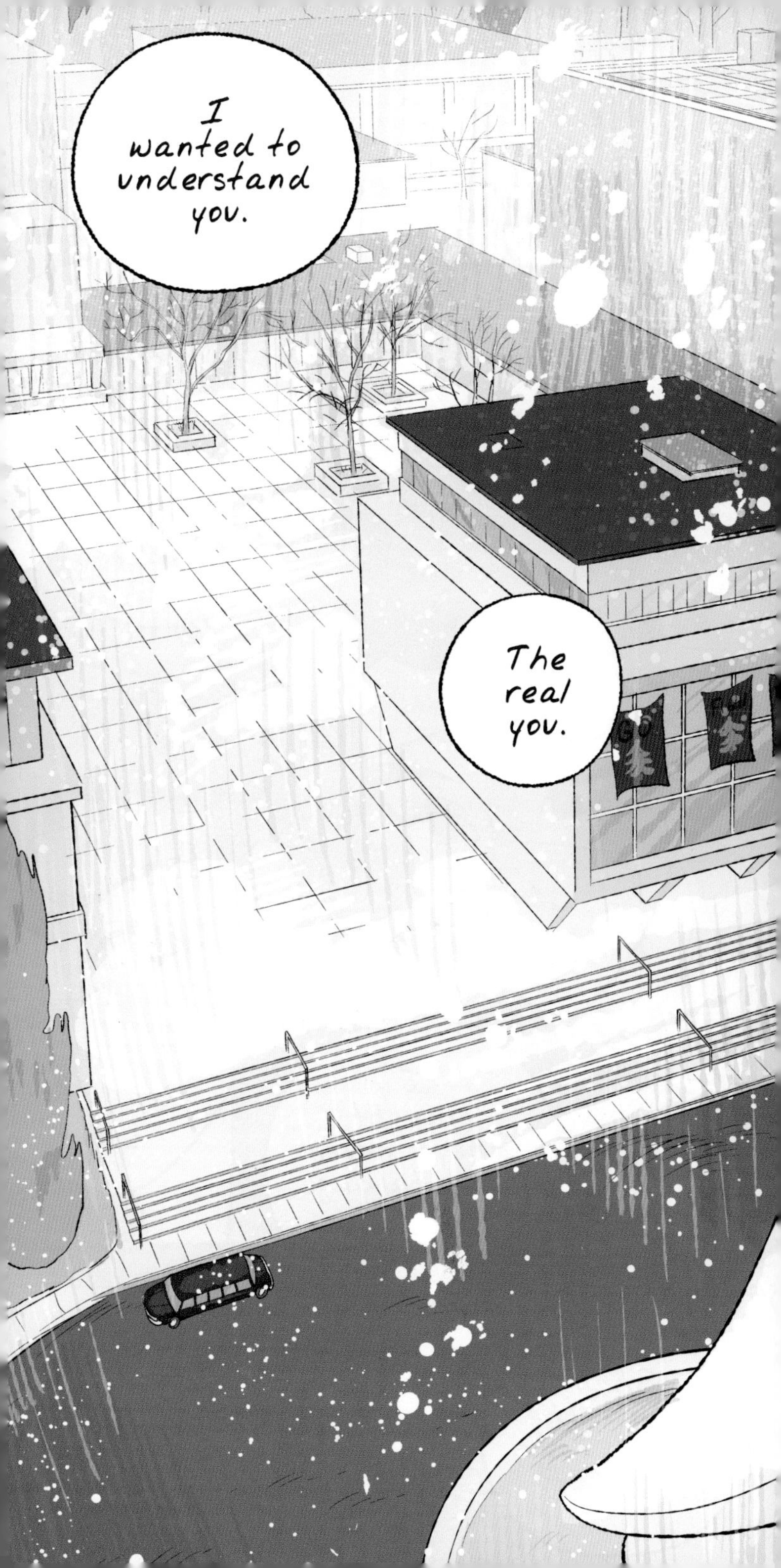
I wanted to understand you.
The real you.

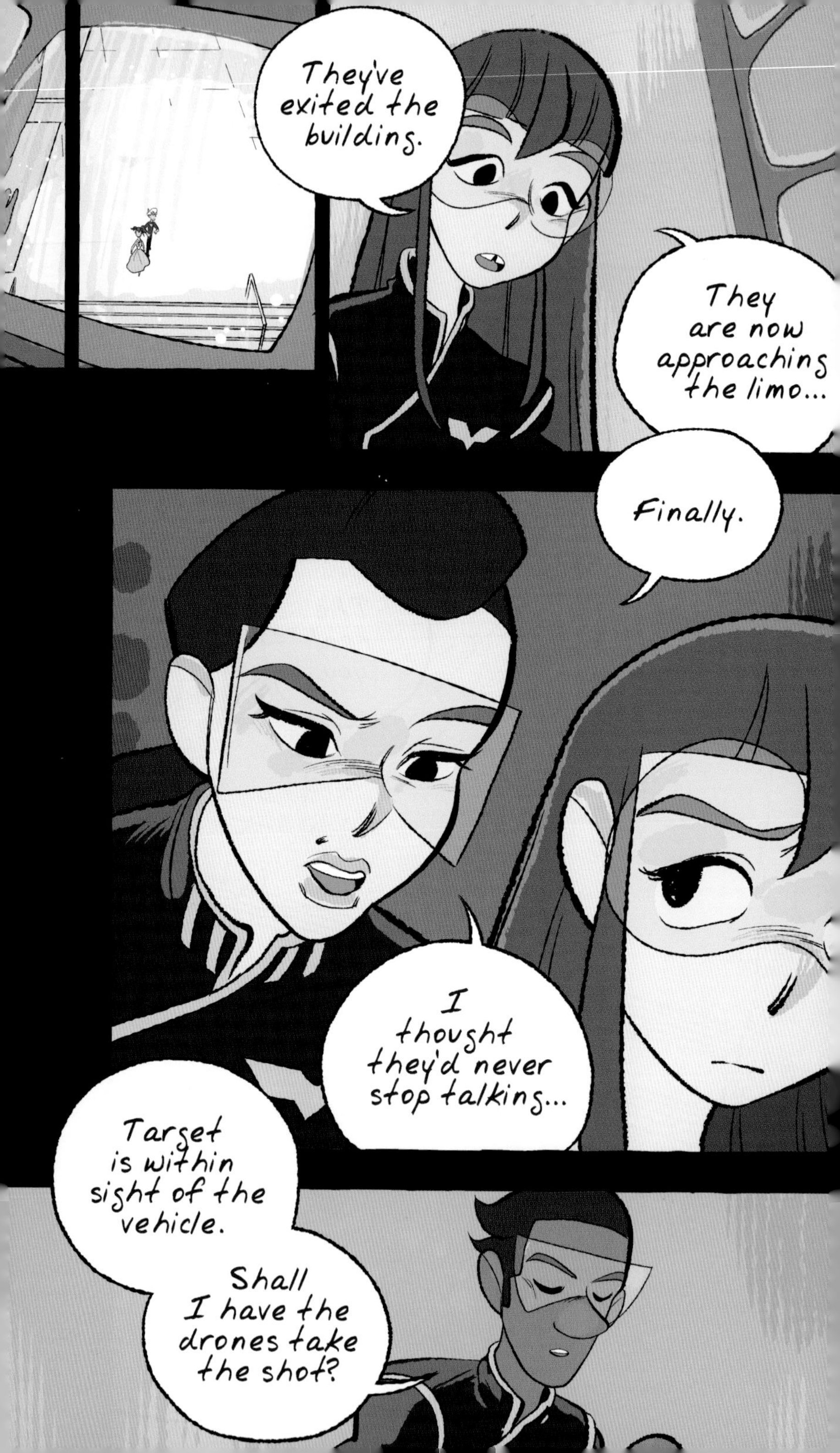
They've exited the building.
They are now approaching the limo...
Finally.
I thought they'd never stop talking...
Target is within sight of the vehicle.
Shall I have the drones take the shot?

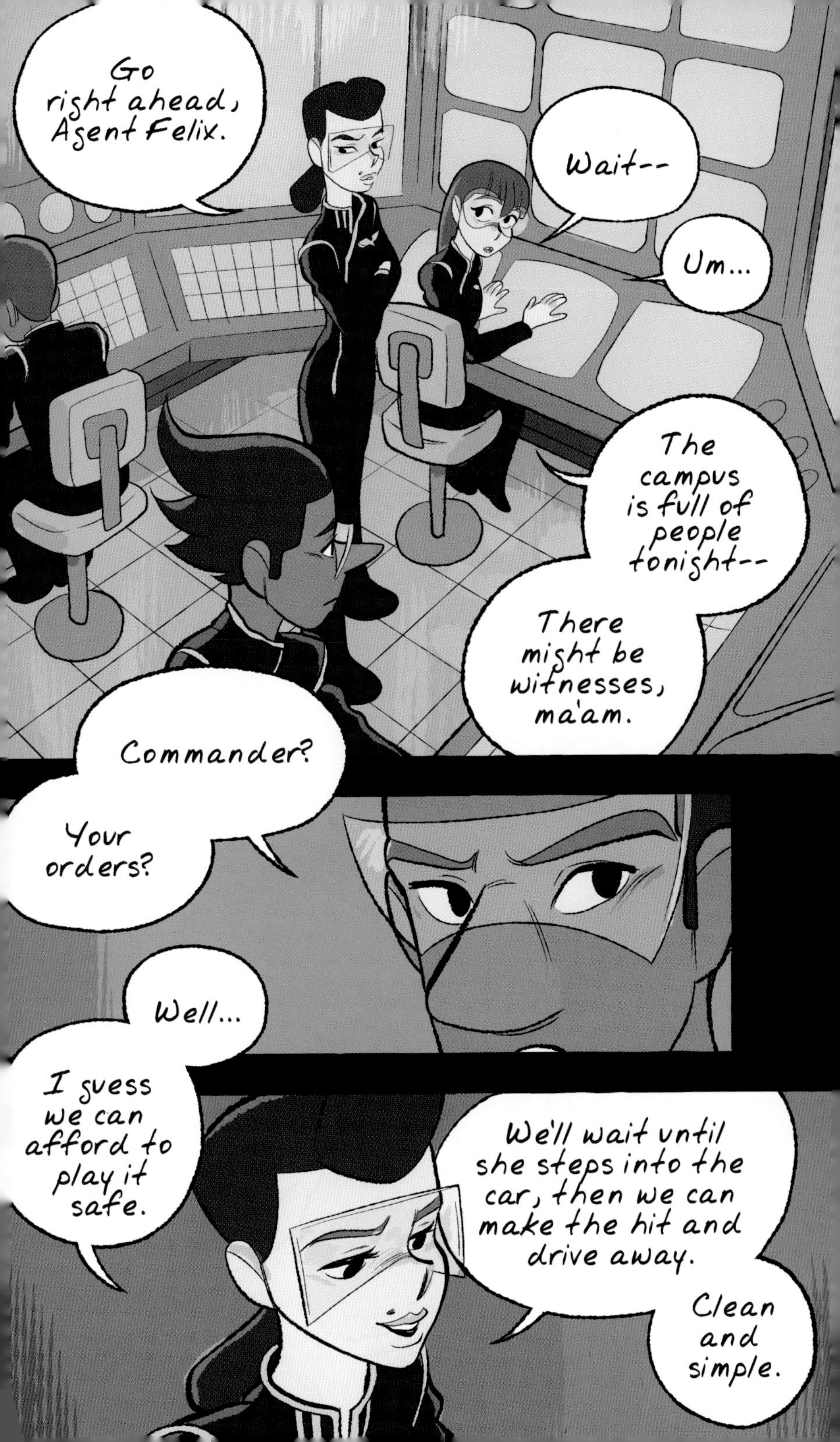
Go right ahead, Agent Felix.
Wait--
Um...
The campus is full of people tonight--
There might be witnesses, ma'am.
Commander?
Your orders?
Well...
I guess we can afford to play it safe.
We'll wait until she steps into the car, then we can make the hit and drive away.
Clean and simple.

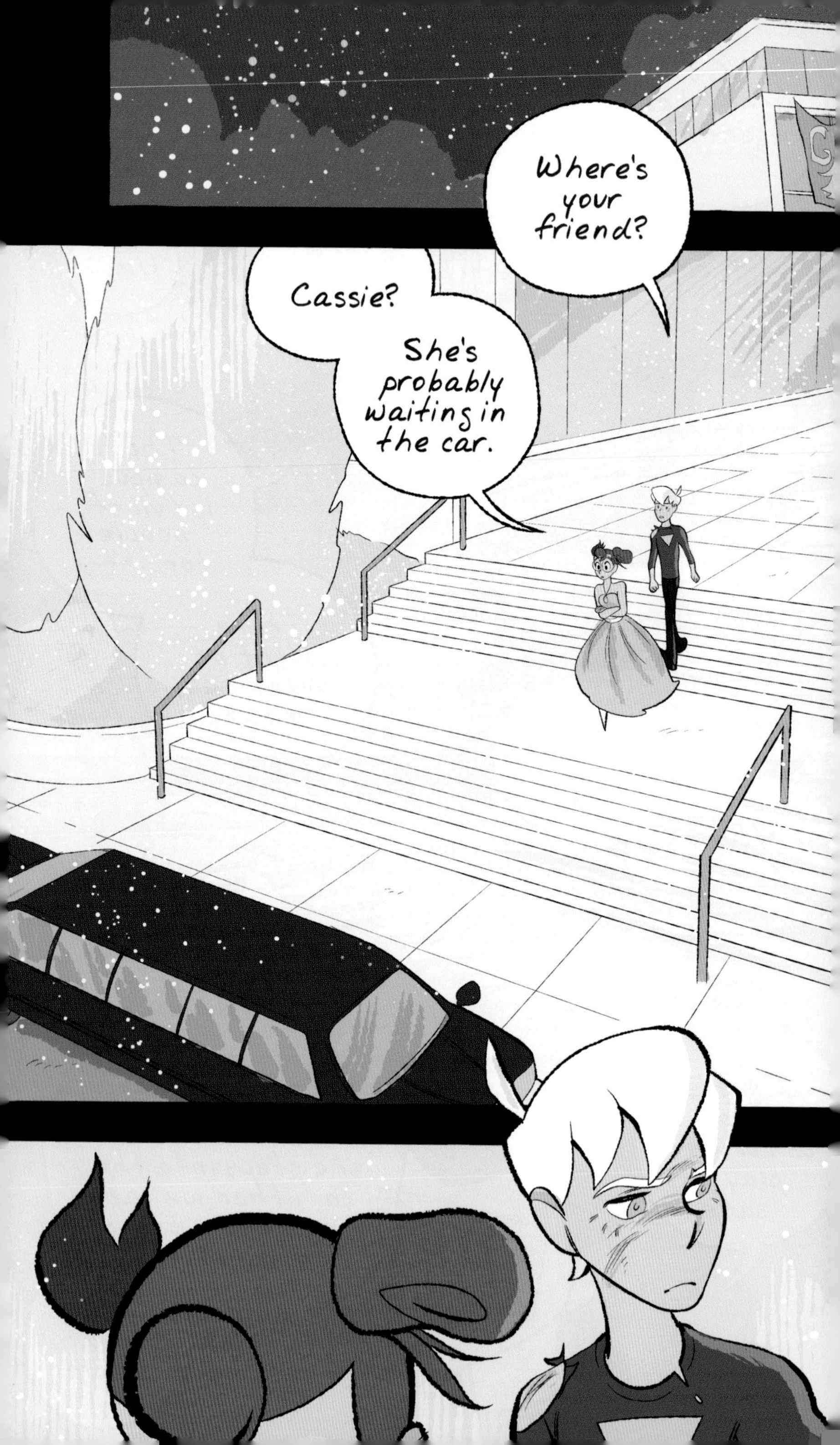
Where's your friend?
Cassie?
She's probably waiting in the car.

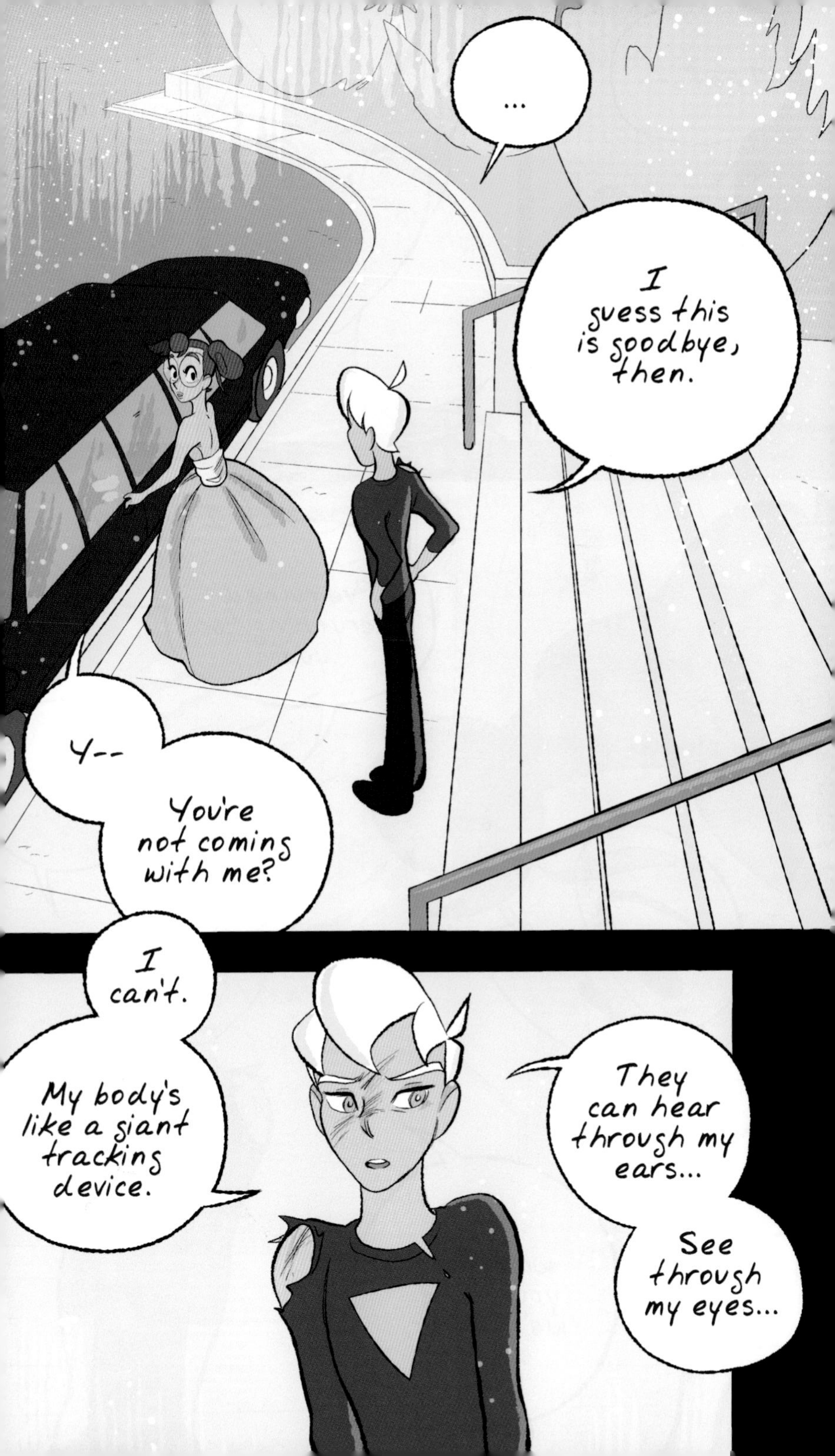
...
I guess this is goodbye, then.
Y--
You're not coming with me?
I can't.
My body's like a giant tracking device.
They can hear through my ears...
See through my eyes...

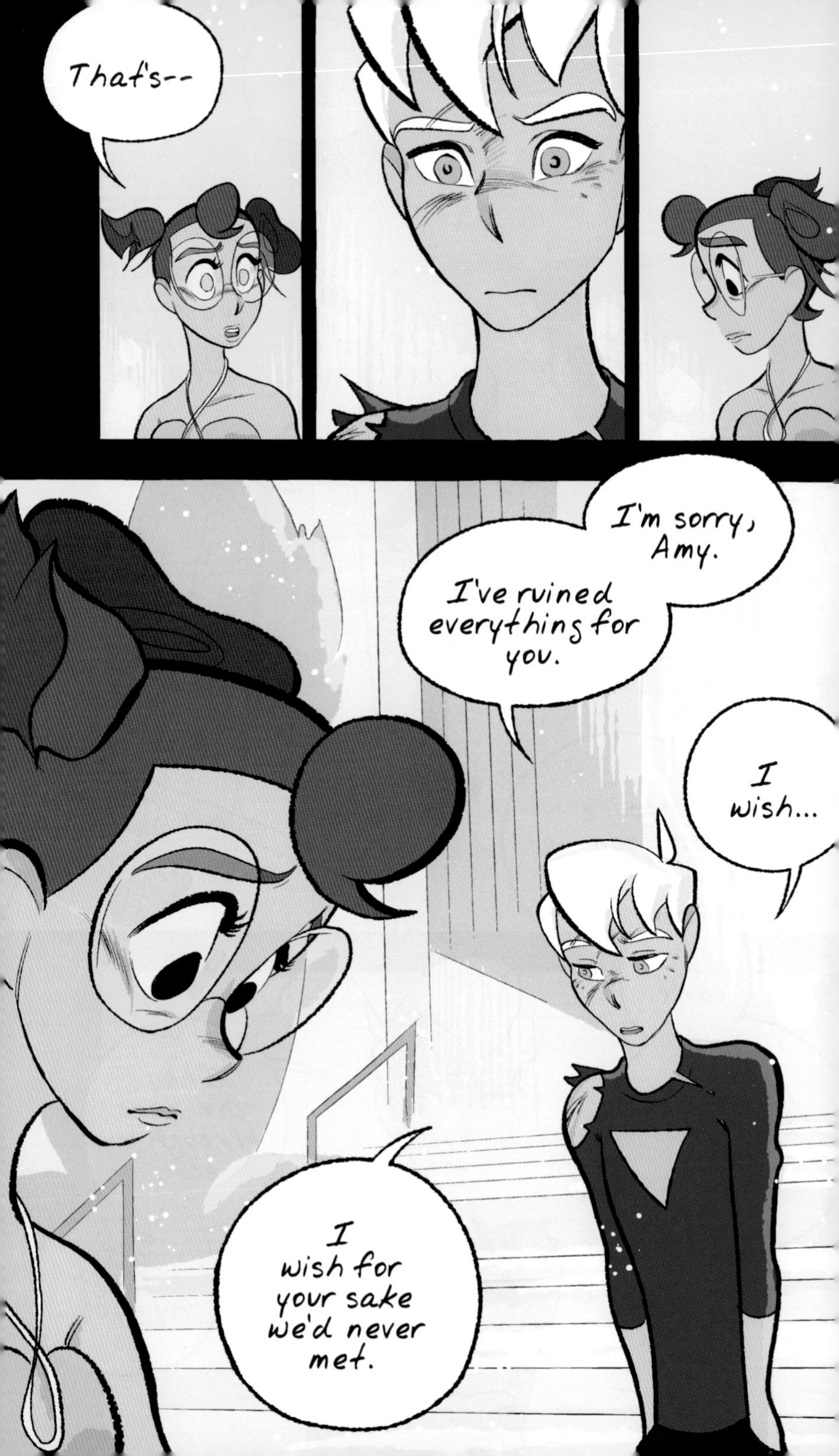
That's--
I'm sorry, Amy.
I've ruined everything for you.
I wish...
I wish for your sake we'd never met.

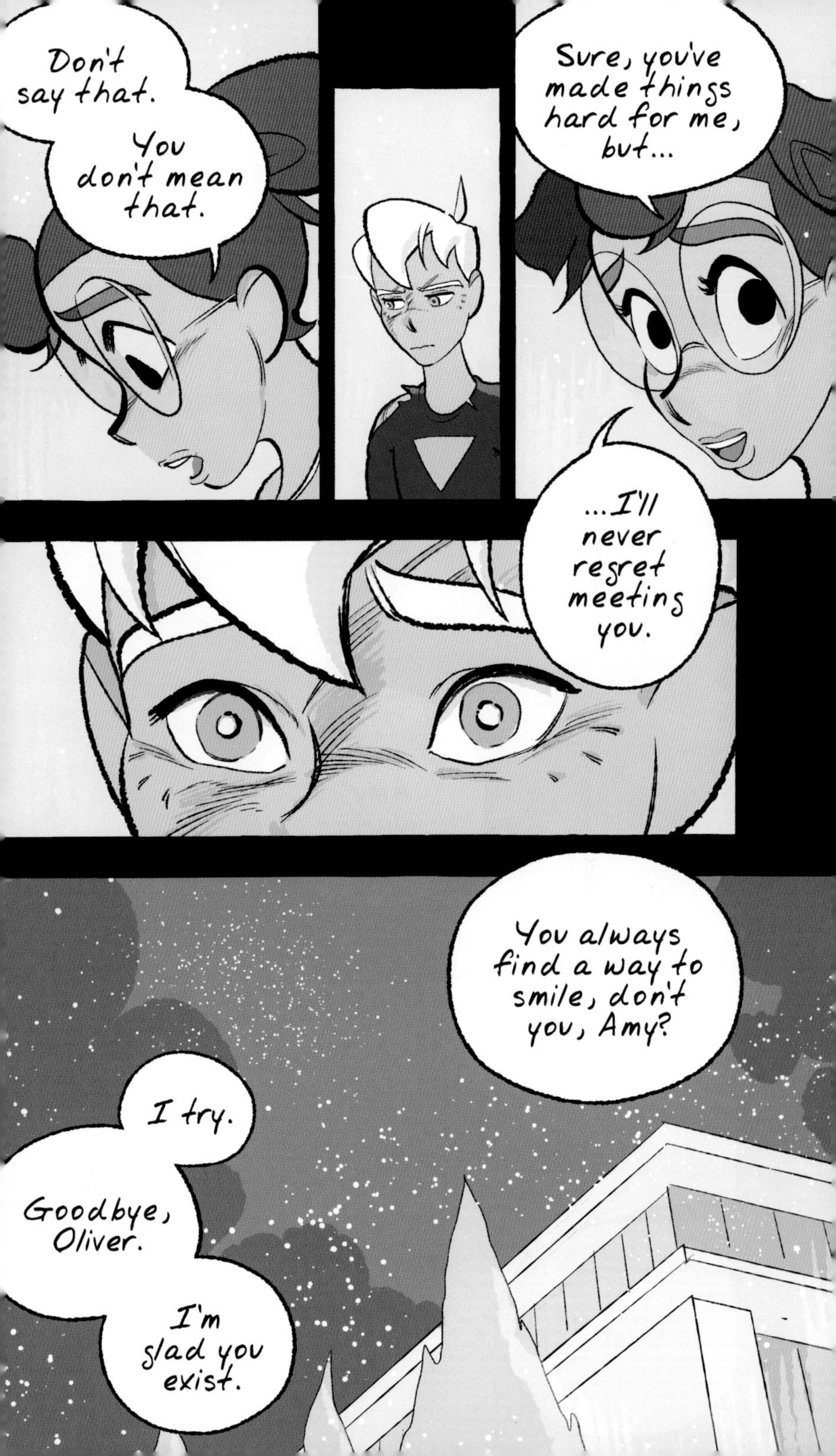
Don't say that.
You don't mean that.
Sure, you've made things hard for me, but...
...I'll never regret meeting you.
You always find a way to smile, don't you, Amy?
I try.
Goodbye, Oliver.
I'm glad you exist.

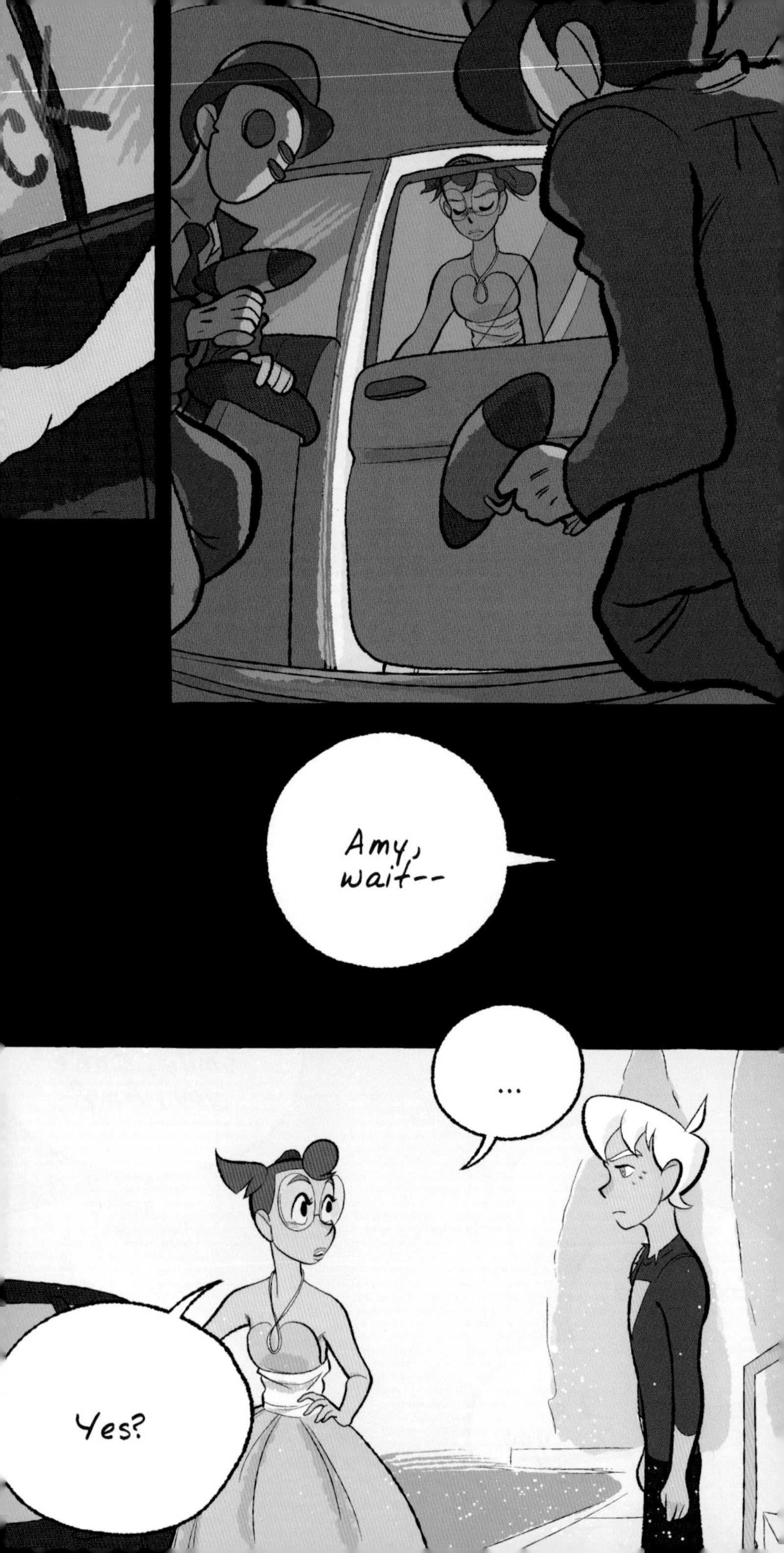
Amy,
wait--
...
Yes?

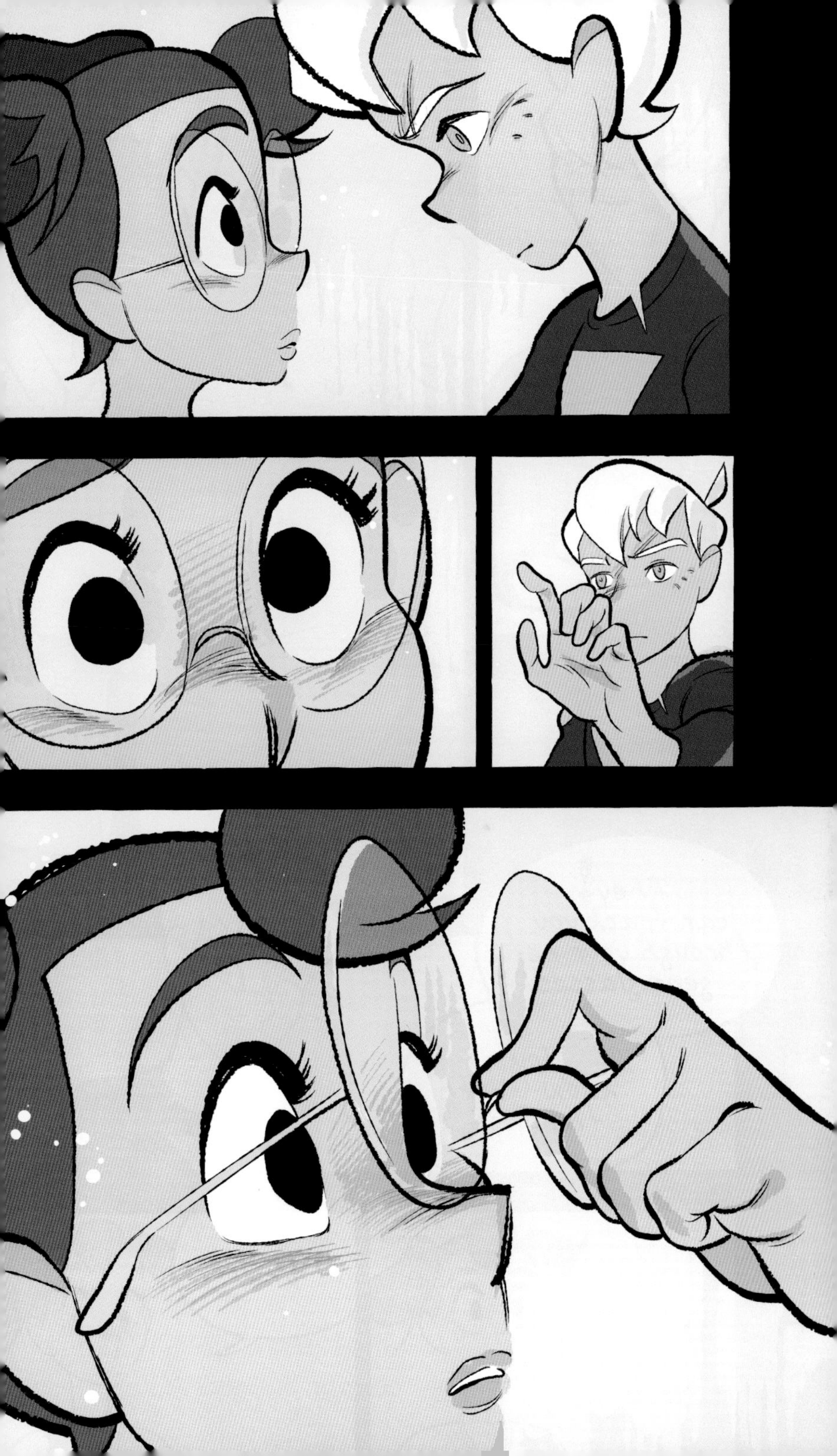

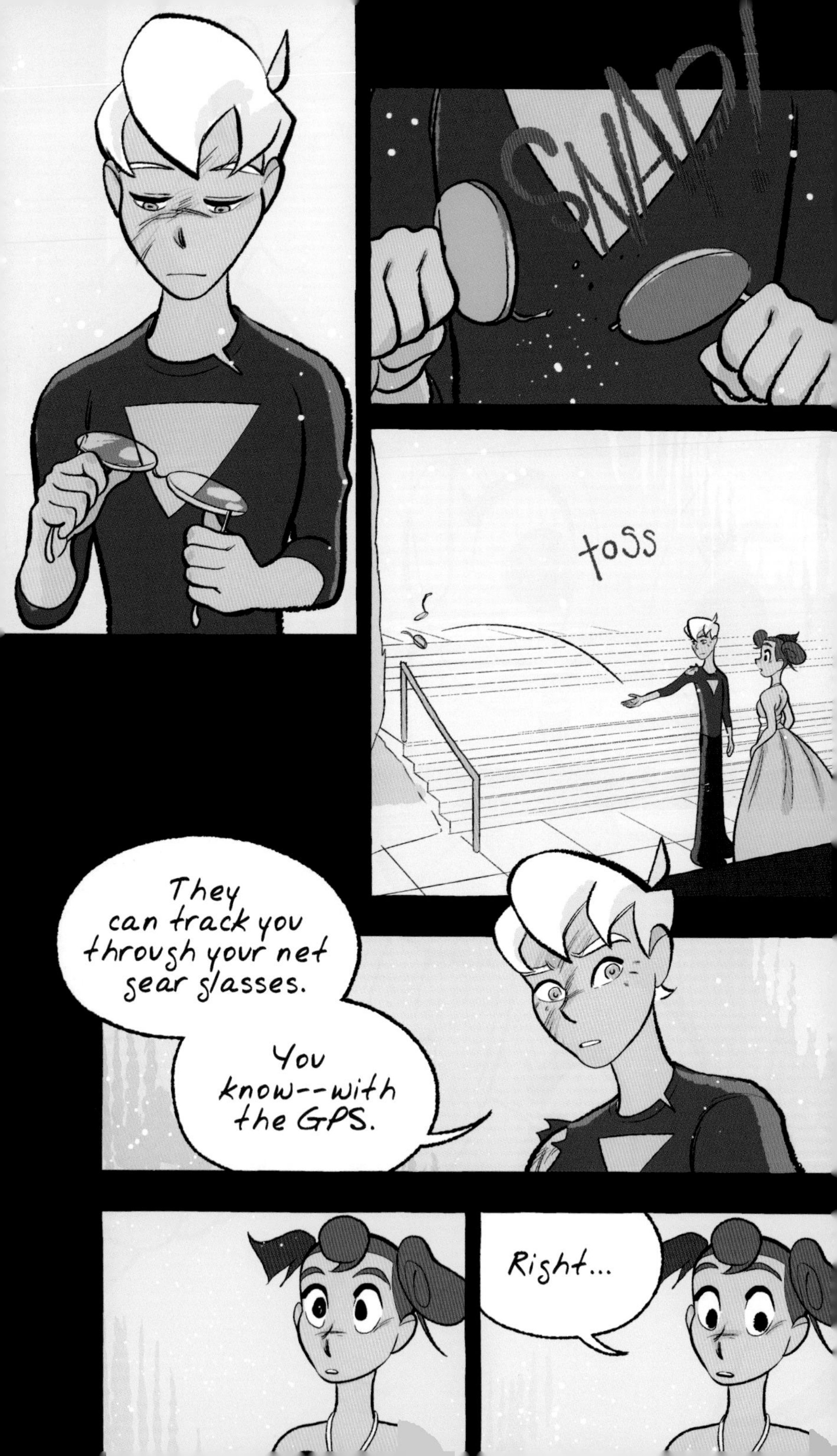
SNAP!
toss
They can track you through your net gear glasses.
You know--with the GPS.
Right...

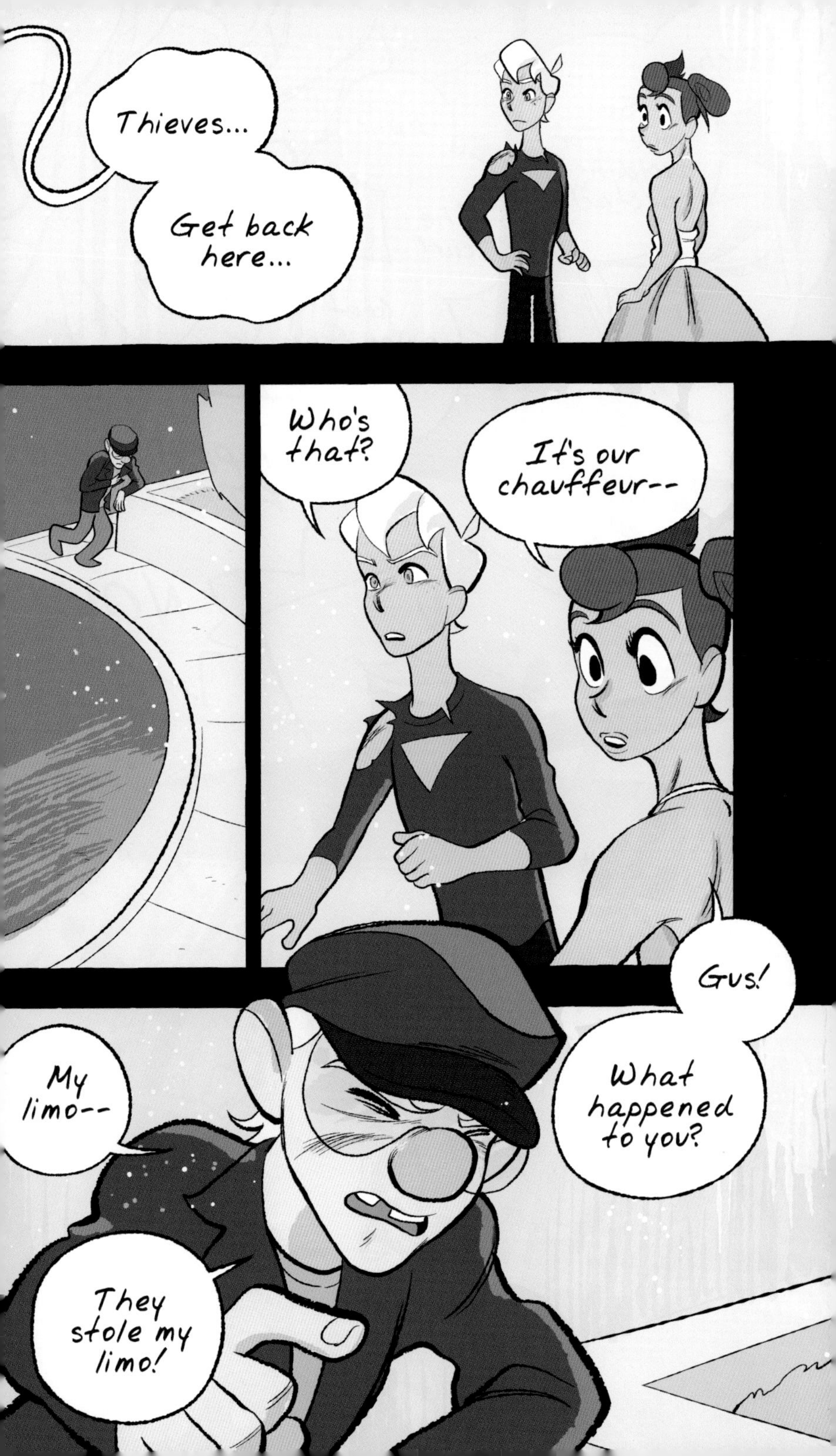
Thieves...
Get back here...
Who's that?
It's our chauffeur--
Gus!
What happened to you?
My limo--
They stole my limo!

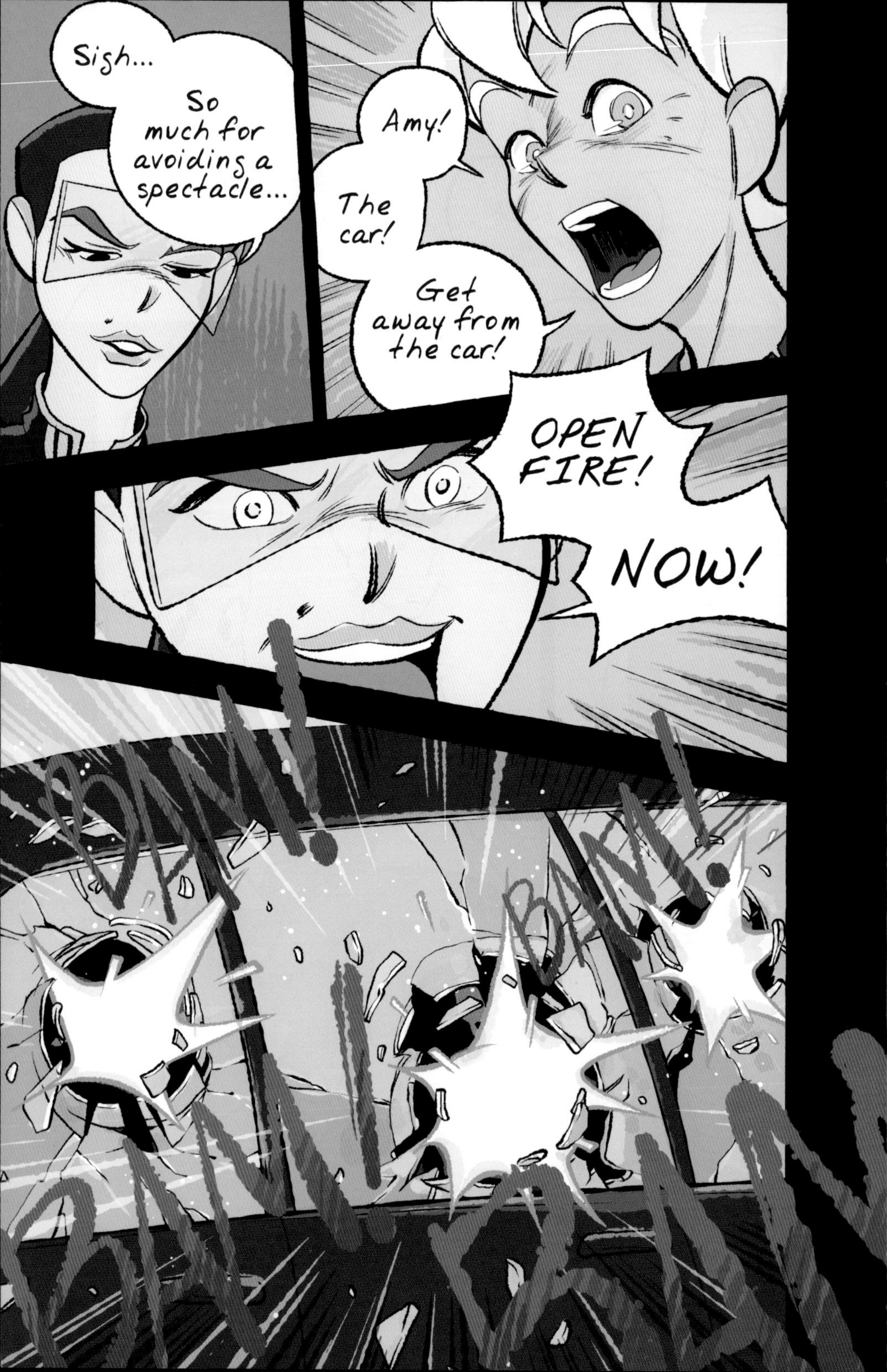
Sigh...
So much for avoiding a spectacle...
Amy!
The car!
Get away from the car!
OPEN FIRE!
NOW!
BAM!
BAM!

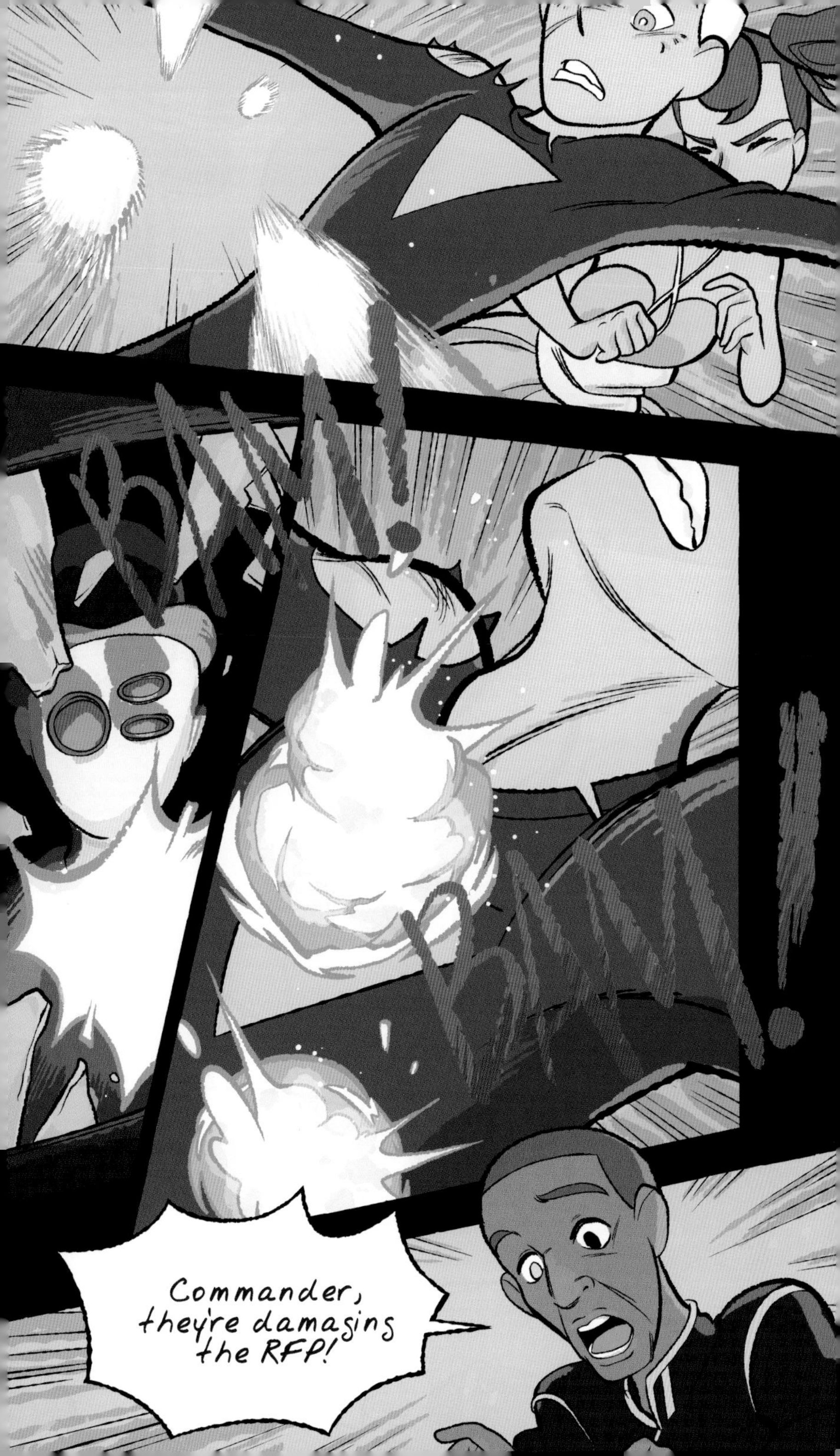
BAM!
BAM!
Commander, they're damaging the RFP!

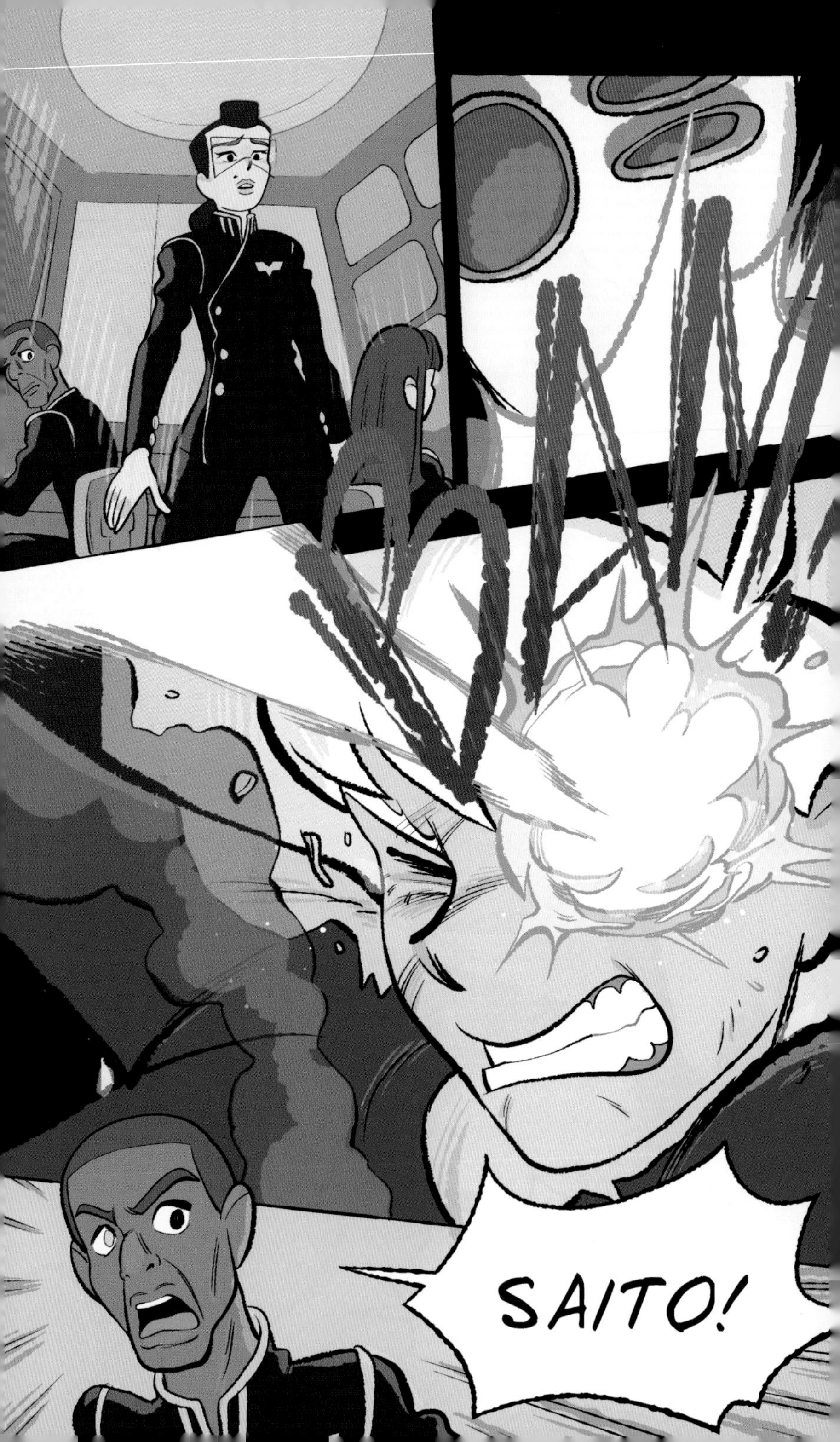
SAITO!

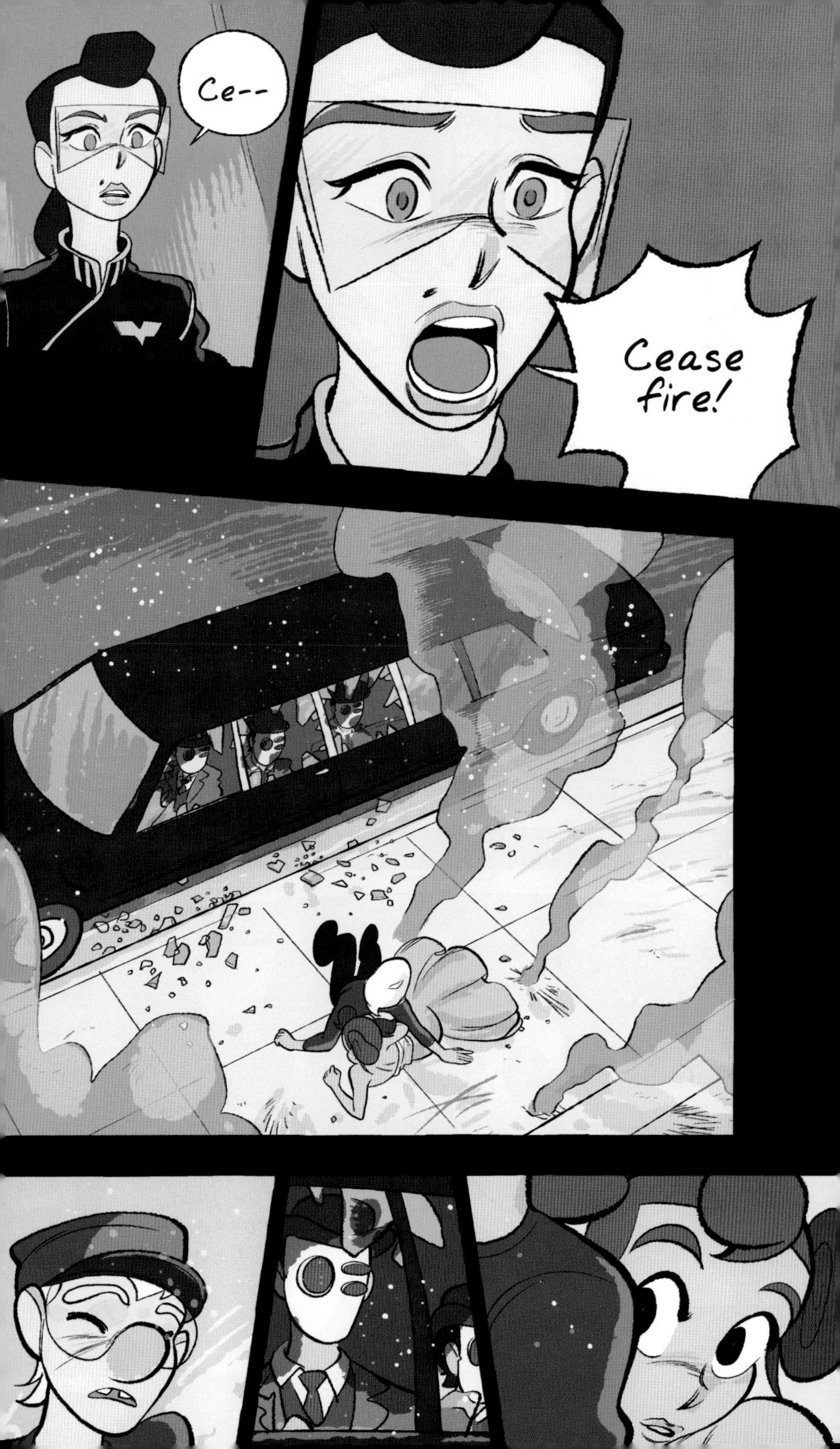
Ce--
Cease fire!

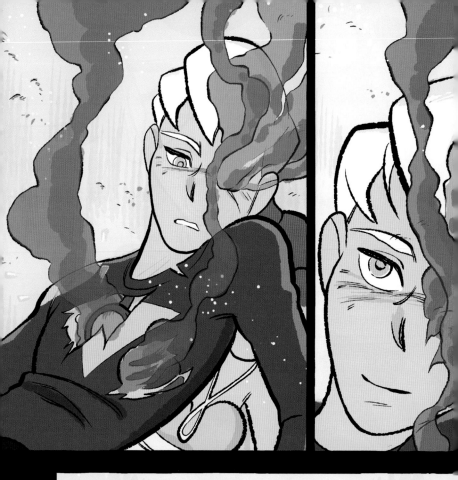

You just crossed a line, Saito.

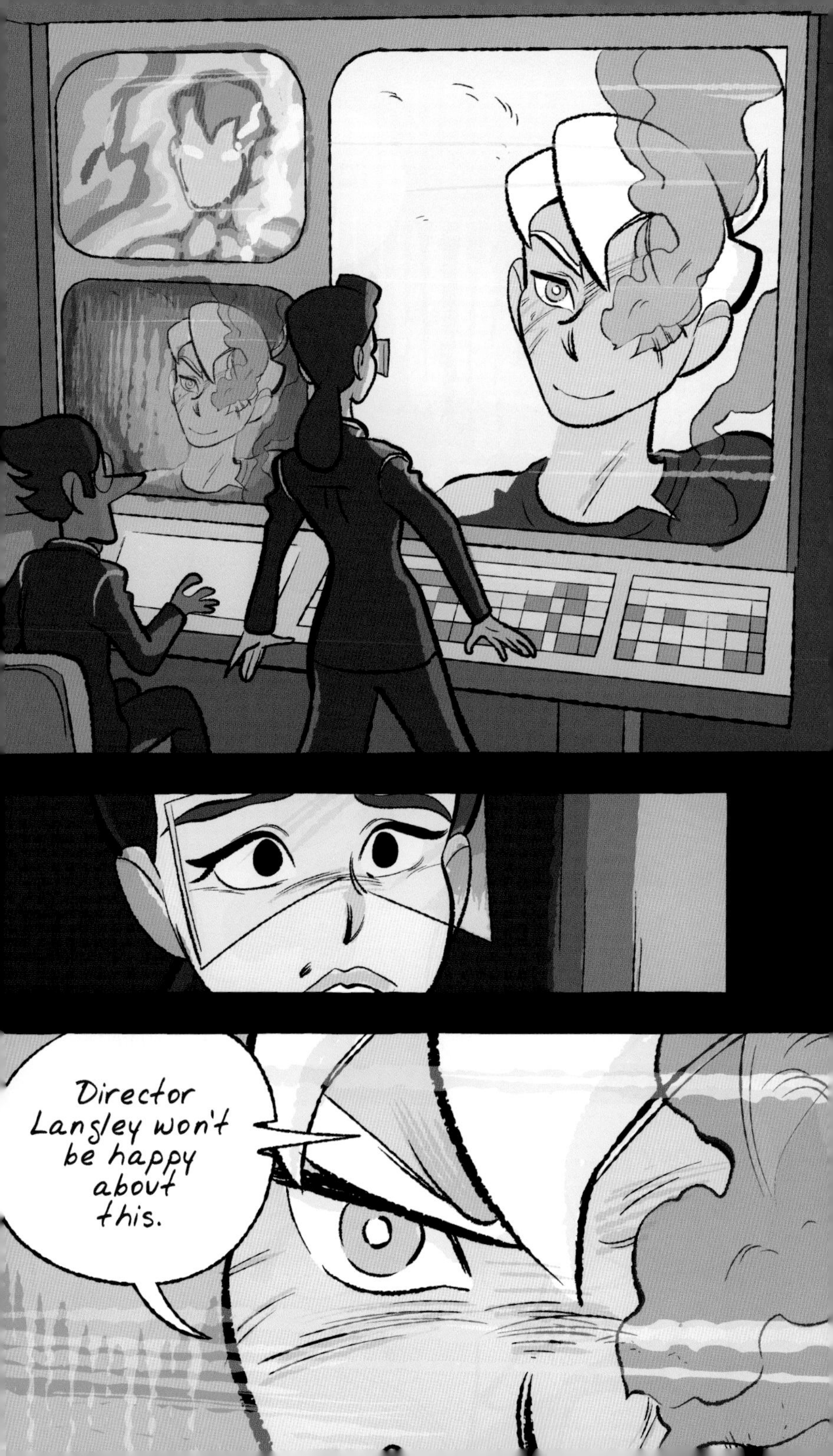
Director Langley won't be happy about this.

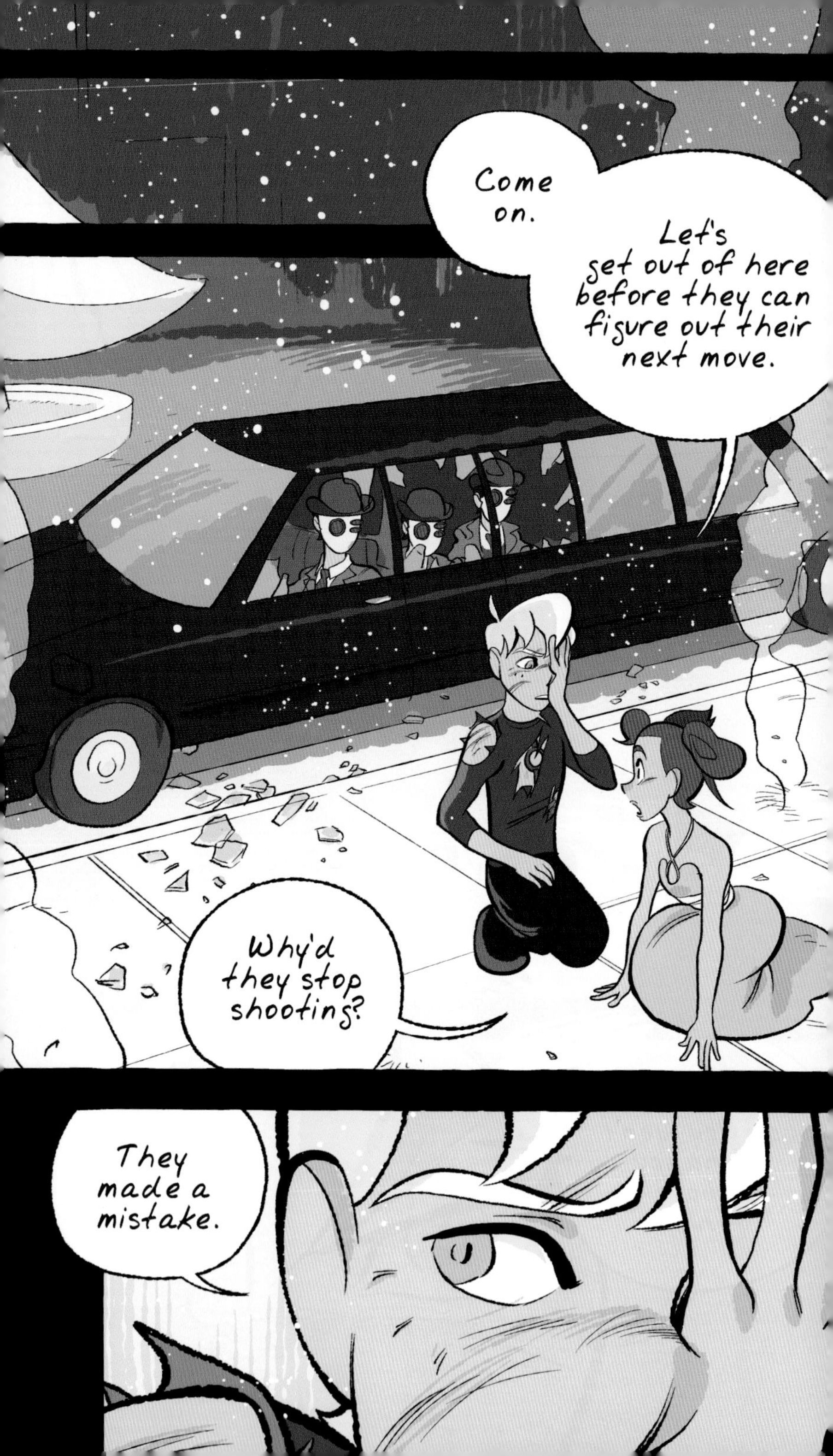
Come on.
Let's get out of here before they can figure out their next move.
Why'd they stop shooting?
They made a mistake.

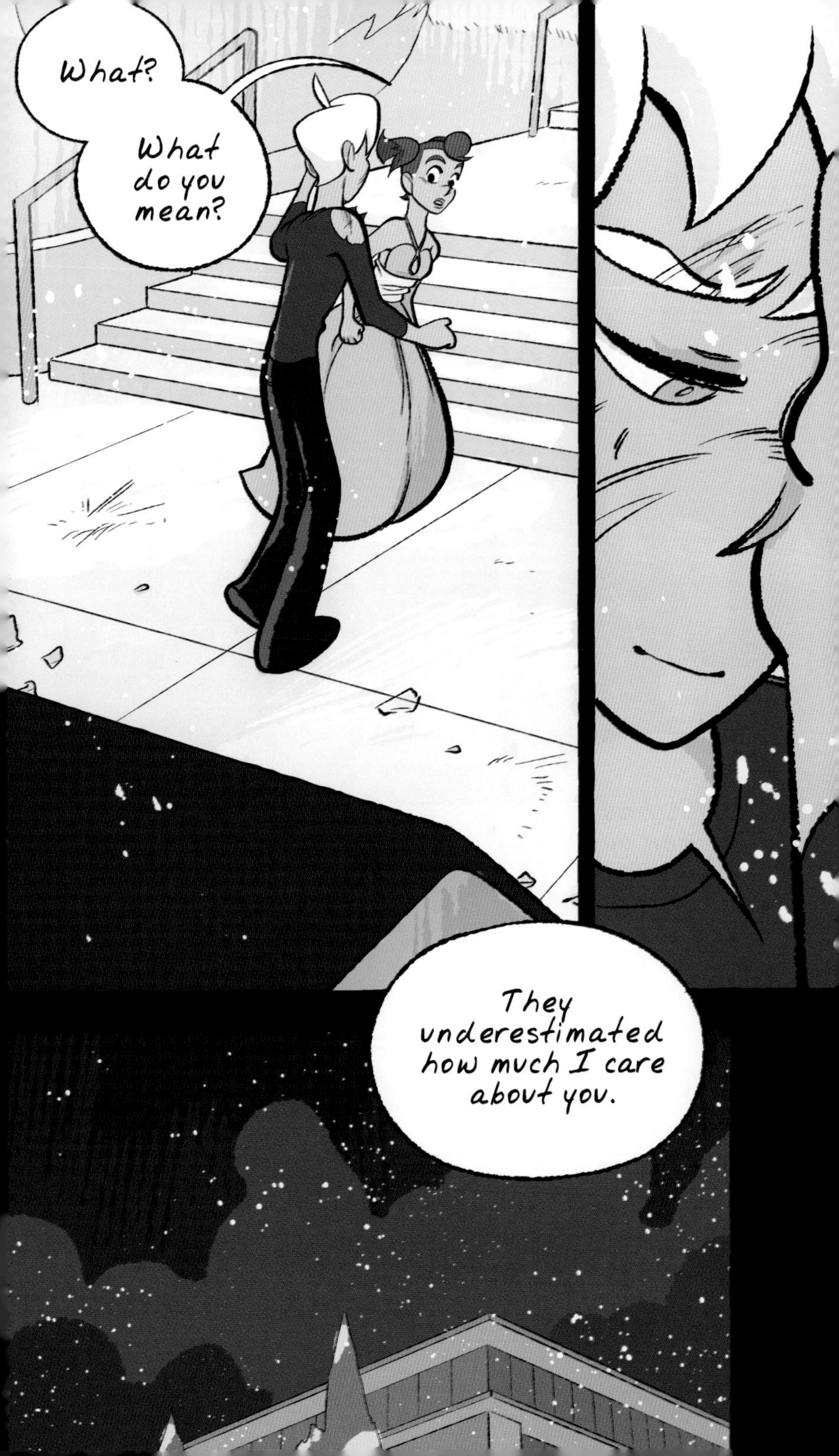
What?
What do you mean?
They underestimated how much I care about you.

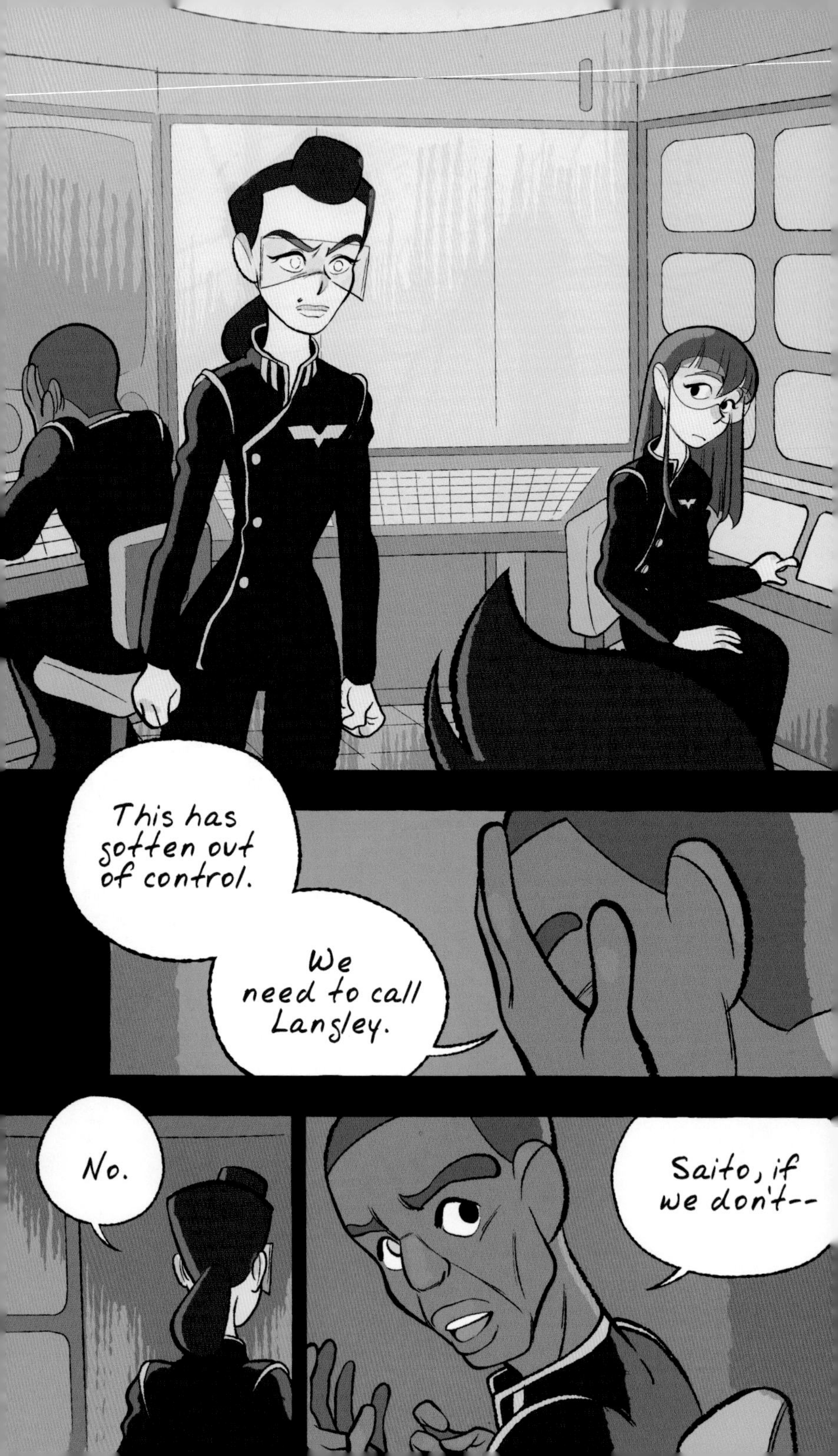
This has gotten out of control.
We need to call Langley.
No.
Saito, if we don't--

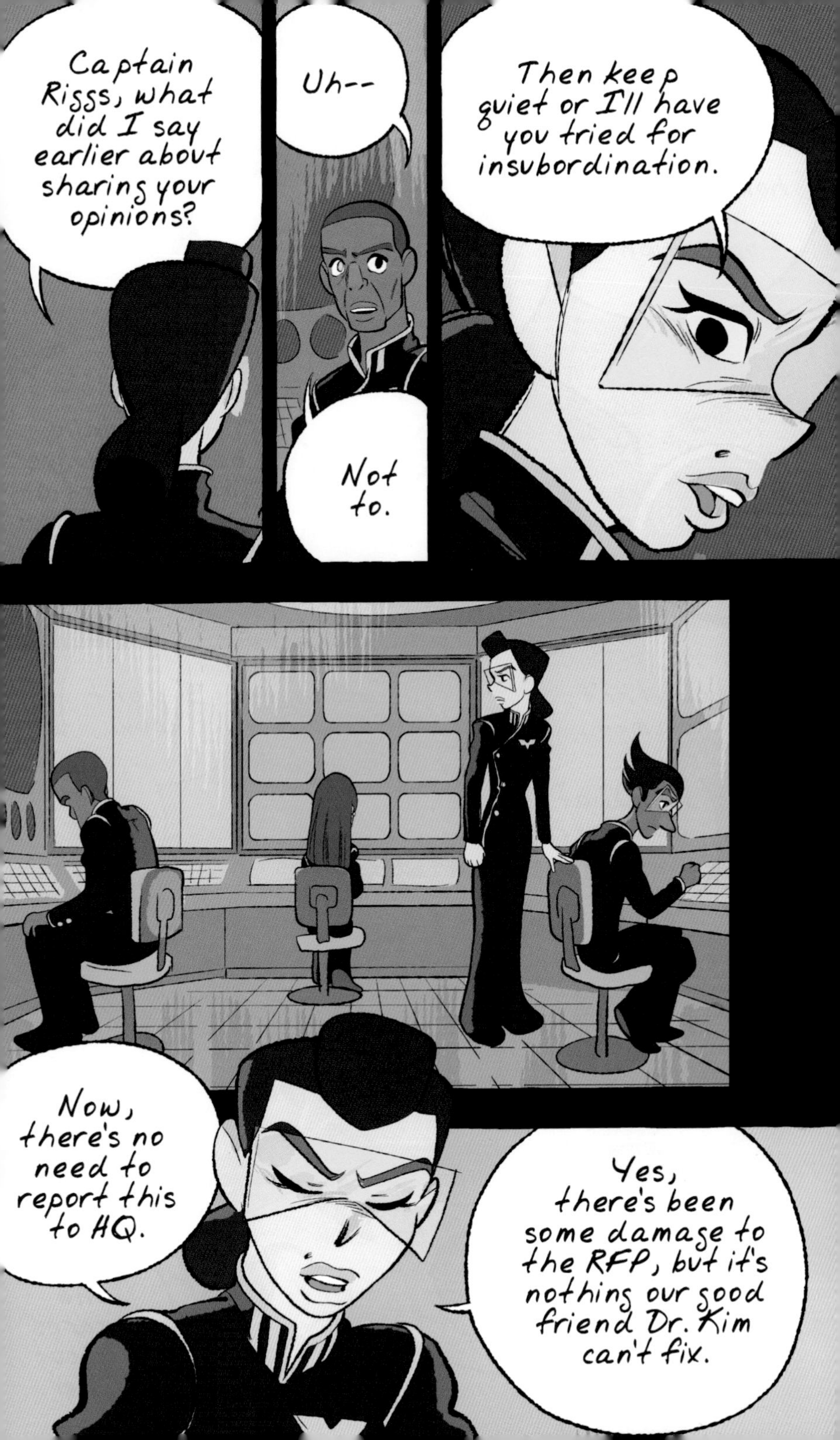
Captain Risss, what did I say earlier about sharing your opinions?
Uh--
Not to.
Then keep quiet or I'll have you tried for insubordination.
Now, there's no need to report this to HQ.
Yes, there's been some damage to the RFP, but it's nothing our good friend Dr. Kim can't fix.

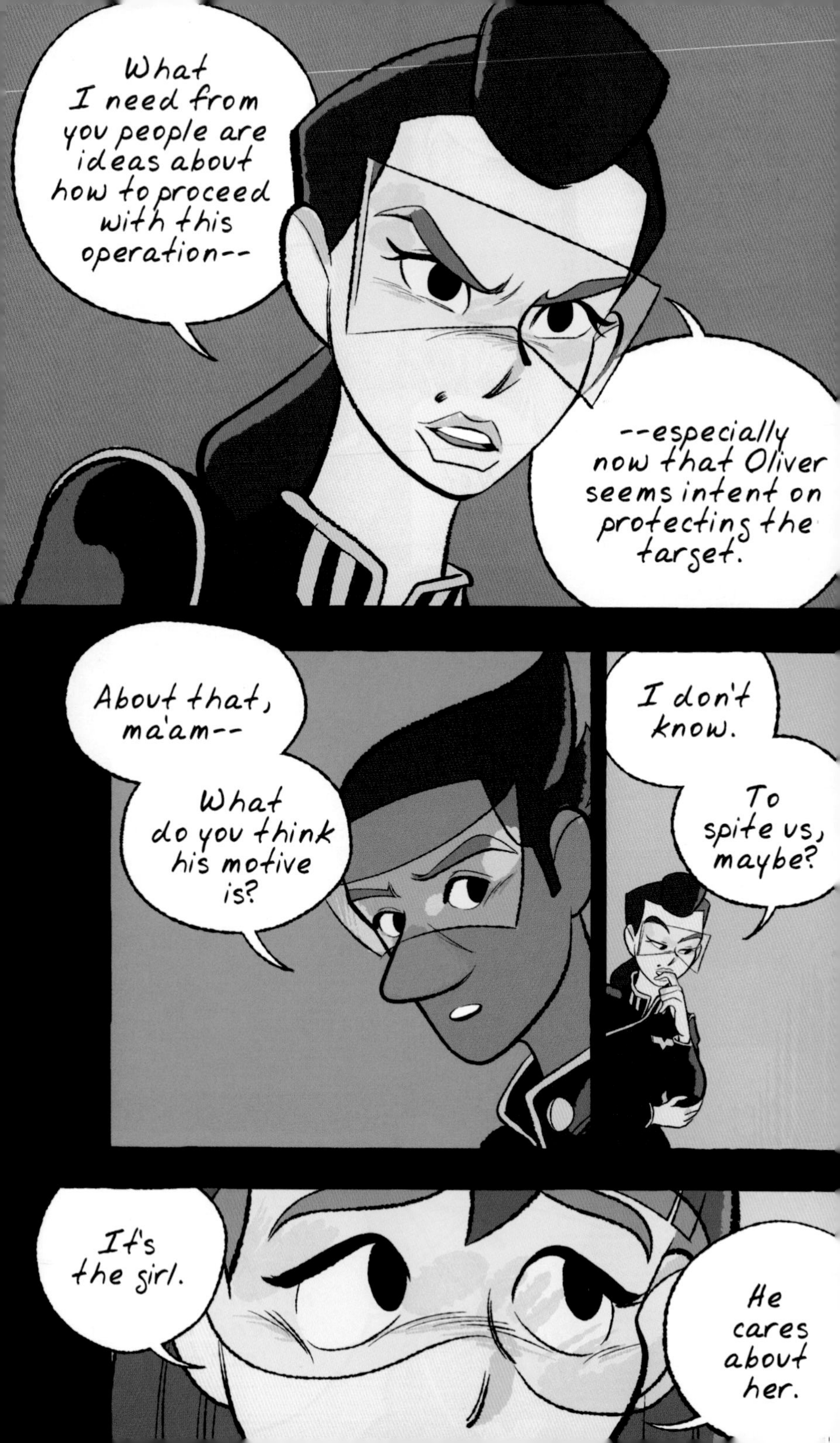
What I need from you people are ideas about how to proceed with this operation--
--especially now that Oliver seems intent on protecting the target.
About that, ma'am--
What do you think his motive is?
I don't know.
To spite us, maybe?
It's the girl.
He cares about her.

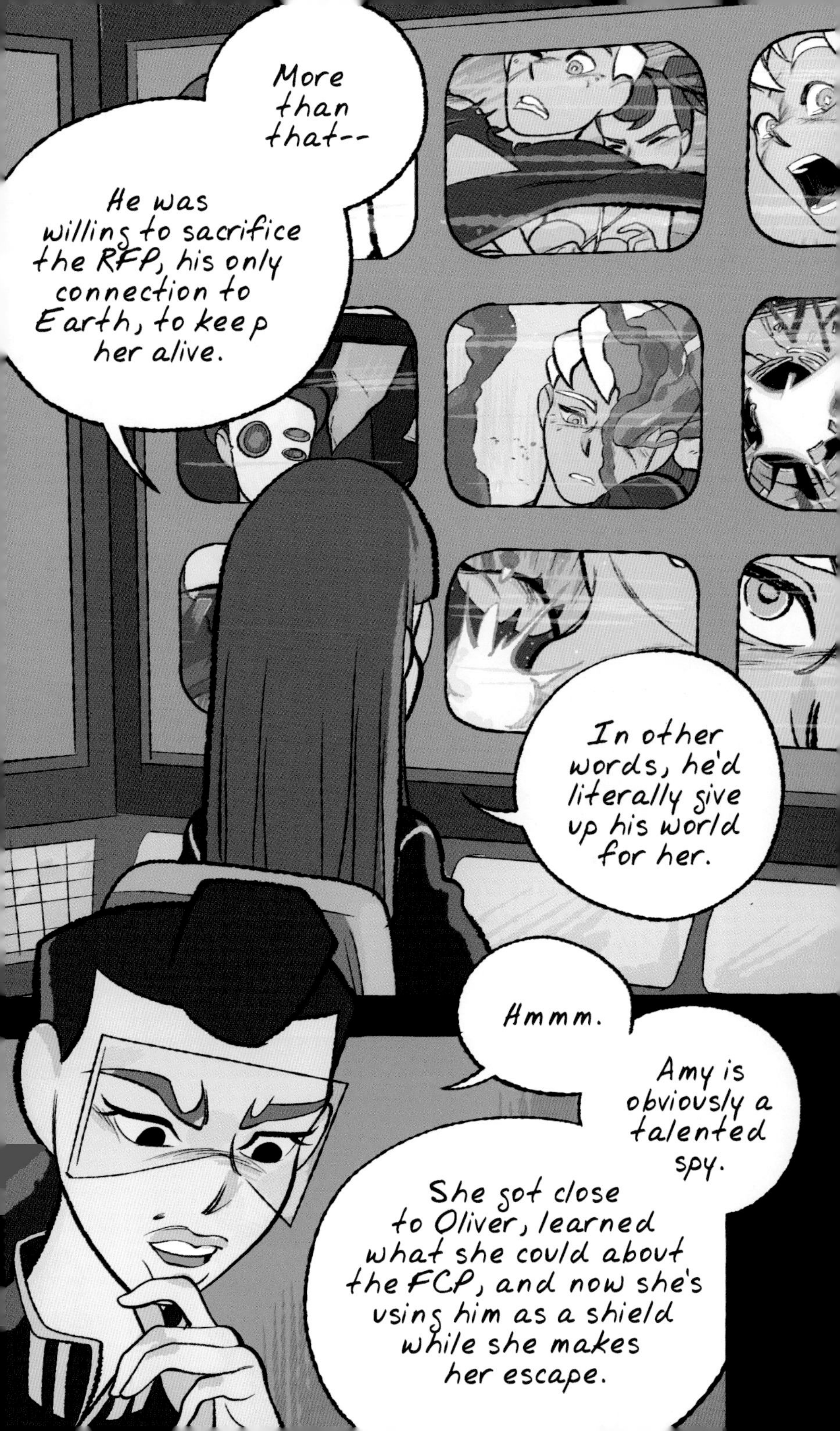

More than that--
He was willing to sacrifice the RFP, his only connection to Earth, to keep her alive.
In other words, he'd literally give up his world for her.
Hmmm.
Amy is obviously a talented spy.
She got close to Oliver, learned what she could about the FCP, and now she's using him as a shield while she makes her escape.

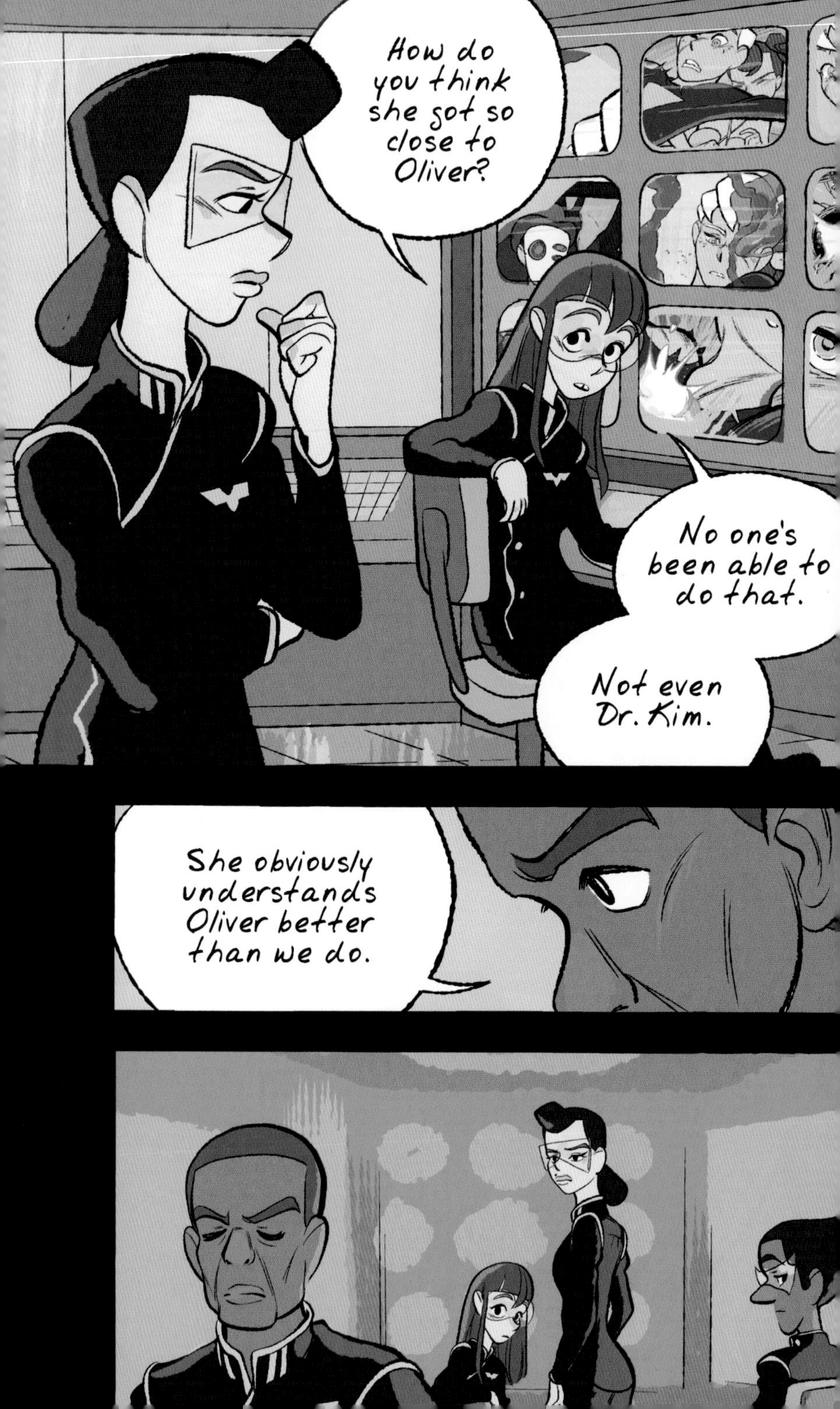
How do you think she got so close to Oliver?
No one's been able to do that.
Not even Dr. Kim.
She obviously understands Oliver better than we do.

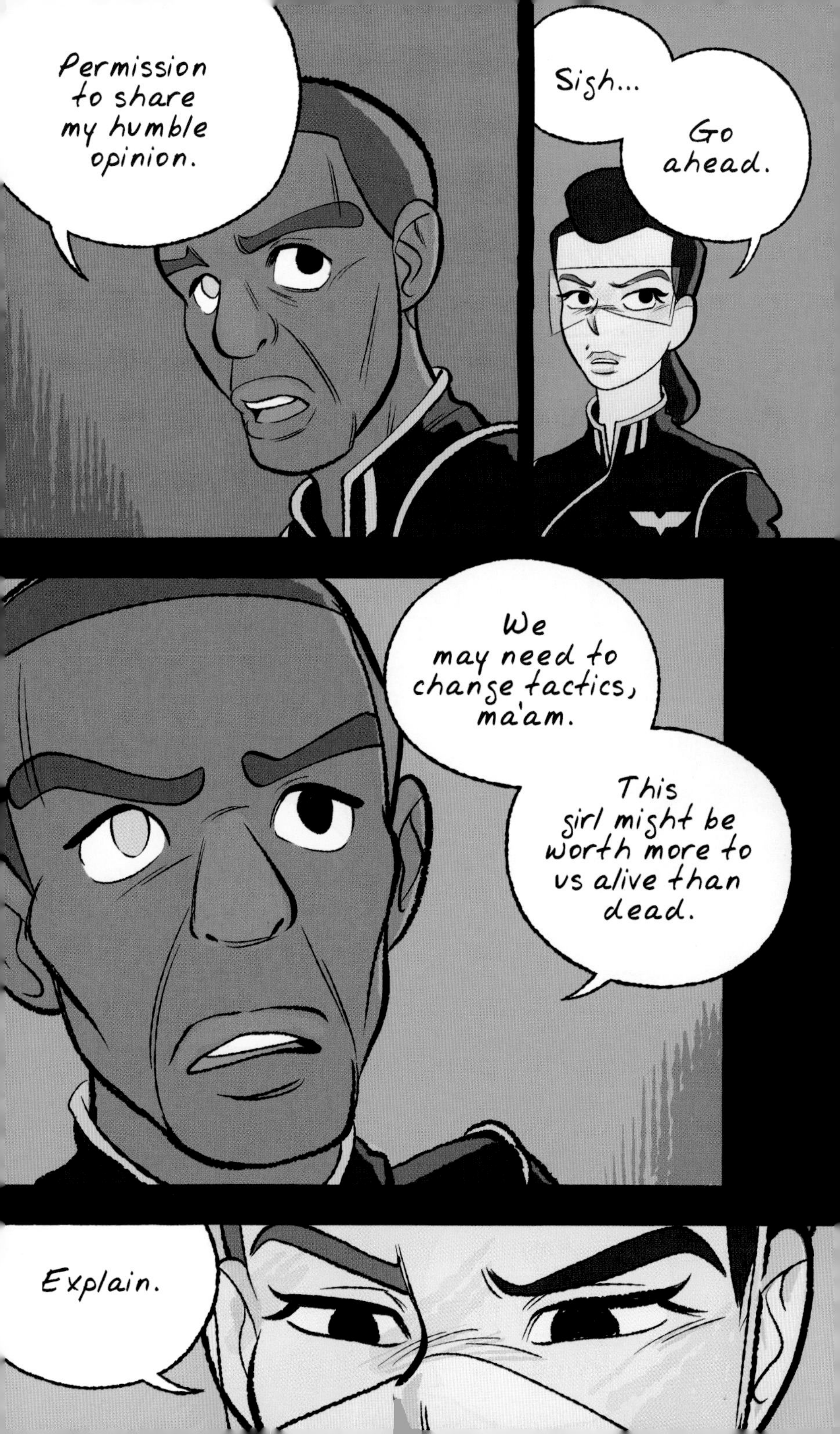

Permission to share my humble opinion.
Sigh...
Go ahead.
We may need to change tactics, ma'am.
This girl might be worth more to us alive than dead.
Explain.

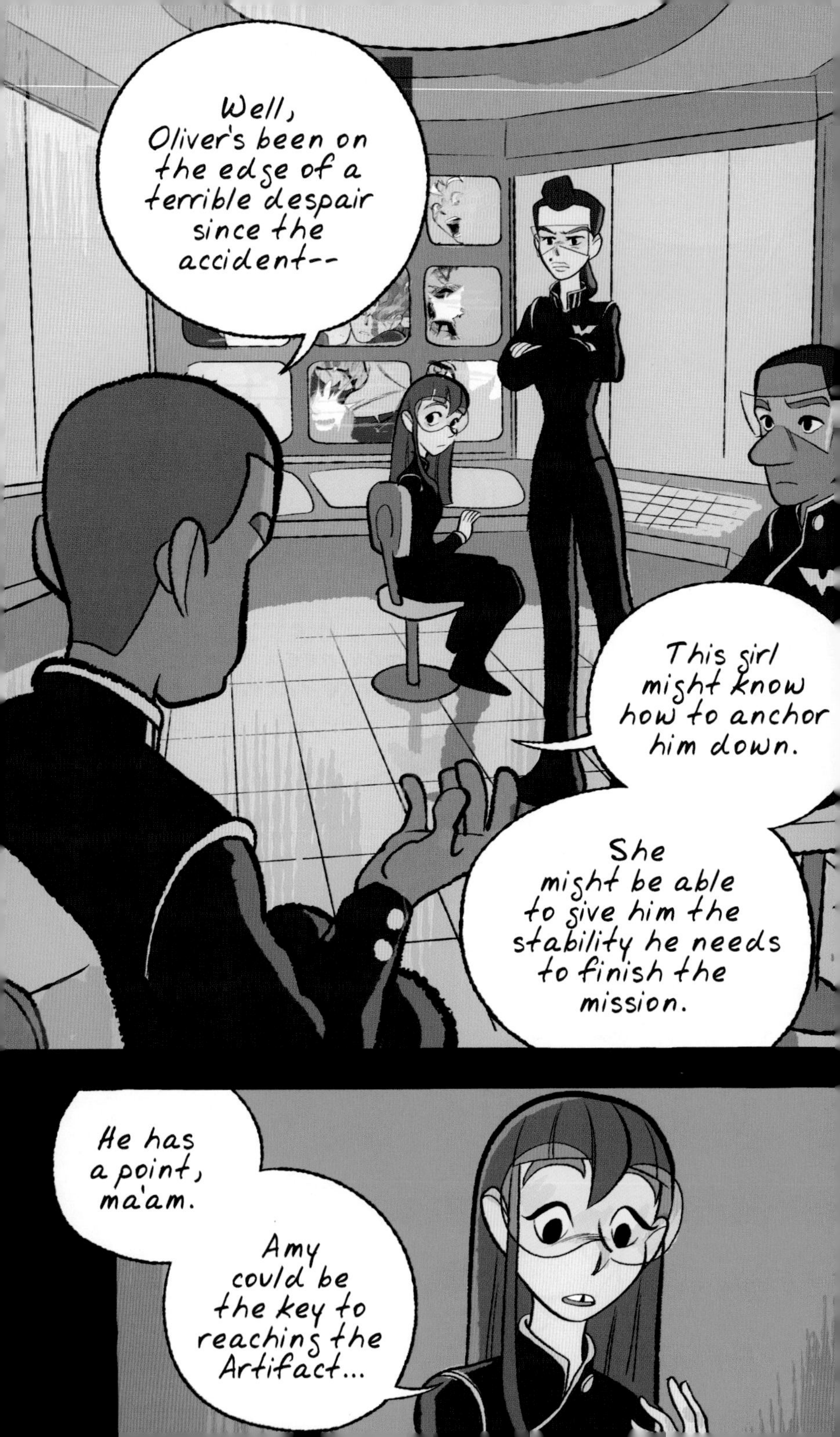
Well, Oliver's been on the edge of a terrible despair since the accident--
This girl might know how to anchor him down.
She might be able to give him the stability he needs to finish the mission.
He has a point, ma'am.
Amy could be the key to reaching the Artifact...

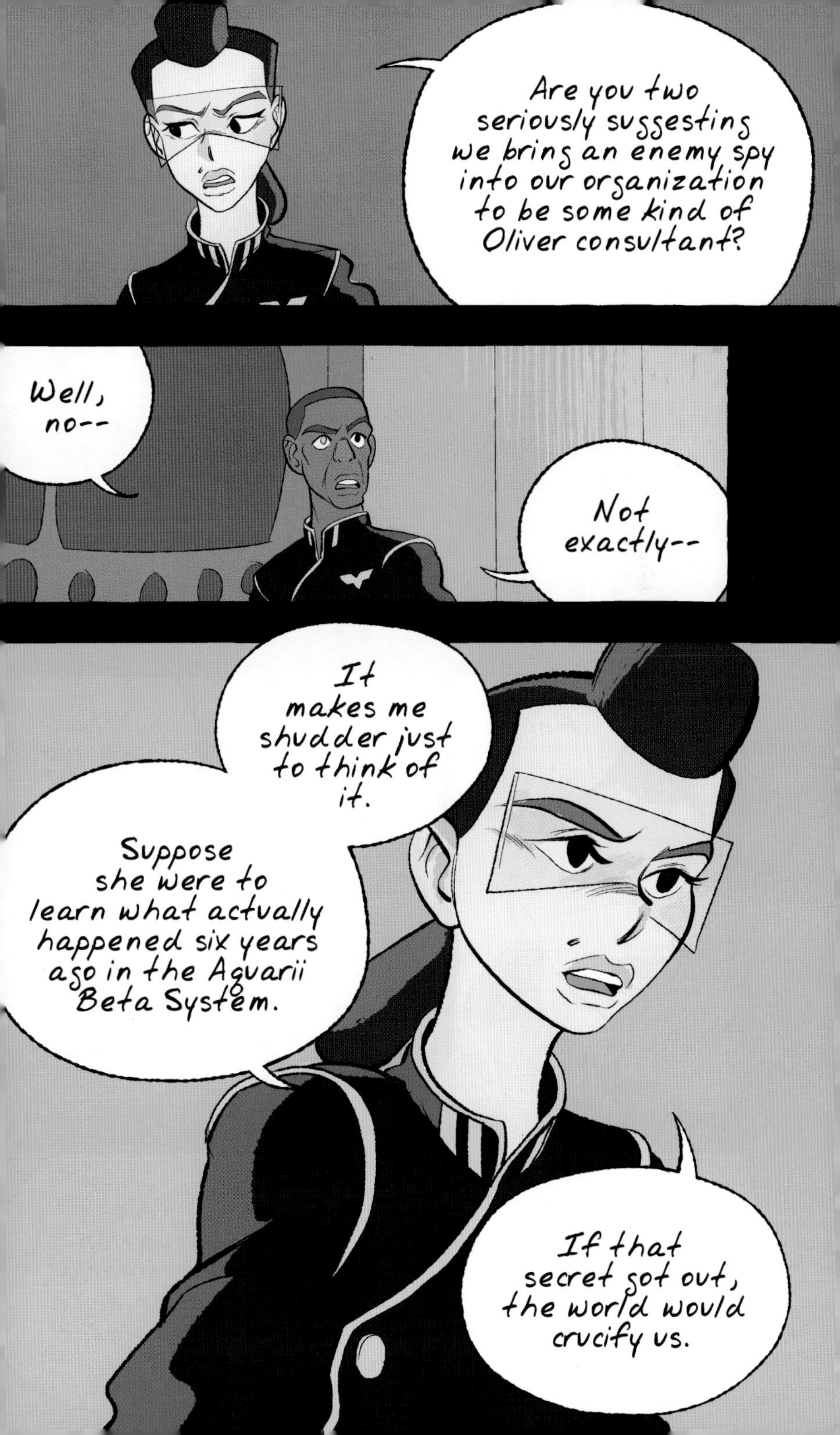
Are you two seriously suggesting we bring an enemy spy into our organization to be some kind of Oliver consultant?
Well, no--
Not exactly--
It makes me shudder just to think of it.
Suppose she were to learn what actually happened six years ago in the Aquarii Beta System.
If that secret got out, the world would crucify us.

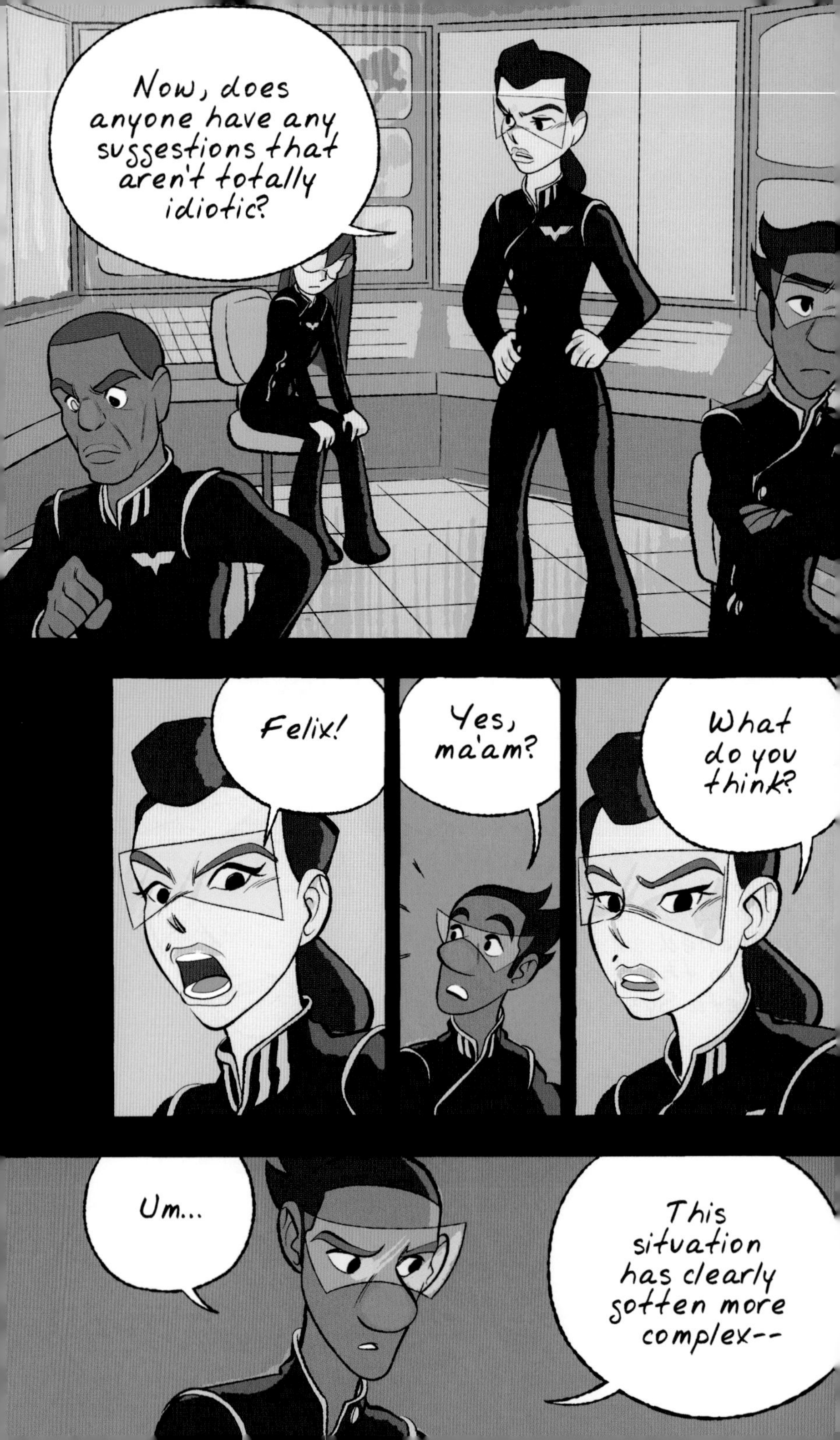
Now, does anyone have any suggestions that aren't totally idiotic?
Felix!
Yes, ma'am?
What do you think?
Um...
This situation has clearly gotten more complex--

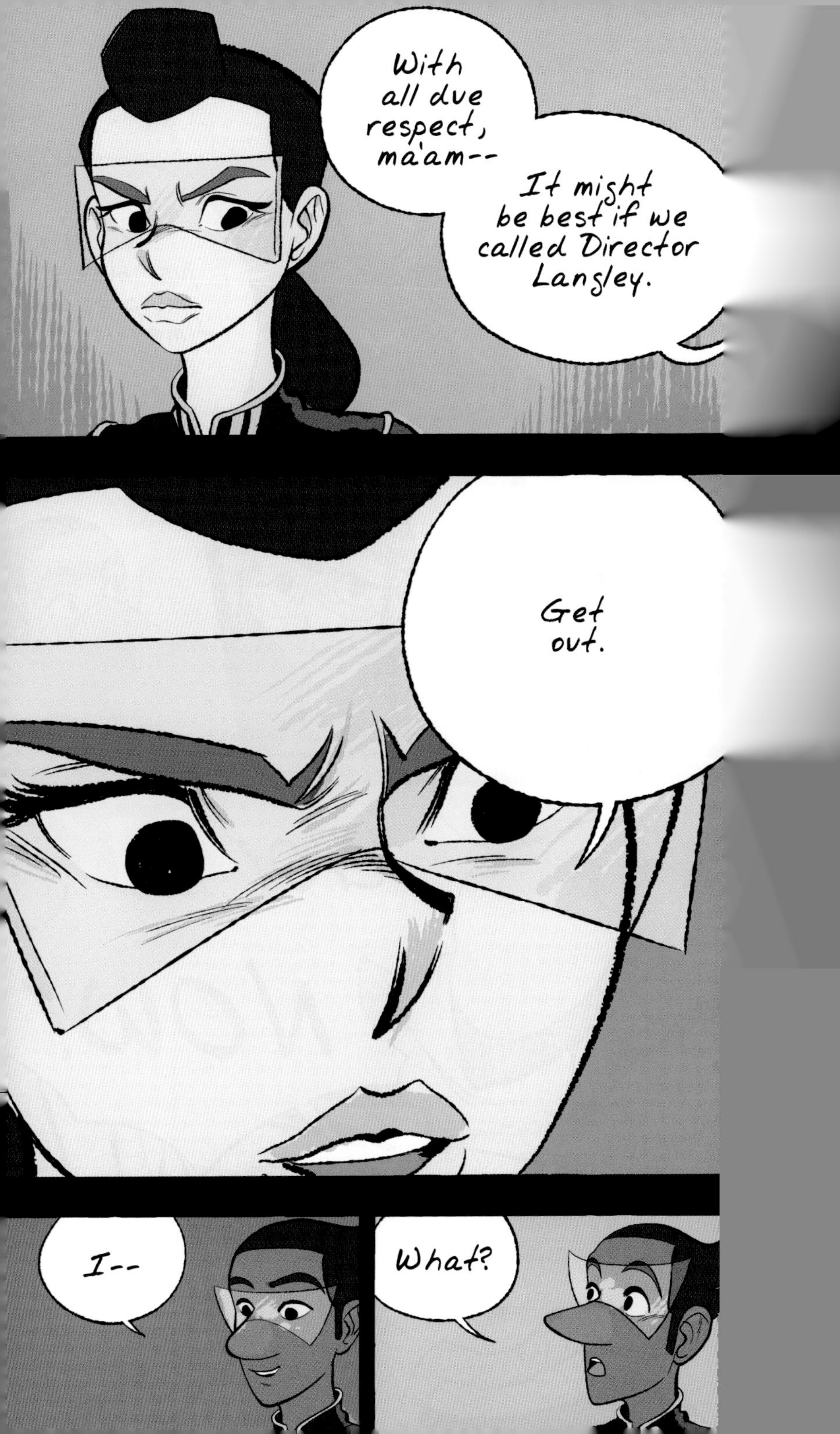
With all due respect, ma'am--
It might be best if we called Director Langley.
Get out.
I--
What?

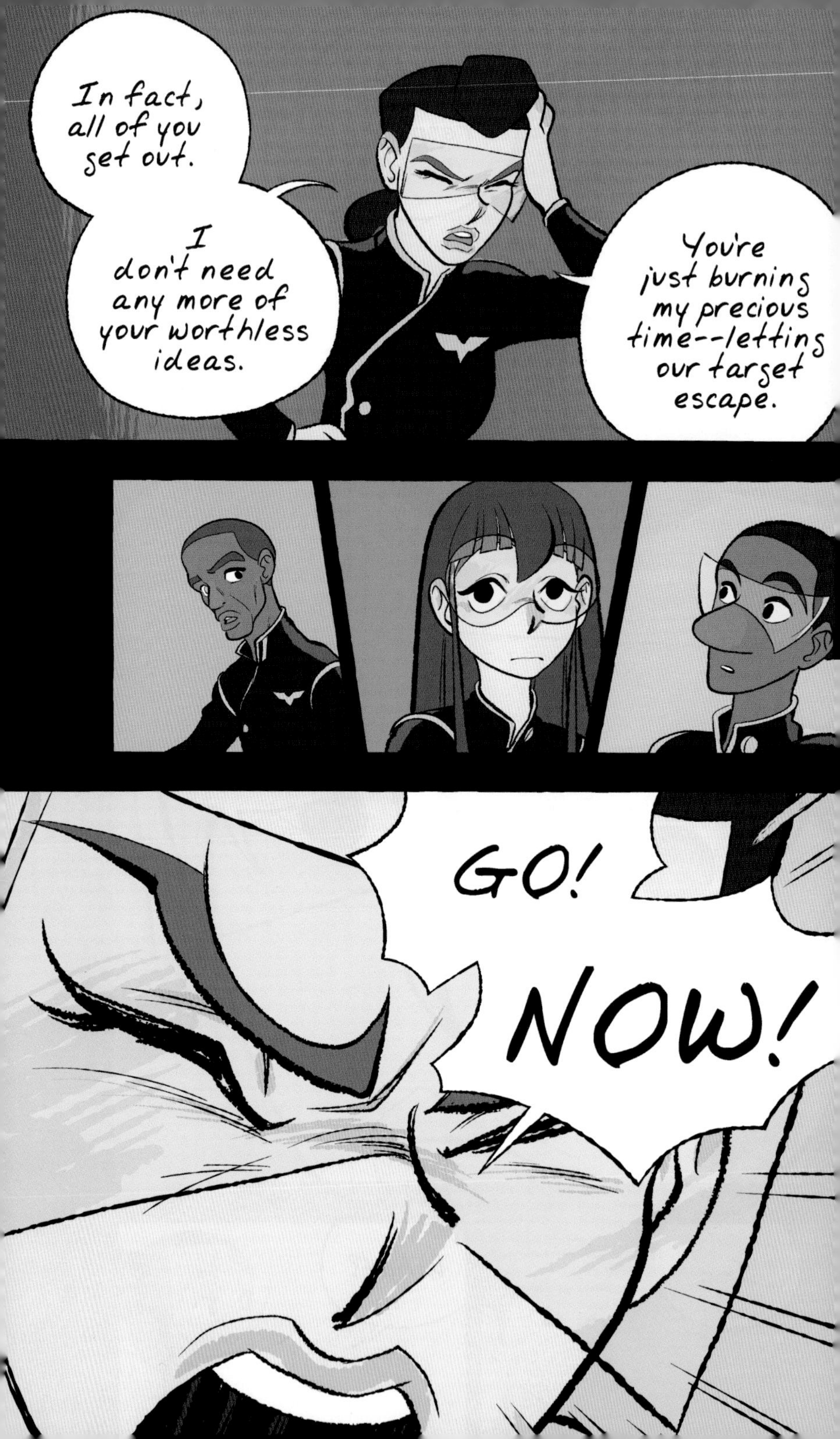
In fact, all of you set out.
I don't need any more of your worthless ideas.
You're just burning my precious time--letting our target escape.
GO!
NOW!

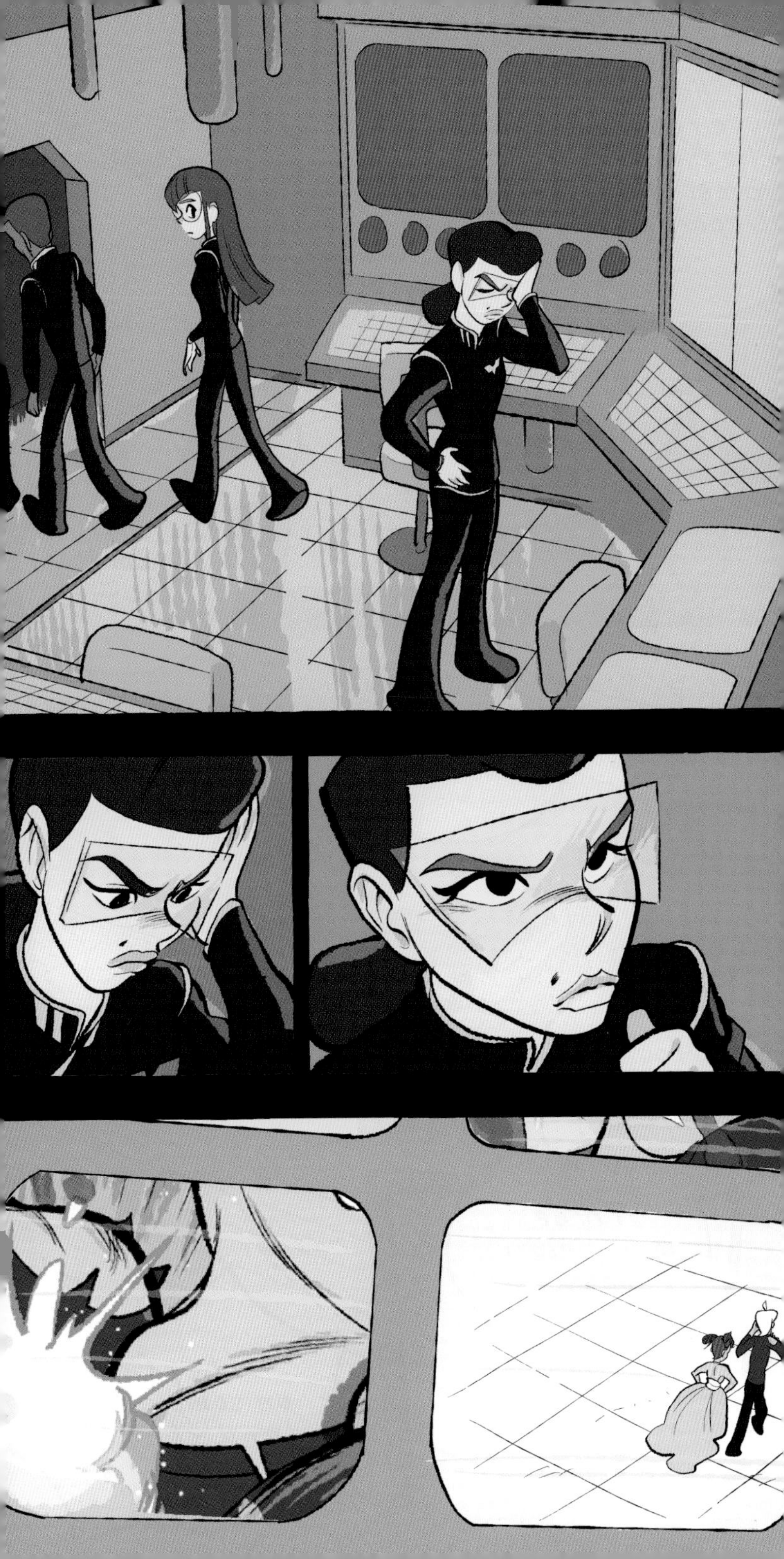

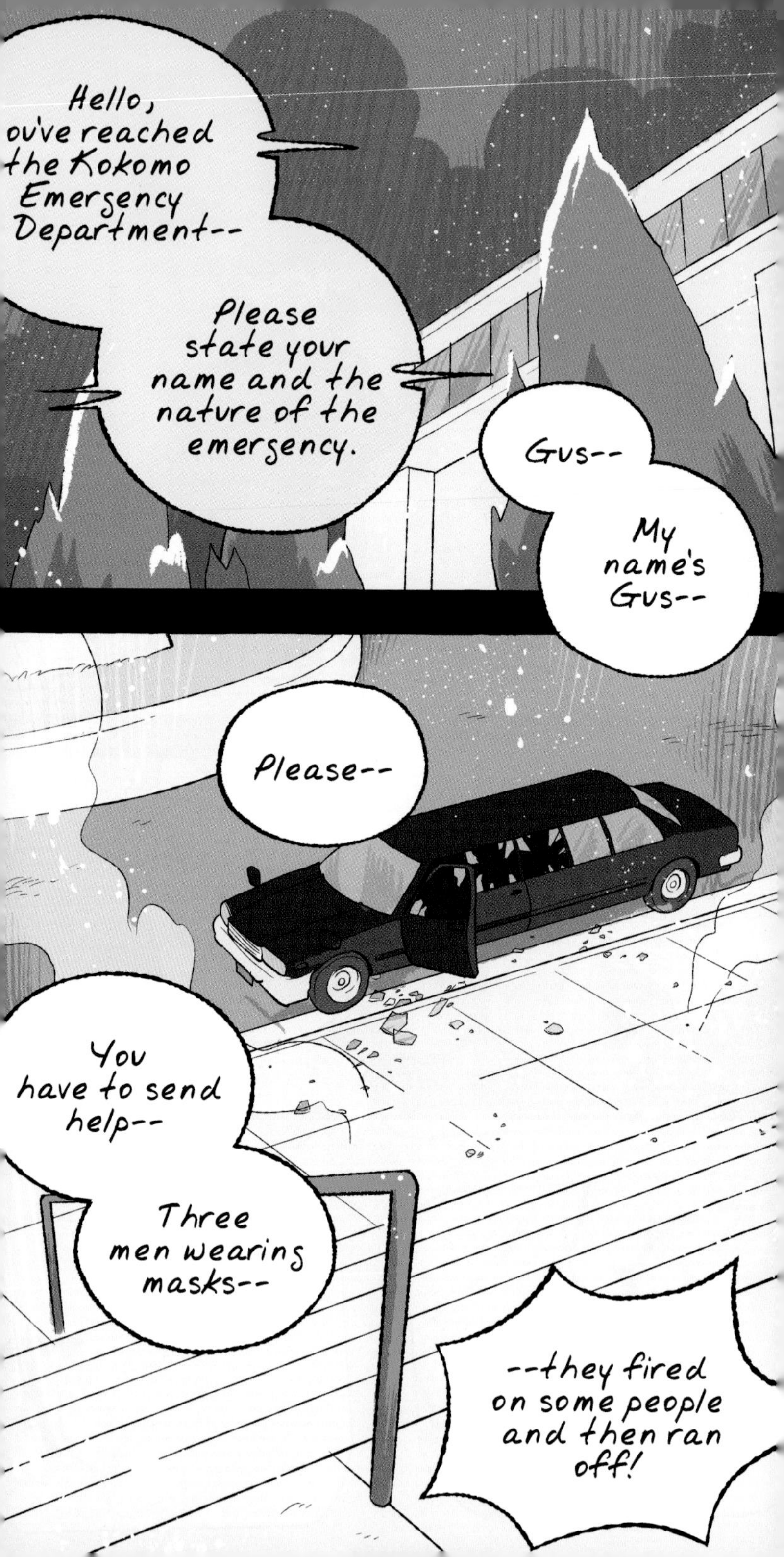
Hello, ou've reached the Kokomo Emergency Department--
Please state your name and the nature of the emergency.
Gus--
My name's Gus--
Please--
You have to send help--
Three men wearing masks--
--they fired on some people and then ran off!

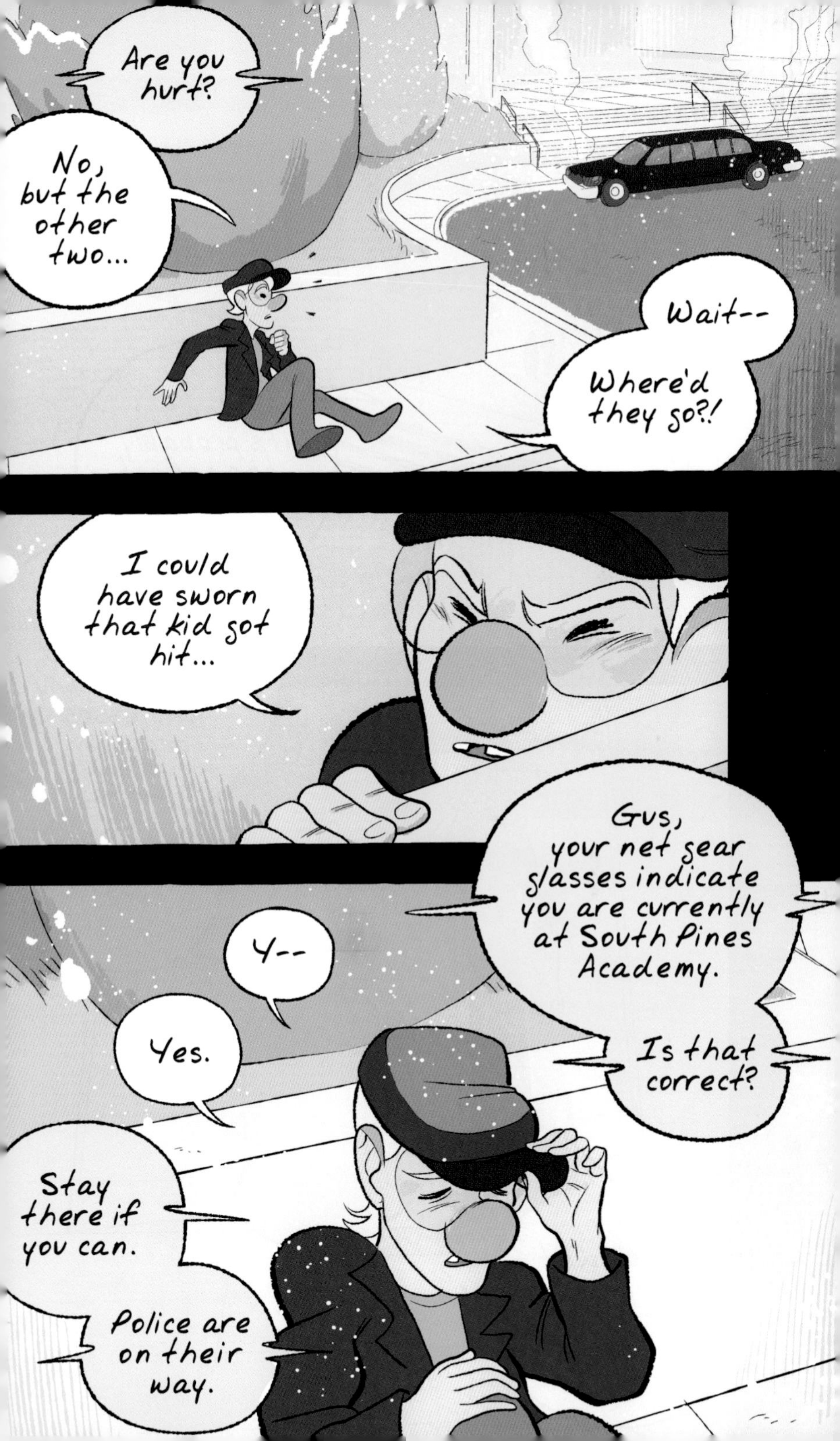
Are you hurt?
No, but the other two...
Wait--
Where'd they go?!
I could have sworn that kid got hit...
Gus, your net gear glasses indicate you are currently at South Pines Academy.
Y--
Yes.
Is that correct?
Stay there if you can.
Police are on their way.

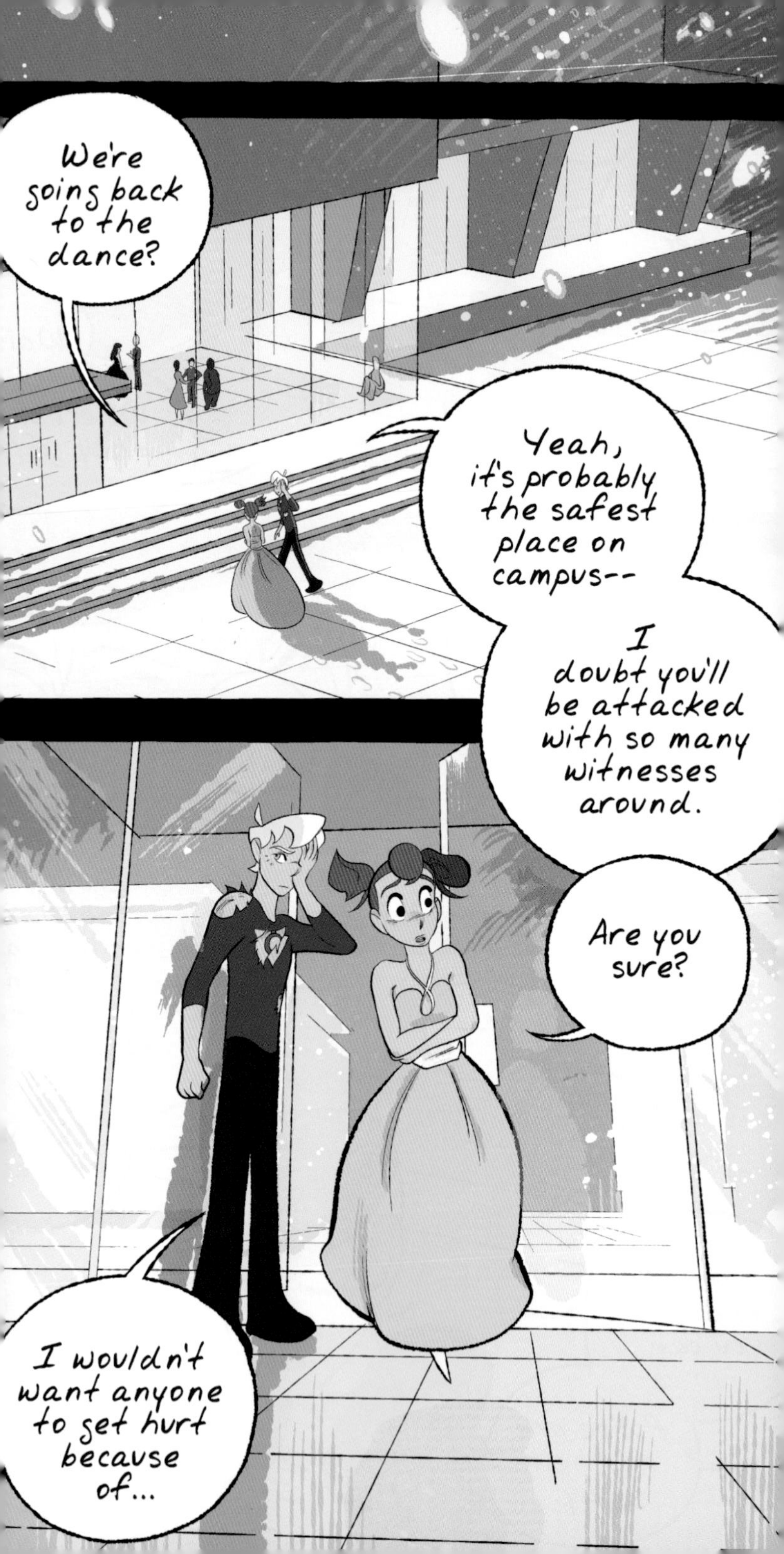
We're going back to the dance?
Yeah, it's probably the safest place on campus--
I doubt you'll be attacked with so many witnesses around.
Are you sure?
I wouldn't want anyone to get hurt because of...

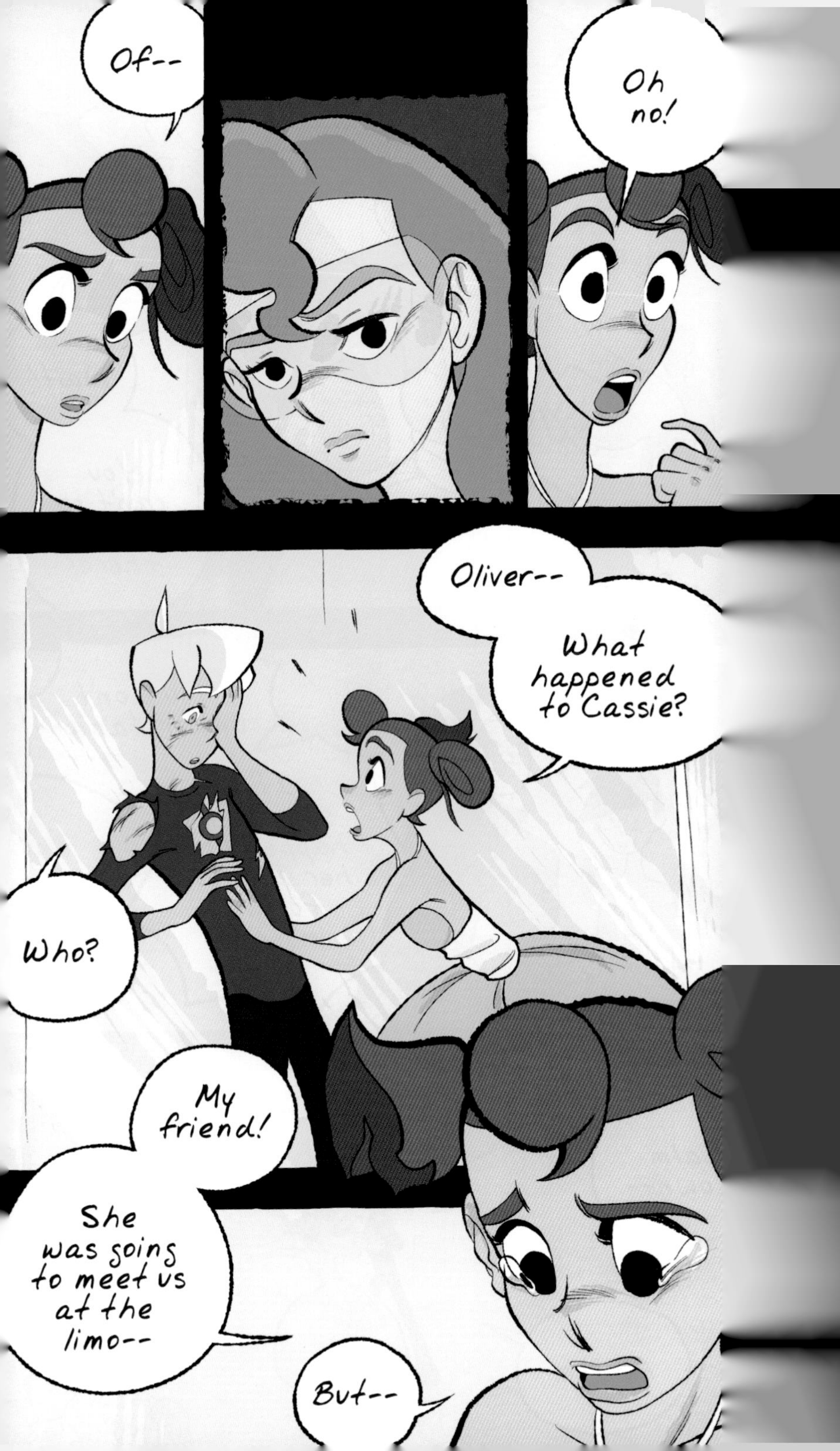
Of--
Oh no!
Oliver--
What happened to Cassie?
Who?
My friend!
She was going to meet us at the limo--
But--

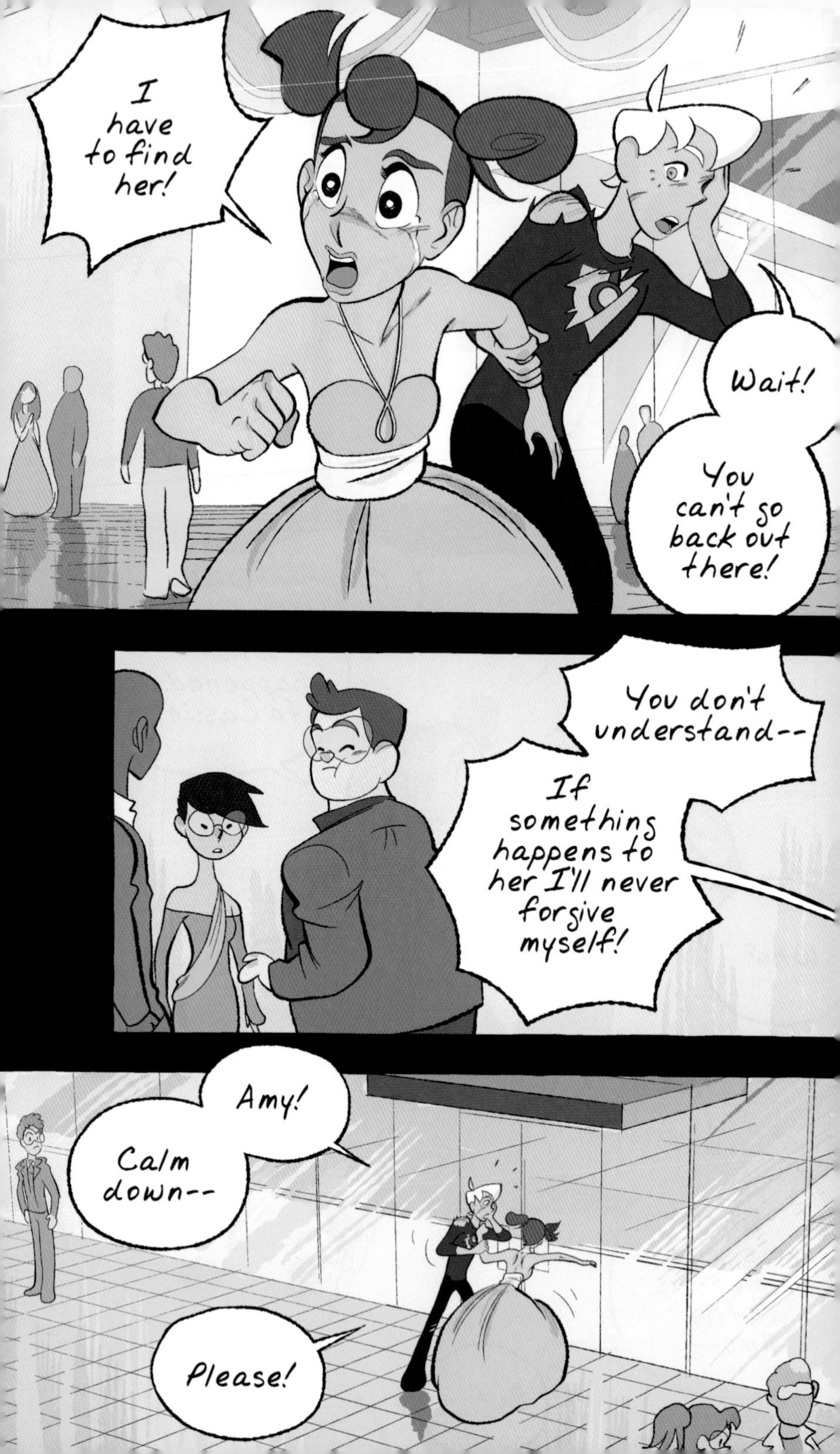
I have to find her!
Wait!
You can't go back out there!
You don't understand--
If something happens to her I'll never forgive myself!
Amy!
Calm down--
Please!

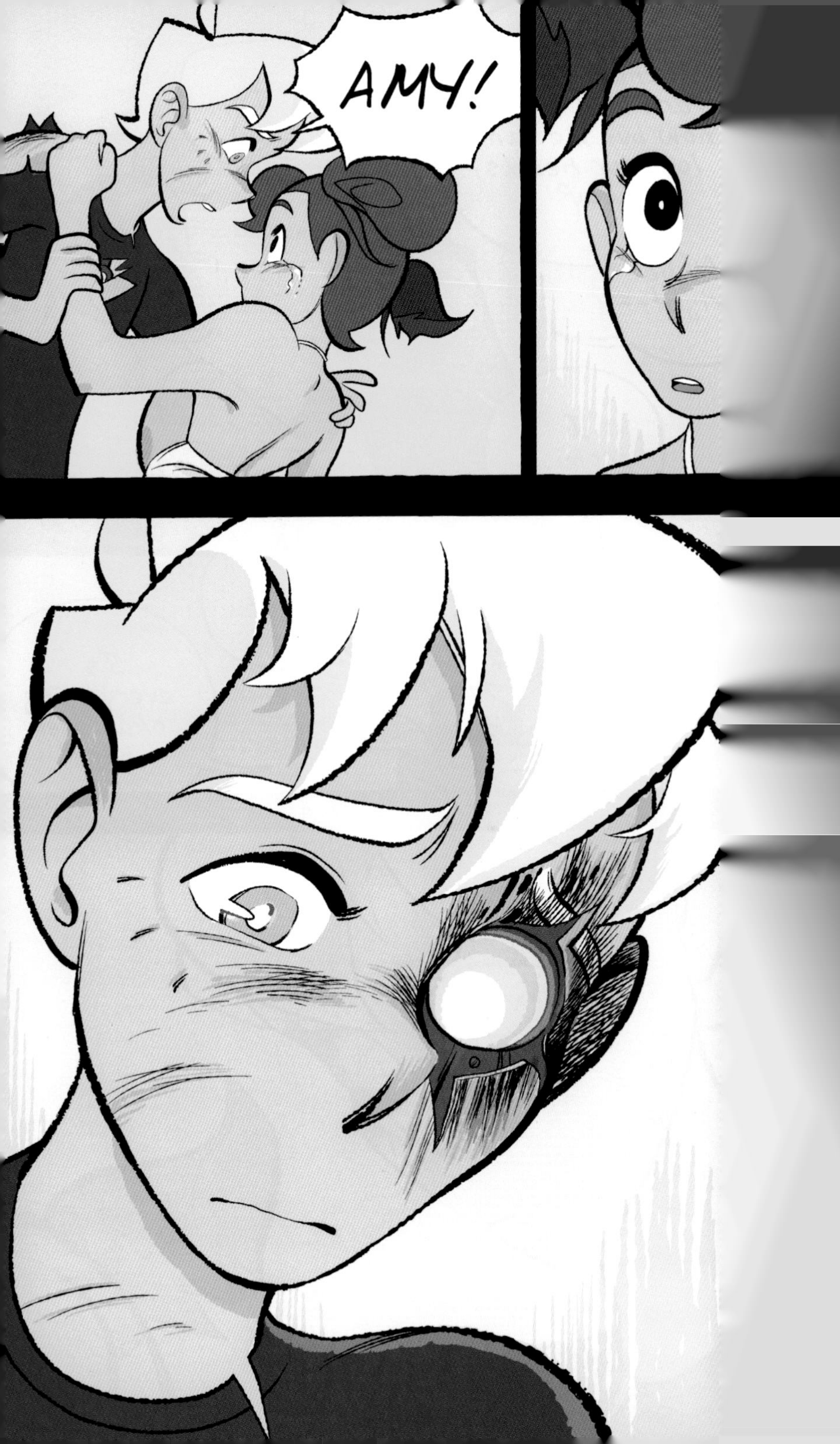
AMY!

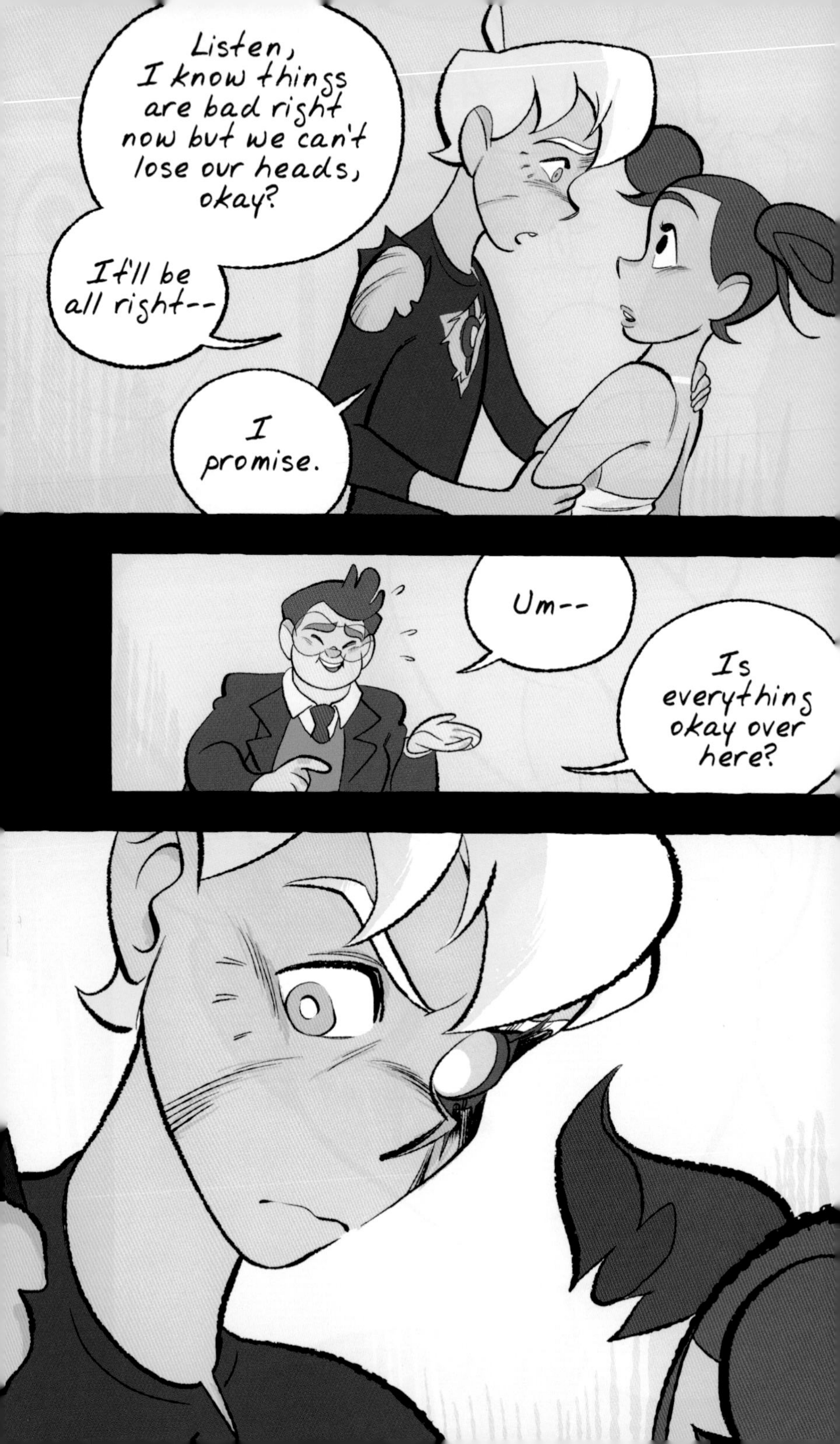
Listen, I know things are bad right now but we can't lose our heads, okay?
It'll be all right--
I promise.
Um--
Is everything okay over here?

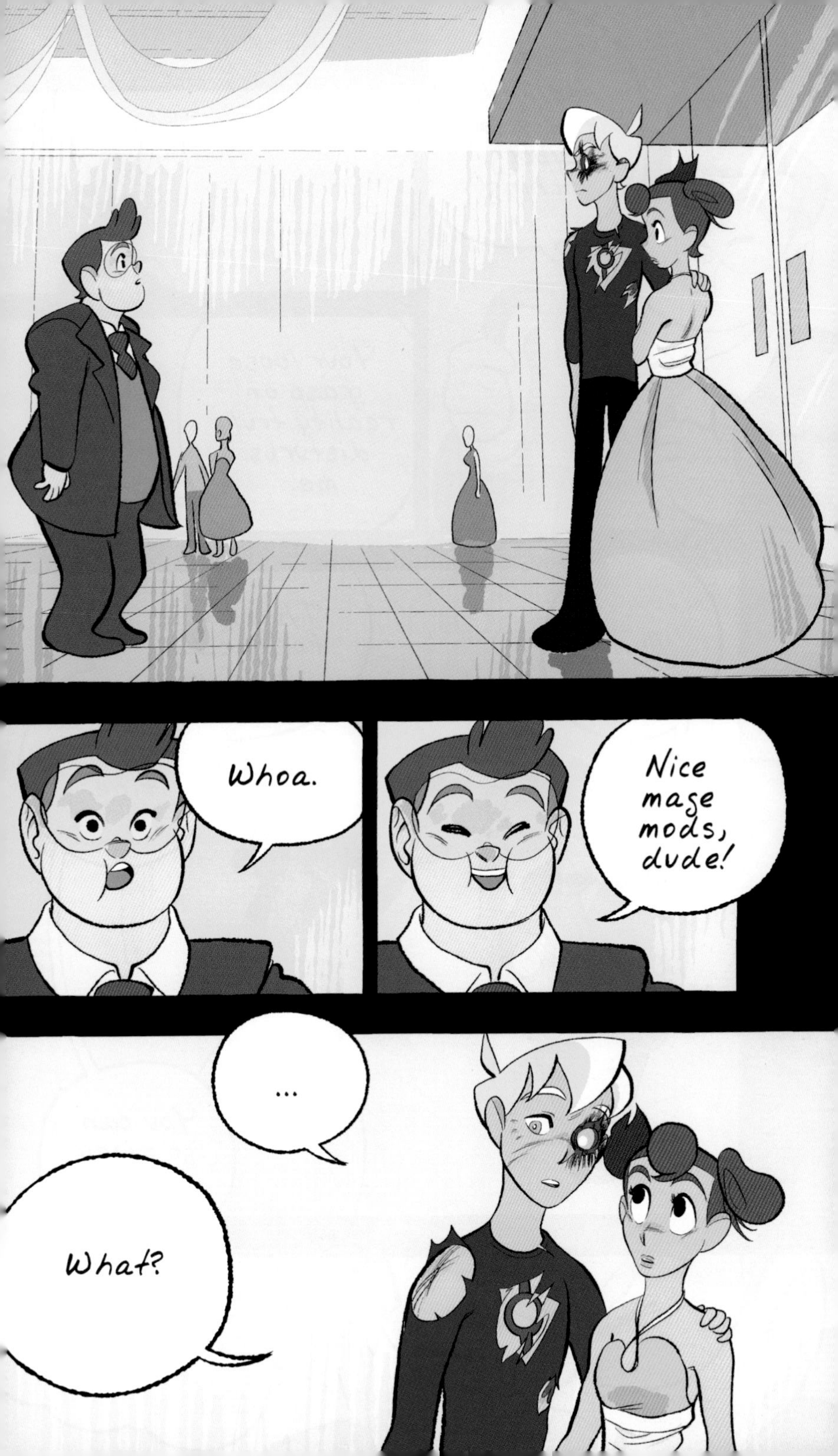
Whoa.
Nice mage mods, dude!
...
What?

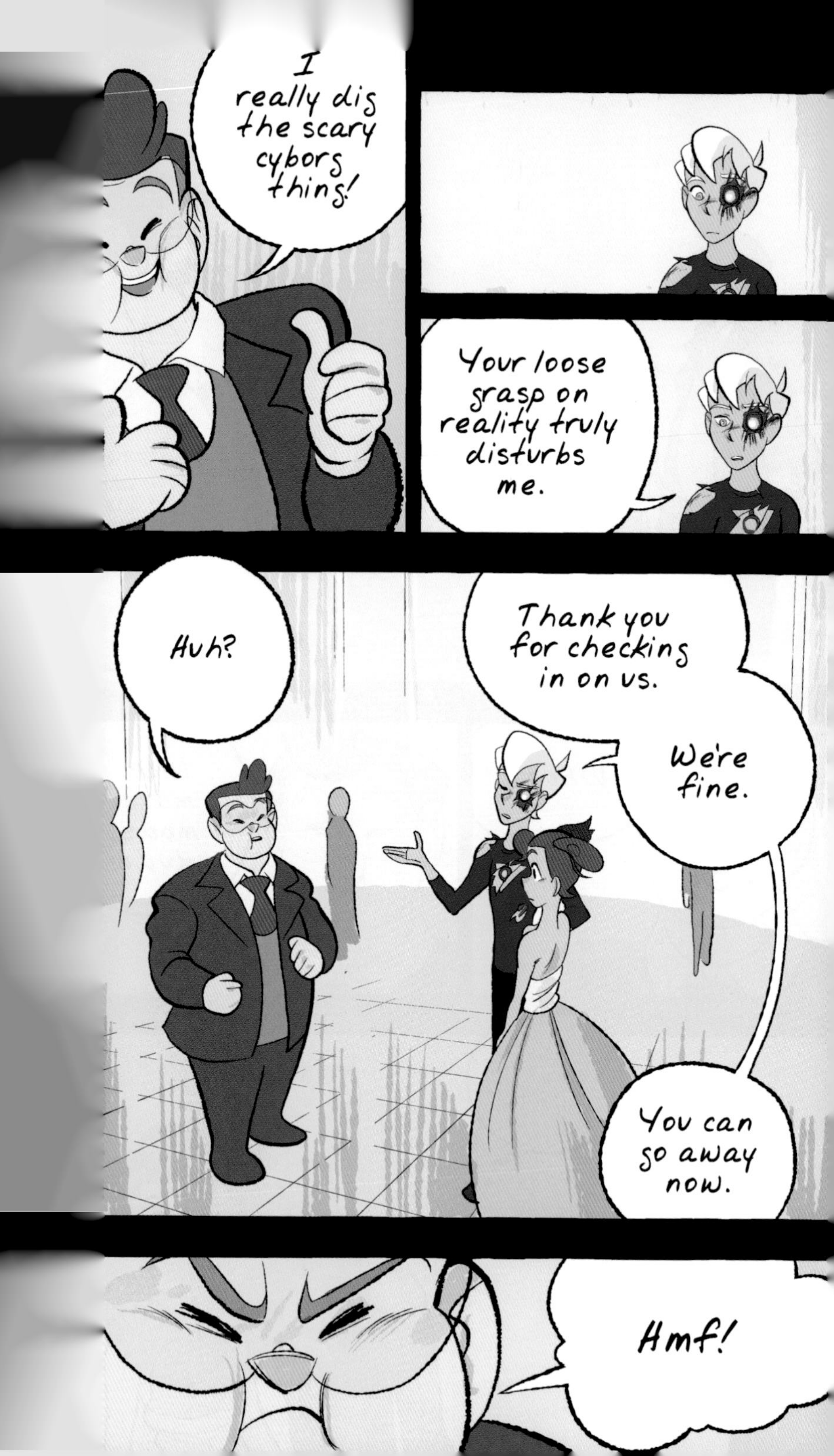
I really dig the scary cyborg thing!
Your loose grasp on reality truly disturbs me.
Huh?
Thank you for checking in on us.
We're fine.
You can go away now.
Hmf!

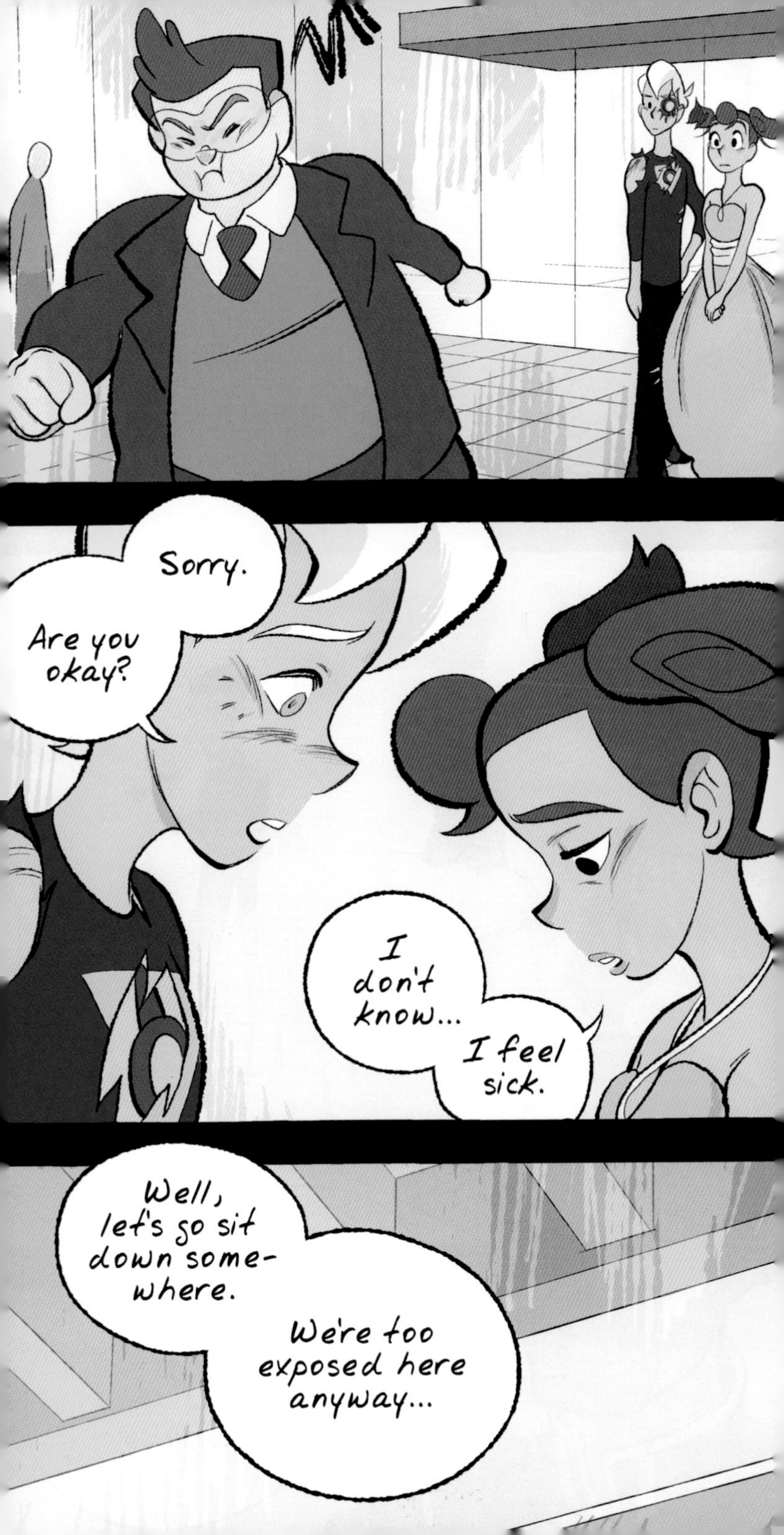
Sorry.
Are you okay?
I don't know...
I feel sick.
Well, let's go sit down some-where.
We're too exposed here anyway...

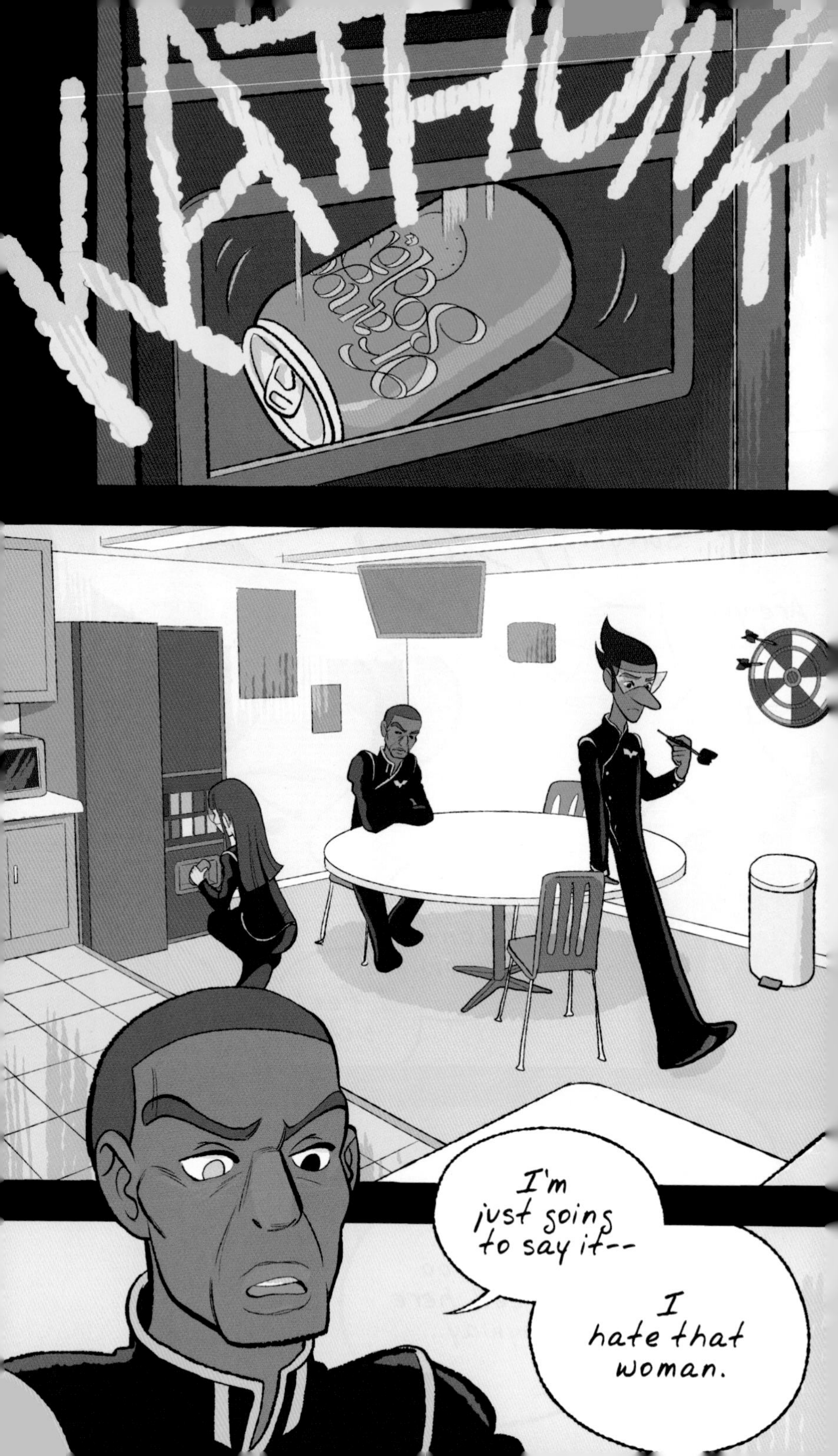
I'm just going to say it--
I hate that woman.

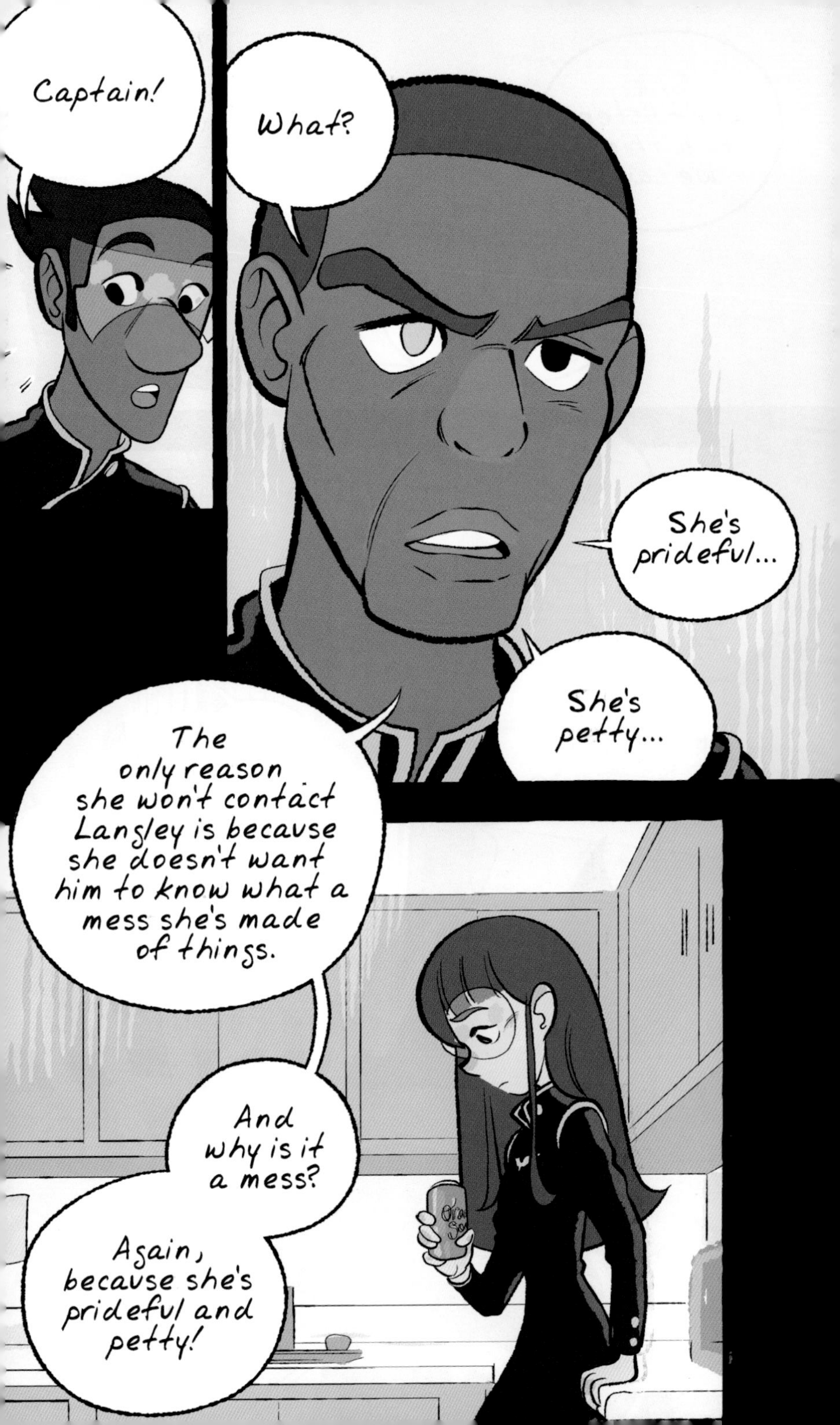
Captain!
What?
She's prideful...
She's petty...
The only reason she won't contact Langley is because she doesn't want him to know what a mess she's made of things.
And why is it a mess?
Again, because she's prideful and petty!

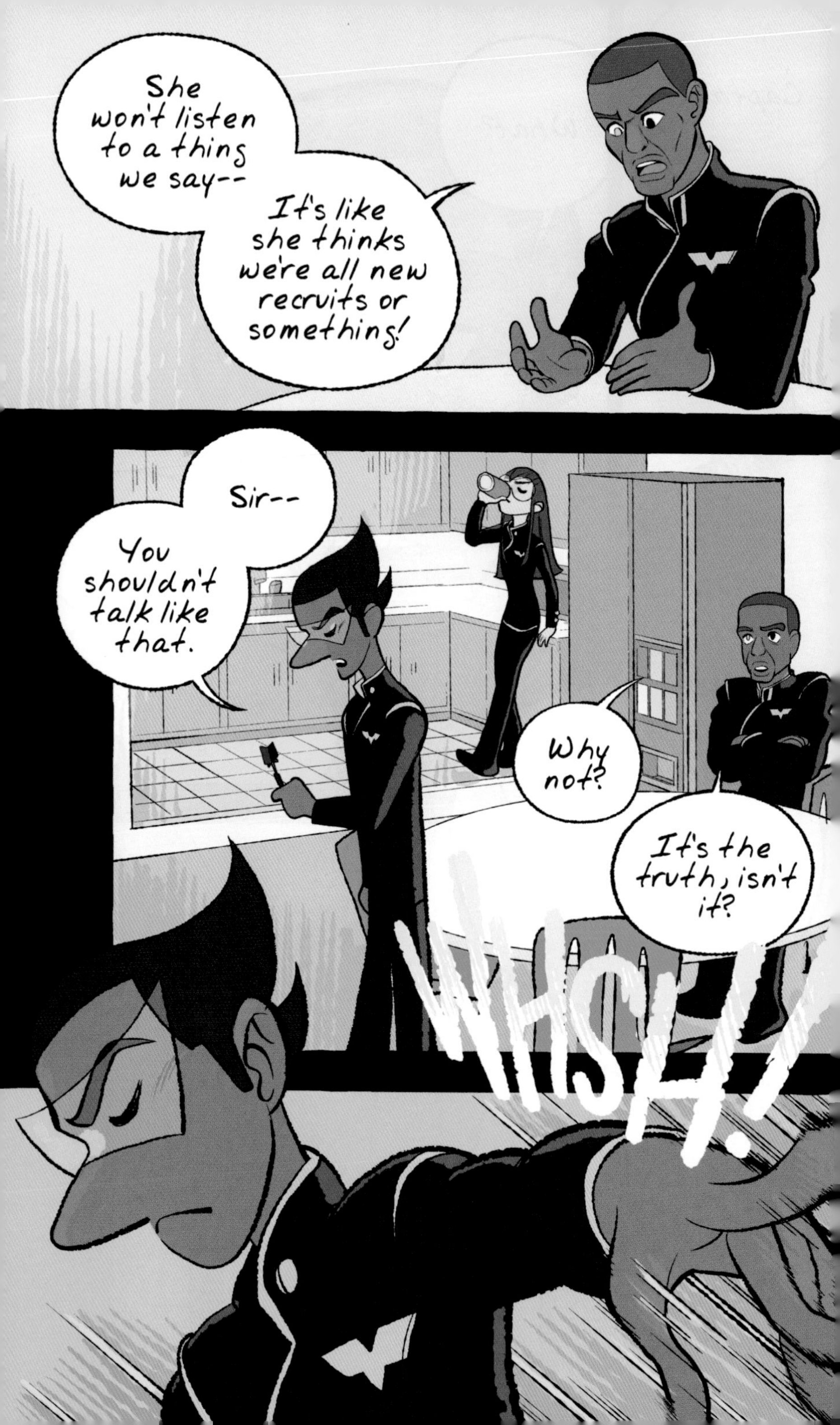
She won't listen to a thing we say--
It's like she thinks we're all new recruits or something!
Sir--
You shouldn't talk like that.
Why not?
It's the truth, isn't it?
WHSH!

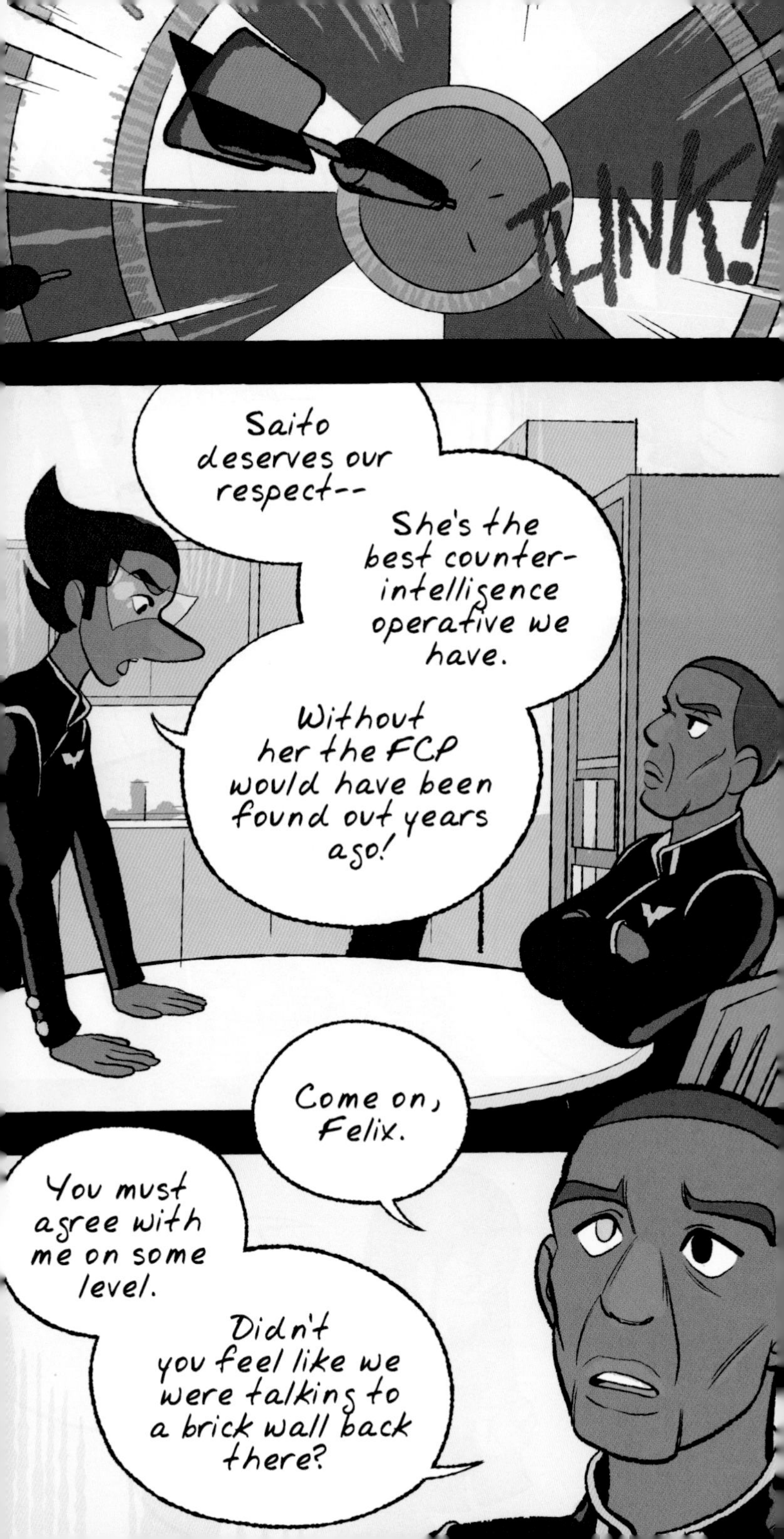
THNK!
Saito deserves our respect--
She's the best counter-intelligence operative we have.
Without her the FCP would have been found out years ago!
Come on, Felix.
You must agree with me on some level.
Didn't you feel like we were talking to a brick wall back there?

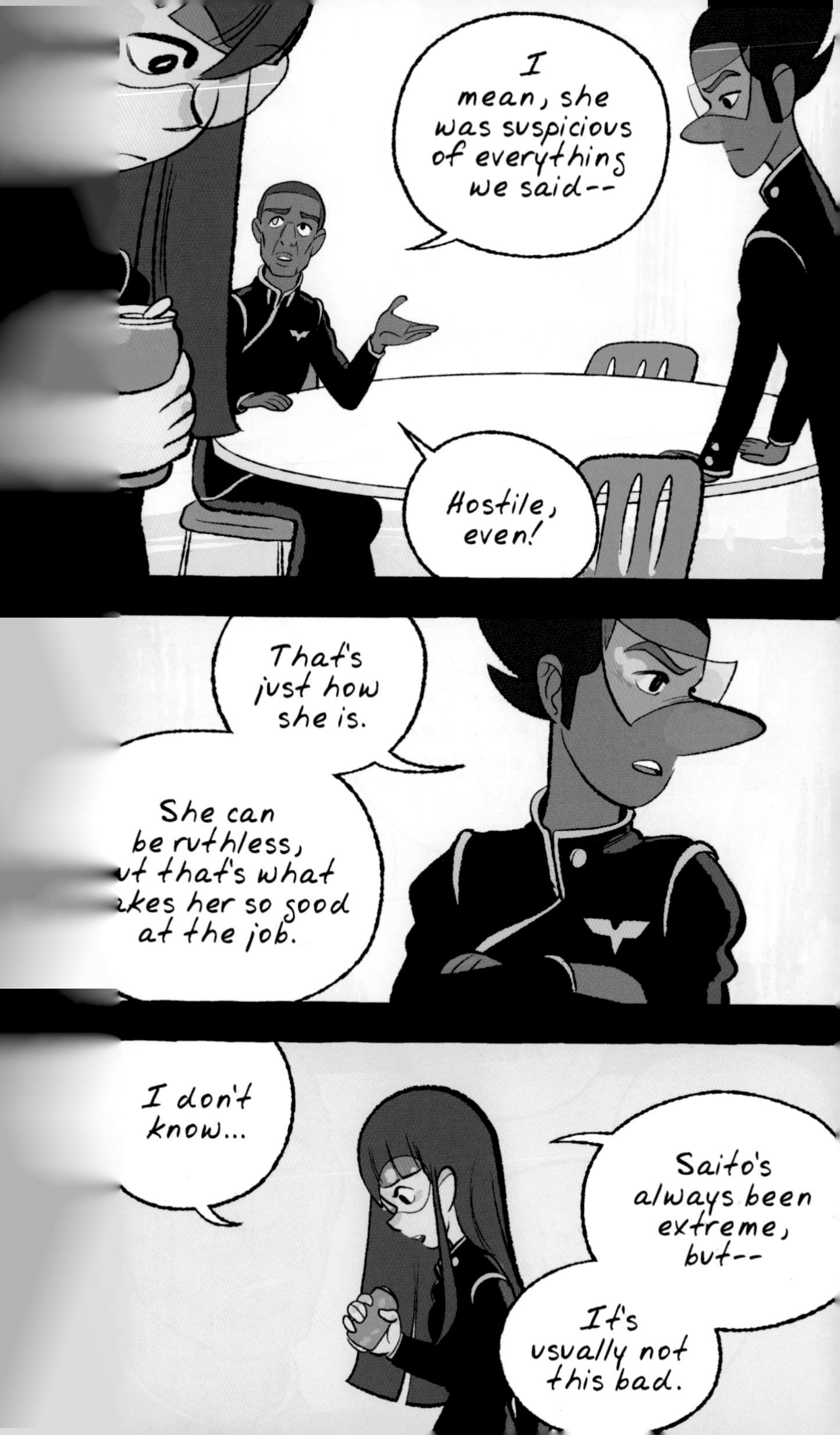
I mean, she was suspicious of everything we said--
Hostile, even!
That's just how she is.
She can be ruthless,
I don't know...
Saito's always been extreme, but--
It's usually not this bad.

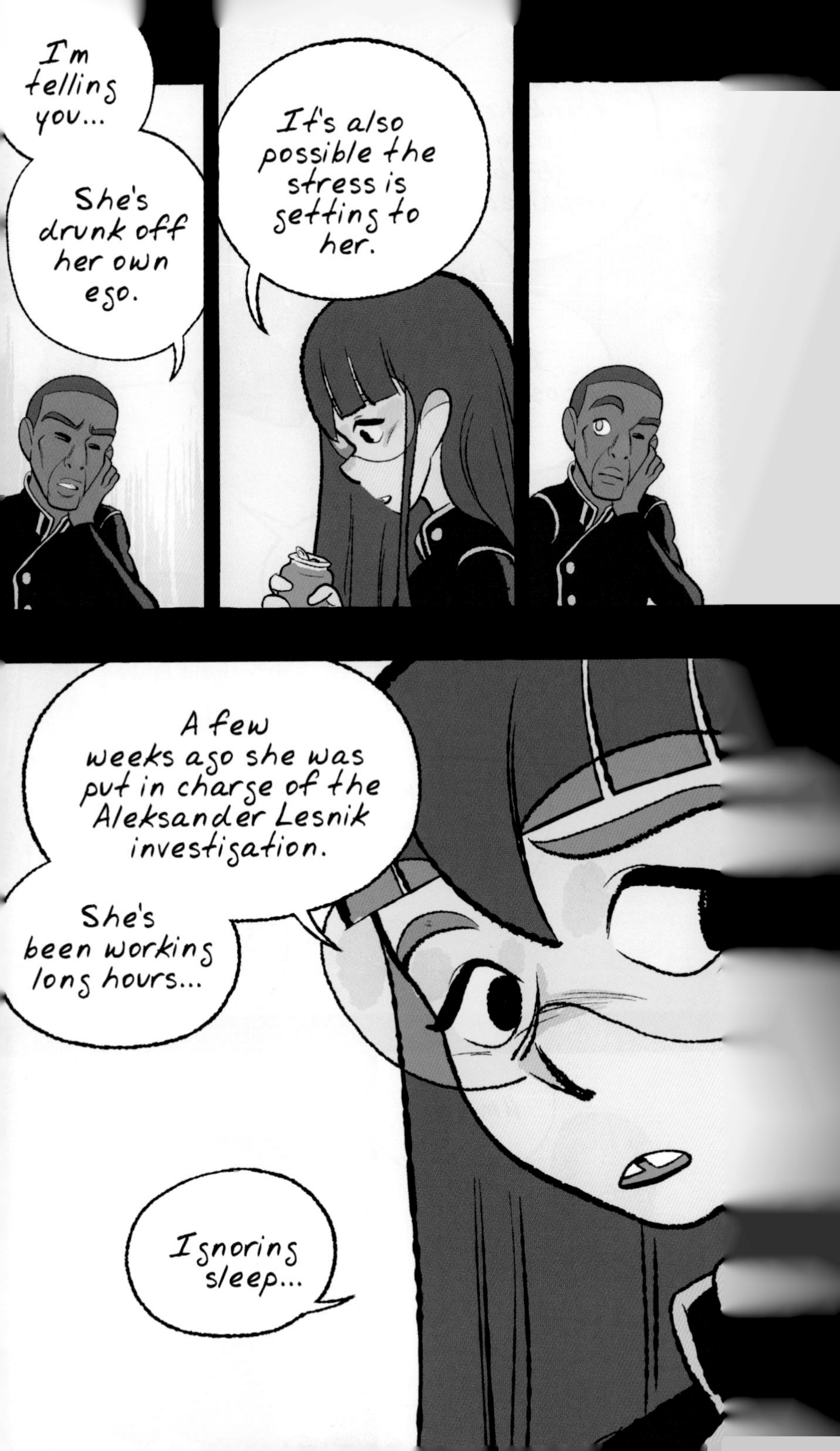

I'm telling you...
She's drunk off her own ego.
It's also possible the stress is getting to her.
A few weeks ago she was put in charge of the Aleksander Lesnik investigation.
She's been working long hours...
Ignoring sleep...

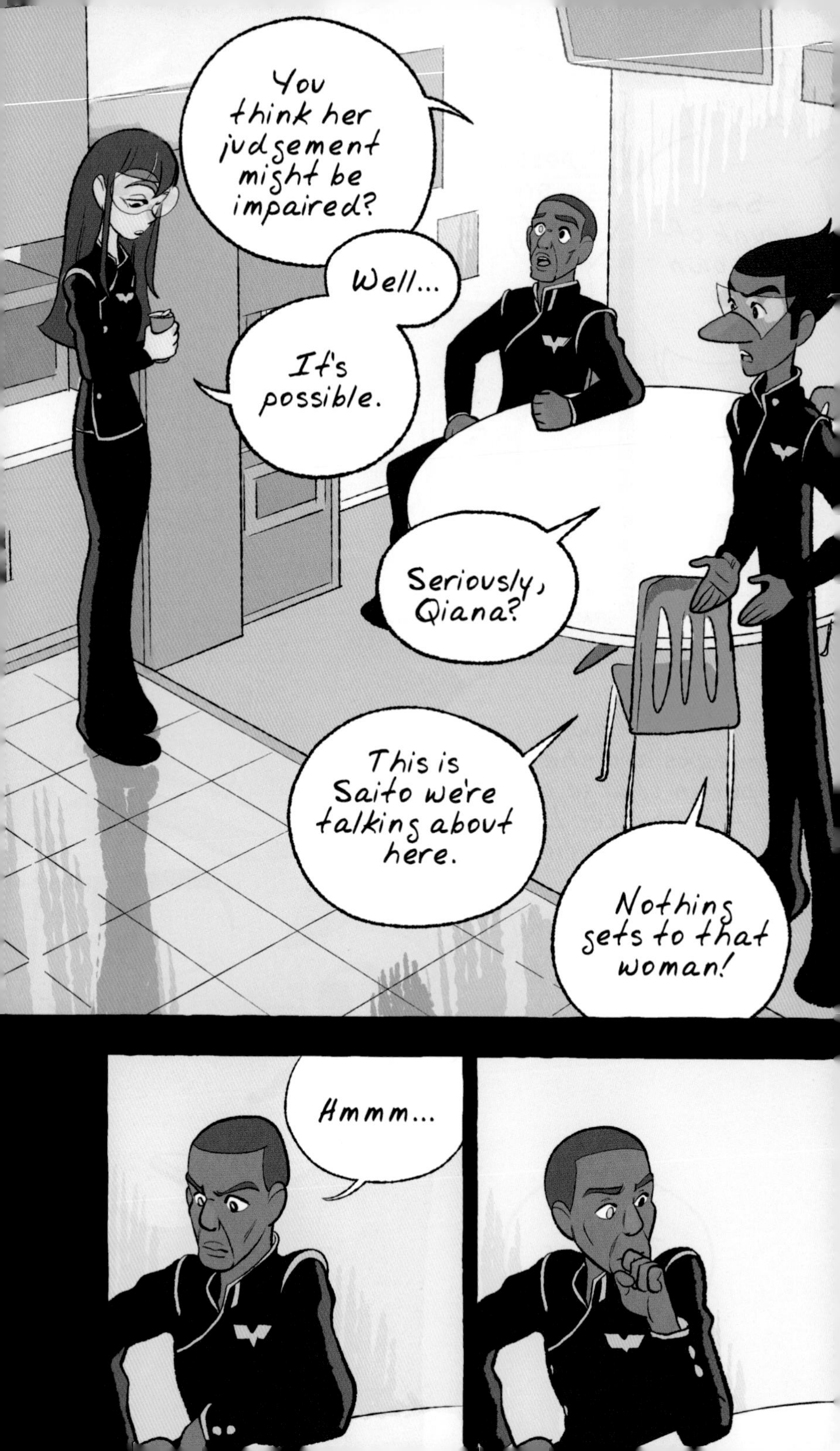
You think her judgement might be impaired?
Well...
It's possible.
Seriously, Qiana?
This is Saito we're talking about here.
Nothing gets to that woman!
Hmmm...

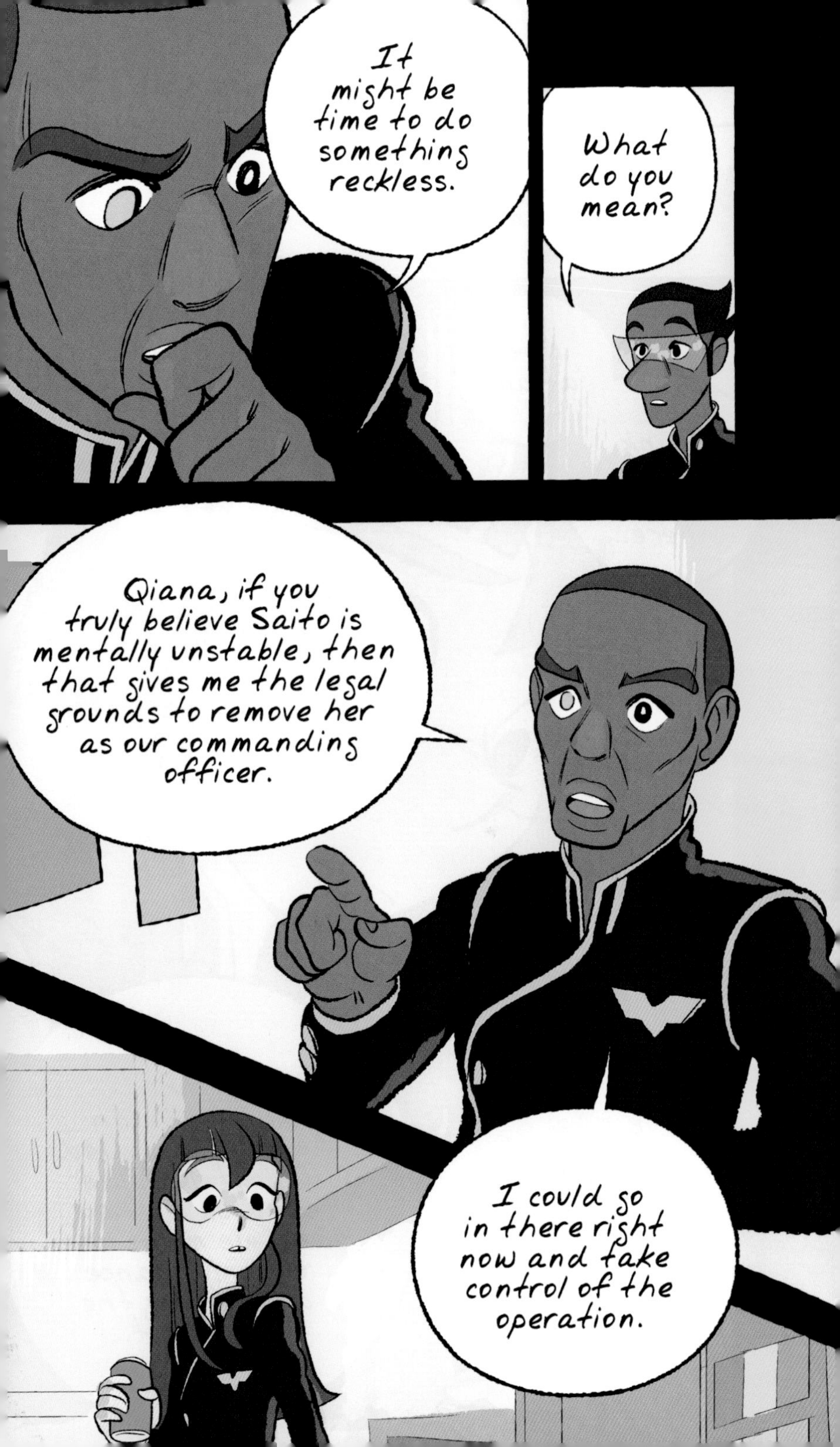
It might be time to do something reckless.
What do you mean?
Qiana, if you truly believe Saito is mentally unstable, then that gives me the legal grounds to remove her as our commanding officer.
I could go in there right now and take control of the operation.

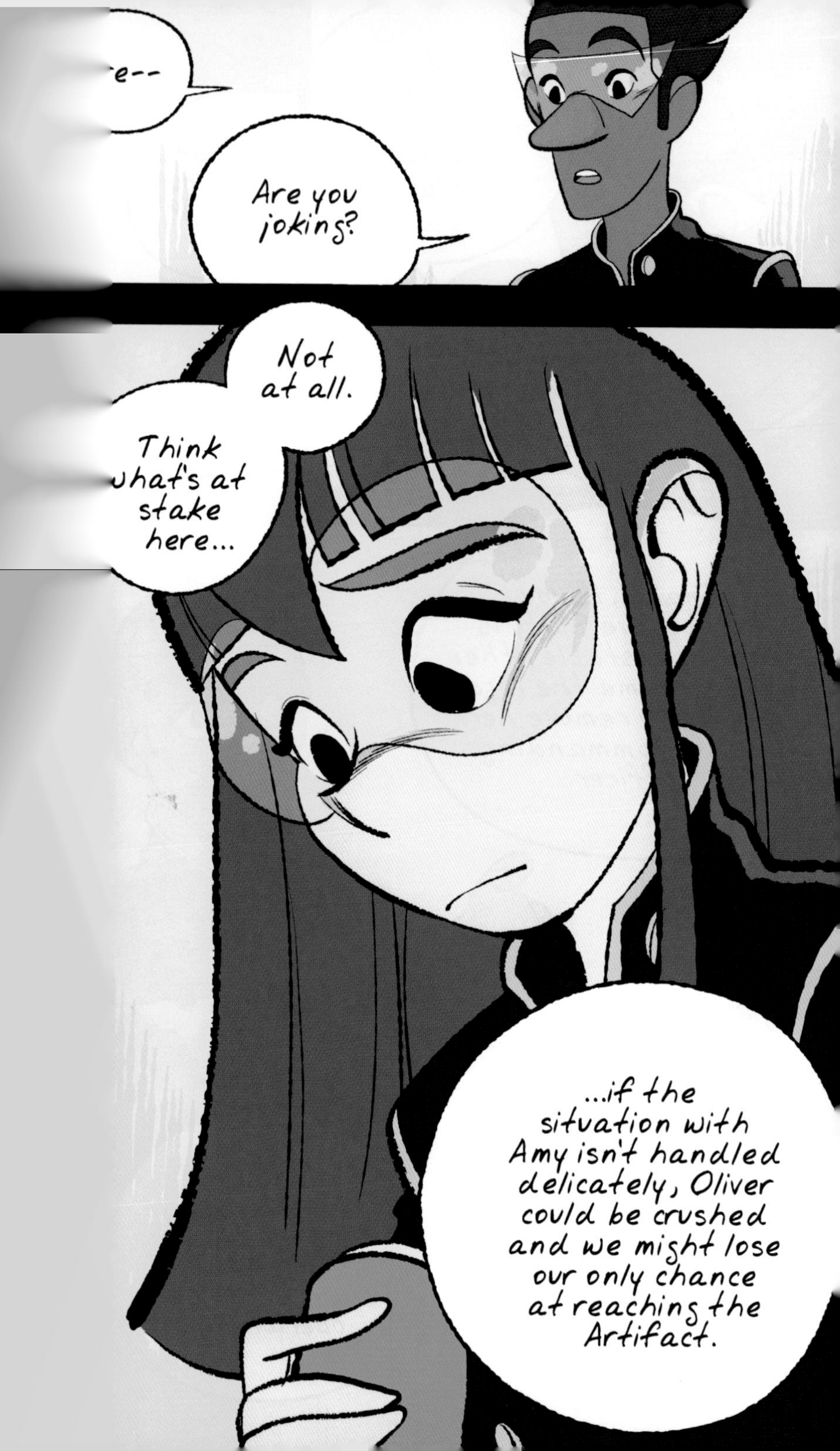
e--
Are you joking?
Not at all.
Think what's at stake here...
...if the situation with Amy isn't handled delicately, Oliver could be crushed and we might lose our only chance at reaching the Artifact.

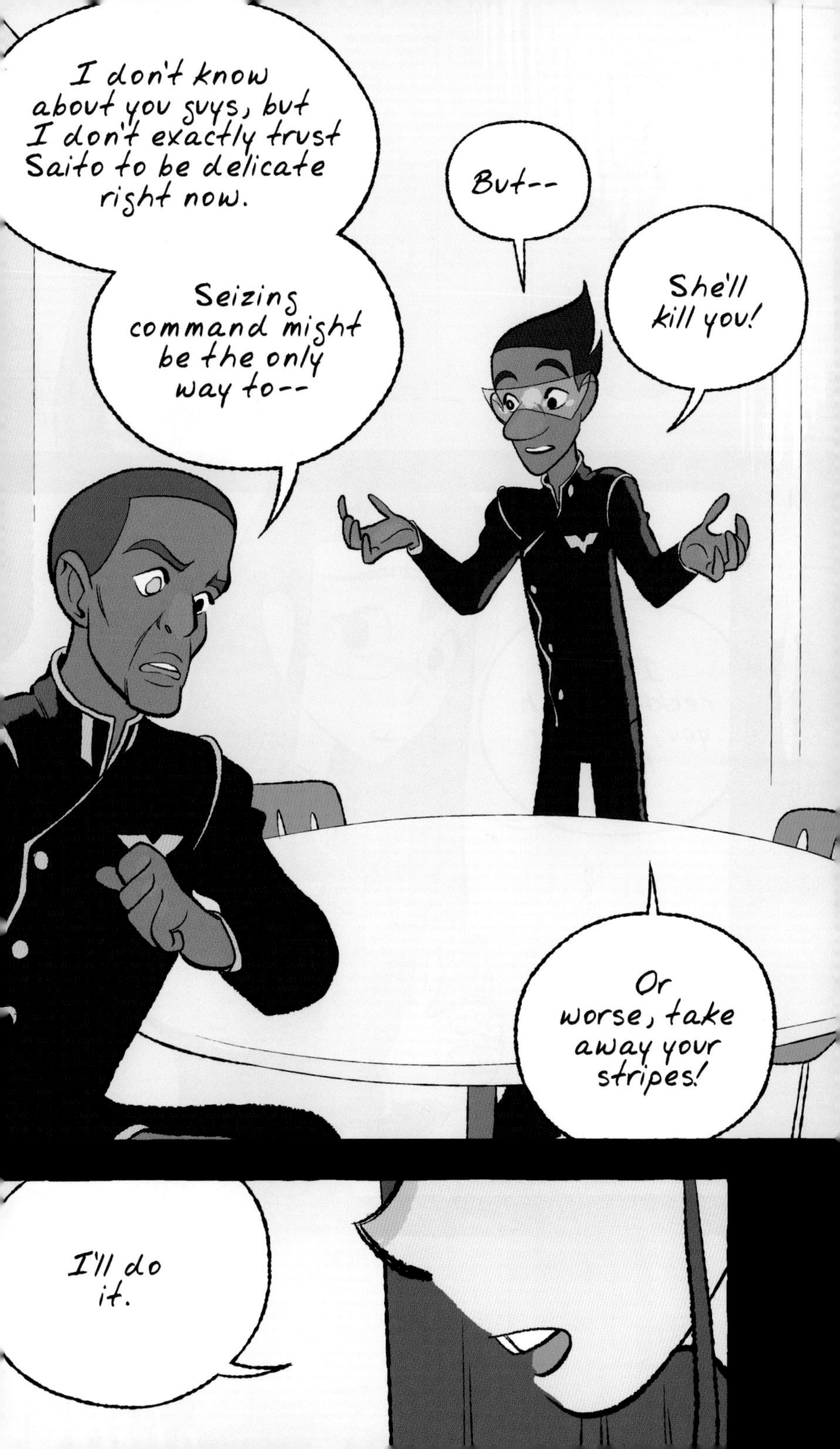
I don't know about you guys, but I don't exactly trust Saito to be delicate right now.
Seizing command might be the only way to--
But--
She'll kill you!
Or worse, take away your stripes!
I'll do it.

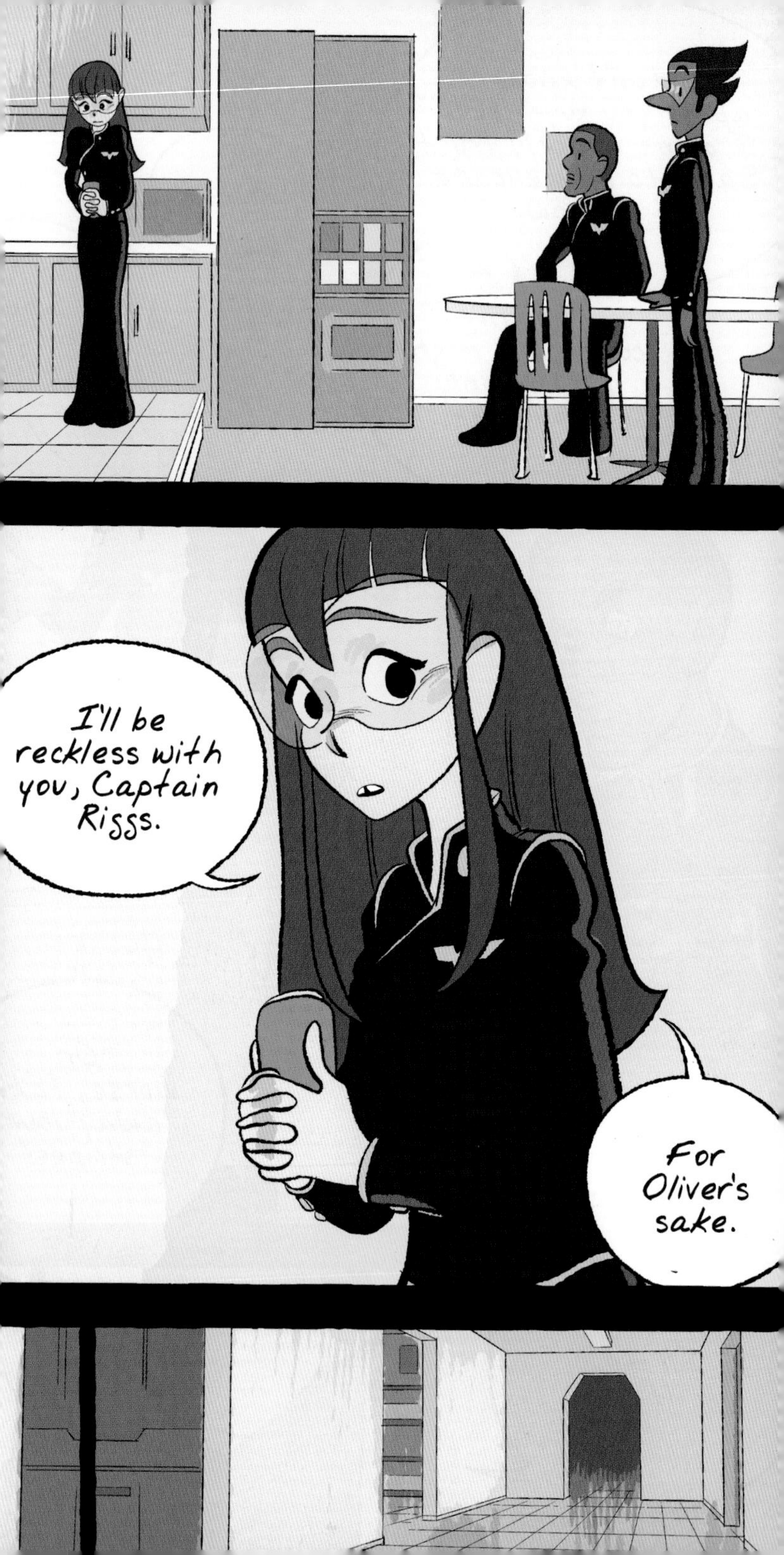
I'll be reckless with you, Captain Riggs.
For Oliver's sake.

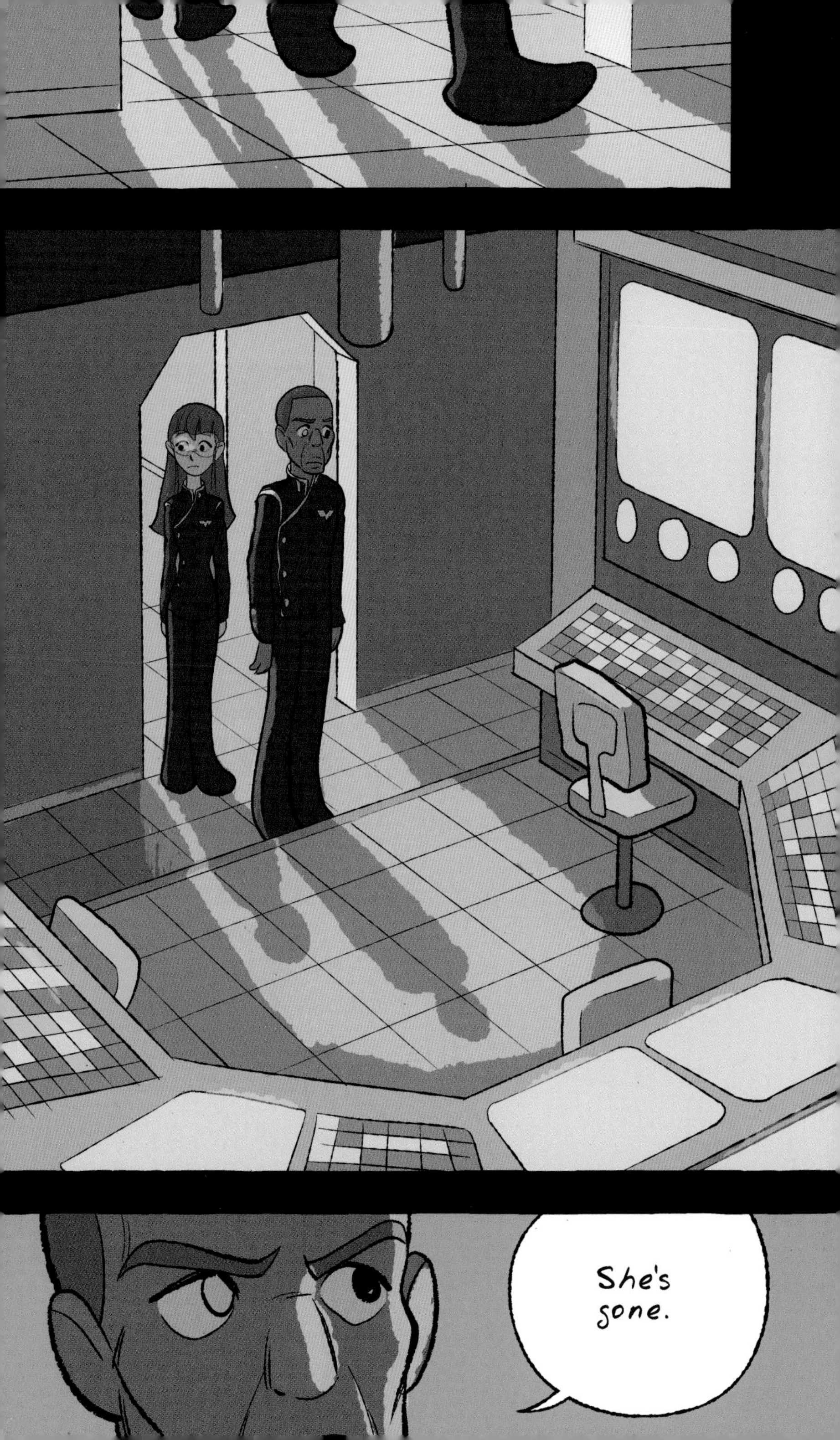
She's gone.

Li'l Amy

by
Stephen
McCranie

Good night, Amy.
Will you stay with me until I fall asleep?
No, you need to learn to do that by yourself, dear.
But when you're here the room is filled with all youramminess.
And I feel safe.
Aw, that's nice.
Tell me more about this "momminess" of mine...
Well...
It's very...
...minty.
Uh--
What?
Z

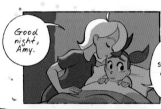

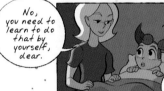

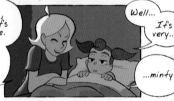

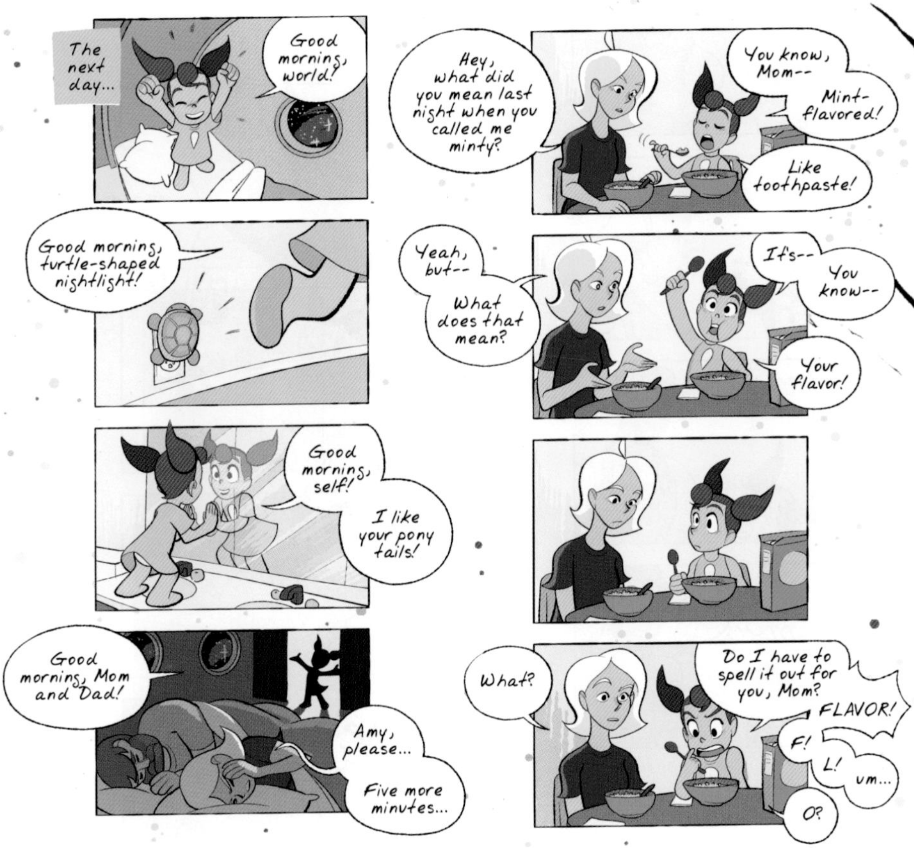

The next day...
Good morning, world!
Good morning, turtle-shaped nightlight!
Good morning, self!
I like your pony tails!
Good morning, Mom and Dad!
Amy, please...
Five more minutes...
Hey, what did you mean last night when you called me minty?
You know, Mom--
Mint-flavored!
Like toothpaste!
Yeah, but--
What does that mean?
It's--
You know--
Your flavor!
What?
Do I have to spell it out for you, Mom?
FLAVOR!
F!
L!
um...
O?

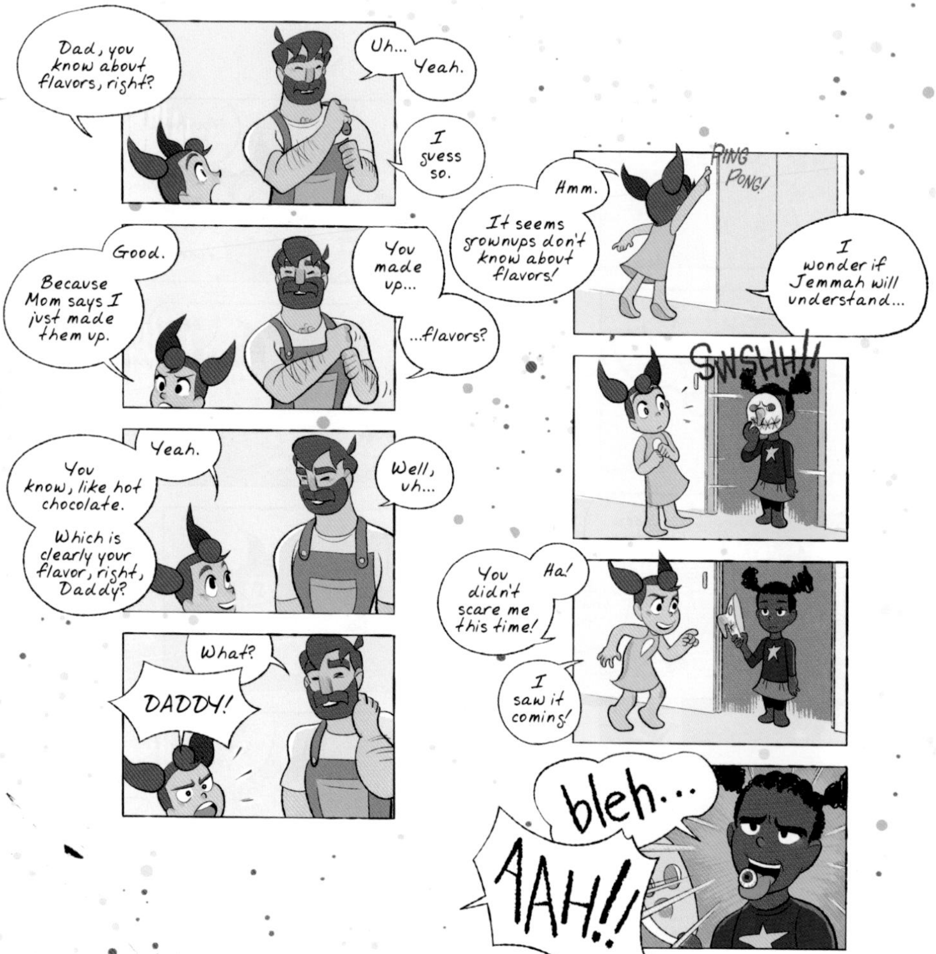

Dad, you know about flavors, right?
Uh... Yeah.
I guess so.
Good.
Because Mom says I just made them up.
You made up...
...flavors?
Yeah.
You know, like hot chocolate.
Which is clearly your flavor, right, Daddy?
Well, uh...
What?
DADDY!
Hmm.
It seems grownups don't know about flavors!
PING PONG!
I wonder if Jemmah will understand...
SWSHH!!
Ha!
You didn't scare me this time!
I saw it coming!
bleh...
AAH!!

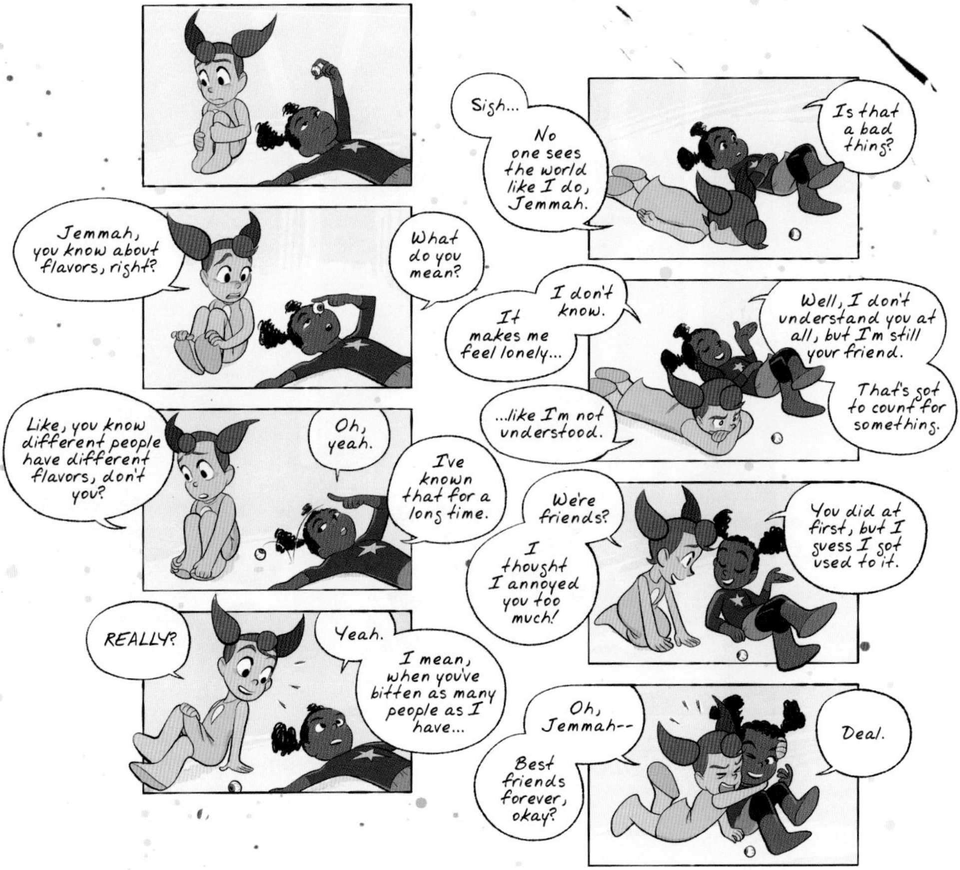
Jemmah, you know about flavors, right?
What do you mean?
Like, you know different people have different flavors, don't you?
Oh, yeah.
I've known that for a long time.
REALLY?
Yeah.
I mean, when you've bitten as many people as I have...
Sigh...
No one sees the world like I do, Jemmah.
Is that a bad thing?
I don't know.
It makes me feel lonely...
...like I'm not understood.
Well, I don't understand you at all, but I'm still your friend.
That's got to count for something.
We're friends?
I thought I annoyed you too much!
You did at first, but I guess I got used to it.
Oh, Jemmah--
Best friends forever, okay?
Deal.

COMING SOON . . .

Stephen McCranie's
SPACE
BOY
9

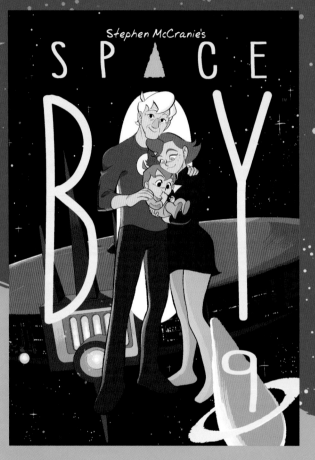

Poison has tainted the flavor of a high-ranking government agent and they are after Amy!

Amy and Oliver survive the drone attack and hide at the dance, hoping for safety in numbers. Little do they know, a rogue agent of the First Contact Project is closing in on them with an EMP grenade that can disconnect everyone at the school—and she's not afraid to get her hands a little dirty. Amy soon learns more about the tragic secret of Oliver and the *Arno* before being taken into custody by the agency controlling Oliver. Find out more in the next volume, available February 2021!